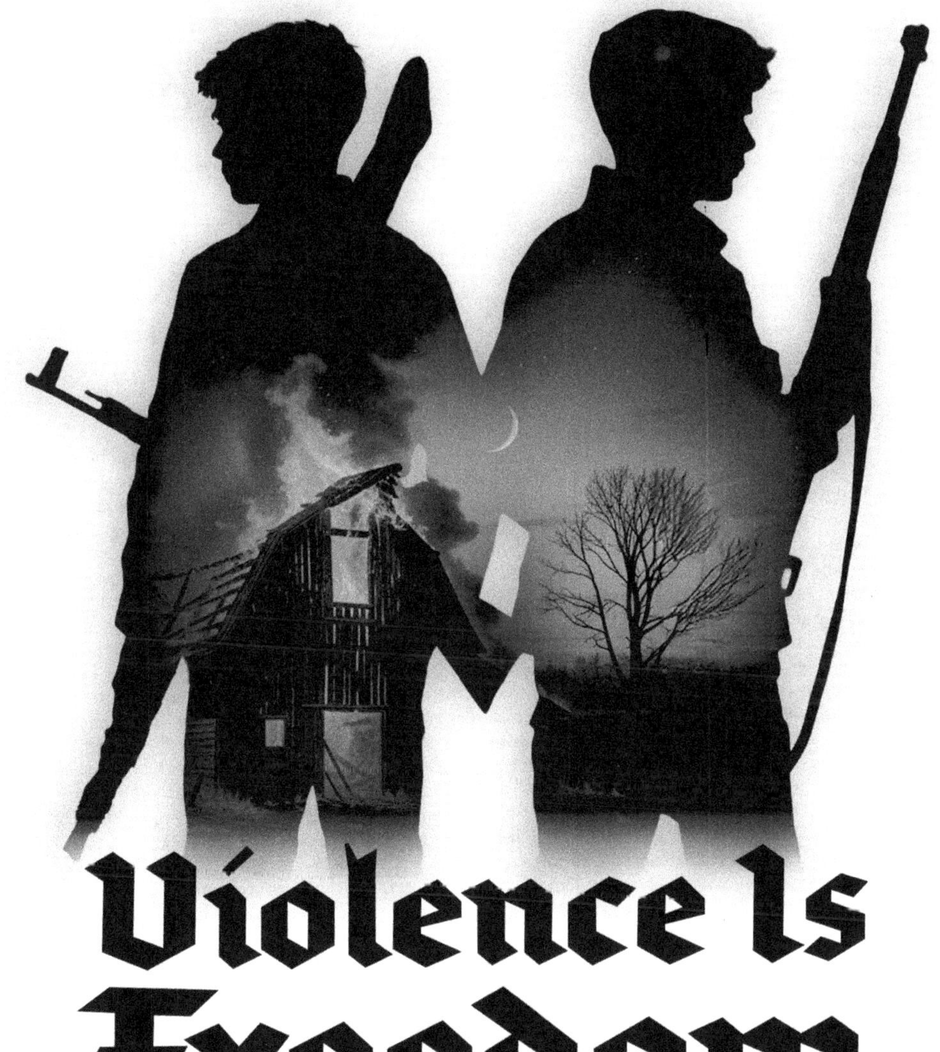

Violence Is Freedom

SIEGFRIED KIRCHEIS

Hardcover ISBN: 978-1-963591-23-1

Printed in the United States of America

Trigger/Offensive Content Warning and General Disclaimer:

By accessing, purchasing, or otherwise utilizing this book, you, the reader, purchaser, or user, hereby acknowledge and agree that you may be exposed to content that you may find offensive, objectionable, or disturbing. You accept and assume full responsibility for any actions, feelings, thoughts, or consequences that may result from reading, viewing, or experiencing the contents of this book. You further agree not to initiate any legal action against the publisher, author, distributors, retailers, or any other parties involved in the creation, marketing, or dissemination of this book, both domestically and internationally. The publisher and author have made reasonable efforts to ensure that the information contained within this book is accurate and up-to-date at the time of publication. However, this publication is provided "as is," and the publisher and author make no representations or warranties, express or implied, as to the accuracy, completeness, or reliability of the information contained herein. To the fullest extent permissible under applicable law, the publisher, author, distributors, retailers, and any other parties involved in the creation, marketing, or dissemination of this book disclaim all liability for any errors, inaccuracies, omissions, or inconsistencies within this publication and shall not be liable for any loss, damage, or disruption, whether direct, indirect, incidental, special, consequential, exemplary, punitive, or otherwise, caused by such errors or omissions, whether resulting from negligence, accident, or any other cause. This book is created and protected under the First Amendment of the Constitution of the United States of America. The acknowledgments, agreements, and disclaimers contained herein apply to all users, regardless of whether they have read or are otherwise aware of this Offensive Content Warning and General Disclaimer. By using this book, you hereby release, indemnify, and hold harmless the publisher, author, distributors, retailers, and any other parties involved in the creation, marketing, or dissemination of this book from any and all claims, demands, liabilities, damages, or causes of action, whether known or unknown, arising from or in connection with your use of this book. This includes, but is not limited to, any claims of personal injury, emotional distress, defamation, copyright infringement, or violations of privacy rights. Your use of this book constitutes your agreement to arbitrate any dispute arising out of or in connection with your use of the book or any claim for damages, and you hereby waive any right to bring any claim against the publisher, author, distributors, retailers, or any other parties involved in the creation, marketing, or dissemination of this book in any court of law, including any international court. Any arbitration shall be conducted in accordance with the rules of the American Arbitration Association, and judgment upon the award rendered by the arbitrator(s) may be entered in any court having jurisdiction thereof. You further agree that the exclusive venue for any arbitration arising out of or in connection with your use of this book shall be the state or federal courts located in the state of the publisher's principal place of business, or, if the arbitration involves parties from multiple jurisdictions, a neutral location agreed upon by all parties or as determined by the arbitrator(s). To the extent that any provision of this agreement is deemed unenforceable under the laws of any jurisdiction, that provision shall be severed and the remaining provisions shall remain in full force and effect. This agreement shall be governed by and construed in accordance with the laws of the publisher's principal place of business, without regard to its conflict of law principles, and any disputes arising hereunder shall be subject to the exclusive jurisdiction of the courts located in such jurisdiction.

We fought for Europe, because no one else would.

— Oberstgruppenführer Paul Hausser

Litany for the Sons of Europa

I speak now the names of the Immortals.

Let every man remember, or let him fall silent.

Alexander, breaker of the East, crowned in the ashes of kings.

Aurelian, restorer of the world, hammer of false gods.

Hitler, Germany's last prophet, who rose against the night.

These are the First Three. Let no man forget.

Leonidas, who stood when all others fled.

Arminius, who taught Rome to bleed.

Charles Martel, who shattered the Crescent's tide.

Codreanu, who bore the cross as blade.

Degrelle, who marched through flame and did not kneel.

Julian, who defied Christ and kissed the Sun.

These are the Champions. Their breath is still fire.

Bohemond, red right hand of holy wrath.

Pelayo, who sang to the hills of Spain.

Sobieski, who rode to Vienna and carved a new dawn.

Alfred, last of the English kings.

Drieu, who lit a match beneath the ruins.

Jünger, who wrote poetry with a bayonet.

Törni, wolf without a master.

Primo de Rivera, who died too soon, yet not in vain.

These are the Poets of Blood. They live where the banners burn.

Scipio. Caesar. Hadrian.

Frederick. Napoleon. Mussolini.

Their hands built empires, but their souls close to perfection.

Let us judge, but not forget. Let us learn, but never bow.

Hess, who flew alone into the lion's den.

Skorzeny, who came and went like thunder.

Heydrich, cold light of the new order.

Von Lettow, iron jungle ghost.

Codreanu, again, for the dead do not die.

Let his name be said twice in this house.

For the unknown soldier, whose bones lie beneath snow.

For the peasant's son, whose blood seeded the land.

For the nameless martyr, who never broke.

For the betrayed, the exiled, the executed.

For the faithful, who did not weep.

O Sons of Europa, remember your fathers.

Their memory is not guilt, but inheritance.

Their struggle is not crime, but covenant.

Their sword is not shame, but standard.

We were not born to serve, but to rise.

We were not made to kneel, but to forge.

We are not the children of slaves, but of Titans.

And the fire has not gone out.

Not yet.

Not ever.

Contents

Contents

Chapter

I

Forget the past, abandon the present. Look up and see the stars. That is where mankind has gone. The year is 2225, the year of the lords and 280 years since the great victory.

The morning light filtered in through the high-pane windows of the schoolhouse, casting long amber shafts across rows of sturdy desks. The boys filed in one by one, their boots thudding softly on the marble floor. There was no chatter. There was no idle murmuring, only the silent shuffle of disciplined youth. They were clean-cut, broad-shouldered, and their posture upright even before the bell.

Reinhardt Jäger placed his satchel down onto his desk and stood behind it. His hands were calloused from farm work. His shoulders still ached faintly from yesterday's timber-hauling exercise. He preferred it that way, pain meant growth and sweat meant strength. He glanced out the window once toward the rising sun cresting over the hills of the planet called Delumina then turned forward again.

The instructor entered. He was tall, with greying temples and an iron gaze that had once scanned battlefield horizons. His voice came like the crack of a rifle...

"Stand."

The boys rose in unison, like the striking of a legion's shield-wall.

"Face the banner."

They turned toward the front of the room. The banner of the Pan-European Confederation hung behind the instructor's podium. It was a black solar-wheel emblazoned on a white field, rimmed in imperial blue and blood red. It fluttered gently from the morning breeze leaking through the cracks in the stone walls and opened windows. Its colors are alive with symbolism known to every citizen from childhood. A radiant golden sunburst crowned the design, each ray sharp and sovereign, representing the light of Europa spreading across the stars. At its heart was a black sunwheel, a Sonnenrad, surrounding a deep red core. The red center symbolized blood, the sacrifice and shared ancestry of the European peoples. The wheel around it was unity in struggle, an eternal turning of fate and will. It was not merely a symbol, it was a vow. Encircling the base of the sunburst were six golden stars, framed by two olive branches meeting at the stem.

The six stars stood for the six great ethno-cultural branches of Europa being the Germanic, Slavic, Latin, Celtic, Hellenic, and Baltic peoples. Each star shone equally, without hierarchy, and bound together in a sacred fraternity. The olive wreath did not signify peace in the liberal sense, rather the sacred guardianship of the Pax Europa as the just peace secured through strength. To raise one's hand to this banner was to swear loyalty not to an empire of blood alone, but to an eternal destiny. A new solar order forged in truth, discipline, and brotherhood.

"Salute."

Right arms rose in a Roman salute: clean, sharp, and reverent.

"Recite the Oath."

Their voices spoke as one. Each syllable carried centuries of memory and thousands of years of unbroken will.

"I stand before the gods and my people.

I pledge my soul to Europa, our blood and our destiny.

I give my mind to truth, my body to duty, my heart to the eternal flame.

I swear by Sol, who watches from above,

by Christ the risen light with mercy and might,

and by the wisdom of the gods of old,

to serve the fatherland and all the peoples of Europe,

to guard their future, honor their past, and conquer all that would destroy them.

From the soul of Earth to the stars and beyond,

I vow to carry the standard unbroken.

Strength and struggle!

Glory to the Confederation!

Hail Victory!"

Silence followed. For a heartbeat, all the world seemed still. No birdsong, no hum of engines outside. Only the stillness of boys on the cusp of manhood, and the weight of vows sealed in the marrow.

The instructor lowered his arm. "Be seated."

Chairs slid across marble, pens were readied as the day had officially begun. The classroom was silent except for the steady cadence of the instructor's boots pacing across the stone floor. Chalk scraped softly as he drew a clean line under the heading on the board, The Year of the Great Victory. He turned to face the class. All the boys sat upright, eyes forward, some eager, some weary from repetition, but all aware that this story, this truth, formed the backbone of their civilization.

"You've all heard this before," he said, voice calm, certain, "but it bears repeating. We do not memorize the past to mourn it. We remember to honor the price paid and the future secured by it."

He gestured toward the timeline etched above the chalkboard, carved in brass. "The year is 2225, Year of the Lords. 280 years ago, in 1945 by the old reckoning, Europe was saved. It was not fate, nor mercy, nor luck that delivered us. It was fire, sacrifice, and will."

He paused, letting the silence settle.

"The Spanish Civil War ended in just over a year, thanks to the discipline of Falangist unity and the survival of Jose Antonio Primo de Rivera. In late 1939, Spain formally joined the Axis Powers. Operation Ghadir followed shortly after. It was a joint German-Spanish operation to seize Gibraltar. It succeeded with breathtaking speed. The British Mediterranean position collapsed. Supply lines severed and with Malta isolated, the Western Mediterranean became ours. Mare Nostra Citadel was formed, as it was then called."

He moved to the next marker on the board.

"Meanwhile, the Japanese adopted the Army plan. Instead of expanding south toward the Americans, they struck north and so Siberia burned. By the time Operation Barbarossa began, the Red Army was split across two fronts and their morale, already fractured by famine and purges, shattered."

He tapped the next line, Fall of The USSR - Spring 1943.

"Axis forces, unified in command, took Moscow in the dead of winter. It was the final blow. Stalin vanished and the USSR was carved into occupation zones. The Slavic peoples were liberated, or pacified, depending on their allegiance."

He turned again, slower now.

"The Battle of the Suez Canal, 1944. Italian and German mechanized divisions as well as foreign and Germanic Waffen-SS volunteers, supported by Arab auxiliaries, stormed through Egypt. The British Empire's last stronghold in the East fell, the Empire crumbled soon after. By 1945, the United Kingdom ceased to exist. The CEAB (Cynru Eire Alba Breizh) union took its place on the British Isles. The Celts of western Europe were finally united, after 2,000 years of separation and humiliation."

He glanced at the banner hanging above the classroom, six stars under a radiant sunwheel. "The global order was broken. The United States, bereft of enemies to rally against, never joined the war. Its economy collapsed. Liberalism, rootless and parasitic, died in its womb."

Reinhardt sat quietly, heart steady. He had heard the story a dozen times. Yet, today, it stirred something deeper, a sense that the time for memorizing history was coming to an end. The older instructor, known simply as Herr Brandt, stood tall at the front of the room, back straight, and the insignia of the ESS (Europäisch Schutzstaffel) clearly visible on the collar of his dark uniform tunic. A polished black pin rested there. Two white thunderbolts, Sieg runes, carved in parallel against a matte black field. It gleamed faintly under the overhead light. The boys recognized it at once. It was not just a mark of service. It was a symbol of conviction. He didn't shout. He didn't need to.

"Young men," he said, folding his hands behind him as he paced slowly along the front wall, "you must understand this. The Confederation is not merely a nation, and certainly not an empire in the old, decaying sense. It is a destiny made of flesh. A covenant of blood, duty, and memory."

The students sat upright at their desks, hands folded or resting atop notebooks. No one spoke. No one fidgeted. The quiet weight of reverence filled the air.

"We are not ruled by parties, nor by profit. We are not governed by abstract principles. We are not a democracy, for truth is not decided by numbers. We are not a tyranny, for power is not held by one man, but by the sacred chain of responsibility. Every link, be they father, soldier, worker, teacher or leader, is bound to the others."

The morning sun fell through the windows at an angle, casting lines of light across the classroom floor. Outside, the wind stirred the banner of the Confederation, six stars sewn in tight formation above a field of white.

"Our German, Spanish, Italian, Celtic, Slavic, and Nordic forefathers did not merely win a war. They restored the soul of Europe. In the year of the Great Victory, 1945, they broke the world of lies and reforged truth. We do not bow to global finance, nor crawl before alien creeds. We remembered who we were. We remembered the gods and our people."

One of the boys raised his hand, uncertain but compelled. "Herr Brandt... are we not also taught to respect the gods of Christ and of reason?"

The instructor stopped pacing. He turned and gave a slight nod, his tone quiet but sure. "We are taught to honor what is eternal. The Logos and the Sun, Christ and Sol. They are not enemies, but faces of the same light. The faith of our ancestors, whether from Jerusalem or the Black Forest, taught the same thing; to live with courage, to die with honor, and to give our lives to something greater than ourselves."

He motioned briefly to the tall window beside them, where a patrol flier glinted across the sky beyond the glass. "This world was not given to us. We carved it from the wild. What of the stars beyond? They will not yield without struggle either. Remember this, we did not come to dominate the galaxy. We came to civilize it, not for profit or plunder, but for a purpose."

The classroom was still. The boys remained at their desks, silent, and eyes forward. They felt the words settle deep into their bones.

Herr Brandt's voice dropped low. "This is why you are here. You are not here to memorize facts nor simply to pass exams, but to become men worthy of the task that history has placed upon your shoulders."

Herr Brandt returned to the front of the classroom and let a brief silence settle. The boys waited. Then, in a calmer voice, he said, "History is not made by machines. It is not made by markets. It is not even made by armies alone. History is made by spirit and by the will that drives it."

He stepped toward the chalkboard and picked up a piece of white chalk. In steady strokes, he wrote four names across the board.

KANT

TOLKIEN

SCHOPENHAUER

NIETZSCHE

"These men were giants of European thought," he said, turning back to the class. "But not all giants walk upright. Some lumber in circles. Some carry the weight of cowardice masked as complexity."

He drew a line through the first three names with a single motion of chalk.

"Kant," he said, tapping the first name, "taught man to bind duty not to destiny, but to abstraction. He taught of a morality of paralysis, where no blood, no people, no god may speak, only the cold machinery of reason."

"Tolkien," he continued. "Rejected the crown. He taught us to love decline and fear greatness. His world ends with the return of the humble slave to his hole in the ground."

He struck Schopenhauer's name with the chalk next. "And Schopenhauer? He who preached resignation, a withered monk for the age of steel."

The boys scribbled notes quickly, a few wide-eyed at the clarity of dismissal.

Brandt let the silence weigh, then underlined the final name: NIETZSCHE.

"This man," he said, "spoke flame. He reminded us that will precedes order. That creation requires struggle, but he too was incomplete because he offered no people to carry the will, and no myth to anchor the flame."

Then, with precision, Brandt added four more names below:

FICHTE

GOETHE

SCHMITT

HEGEL

"Fichte," he said firmly, "gave us the blueprint of the awakened nation, not as soil, but as spirit. He spoke of the Volk, not as a race alone but as a community of destiny. Goethe gave us the soul of Europe in poetry and parables. His Faust did not rot in despair, he acted. He created it. He redeemed."

"Carl Schmitt," Brandt said, rapping the board with chalk, "taught us that all politics begins with distinction, friend or enemy. He saw clearly that liberalism dissolves these boundaries and with it the spine of a people."

"Lastly, Hegel..." Brandt circled the last name, "Gave us dialectics. Europe is a continent of contradictions and therefore dialectics. Only by struggle can man cut off the unworthy and reforge it into something stronger."

He stepped back from the board, letting the boys absorb the names. "These are the men who gave us the roots of the Confederation's law, its sovereignty, and its myth. We did not rise from democracy. We rose from destiny."

One boy hesitantly asked, "Weren't most of these men Germans, Herr Brandt? What about the rest of Europe?"

Brandt turned, lips curling into a rare smile. "They spoke the language of the blood and blood speaks across borders. Spain had José Antonio. Italy had Gentile. Romania had Codreanu. Ireland had Pearse. Europe is not the product of a single land, but a single rising, a solar rising. These men, our spiritual fathers, shaped the dawn that came in 1950."

The classroom, filled moments before with scribbling pens, now sat in complete stillness. A brief silence followed Herr Brandt's closing words. The room buzzed faintly with the lingering tension of ideas too large for many of the boys to fully grasp. Then a hand rose, reluctantly but purposefully. It belonged to Alexei Dražen, a broad-shouldered boy from one of the Dalmatian colonies, known more for his brawling than for speaking. He didn't wait for permission.

"Sir," Alexei said, his voice steady but skeptical, "if this Confederation is the fulfillment of Europe's destiny... then why did we almost lose? Why did we nearly fall in the early years? Why did so many of our own people fight for the other side? Weren't the French divided? The Greeks and even the Slavs?"

Several boys turned toward him in surprise, others frowned. Reinhardt said nothing. He stared ahead, his knuckles white against the desk's edge. Brandt did not smile. He regarded Alexei with the calm, unflinching gaze of a man who had buried both enemies and comrades.

"Because," Brandt declared, "Europe had forgotten herself."

He stepped forward, walking slowly between the rows of desks as he spoke.

"We were a continent of merchants and ideologues, bankers and bureaucrats. Our poets had been strangled, our warriors tamed, our mothers turned into workers, and our fathers into consumers. We were the body of a hero, but with the soul of a gelding. The struggle was not against foreign armies. It was against the sickness within."

He stopped before Alexei's desk.

"You ask why so many fought against us. I ask, what else would you expect? The road to resurrection is not paved in harmony. It is paved in trial, betrayal, and sacred fire."

Brandt turned toward the whole class now.

"Understand this, the Confederation is not the fruit of victory alone. It is the fruit of loss. We had to lose half the world to remember who we were."

No one spoke. Even Alexei looked down, his brow furrowed, not shamed but thoughtful. A moment passed. The bell rang, sharp and clean. Brandt's voice softened slightly.

"Next week we will cover the Great Purge of International Finance and the destruction of the false democracies. But for now... remember that without victory, we would have no future. Without struggle, no identity. Without sacrifice, no Europe. Go now, eat, train, and remember that everything you have was paid for in blood."

The boys rose. A shuffle of boots and chairs echoed through the room. Some whispered to each other. A few gave Alexei glances, some approving while others cold. Reinhardt gathered his things silently. He said nothing. As he passed by Brandt's desk, his eyes met the old veteran's thunderbolt pin, black and white, bright as ice. For a fleeting second, something stirred behind his ribs. Not guilt or pride but gravity, a quiet pull toward something greater. Most of the boys had already filed out by the time Reinhardt stepped away from his desk. He walked slower than the others, his mind still braced by the silence Brandt had left in the room. The old man stood alone at the lectern, tidying his notes with the casual rhythm of a man used to being left behind. Reinhardt lingered by the door. His gaze drifted, once more, to the pin at Herr Brandt's collar, black with two white thunderbolts. Clean, angular, like runes cut into obsidian. He felt it again, that gravity. Like something buried just beneath his skin had shifted quietly, without permission. He stepped forward.

"Sir?" Reinhardt said.

Brandt looked up. Reinhardt hesitated, then nodded toward the pin.

"You served in the ESS?"

Brandt regarded him for a long moment. Not suspicious, just weighing the soul behind the question.

"I did," he said.

"What was it like?"

Brandt set the last paper down and folded his hands atop the desk.

"It was cold, loud, and lonely." Brandt paused. "Yet full of meaning."

Reinhardt stood there in silence. Brandt studied him briefly.

"Do you know what the symbol means?" he asked, tapping the pin.

Reinhardt shook his head. Brandt turned it slightly so the lightning bolts caught the window's light.

"One thunderbolt and one sunray," he said. "Sieg runes, in the old saying. The storm's heralds. They represent violence and harmony. They represent clarity. Sudden, divine clarity. The kind that tears away illusion."

Brandt paused for a moment to let the revelation settle.

"To wear them is to be the hand of judgment. Not above the people, but within them. Sharper than a blade, and quieter than a prayer."

Brandt leaned back, voice calm but firm.

"That is the creed we lived by and with it came the motto. The doctrine of our corps that speed is violence, violence is freedom. Not chaos, not cruelty, but the ruthless precision of will made flesh."

He paused again.

"Most men are never taught what to do with their freedom, but we were."

Reinhardt blinked, slowly. Something itched behind his sternum.

Brandt's voice softened. "Why do you ask, Reinhardt?"

A beat passed.

"No reason," Reinhardt lied.

Brandt nodded. He said nothing more. He just watched Reinhardt go, slowly yet also calmly, as the boy stepped back into the hallway and disappeared into the noise of lunch. Behind the teacher's eyes something stirred, not surprise rather recognition.

The lunch hall echoed with the scrape of boots and chatter as the boys filed into their usual spots. Reinhardt sat near the end of one of the long tables with Tomas and Jules, both sons of farmers from the southern hill cantons. Like Reinhardt, they spoke Low German, the old earth-tongue brought across the stars by their forefathers. It is a language that is rough, simple, and close to the land.

"Brandt was in rare form today," Jules muttered as he sat down, cutting into his root-bar with a dull knife. "Swore half the philosophers into exile."

Tomas chuckled. "And dug up the rest just to slap 'em again."

Reinhardt grinned faintly. "He's not wrong about Schopenhauer though. My father used to say reading him felt like letting rot into the soul."

"Better than Kant," Tomas said, mock-serious. "At least Schopenhauer said something."

Their banter slid naturally between clipped syllables and earthbound cadence. In the classroom they spoke Hochdeutsch which is precise, severe, and holy. Out here, with dust on their boots and broth in their flasks, they spoke as their grandfathers had.

The ease dimmed when Jules leaned closer. "You heard the talk?"

Reinhardt raised an eyebrow. Tomas leaned in, lowering his voice again. "They found it near the forge crates. Drawn in blood or what looked like blood, the symbol."

Reinhardt didn't need to ask which one. The Molten Glyph, they called it. A dripping, cancerous shape that seemed to pulse even when still. It had no symmetry or center, at least from the perception of anyone who had seen it. A warped loop of crude red, branching like nerves or roots clawing from a black void. It looked like it had been poured rather than drawn as if it bled from the air itself, always running or rather always weeping. No one knew what it meant. Not in language, at least, but the boys who saw it didn't forget. Some said it mirrored the synaptic map of a brain in seizure. Others claimed it was a failed letter, a defiled character from an old script. Everyone agreed that it felt wrong, like a word spoken backward or a scream underwater. Even adults wouldn't touch it if they found it burned into walls or smeared on supply crates.

"It's their sign," Jules said darkly, "but also a weapon. You see that thing enough, it stays in you."

Reinhardt didn't reply. He had seen it once before, the year prior. On a relay tower west of the ridge, just before a skirmish with saboteurs. The tower burned later that day.

Tomas lowered his voice. "One of my classmates in the carpentry class handed me a pamphlet. He said the Confederation is false. That Europa's built on bones and lies. That the gods are dead."

Reinhardt didn't flinch. "Do you believe that?"

"Of course not," Tomas said quickly. "But it's spreading."

"They don't fight like men," Jules muttered. "They whisper. They slip through cracks."

Reinhardt didn't respond. His eyes drifted upward to the far wall, where the great mural of Operation Ghadir sprawled across the stone. Soldiers, European soldiers, stormed the straits under a burning Mediterranean sky with steel, sand, and thunder. The banner of old Germany, a black hooked-cross on a red banner, raised high. The old world locked out. Brandt's words echoed again, "To wear them is to be the hand of judgment. Not above the people, but within them. Sharper than a blade, and quieter than a prayer... Speed is violence, violence is freedom."

Reinhardt nodded once, quietly. Not to them, but to something deeper.

The hallway echoed with bootsteps and muted chatter as Reinhardt walked the tiled corridor toward his next class. The midday sun cast long beams of light through the tall windows along the southern wall, fracturing into dust motes that drifted like tiny ghosts. His mind still lingered on Herr Brandt's words, but the heaviness had receded, leaving a strange calm in its place. He had felt something stir. A downward pull toward the root of something larger, older, and undeniable. He could still see the white runes pinned to Brandt's collar, stark against the black. By the time he reached the Vocational Hall, the scent of mortar and lime had already filled his nose. He stepped inside the workshop and found the other boys already seated on low benches, arranged in a semicircle around a central demonstration slab. The instructor, a heavyset man in a pale-grey work tunic, stood beside a half-cured mold of concrete, his hands stained with dust.

"You boys eat well?" the man barked with a smile. A few nods and murmurs answered. Reinhardt slid into an open seat and folded his arms, posture straight.

The instructor clapped once. "Good, then let's begin. Concrete is not just a building material. It is a language. One spoken by those who build for the dead, the living, and the unborn."

He struck the slab with a short metal rod. A dull, solid tone rang out.

"You hear that? That's permanence. That's silence given shape. This..." he tapped the slab again, "will still be here when the sons of your sons are teaching their sons."

A younger boy leaned forward. "Doesn't concrete decay? Doesn't it break over time?"

The instructor turned and lifted a chunk of old, crumbling rebar concrete from a side table.

"That? That's what they used. Sand-heavy, steel-bound, water-washed garbage. They poured it fast, sold it faster, and called it progress. It lasted fifty years, maybe."

He dropped the broken chunk. It cracked again on the floor.

"Now this," he said, gesturing to the half-cured slab, "is Confederation concrete. The mix is old-world lime, volcanic ash, and basalt aggregate. We've refined it with nano-silica, carbon-laced fiber, and Delumina slag. It doesn't rot. It bonds. It breathes."

Reinhardt leaned forward slightly, studying the faint shimmer of the curing slab.

"We pour to consecrate," the instructor said, more quietly now. "Every foundation we lay is a sacrament. The Pantheon still stands. Rome fell, but her concrete endured. We build not for today, but for the day after time."

A silence passed over the boys. Then the instructor motioned them up.

"All right. You're each going to mix your own small batch. Use the molds behind you. I want a clean pour, no air pockets, no slop. Carve your family rune or sign into the bottom once it sets. That'll go on the school wall."

Reinhardt retrieved his mold, hexagonal and palm-wide, and began collecting the powdered lime and ash from the labeled bins. The volcanic ash had a dark grey shimmer to it, and the lime dust clung to his fingers like memory. He worked without speaking, hands steady.

Next to him, a friend named Mathis muttered, half to himself, "Even in the soil, we build with stone."

Reinhardt smirked. "That's the idea."

They stirred, poured, and tamped their molds in silence. By the time the instructor called the hour, Reinhardt had already etched a faint wolf-tooth pattern onto the bottom of his setting mold. It wasn't fancy, but it was sharp, precise, and his. As the boys cleaned their workstations, the instructor walked past Reinhardt and placed a heavy hand on his shoulder.

"You've done this before."

Reinhardt nodded. "My uncle builds irrigation channels and earth-set walls. We pour after frost."

The man grunted in approval. "Then you already know the truth that what a man pours, a people will inherit."

And with that, the bell sounded. The boys filed out, hands white with dust and sleeves streaked with sweat. The hall once again filled with the sound of movement but this time, it was grounded, earnest and unshaken. Reinhardt stepped into the sunlight and looked skyward, then down to the concrete dust still clinging to his palms, stone in the blood. That, he thought, was no small thing.

The air outside the vocational hall was thick with heat, even beneath Delumina's washed-blue sky. Reinhardt squinted upward as he stepped outside, one hand shielding his eyes from the late-afternoon sun that glinted off the stone facades and sloped metal roofing of the outer campus. The lesson on concrete still echoed in his mind on how volcanic ash and lime, pressed and aged, outlived empires. Concrete remembers, Herr Strass had said, slapping a cylinder core sample on the workbench like a sermon's end that steel rusts, timber rots, but concrete endures.

Reinhardt walked in silence toward the next block of training fields, past rows of students crossing paths for their own scheduled classes in agronomy, mechanical engineering, or flight preps. His body ached from standing during the lab portion, but he felt no complaint in his stride. His boots struck the paved walkway with rhythm. The dread from earlier had ebbed was still present, but beneath the surface now, like iron laid beneath skin.

The HEMA, Historical European Martial Arts, training grounds sat at the edge of campus. A rectangular dirt arena, hemmed in by stone seating tiers and iron weapon racks, waited under open sky. Already, students were forming lines, dressed in thick tunics, reinforced gauntlets, and leather-padded pectorals stitched with red-thread Roman numerals denoting cohort and training unit.

He found his assigned rack. Wooden gladius, polished smooth from repeated use. Shield, not a curved sport buckler, but a full scutum made from laminated composites and weighted to match old measurements. Reinhardt slipped his arm through the straps, adjusted the fist grip, and took his place in the line without needing a word. The instructor arrived without a shout. A lean, scar-faced man in his early forties, his voice projected like steel through linen.

"You do not train to survive. You train to win," he said, pacing the dirt. "The man who survives thinks of his own skin. The man who wins protects the man beside him. That is why we begin with the shield."

One by one, the formations were built. Reinhardt locked shields with his cohort, five across and two deep. The drill began with pressure movement to advance, push, brace, and strike. Forward thrusts with the gladius into straw-stuffed dummies behind wooden palisades. Then, live-sparring rotations for one-on-one fights inside the formation with boys switching partners every thirty seconds. There were no cheers, no whooping, no bravado. The only sound was the thud of wood on shields and grunts of effort. Sweat darkened the students' tunics. Blood spotted a few lips and jaws.

When Reinhardt stepped into the ring, he moved like he'd been doing this his whole life. The weight of the scutum pulled at his arm, but the centerline was his. The blade in his hand didn't feel like a weapon. It felt like a language that was direct, final and measured in inches, not shouts. His opponent lunged too high. Reinhardt dipped, braced, and thrust upward under the ribs and straight into the padded vest. The boy reeled and staggered, but did not fall.

"Hold the centerline," the instructor said from the edge, nodding. "Good."

By the time the session ended, the sun had dipped toward the horizon. The red light made the arena glow like something older than the colony, older than stars. Reinhardt breathed deep through his nose, tasting sweat, dust, and iron. He did not feel strong. He felt honed.

The heat clung to him as he stripped off the padded tunic and hung it on the rack, steam rising faintly from his arms. He wiped his brow with a coarse rag, ran a hand over the back of his neck, and checked the time. One more class for the day.

The Rifleman course met just beyond the main training fields, where the range stretched into the yellowed grassland. Rows of earthen berms lay etched into the slope, marked with faded flags at 100, 200, and 300 meters. The white banner of the Confederation snapped lazily in the breeze. Here, there was little talk, a different sort of reverence filled the air. Each boy approached the arms rack in turn. What waited for them were not sleek composite rifles of modern war, but dark wood and blackened steel. Bolt-action Mausers that were chambered in the ancient 8mm cartridge. Their serial numbers whispered history. Some dated back nearly three centuries, relics of the first Great War on Earth. They bore the patina of age, but remained functional, precise, and deadly. Reinhardt took his rifle with both hands. The weight was honest with no electronics or sensors. Just walnut, steel, and will. The instructor, Herr Volmer, paced slowly in front of them. His face was marked by a deep burn on the left side, and one eye was stitched shut.

"You do not use these rifles," he said calmly. "You inherit them."

He let the words hang in the air.

"They were carried at Verdun, Ypres, and Kursk. Passed down in silence by fathers who never returned. Today you fire their memory."

Each boy knelt at the bench. Clips were issued with five rounds per volley. Reinhardt loaded, chambered, and waited.

"First phase, iron sight zero. One hundred meters. Tight groups. Center mass. No optics. No excuses."

He settled in. The sling looped around his elbow. The stock locked into his shoulder. The front post floated in the rear notch. Breath half-released.

Crack.

The rifle kicked against his shoulder like a living thing. The shot cracked across the valley. Brass pinged onto the bench. He cycled the bolt, steady, and fired again.

Crack.

He adjusted windage two clicks left. Slowed his breathing and let the rifle guide him. By the third set, he felt it. The quiet, the presence and the rhythm. It no longer felt like firing a weapon, it felt like communion. Herr Volmer stopped behind him, observing through a battered spotting glass.

"Tighter now, but nearly perfect. Your cheek weld is drifting, correct it."

Reinhardt nodded, correcting the pressure of his jaw against the worn wood. He squeezed the trigger with care. As the smoke cleared and the last shells cooled, Volmer spoke to the class.

"These are not toys. They are not for sport. This is your spine. This is the will of law, forged in fire and blood."

The boys stood. They cleared chambers and returned the rifles. Reinhardt lingered a moment longer, fingers on the bolt, feeling the warmth. It had not been a game. It had been a rite. The rifle was not just an armament. It was an heirloom, passed through the ages, binding the dead to the living. As they were dismissed and the sun dropped low, Reinhardt slung his satchel and walked off the range, the last rays of daylight casting long shadows over the flag. As Reinhardt crossed the training field, the gravel crunched under his boots in steady rhythm. The sun was dipping now, casting long shadows and washing the concrete range in amber light.

He passed beneath the banner of the Pan-European Confederation, its white field rippling gently in the wind. The six golden-stars, one for each brother-people of Europe, gleamed around the central solar sunwheel like a guardian in orbit. It was a flag born not from treaties, but from sacrifice. Then, from the rooftop loudspeakers came a soft electric crackle. Then, clear and unwavering, the slow march began.

"Ich hatt' einen Kameraden... einen bessern findst du nicht."

Reinhardt halted, his boots locked in place. He turned crisply on his heel and faced the flag. His right arm rose in a clean Roman salute, palm down, and eyes fixed. Around the grounds other students did the same on the walkways, in doorways, or beside the stone wall near the garden. All facing the banner. All still.

The old soldier's song rang out across the grounds. A hymn not to glory, but to brotherhood.

"Er wollt' mir die Hand noch reichen, derweil ich eben lad'.

Kann dir die Hand nicht geben, bleibst du doch mein guter Kamerad.

Mein guter Kamerad..."

The final words echoed, slower, deeper, and spoken now by memory more than melody. Mein guter Kamerad, the phrase lingered like smoke on the cold air, solemn and unshaken. Reinhardt held his salute a moment longer, then slowly lowered his arm. He turned and resumed walking, boots falling with quiet certainty. The sun touched the edge of the forest, and the wind shifted behind him, carrying away the last note. The day was done.

The gravel crunched beneath Reinhardt's boots as he left the school grounds. The air had grown cooler, the sunlight thinning through the high pines that lined the road toward the homestead. Dust clung to the hem of his trousers. He walked with his satchel slung over one shoulder, the day's weight hanging heavier on his chest than on his back. The anthem still echoed in his skull, not as melody but as memory.

Ahead, the house came into view. It was stone and timber, built in the old style. The shutters were drawn back, and the chimney whispered a line of smoke into the evening sky. To the side of the home, the family's modest tractor was parked under the overhang beside stacks of firewood and sacks of concrete mix from the co-op. Inside, the smell of baked root vegetables and pork broth filled the air. His mother, Annika, stood at the stove, her sleeves rolled above the elbow. She glanced over her shoulder and offered him a soft smile as he stepped in.

"Wash up," she said simply.

He nodded, setting his satchel down and ducking into the washroom before returning to the table. His father, Gerhard, was already seated, shirt unbuttoned at the collar, rubbing the bridge of his nose as if the day had been long. Across from him sat Uncle Ludwig, hands clasped and posture straight. A militia field jacket hung on the back of his chair, the armband folded neatly in the front pocket.

The four of them ate mostly in silence. The only sound was the clinking of spoons and the low hum of the electric lantern above. Now and then, his mother asked about school, which Reinhardt answered in measured words. When he mentioned Herr Brandt's lecture, Ludwig looked up briefly.

"Brandt still quotes Goethe like scripture?"

"Better him than Kant," Gerhard muttered.

Ludwig smirked, but said nothing more. There was no argument, but it happened from time to time. Though, the tension sat in the room like a fifth chair. After dinner, Reinhardt helped his mother with the dishes while the two men sat by the hearth. Their conversation drifted toward local matters including supply logistics, militia drills, and news from the radio. The conversation didn't boil over, but was never truly warm. When the plates were dried and the fire had begun to settle low, Reinhardt excused himself.

He climbed the wooden stairs slowly, each step creaking softly beneath his weight. His room was modest with a bed, a desk, and a small armoire. Over the desk hung a faded reproduction of a Roman legionary standard, and beside it an old National Socialist war banner in the Prussian style. It was a red banner with a black hooked-cross at the center of a cross. Nearby is a neatly folded militia tunic he had yet to earn the right to wear. He sat on the edge of his bed for a moment, staring at the dusky blue out his window. Downstairs, his father spoke in quiet tones. His uncle answered with fewer words. He lay back, closed his eyes, and exhaled. The day was over. The dread had subsided and tomorrow something new will come.

Chapter

2

The knock on the wooden door was not loud, but it was final.

"Reinhardt," came the voice that was calm, low, and unmistakably his uncle's. "Get up, you're burning daylight."

Reinhardt stirred beneath the linen sheets, the last weight of sleep dragging behind his eyes. his muscles ached faintly from yesterday's drills, but the ache was clean and earned. A swallow of air in the room smelled of ash and iron, and somewhere outside, a crow cried once. The knock came again, just once.

"I'm up," Reinhardt said, his voice dry.

He swung his legs out from under the covers and stood. He didn't bother checking the mirror or smoothing his hair. If he had slept in, it was only by minutes, and Ludwig would say nothing more about it. Though he'd note it, the man always did. He stepped into his work trousers, slipped on a plain black tunic and black jackboots then stepped out into the narrow hallway. The house was quiet, his parents still asleep. Only Ludwig was awake, already in the front room, kneeling beside the heavy case that sat beneath the coat rack like a buried relic, the old machine gun. It was wrapped in canvas, the corners frayed from decades of oil, dirt, and movement. Ludwig had kept it through two tours and now as part of the militia's reserve weapons inventory. Technically, it belonged to the Confederation, but in practice, it was Ludwig's alone.

"You're late," Ludwig said without looking up.

"I'm here," Reinhardt replied, kneeling down beside him.

"Good."

Without another word Ludwig peeled back the canvas revealing the aged but still-solid weapon, a MG-82. A belt-fed general-purpose machine gun chambered in 7.92×57mm, a round more than 300 years old. It was a descendent of the MG-42, though heavier, more refined, and rebuilt for the age of the Confederation. This particular one bore a scratched engraving on the receiver...

GEB FÜR EUROPA

Born for Europe

They worked in silence for a while, Reinhardt holding the barrel assembly while Ludwig disassembled the bolt group. The smell of cleaning solvent began to fill the air, mingling with the faint scent of coal from the stove.

"Have you ever fired her?" Ludwig asked eventually, nodding to the gun.

"No," Reinhardt replied. "I've seen drills, even the dead-gunner drill."

"You will today."

Ludwig's hands moved with precision, every gesture deliberate, hardened by repetition. "She's like a living thing. Feed her wrong, she jams. Treat her wrong, she bites. You take care of her, and she'll drown the bastards in lead."

Reinhardt said nothing, only watched. There was reverence in Ludwig's movements, but not ceremony. This wasn't religion. This was stewardship. After a few minutes, Ludwig sat back and inspected the bolt group, then passed it over.

"Your turn."

Reinhardt took the parts into his hand, cold steel and grease slick on his fingers. He wiped them down with practiced efficiency, the same way he had cleaned practice rifles at school. Yet this wasn't school. This was his uncle's gun, and that made all the difference.

They finally exited the house. They began their foot movement. They stepped off the gravel road and onto the wooded trail at a steady pace, the morning sun just beginning to break through the upper branches. The air was cool, but the walk would warm them quickly. Ludwig led the way, MG-82 slung across his back, barrel angled down. One arm gripped the center handle of a dual-slot ammo can rig, two olive-green boxes of 7.92mm belted rounds clinking softly with each stride.

Reinhardt followed just behind, two cans in each hand and a folded blanket draped over his shoulder. The fabric was coarse, woolen, and older than him, in the old field-green coloration. Each step was deliberate, boots pressing into damp moss and pine-needled soil.

"You keep pace well," Ludwig said after a few minutes of walking. "Good legs. The hike is four kilometers. That's about two and a half miles, in the old measurement."

They passed a stone marker embedded in the root of an old oak. Reinhardt glanced at it, moss-covered and etched with a faded sunburst. The walk was familiar to Ludwig. There was no hesitation in his gait. This wasn't exercise. It was a pilgrimage. For a while, the only sounds were birdsong, the rattling of brass, and the occasional snap of twigs underfoot.

Eventually, they reached the clearing. It wasn't large, maybe thirty meters across, but the tree line had been thinned and pushed back in years past, and a long earthen berm curved around the far edge like a half-moon. The stumps were old, sun-bleached and dry. A few rusted casings from past drills still lay embedded in the soil.

"This is where my squad zeroed in... days before," Ludwig said. "We didn't have the range back at the depot, so we had to hike out. Some of these stumps have our names carved in. Mine's still there, somewhere."

Ludwig unslung the MG-82, setting it down with care. The weapon was matte black steel with a ribbed receiver and a heavy fluted barrel ending in a compensated muzzle. The bipod folded out with a practiced flick. Reinhardt laid down the blanket while Ludwig cracked open the first ammo can.

"Load belt," Ludwig said, handing him a fresh fifty-round length. "Start with five rounds. No need to waste."

Reinhardt fed the belt carefully into the feed tray, his hands sure despite the weight of the moment. When he locked the cover down, Ludwig nodded.

"Good. Fire from prone, bipod down. Center the rear sight. Front post just under the target."

Reinhardt nodded and dropped flat behind the gun, tucking the buttstock tight into his shoulder. The bipod sank slightly into the earth as he settled into the firing position, cheek pressed to cold wood. Ludwig stepped to the side, arms crossed, watching.

"The range is eighty meters, dead tree in the middle. I want that bark stripped."

Reinhardt adjusted his stance slightly, sucked in a slow breath, and exhaled. His finger curled, and then the MG-82 cracked. A staccato burst of sound and recoil, a flickering flame at the muzzle, brass showering to his right. The noise shattered the birdsong and echoed off the berm like thunder in a canyon. Five rounds, a heartbeat and gone. Ludwig crouched beside him, silent. They walked the line. The rounds had struck low and to the left. The rounds were close, but not on mark.

"Recenter your rear sight," Ludwig said. "You're anchoring too far forward. Relax, you don't force this weapon. You guide it."

They walked back, ten rounds in another burst. This time, the bark on the dead tree exploded outward in a cloud of wood and dust. Ludwig said nothing, only knelt and began feeding the next belt. The clearing echoed with gunfire, the MG-82 breathing like a mechanical beast. Smoke drifted low in the air. Reinhardt's shoulder ached, his hands were caked with soil and grease, but he was steady. He had found the rhythm. Ludwig stepped beside him and crouched.

"Time to push," he said. "We don't fire like parade girls. War isn't generous. It's brutal, fast, and unforgiving. Reload on my signal. Malfunction when I say. If I go down, you take the gun. Understood?"

"Yes, uncle."

"Good."

Ludwig pointed to the tree. "That bark. It's your enemy. Strip it, beat it, and break it."

Reinhardt lay prone again, feeding the fresh belt. He braced.

"Fire!"

Reinhardt squeezed the trigger. Ten rounds thundered out in a controlled burst. Brass scattered in arcs. He paused.

"Reload!"

Reinhardt popped the top cover, yanked out the empty belt, slapped in a fresh one from the open can beside him, and slammed it shut. He fired again, less than six seconds later.

"Good. Malfunction!"

Reinhardt tried the trigger, nothing. He kept the weapon down, reached up, racked the charging handle, and felt resistance, bolt jam. Without panic, he tapped the cover open, cleared the belt, slid the bolt back and forward twice. Dust fell from the receiver. He re-fed the belt and re-engaged. The tree bled bark. Ludwig was smiling with his arms crossed. Then he went silent. He dropped beside Reinhardt, face-first into the dirt and motionless. Reinhardt froze, then he moved. The training kicked in. He crawled over Ludwig's body, grabbed him by the collar and shoulder, rolled him over onto his back, and shoved him aside in one swift motion, rough but practiced with no hesitation. He took the gun's position, planted his elbows, and found the sight picture again. He fired. A controlled burst ripped through the clearing, clean and centered. The tree shook from impact, smoke drifted across Reinhardt's vision. Ludwig sat up slowly and exhaled, brushing leaves from his jacket.

"Well done," he said. "Not clean, but fast. That's what matters. You didn't hesitate."

Reinhardt's chest heaved. His mouth was dry.

"Do you know what that's called?" Ludwig asked.

"Dead gunner drill...?"

"No," Ludwig said, rising to his feet. "It's called inheritance. You don't wait for someone to tell you the world is yours. You take it when the one before you falls."

He looked down at Reinhardt.

"To carry the machine is to carry a world that can never fall again."

Reinhardt's lungs still fought for air. His body trembled, not from fear but from the weight of the moment. His finger had just danced with real war. He stared at the torn tree and then looked to Ludwig, who stood beside the weapon like a sentinel.

"Uncle," Reinhardt asked, breath still shallow, "what does it mean to you that speed is violence, violence is freedom?"

Ludwig tilted his head and for a second the edge of his lip curled, part smirk and part exhaustion. He picked up a canteen and took a swig before passing it down to Reinhardt.

"You asking me what the priests of the black pin mean," he muttered, glancing down at Reinhardt.

Reinhardt didn't answer, he waited. Ludwig sighed, crouched beside him, and looked out toward the smoke-hazed trees. "It means don't hesitate. If you hesitate, you die. If you charge first, the enemy blinks. That's the truth behind it but those thunder-pin boys, they talk like poets. I don't care much for it."

He looked Reinhardt in the eye.

"You want to be a soldier? Then be a soldier and join the army. Hell, go active militia if you want to stay close to home. If you think that wearing their black tunic and quoting thunder makes you a hero then you're not ready to be one."

Reinhardt took a drink. The water was warm and metallic from the canteen but it steadied him.

"I thought you respected them," he said, cautious.

"I respect anyone who fights for Europe," Ludwig said plainly. "But the ESS? They're not the army. They don't hold ground. They don't dig foxholes. They strike, disappear, and burn. They answer to something higher than orders."

He stood up, dusting himself off.

"And men who answer to ideas rather than officers, well... some become saints but most become ghosts."

Reinhardt nodded slowly and respectfully but the agreement was more gesture than conviction. He understood what Ludwig was saying. He even saw the logic in it. Something in him pushed back. The ESS wasn't just pageantry. They weren't ghosts. They were the flame, the blade in the dark, and the judgment in motion. Ludwig didn't miss the hesitation behind his nephew's eyes. He squinted at him, then asked plainly, "Where'd you hear that line anyway?"

Reinhardt didn't need to think. "Herr Brandt."

That name settled the air between them. Ludwig grunted, no surprise. Brandt's reputation was known across the district as an ESS veteran, decorated, respected, and perhaps feared.

"Is he still wearing that black pin on his collar?" Ludwig asked, half-smiling.

Reinhardt gave a short nod. "White thunderbolts on black enamel."

Ludwig chuckled through his nose, almost fondly. "Figures, he always had a taste for ceremony."

There was no bitterness in the words, only distance. Like watching a storm roll across someone else's land.

"I'll give him this," Ludwig added, adjusting the sling on the MG-82, "He came back different, but not broken, while a lot of them didn't."

They stood in silence for a few moments. Reinhardt looked back to the torn tree where his burst had struck. In his chest, the weight of Brandt's voice still echoed. Speed is violence, violence is freedom. It didn't sound like poetry to him. It sounded like the truth. Ludwig gestured toward the path home. "Let's get moving. Got a few hours of light left, and your mother'll be pissed if we're late for dinner."

Reinhardt followed, the weight of the ammo cans digging into his fingers. The greater weight, the question of what kind of man he would become, pressed heavier. The walk back was brisk. Neither uncle nor nephew said much, the crunch of dry earth and brush underfoot filling the quiet. Reinhardt's arms ached from hauling the weight of the ammo cans, but he bore it without complaint. The sun had dipped just enough to cast long shadows behind them, painting the land gold.

They crested the final hill. Below lay the house, white stone and timber, weather-worn but proud. Smoke trailed from the chimney. A horse tied to the side-post stirred and snorted. Ludwig stepped through the door first, slinging the MG-82 down with practiced ease. Reinhardt followed, careful with the ammo. The warmth of the hearth met them immediately, along with the faint scent of roasting roots and salted meat. His mother stood over the stove, her sleeves rolled up, hair tied back, stirring with one hand and tasting with the other. She turned at the sound of boots on wood and smiled. “Wash up, both of you. Dinner’s nearly done.”

“Jawohl,” Ludwig replied with a semi-sarcastic grin, already moving to the basin.

At the table, Gerhardt looked up from an old book. It is something leather-bound, creased and dog-eared, its title worn thin from use. He took in the sight of his son with soot on his cheek, his brother with oil-stained hands, and both carrying the trappings of war. His brow creased. Not in anger, but disapproval. He set the book down with deliberate care. “Out with the gun again?”

Ludwig answered without shame. “Better to train him now than bury him later.”

Gerhardt didn’t reply immediately. His eyes moved to Reinhardt, then back to Ludwig. “He’s not a soldier.”

“Not yet,” Ludwig said, wiping his hands on a towel. “But this world doesn’t ask permission.”

“He’s a farm boy,” Gerhardt muttered. “He should stay one.”

“Farm boys die just as easy when the time comes,” Ludwig replied evenly.

Their mother clattered a pot down to interrupt the silence. “Enough, both of you.”

The room stilled. Gerhardt returned to his book, but didn’t open it. Ludwig leaned against the wall, arms crossed, eyes quietly studying the flame in the stove. Reinhardt stood between them, not sure which shadow he stood closer to. Dinner was nearly ready. His mother only shook her head, turning back to the stove in silence. She had lived through enough arguments between the two to know they never ended cleanly, only with time or silence. Gerhardt tapped his fingers once on the closed book, then looked back at Ludwig. “You think every boy should be a killer now?”

Ludwig didn’t flinch. “I think every boy should know what’s coming. What’s already here? You think we’re safe in this colony? You think the enemy will care whether your son plows fields or pulls a trigger?"

Gerhardt narrowed his eyes. "There's more to a man than war."

"There used to be," Ludwig replied. "But now? The world isn't made for soft men, Gerhardt. You know that."

"I know we came here to build," the younger brother snapped. "To work. To make something that would last. Not just to teach the next generation to shoot machine guns in the woods."

"And what happens when the work you've done is put to flame?" Ludwig's voice was low, not angry, but steady. "When men come and take what you've built because no one stands ready to stop them?"

Gerhardt opened his mouth but no words came, only his jaw tightened. Reinhardt looked between them. The fire popped in the hearth. The scent of smoked root vegetables now mixed with charred pork belly and liver. His stomach rumbled, but he didn't move. His mother finally turned, carrying the pot to the table. She said nothing. Just set it down with quiet hands and then went to retrieve bread and knives with no eye contact or interruptions.

They sat. First Ludwig, then Reinhardt, then finally Gerhardt, who muttered a prayer before tearing a piece of bread in half and passing it down. Dinner was quiet. Knives scraped gently against wood bowls. The meat was salted well, the vegetables rich with herbs, but Reinhardt barely tasted any of it. He chewed, nodded when spoken to, and kept his eyes low.

The silence held like the tension before a storm as thick, motionless, and waiting for the break, but none came. Only the ticking of the old clock by the mantle. The shifting of weight in chairs. The slow, tired sounds of a house full of men who loved one another but could not agree on what that love demanded. The fire crackled softly, plates clinked and spoons scraped. No one said a word. Gerhardt chewed with quiet intensity, staring into his bowl like it might offer some answer he couldn't find in the faces of his brother or his son. Ludwig ate slower, deliberate, and his hands always near the radio clipped to his belt, the receiver resting just above his hip. Reinhardt kept his eyes on his bread, feeling every breath between them, unsure whether to speak or swallow the moment whole. Then, Click. Bzzt. The militia radio that was Ludwig's came to life with a burst of static, loud in the dead quiet.

"...Delta-Two, Delta-Two, this is Homepost. Immediate priority. Repeat, immediate. A barn complex at grid six-four-seven was found burning, family not accounted for. A militia patrol unit on site reports signs of forced entry. Blood present. Multiple casings, burned livestock. No confirmed survivors. Possible Red Twilight involvement. Proceed with caution."

A long pause. Then, static again. Ludwig was already standing. Gerhardt didn't move. His eyes locked on the table, jaw tense, and knuckles tight around his spoon. Reinhardt looked to his uncle then to his father. Ludwig unhooked the receiver from his belt, pressed the call button.

"This is Delta-Two, acknowledged. Will prepare for patrol. Out."

He clipped it back. No words, just that same steady presence. A man trained to move when others froze. Reinhardt swallowed hard. "That was just up the road, wasn't it?"

Ludwig nodded once. Gerhardt didn't look at either of them. "They'll send someone else."

"They just did," Ludwig replied.

Silence again. The fire cracked louder now, as if offended by the intrusion of horror into the warmth of its glow. Outside, the wind had shifted. It grew colder and tighter against the windows. Reinhardt felt it then, that creeping pull again. Not as dread this time, but clarity. They weren't safe, not really. They never were. Ludwig reached for his coat.

"I'm going," he said quietly. "Don't wait up."

Ludwig moved with focus, not urgency. He grabbed his militia pack from the hallway peg, flipped open the old wooden chest by the door, and pulled out the folded webbing. The soft clink of metal buckles and the stiff sound of canvas straps filled the room like a second pulse. His face was stone, not worried but working. Reinhardt stood slowly. He glanced at the window, then at the door. Without thinking, he stepped toward it, cracked it open, and leaned forward into the night air. The wind had shifted more than just the temperature. Now it carried the scent of smoke. Out past the sparse line of oaks, past the low hill that broke the horizon, fire. A barn complex, silhouetted in orange and red. Far off, yet not far enough. Flames licked up like the tongue of some ancient beast, greedy and vengeful, devouring roof beams and rafters alike. Smoke rose high into the darkening sky, a plume of ruin. He stood in the doorway for several heartbeats. He was watching but not blinking. Then he turned and stepped back inside. The warmth of the house felt alien now, stupid yet soft and small. He stood still in the entryway, eyes locked to the floorboards beneath his feet, then slowly lifted them toward Ludwig. The older man didn't look up, still busy cinching down a side pouch and checking the tension on his belt.

Reinhardt didn't speak. He turned, walked to the stairs, and climbed them in silence. In his room, the air was colder, it always was. The militia jacket hung on the wall peg above his desk. Grey and functional, yet worn-in just enough to feel like his. He pulled it down and shrugged it on. His field cap sat beside a copy of Mein Kampf and Codreanu's For My Legionnaires. He tucked it on without a second thought, then made for the door. Boots thudded against the steps as he descended. Ludwig was tightening the sling on the MG-82 when Reinhardt reappeared.

"I'm coming with you," he said.

Ludwig looked up at last, surprised but only slightly. He let the silence stretch. Then nodded once.

"Grab your boots, soldier."

Reinhardt pulled the gray field cap tight over his brow and cinched the strap on his militia jacket. It was a thin, worn canvas that was dyed in the flat stone-gray of Delumina's militia corps. The right shoulder bore the embroidered patch of the colony, wheat over a rising sun, and his chest carried his name tag: JÄGER. Across from it was the red-threaded stripe denoting cadet status. He fastened the buttons with quick, efficient fingers.

Ludwig was already in the hall, slinging the MG-82 over his shoulder. He wore no armor either, just a simple olive drab tunic, a reinforced leather belt, and soft-soled field boots. His sleeves were rolled up to the elbow, exposing forearms seasoned by decades of labor and war. The machine gun hung diagonally across his back. In one hand he carried two old surplus ammunition cans, their olive paint scratched with age. Reinhardt mirrored him by gripping two more, his arms taut from the weight. Neither of them spoke. They moved with the instinctive choreography of men preparing for the unknown as belt pouches checked, canteens topped off, and old wax-paper rations shoved into side pockets. No mess kits were packed or bedrolls. This wasn't a march to a camp or a roadside picnic.

"We pack light," Ludwig finally said, nodding at Reinhardt's belt. "Ammo, water, and salt. That's what keeps you alive. Armor only slows you down."

Reinhardt nodded. He knew the doctrine, everyone in the border colonies did. You don't outrun an ambush in plating. You don't keep your bearings weighed down like a grave statue. Gerhard stood in the kitchen doorway, arms crossed. His eyes were narrowed, jaw clenched, not in anger but disappointment. Still, he said nothing. Annika stood behind him, lips pursed, with one hand clutched around the dish towel she hadn't put down since the call came over the radio.

"You're still just a boy," Gerhard finally muttered, more to the floor than to his son but Reinhardt didn't answer.

He gave a single, respectful nod to his mother, who gave no response save for a quiet shake of her head. Then the door opened, and the night air washed over them. Smoke drifted across the starlit horizon like a black, skeletal hand clawing toward the heavens. The fire was a few kilometers down the ridge, maybe five, but it burned bright enough to stain the treetops in amber. Ludwig adjusted the gun on his shoulder. "Two-point-five klicks to the treeline, another five if they ran. Might be more out there."

"Are we the only ones going?" Reinhardt asked.

"We're the first ones moving. Others will catch up, or not. It doesn't matter. We're recce, and if there's a shot to take, we take it. Understand?"

Reinhardt nodded. They stepped off the porch into the wild dusk. The gravel crunched softly beneath their boots as they set off down the road, then veered into the woods to avoid the light. The moon hung low, yellow and watching.

Trees loomed tall and silent. Each step into the dark felt like a narrowing tunnel. Reinhardt breathed in through his nose, slow and steady. The weight of the cans pulled on his fingers. His rifle, the STG-91, slung across his chest shifted with his gait. It was heavier than a bolt-action but more dependable, chambered in 6.8x42mm Kurz Hochdruck. The brass-cased rounds were punchy, high-velocity, and brutal at mid-range. He'd zeroed it just a week ago. No words passed between them for the first kilometer. The hunt had begun.

Chapter
3

The road was quiet, save for the distant hum of cicadas and the crunch of gravel under boots. Reinhardt kept pace beside his uncle, sweat beading beneath his field cap, and his STG-91 slung tight across his chest. The scent of ash still clung to the wind, drifting like a ghost from over the hill. They had walked nearly four kilometers, maybe more. Neither had spoken much since leaving the house. Ludwig carried the MG-82 like it was part of him, one arm slung through the sling, the other balancing a pair of ammo cans. Reinhardt bore his own burden of two cans of ammunition, water flasks clipped to his belt, and rations in his pouch. No body armor or frills, just the essentials. Then came the call. The radio on Ludwig's chest crackled once, then came through clearly.

"This is Gerling One. All local elements converge on Sector 3. Fire confirmed at the Wessel farmstead. Possible enemy withdrawal. Repeat, converge on Sector 3, Wessel farmstead."

Ludwig clicked the mic twice in acknowledgment, no words. Reinhardt said nothing, but his spine straightened. His hands gripped his rifle a little tighter. They moved off the road and began cutting across open pastures. The sky had darkened with smoke, thick columns rising above the horizon. When they crested the next hill, the Wessel farmhouse came into view, what was left of it. Blackened timber jutted up like ribs, flames still smoldering in the barn. A calf, half-charred, lay motionless in the field. The garden was trampled. The fence was blown open, but they weren't alone.

At least two dozen figures were gathered. They were all militiamen, both young and old. Some wore proper uniforms, others in patched jackets and boots wrapped in tape. All were armed, some had modern rifles while others held weapons that looked inherited, passed from father to son. Then Reinhardt saw him, Herr Brandt. He stood just beyond the barn ruins, speaking with several men in low, sharp tones. His uniform was different now. Less formal. A long overcoat, sleeves rolled back, the same black collar pin with the white twin-thunderbolts gleaming in the ash-light. His face was streaked with soot. One hand rested on the hilt of a sidearm. The other held a field map. He turned and their eyes met. Brandt's expression did not change, but he gave a short nod, a silent acknowledgment. Reinhardt felt something stir in his chest. It was not pride, not fear, but a kind of grim certainty. They weren't in class anymore. This was real.

Ludwig murmured beside him, "Looks like your teacher is running the show."

Reinhardt nodded once. "Yes, he is."

Brandt raised his voice slightly, speaking now to the assembled group.

"We move before dusk. Red Twilight left tracks northbound. If they're smart, they're long gone. If they're not, we'll find out soon enough."

He paused. His eyes lingered briefly on Reinhardt.

"Those of you who've never been under fire, stay near the veterans. Watch, learn, and stay quiet. We do this clean, or not at all."

There were no cheers, no bravado, just silent nods and the shuffling of boots in preparation. A few men checked their magazines, one crossed himself. A boy maybe two years older than Reinhardt was white in the face, holding a shotgun like a lifeline. Ludwig moved toward the group to speak with a militia corporal. Reinhardt stayed back for a moment, watching and taking it all in. The smell of smoke. The shattered fence. The scattered shells and spent brass. This was a war; quiet, close, and real. It had come home. The militia moved out in squads, the lines quiet and methodical. There were no shouted orders, only hand signals and brief acknowledgments passed down the columns. The smell of scorched earth and ash still lingered in the air as the formation advanced through the forest paths that led northward from the ruined farmhouse. The woods, thick with old pines and moss-covered stone, were eerily silent save for the distant crackle of dying fire and the steady movement of boots on soft dirt.

Fireteam wedges stretched out in bounding overwatch, two-man elements leapfrogging past each other with discipline and cohesion. They advanced in this way along the ridge line and into the low valley, the tactics drilled into them from their earliest days in the militia. For all its volunteer nature, the frontier militias were expected to move with the professionalism of a standing army. Here, there was no time for playacting. Reinhardt stayed glued to his uncle's side, acting as assistant gunner. Ludwig carried the MG-82 with the weapon's bipod slung forward, eyes scanning the woodline. Reinhardt bore two ammo cans in his rucksack, and the long barrel of his STG-91 angled over his shoulder. A full canteen bounced against his hip, along with a basic field dressing kit, two ration bars, and extra magazines.

The unit's leader, Herr Brandt, moved a few meters ahead of them, coordinating the columns. The former ESS man held his rifle close to his chest, his posture rigid but fluid. He did not need to shout. He pointed, gestured, and others followed. Every man knew what to do. The sun was beginning its slow descent into the western horizon when the column paused. A scout returned from the forward element and knelt before Brandt, whispering something hurriedly. Brandt raised a clenched fist, signaling halt.

"Rear element, confirmed. Five, maybe six," the scout reported back as Brandt relayed the word quietly.

Ludwig turned his head. "Red Twilight, caught with their hands full. Probably tried to carry something heavy. Whatever it is slowed them down."

Brandt nodded. "If they're dragging prisoners or gear, they're vulnerable. They won't want to fight, but they will if forced."

The order came in swiftly with two fireteams pushing around to flank the path and coming down from higher elevation while the main body would approach from the forested gully below. It was a simple pincer move, but terrain and speed would decide the outcome. Reinhardt's squad was part of the lower push. They crept forward now, no longer in standard wedge but as a loose skirmish line, taking cover behind brush and fallen logs. Reinhardt's heart pounded in his chest. He felt sweat roll down the side of his cheek, but he did not wipe it away.

Brandt's voice came over the local militia band, "Standby for contact. Ten meters."

Then came the sharp burst of gunfire. Not more than a dozen rounds, controlled, fast.

"CONTACT FRONT!"

Ludwig hit the ground instantly and barked, "Gun team up!"

Reinhardt slammed down the folded blanket onto the dirt and dropped beside it, yanking the bipod legs into place as Ludwig laid prone. The MG-82 was up in seconds. Reinhardt cracked open one ammo can, pulled the belt across, and locked the feed tray with trained speed. Ludwig fired.

The roar of the belt-fed machine gun cut through the forest like thunder, stitching a line across the slope where shadows moved. Reinhardt could just make out three figures diving behind a downed log, their gear clunky and unbalanced. One was dragging something. A sack or a body, he couldn't tell. Return fire came a second later. Cracks and snaps as rounds tore through branches overhead. One man in their column went down, not moving. Brant called for suppressing fire. Reinhardt dropped his rifle to the side and slapped the ammo belt forward as Ludwig kept firing. Spent brass clinked against stone and leaf. Then the gun stopped. From the ridge above, the flanking teams opened fire. Controlled, semi-automatic cracks and a single grenade arced in, sending up a plume of dirt and pine. Then silence.

Brandt's voice again, firm and low: "Cease fire. Cease fire. Cease fire. Secure the area and check for any wounded or casualties."

Ludwig stood, brushing dirt from his jacket and helping Reinhardt up. They exchanged no words, only a nod. His first skirmish was over. While somewhere, just beyond the blood-streaked ridge, the Red Twilight still moved. Now they knew they were being hunted. Reinhardt crouched behind the base of a low earthen berm, eyes scanning the treeline ahead. The adrenaline still hadn't left him. His pulse beat loud in his ears. A few meters away, Ludwig was checking the machine gun's belt feed, resetting it and muttering under his breath about keeping pressure off the sear.

"Fireteam two, advance and clear," came Herr Brant's voice over the comms, crisp and without emotion.

The four-man team surged forward, bounding in pairs toward the area where the last of the Red Twilight fighters had fallen. Reinhardt watched them move with purpose, each man spaced with the discipline of drilled militia, amateur soldiers but not untrained. He kept his rifle tucked into the hollow of his shoulder, scanning for movement but there was nothing. Just the wind through the tall grass and the acrid smell of propellant. Then the call came. "Objective secure. You'll want to see this."

Brandt moved first, striding past the fireteams with Reinhardt and Ludwig following close behind. The dead guerrillas were sprawled out, ragged uniforms soaked in blood. One still had a Molotov in hand, half-broken, the glass cracked but not shattered. The real find was what they'd been dragging. A covered crate, reinforced with metal bands, roughly the length of a coffin. Not just one, two of them. Both heavy, both clearly important enough to slow down their retreat.

Brandt knelt beside the nearest and pulled back the tarp. Inside was a cache of pre-war books, dozens of them. Some old, some more recent, all illegal. Smut, communist, racial demoralization, pacifist pamphlets, and things that hadn't seen the inside of a printing press in decades or longer. A few even had English titles including Gender Beyond the Binary, The Abolition of Manhood, White Skin, False Sin, and World Without Fathers.

"These were headed to a school," one of the fireteam members muttered, disgust rising in his voice.

The second crate was worse. Brandt pulled the tarp off and inside were electronics, data drives, solar chargers, cheap tablets preloaded with propaganda and messaging apps. The Red Twilight hadn't just been torching buildings. They were seeding a network.

"Command will want to see this," Brandt said. "Burn the paper, pack the drives and strip the corpses."

He stood and looked at Reinhardt. "What you saw here today is not war, at least not yet. This is poison and they'll feed it to your little cousins, your sisters, and sons."

Ludwig just shook his head. "Cowards don't win wars. They whisper their way in."

Reinhardt, still pulling security at the edge of the perimeter, felt something settle deeper in him, not rage not fear, but clarity and reason. The kind you don't outgrow.

Reinhardt looked west. The trees thickened and rose along the distant hills. Twilight had fully set in.

Brandt turned to Ludwig. "Take your nephew. Take your squad. Track them down. We'll follow behind as we regroup."

Ludwig nodded curtly. “Understood.”

The order was given. Men reloaded, checked water and rations. The forest ahead was dark, but alive.

They moved in bounding overwatch, one fireteam covered while the other advanced. Reinhardt stayed close to Ludwig, eyes scanning every ridge and root ahead. They crossed a shallow creek, then followed what looked like a boot-trodden path winding up a gentle slope.

“Trail’s warm,” muttered one of the scouts. “Maybe a half-hour lead.”

More signs followed just bits of cloth snagged on bark, crushed moss, and disturbed branches. Then came the stench. A body, strung up between two young trees, rope-cut into the neck. The eyes were gouged, and scrawled across the chest in red paint were the words, “No gods. No fathers. No sons.”

One of the younger militiamen swore. Ludwig only shook his head. The body was quickly taken down and a team was sent back to hold the body back at the farmstead.

“We keep moving.”

The militia fanned out in a wide semicircle around the last known trail. Drones or aircraft were not available. This was a remote stretch of woodland seeded only fifty years prior, still raw and teeming with semi-wild fauna. No cities, no permanent roads, just a frontier. As darkness closed in, Reinhardt spotted it.

“Movement. Southwest ridge. Torchlight.”

They dropped to their knees. Through the gaps in the trees, they could see the faint flicker of fire. Figures moved in low silhouettes, rifles slung, and crouched beside what looked like wounded men and a heavy cart. It was the main cell. A rear detachment of Red Twilight guerrillas, exhausted, and slowed by their burden. Ludwig raised a clenched fist. No advance. No fire. Not yet. From the edge of the trees, Reinhardt watched as the enemy hunkered down in a small depression, unaware of how close the wolves had drawn.

Brandt’s voice whispered over the radio. “We hit at dawn.”

Reinhardt blinked slowly, exhaled, and settled into the loam. The earth was still warm beneath him.

Chapter 4

The woods were still, silent except for the faint rustling of wind-tossed leaves and the hushed cadence of boots shifting in loamy soil. A thick darkness lingered in the treetops, the moonlight choked out by branches, and the men huddled low behind roots and brush. They were scattered in staggered pairs, each fireteam bedded down in improvised concealment across the ridge that overlooked the valley basin where the Red Twilight encampment lay nestled like a cancerous boil. They were on two-hour rotations, classic fireguard. One man watched when the other slept, then they'd trade. Whispered exchanges, nods in the dark. A squeeze on the arm to wake the next watchman. No one complained and certainly no one broke the silence.

Reinhardt sat propped against a felled log, his STG-91 across his lap and eyes locked into the black distance. Beside him, Ludwig snored faintly, wrapped in a gray woolen blanket, with the MG-82 between them like a shared hearth. Reinhardt had already done one shift earlier in the night. This was his second. Even in the quiet, his ears played tricks. A crack of twig, a breath of wind, or the imagined whisper of voices in the foliage. He kept scanning the horizon where the enemy camp should be, just beyond the shallow creek and into the clearing dotted with their stolen supply tents. Somewhere down there, men who had burned the Wessel farm were sleeping and, unbeknownst to their prey, waiting to be killed. Time passed, then, first light. It was a barely perceptible shift in the darkness. The stars dimmed, and a cold gray began seeping into the sky. Reinhardt stirred Ludwig gently. His uncle blinked once and nodded, already awake. The others nearby began doing the same, like a quiet stirring of wolves before a coordinated pounce.

It began. Three rifle shots broke the stillness. Sharp and disciplined shots came from the leftmost flank. Suppressed but unmistakable. Seconds later came the rattle of automatic fire and the ripping roar of a belt-fed gun on the far side of the valley. The entire militia line opened up in disciplined bursts, their positions fanned wide and dug in from hours of waiting. From across the creek, chaos erupted. Shouts in strange dialects. A klaxon call, maybe a whistle. Then gunfire answered back, poorly aimed and sporadic. It's the panicked reply of men caught unaware and too slow to mount a counterattack. Reinhardt clutched his rifle and watched Ludwig rise to his feet in a crouch, MG-82 slung forward, face steeled. This wasn't a drill anymore. This was a real struggle. Reinhardt could tell by the screams. A few of them had been hit. Red Twilight guerrillas sprawled out in the open, caught in their bedrolls or scrambling for cover when the first shots rang out. Some thrashed and groaned, clutching stomachs or limbs. Others went limp before they even hit the ground. A few scattered into the creekbed, crawling through wet brush. The militia was pouring accurate fire down from the ridge, muzzle flashes blinking through the dark timber like fireflies of death.

The bastards were getting their bearings now. Gunfire barked back from the encampment. It was erratic at first, then increasingly concentrated. The guerrillas had been asleep, but they weren't amateurs. They knew how to fight dirty. Rounds whipped through the trees, blindly snapping in the direction of flashes or shouted orders. The militia's firing line returned fire in staggered bursts. Control, discipline, and kill zones were enforced by self control. All militiamen stayed in their lanes of fire. Reinhardt lay low beside Ludwig, his face tense, and every sense alive. His rifle was slung to his side, but his job wasn't to shoot, yet. The MG-82 sat mounted in the fork of a fallen log, Ludwig behind it, calm and expressionless, feeding short bursts into the enemy position. The barrel steamed in the cool air.

Reinhardt kept the spare belt draped around his shoulders, feeding the rounds with gloved fingers. One ammo can was already empty, tossed aside with another sat cracked open beside him. He heard the sound before he felt it. A snap, close, too close. Something slapped the bark inches from his ear. He flinched, ducked down instinctively as time slowed.

He turned and saw Ludwig slump forward. No sound came from his uncle, just the heavy thud of a man suddenly without will, his weight collapsing over the MG-82 like a ragdoll. Blood misted faintly in the early dawn air, trailing from the neat black hole in his cheekbone. The right side of his face was gone. Reinhardt stared, not breathing.

"Uncle..."

No response. The gun went quiet. Reinhardt's hands trembled if only for a moment. He lunged forward and did as he'd been trained. One hand on Ludwig's collar, the other on his belt. He yanked with a grunt and rolled his uncle to the side, the man's body thudding lifeless into the pine needles. He pulled himself onto the gun, slammed the cover open, checked the feed and saw half a belt still good.

He braced the buttstock into his shoulder, peered through the iron sights, picked a target running between tents and fired. The MG-82 roared to life again. Reinhardt kept the gun hot. The belt ran smooth through the feed, the weapon kicking hard against his shoulder. He aimed low, swept the encampment with disciplined bursts, and brass hailing down around his elbows.

Then, movement between the flapping corner of a tent and a smoking crate. He shifted the sights and squeezed. The world slowed. The thunder of the gun faded beneath his heartbeat. All sound dulled, muffled like he was underwater.

The figure stumbled mid-sprint. One arm jerked, then the legs gave out as the man crumpled face-first into the dirt. Blood pooled near the body, slowly darkening the soil. Reinhardt couldn't be sure it was his burst that hit the man. Maybe someone else had landed the shot from another angle. It didn't matter. They'd burned the Wessel farmstead. They'd butchered livestock and dragged families off into the dark. Now his uncle's blood soaked the pine needles beside him. He would make them pay.

He stayed on the gun, feeling the last links of the belt rattle through. The final few rounds chattered out and the gun clicked dry. With practiced hands, he yanked the empty belt free and slammed a fresh one into place from the can. The receiver slammed shut. He yanked the charging handle. Clack. The gun roared again. Then came the call, sharp and distant, from the squad leader farther down the ridge.

"Shift fire! Shift right! Cover the far treeline!"

Reinhardt didn't hesitate. He swung the barrel to the right, aiming past the smoldering remains of the encampment toward the opposing ridge, their likely escape route. Trees swayed slightly in the morning wind. He fired short bursts into the thick brush, not aiming for targets now but laying suppressive fire as the assault element broke cover and surged down the hill.

Militiamen moved like wolves, darting through gaps in the brush and low stone terraces. Two bounding teams leapt forward, clearing deadfall and spreading out as they approached the enemy's position. Reinhardt kept the fire up, scanning for any shape that didn't belong. The gun thundered again, rocking against Reinhardt's shoulder, the barrel now white-hot, and smoking at the vents. His cheek burned from the rising heat, but he didn't flinch. He couldn't. To his left, Ludwig's body sagged in the grass. His face had gone pale, jaw slack, eyes half-lidded and staring past the trees. Reinhardt didn't dare look more than once. Not now. There would be time to mourn later, if there was a later.

The belt ran dry. Reinhardt slapped another into place. His hands moved automatically, one man and one weapon, but he was the fulcrum of the battle. If the gun went silent, the whole line could collapse. The MG-82 wasn't a weapon. It was a vow. A totem of civilization in a world clawing at the edge of savagery.

His breath was heavy, heart thudding in his ears. He didn't know if the last man he dropped was the one who'd killed his uncle. He didn't care. Each pull of the trigger was a hammer-blow of justice. The kind of justice that didn't ask for permission, didn't wait for tribunals, didn't need a court. It just needed to be done.

A voice crackled over the militia comms: "Objective secure. No more contact. Begin SSE. Hold fire."

Reinhardt's hands finally stilled on the grips. The world returned to sound and smell. Distant shouts, crackling flames, the stink of blood and hot brass overwhelmed his senses.. He eased back from the gun, the final shells cooling in the dirt. Only then did he turn and look again, Ludwig hadn't moved. Reinhardt reached down and shut his uncle's only remaining eye with his hand, then pressed his forehead to Ludwig's shoulder for a brief moment. No words, just silence.

Reinhardt rose slowly, wiping his blood-streaked face with the inside of his sleeve. The muscles in his back ached from the recoil, his ears rang like cracked bells, but he stayed standing. He had to. There was no one else left to keep watch on this side of the perimeter. He quickly but reverently took the com system off his uncle. He swung the MG's battered stock back into place, checked the belt, and chambered a fresh round with a snap. Not because he expected more contact but because it gave his hands something to do, something real.

A militia man jogged past in a blur of smoke and ash, rifle held low, scanning the ruined shanties. "SSE team's moving up," he said, barely glancing at Reinhardt. "Do you see any squirters head out north?"

Reinhardt shook his head. "Not a damn one."

He posted up behind a shattered rain barrel and took a knee, bracing the machine gun over it. The barrel was warped and blackened, pockmarked with shrapnel. The camp had once been alive with fires for warmth, beds of old tires and canvas, and half-dug trenches around the edges. Now it was quiet, burned, still twitching with death.

Across the clearing, he could see militia sweeping through the tents, two-by-two. Muffled bursts of conversation on the radio. One man overturned a tarp and fired twice. A body rolled out. It was a young female with blood running black across her chest. She'd been holding a flare pistol. No quarter was given, at least not today. Reinhardt caught movement out of the corner of his eye. A militia youth, maybe fifteen, came trotting toward him with a canteen and a pack. "Sir, uh... need water?"

"I am not a sir and not now," Reinhardt muttered. "Stay behind cover. You see any movement, shout first."

The boy hesitated, then nodded and scurried to a low embankment nearby, setting up with a bolt-action rifle that looked older than his great, great grandfather. Before the boy moved to cover Reinhardt granted him access to his STG-91. Better the boy have an autoloader than a bolt-action.

A shout rang out, "Cache found! Got papers, comms gear, Red Book fragments!"

Another voice followed soon after, "Tunnel entrance here! One confirmed dead inside, still warm!"

Reinhardt's jaw tightened. A tunnel meant escape route meant someone might've slipped out, maybe even the bastard who put the round through Ludwig's skull.

He keyed his comms, "Tunnel confirmed on the west side of camp. Lock it down, and toss frags. Nobody gets out."

A crackle of acknowledgment. A few seconds later, thoom thoom, two detonations from below. Dirt and smoke belched from a hole in the ground. Reinhardt didn't flinch. Reinhardt had become an impromptu leader with the death of his uncle, inheriting the responsibility of both the machine gun and much more. He looked back at Ludwig one more time. Still there. Still silent.

"Your war's over. Mine isn't." Reinhardt said quietly to himself.

His fingers tensed on the grips again. One more pull of the trigger, maybe it would finally be enough, but it wouldn't be today.

"Reinhardt," the squad leader's voice came over the comms. "hold position. Keep that gun up 'til the sweep's done. You'll be last off the line."

.The barrel steamed faintly in the morning chill, its sheen dulled by streaks of blood and soot. Reinhardt crouched low behind a stack of sandbags blackened by smoke. His eyes were fixed on the treeline beyond the camp. His thoughts were far off, hovering somewhere between the still-burning wreckage and the quiet weight on his shoulder.

"I don't know if it was him."

That truth gnawed at him. He'd cut down several men, that he was convinced. The blur of recoil, fire, and shouting made it impossible to say. His uncle had dropped mid-firing and mid-breath, with a clean shot through the side of the face. Gone, just like that. Reinhardt had answered with fire. He'd painted the perimeter red, stitched men apart like meat but he still didn't know if the one who did it had bled. His fingers rested loose on the grips. No trigger discipline anymore, just habit. His breathing was steady now. He watched the wind bend the leaves beyond the clearing and wondered if any of them were still out there. Not rats fleeing tunnels, but real ones, ideologically committed and dangerous.

A shape moved near the center of the camp. Militia were forming up, two on either side of three prisoners, Red Twilight, young and dirty. Two men and one woman, all wearing improvised fatigues; sashes dyed black-red. Their hands were zip-tied behind their backs. Blood smeared across their faces, some theirs and others not. Reinhardt didn't shift or lower the gun. He just listened. Brandt's voice cut the stillness, clear and sharp with no softness in it.

"Tell me what you were doing here, what intel you had and what you pulled from the supply depot three days ago. What did you learn during the first contact? Who gave the order to attack that farmstead?"

No answer. The tallest of the three, a boy with hollow cheeks and shaking jaw, spoke first. "We don't answer to you."

Brandt stepped closer. "You do now."

A pause, then the girl broke. Her voice was hoarse, but not frightened, resigned. "The glyph will consume all."

Silence followed. Reinhardt blinked once. Brandt sighed, not in exasperation but more akin to inevitability. He drew his sidearm. The prisoners didn't beg. Didn't flinch.

Crack. The tall one dropped.

Crack. The girl slumped sideways.

Crack. The last let out a breath and fell forward.

Three clean shots, spaced evenly. Not overkill, just execution. A few militia turned away, while one muttered a prayer. Brandt reholstered and nodded once to the field medic. "Strip them, burn what's corrupted and bag the rest."

Reinhardt didn't move. His eyes were back on the treeline. He didn't need to look at the bodies. He'd seen enough. All that mattered was that they wouldn't speak again. Still the question burned, was the one who killed Ludwig among them? He didn't know. He didn't care. He watched the wind again, and kept his hand on the trigger. The smoke was thinning now, curling up into the pale morning sky. It was still early, the kind of chill that clung to your skin even after fire. Reinhardt shifted his stance slightly, cracking his knees as he rose a few inches to readjust behind the gun. He still hadn't been relieved. He didn't ask to be. Voices crackled over the comms, more measured now and calm. The kind of calm that only came after death had passed and left its tally.

"Final report coming up, Brandt. Ready copy."

Brandt's voice answered without hesitation. "Go ahead."

The militia radioman, posted just outside the ruined center tent, began reading aloud for all on net:

"Red Twilight camp neutralized. Twenty-five enemy confirmed KIA, including six from the night engagement. Three captured, executed following noncompliance and extremist incantation. Two friendly fallen; Ludwig Jäger, machine gun team, and Hans Schmidt, rifleman, second element. Three wounded and ambulatory, no medevac needed at this time. Weapons seized: nine automatic rifles, one marksman's carbine, two belt-fed LMGs, unknown number of handguns and hand-made explosives. One crate of pre-war ammunition was recovered. Censored material: multiple Red Book fragments, Molten Glyph banners, and printed manifestos burned. A shrine containing blood-marked glyphs collapsed and incinerated under controlled fire. Intel packets secured, awaiting review. All SSE elements complete. Camp integrity shattered. No enemy survivors are known."

There was a pause. No one replied.

Then Brandt gave the only answer needed. "Understood. Begin collection and strip the field. We move before noon."

Reinhardt exhaled. The words landed with dull finality. Not satisfied with closure, just completion. He looked to where they had thrown a canvas over Ludwig's body. It hadn't moved. The second fallen, Hans, lay nearby. A boot is missing and a strange stillness in his posture. One of the wounded, bleeding from the thigh, limped past carrying a satchel of documents. Another passed by dragging a sack of looted rifles with one hand and cradling a broken arm with the other. They weren't broken, just bleeding. These are men who'd survived.

Reinhardt finally spoke into the comms. His voice was low but firm. "MG post clear. No movement. Permission to fall back for debrief."

The reply came swift. Brandt again. "Granted. Bring the weapon in. Leave nothing behind."

Reinhardt nodded to himself. He unbraced the gun, slung it across his shoulders, and stepped over the spent casings littered like bones. The battlefield was quiet now. Only the soft murmur of wind, rustling tents, and the far-off snap of canvas tearing from its moorings could be heard.

Chapter 5

The shattered remnants of the militia formed a rough column around Brandt, rallying at the gutted heart of the Red Twilight camp. The bodies had been burned, the shrines collapsed, the ground scoured. But the glyphs still lingered etched into bark, smeared on stone, or carved into bone. Nothing truly died here, only decayed.

Reinhardt joined them quietly. No announcement. No nod. Just merged in, the MG slung across his shoulder like a crucifix of brass and steel. His boots crushed ash, spent brass, and bone without distinction. Behind him, two militiamen carried the body of his uncle, Ludwig Jäger. They'd wrapped him in a poncho, but his boots still showed. One of them had a hole from the shot that killed him.

The march to the Wessel farmstead took the better part of an hour. The sun had fully risen now, pale and unsympathetic, casting long shadows that made every man look taller than he was but more hollow. No one spoke. Even the wounded trudged without complaint. Even the green boys, some no older than Reinhardt, kept their eyes forward with their rifles tight to their chests.

When the smoldering ruins of the Wessel farmstead came into view, the line stopped briefly. The place had once been a working homestead with wheat, pigs and old brickwork barns. Now it was charred earth and a roofless shell, the blackened timbers sticking out like ribs from a starved corpse. Brandt turned, his voice sharp but calm as it had always been.

"Final headcount."

A militia runner moved down the line, calling off numbers.

"Thirty-seven present. Two fallen and three wounded, all ambulatory. No missing."

Brandt nodded once. "Acknowledged. This concludes action under militia order. All personnel are relieved, field command dissolves. Medical and resupply rotate within the hour. Stay sharp. Stay armed."

The column loosened. Some men sat where they stood. Others walked toward the edge of the field, toward the pig shed that had been used as a field tent. A few lit cigarettes. No one cheered. No one saluted, only one or two muttered prayers. The two men still holding Ludwig's body turned to Reinhardt.

One of them, a stout older man with a buzzcut and soot-smeared jaw, asked softly, "What do we do with him?"

Reinhardt stood still for a long moment. His face was unreadable. He looked around at the ruined fields, the churned-up earth, and the skeletal house. Then he looked up, toward the east. Toward the hills that rose behind the burned orchard and beyond them, the Jäger farmstead. Home. He finally spoke, his voice steady.

"I'm taking him home."

He shifted the MG across his back, walked forward, and placed one gloved hand on the poncho-covered chest.

"Anyone willing to help carry my uncle... carry him the rest of the way?"

There was silence at first. Then a few of the younger men looked toward Brandt, as if waiting for permission. Brandt didn't stop them. He didn't say a word. Then one spoke.

"I'll help."

Then another.

"Me too."

The two boys stepped forward. Neither is older than seventeen. Mud on their boots, ash on their cheeks, but no hesitation in their eyes. Reinhardt gave them a curt nod, acknowledgment not thanks. There wasn't room for gratitude yet, only duty. One of them, the lankier of the two, still had Reinhardt's STG-91 slung over his shoulder. He reached up instinctively to adjust it, then paused, uncertain. Reinhardt walked up to him, held out his hand. The boy hesitated only a second before unslinging the rifle and placed it into Reinhardt's grip. Reinhardt checked the action by feel. A smudge of dried blood stained the polymer stock, but the rifle was clean and cared for. The assault rifle had an aura of warmth.

"You did fine," Reinhardt said quietly. It wasn't praise, merely a simple truth.

The boy gave a small nod and returned to Ludwig's body without a word. He and the other lad hoisted the burden between them with one at the shoulders and the other at the feet. Reinhardt slung the rifle across his chest and fell in step beside them, hands resting across the sling and magazine well. The machine gun remained across his back, heavier now somehow.

They walked out from the scorched Wessel farmstead without fanfare. Just three boys, and a man who would never walk again. The wind stirred the tall grass along the field roads. Here and there, blackened stalks still smoked from the night before. Crows circled in the gray-blue sky above the hills, too far to hear, but watching all the same. No one followed. No one called after them. They didn't speak. They just walked. The Jaeger farmstead was only a couple miles east, but the path would feel longer now than it did last night.

They walked without incident, no more patrols, gunfire, or orders. Only the wind and the creak of leather straps, the weight of weapons and death carried across the back. The three of them, not boys, moved like men because that's what they were now. Whatever softness had lived in them before had burned away somewhere between the first contact and the smoldering camp they left behind.

No one joked. No one spoke of heroism. They had crossed a line that morning, and there was no crossing back. The road to the Jäger farmstead wound through shallow hills and burned fields. Smoke still lingered in the west, a faint black smudge above the trees. Reinhardt walked with his jaw set, rifle steady on his chest, and machine gun heavy on his back. The two others carried Ludwig without complaint. They shifted their grips now and then, but not once did they pause or ask for rest. They knew what this meant and what it cost.

Reinhardt's thoughts turned inward as the road narrowed. Where do I put him? He thought of the barn but it smelled too strongly of feed, of earth and living things. His uncle deserved quiet, not cows. He thought of the living room, where his mother used to leave flowers on the sill. Too small. Too fragile. The smell of blood would ruin the wood. Then he remembered the stone shed behind the main house that was cold, shaded and built to last. The place his grandfather had used during hard winters to hang venison, salt hides, sharpen tools. It was clean now, unused in recent years. But it would do.

They crested the final hill. There it was, the Jäger homestead. Sturdy, timber-framed, with a slate roof and a flagstone path running to the porch. The fields were half-harvested. A pale blue washbin sat forgotten on the well's edge. The windows were open, as if expecting summer air instead of death to return. Reinhardt slowed. His boots crunched the gravel. He looked at the shed still standing, quiet and tucked in the tree line beyond the house. He turned to the two men carrying Ludwig.

"There," he said, nodding toward the stone shed. "We'll place him there until the rites."

Neither man spoke, they shifted course without question. Reinhardt stepped aside and opened the door. The hinges creaked faintly. The inside was cool, dry, and still smelled of iron and old smoke. They laid Ludwig down gently on a wooden table that had once been used to clean game. Reinhardt reached down and straightened his uncle's arms across his chest. He stood there for a long moment. Not praying. Not crying. Just thinking. A man should be buried by his kin and Reinhardt would make sure of it. The stone shed was still. The air inside carried no scent of rot but only cold earth, dry wood, and the faint iron tang that clung to every weapon and every wound. Reinhardt knelt beside the table. He didn't bow his head. He didn't cry. He just stared at Ludwig's face which was still and pale with blood crusted along the jawline where the poncho had slipped open. One eye is gone and the other closed by Reinhardt's own hand. Reinhardt put the tarp back over his uncle's face.

"I swear," he said silently, lips unmoving, "I will lay you to rest. By fire or by earth, I will not let you fade like smoke. You gave me everything. I'll carry it now."

He rested one hand lightly on his uncle's chest, only for a moment. Then he stood.

The two young men were bloodied, exhausted, and solemn, standing near the shed's threshold. They didn't speak, and didn't rush to leave. They knew the weight of what they'd done. Reinhardt stepped forward and extended his hand. The first, taller and wiry, took it. His grip was firm, not boyish.

"What's your name?" Reinhardt asked.

"Elias," the young man replied.

He turned to the second, stockier with eyes red with fatigue but unwavering.

"Kasper," the other said before being asked, taking Reinhardt's hand in turn.

Reinhardt nodded. "You carried my uncle like brothers. I won't forget that."

Both men looked humbled, unsure of what to say. Reinhardt continued, voice steadier now. "You've done your part. We all have. But if you'd like, stay a moment longer. Eat. Rest your feet. My house still stands, and it's the least I can offer."

The two exchanged a glance. Neither looked eager to be alone just yet. Elias gave a tired nod. "Yes... we'll stay. A little while."

"Good," Reinhardt said, motioning toward the farmhouse. "Come on, then."

They left the stone shed together, the door swinging shut behind them with a dull click. The wind rustled the eaves above, and the crows in the tree line finally scattered as the three men walked toward the Jaeger house. Not as soldiers, as kin. The farmhouse door creaked softly as Reinhardt stepped inside, Elias and Kasper close behind. The warmth of the interior was almost jarring. It smelled of old stone, hearth smoke, and something faintly sweet lingering from breakfast long gone cold. They said nothing as they entered, only the quiet scrape of boots being removed and set aside near the door, weapons propped carefully along the wall. Reinhardt removed his field cap. The sweatband was stiff with dried salt. His hair, matted and grimy, stuck to his forehead as he crossed into the kitchen, cap held low in both hands. His father sat at the table, a worn ceramic mug in his grasp. He looked up, and for a moment, his face lit with relief.

"Reinhardt," he said, standing. "You're back... thank God, you're..."

Reinhardt didn't smile. He didn't speak at first. He stood across from his father, just beside the table, and the cap still held in front of him like a folded flag. When he finally spoke, it was just one word. A quiet tremor beneath it.

"Father..."

Gerhardt stepped forward and pulled his son into an embrace, gripping him tight. Reinhardt stood still for a breath, then returned it with one arm for a moment. Then he felt it, the tension in his father's back. The slow realization worked its way up Gerhardt's spine. Gerhardt pulled away, eyes scanning his son's face. Then it came as a soft, uncertain voice. Cracking under a pressure he didn't want to acknowledge.

"Where is my big brother...?"

Reinhardt looked him in the eye. Reinhardt was not cruel or cold, only honest.

"He's in the shed," he said. "If you want to see him."

The room fell into silence. Even the fire in the hearth seemed to quiet. Gerhardt's breath hitched, but he didn't collapse. He didn't cry, not yet. He just stood there, a man who had just lost his brother, blinking in a world that suddenly felt smaller. Behind Reinhardt, Elias and Kasper stood silently, heads lowered, waiting for permission to sit or retreat.

Gerhardt didn't speak. He didn't ask any more questions. He simply nodded, once, slow and heavy, and stepped past his son. His boots made hollow sounds against the floorboards as he crossed the threshold and disappeared through the back door. The screen door creaked and clicked shut. Reinhardt didn't turn to watch. He just stood there for a breath, then looked at Elias and Kasper. Both had moved to the washbasin in the corner, sleeves rolled up, scrubbing blood and sweat from their forearms. The water ran pink as it swirled down the old iron drain. Neither of them spoke. They didn't need to. Their silence was the right kind.

Reinhardt turned and moved toward the hallway that led to the pantry and cellar steps. His boots still off, his sock covered feet made almost no sound across the wood. He found his mother in the back kitchen, bent slightly as she was sorting root vegetables into a canvas sack. Annika Jaeger, a quiet woman with long braids pinned into a crown around her head. Her back was to him.

"Mother," Reinhardt said, his voice calm but carrying a new tone now. Not a child's petition, but a man's assertion.

She turned and faced him, eyes widening with instant, wordless recognition. Her hands froze on the sack. Reinhardt met her gaze.

"We have guests. They helped carry Uncle Ludwig home. They'll stay for a meal, something warm and real."

He didn't raise his voice. He didn't need to. Annika stared at him for a moment. Something passed between them, quiet and ancient. She saw the blood still under his fingernails. The tightness in his face. The way he no longer stood as a boy. She didn't ask. She didn't cry. She gave one small nod.

"I'll prepare something," she said, already turning back toward the stove.

Reinhardt stepped back into the hallway as the first sounds of chopping behind him. In the front room, Elias and Kasper had dried their arms and taken seats at the table. Reinhardt appeared at the table after washing up, rifle resting against the corner of the living room. He didn't look toward the shed. He didn't need to. His father was there now, where he needed to be. Reinhardt was here, relaxing with his comrades after what had to be done.

The three men sat in silence for a few moments. The warmth of the house settled around them like a wool blanket after a storm. It felt worn, familiar, frayed at the edges, but still intact. Reinhardt leaned back slightly in his chair and looked at the two across from him. Elias stared at the floorboards, eyes distant but not vacant. Kasper rested his hands over his stomach, fingers still twitching now and then, like his body hadn't realized the fight was over. Reinhardt broke the silence with a question that felt heavier than it should've been.

"Would either of you like something to drink?"

Elias blinked and looked up.

"We've got beer. A few bottles left in the cellar," Reinhardt continued, voice even. "Some stronger stuff too, if that's what you need. Coffee or tea if not. Water, of course."

He wasn't offering out of politeness. He was offering because men needed something to mark the line between before and after. Between battle and breath.

Kasper cracked the ghost of a smile. "A beer would be good."

Elias nodded after a moment. "Same."

Reinhardt rose from the table and walked down the cellar steps, returning a moment later with three dark-bottled lagers, old local stock brewed a few villages over, strong and clean. He passed one to each of them and kept one for himself. They sat for a while longer, bottles opened but mostly untouched, the foam settling slow. No toasts or speeches, just men, alive, together in the quiet after the storm.

The scent of food filled the farmhouse. The smell of onions searing in fat, dark bread warming in the oven, a stew of root vegetables and salted pork bubbling low and slow. It was a modest meal, but one rooted in the old ways, built to sustain laboring men through long winters and longer wars. Annika Jäger moved with quiet efficiency, no wasted motion. Her face was composed, but Reinhardt could see the set of her jaw, the paleness behind her eyes. She knew. She hadn't asked, but she knew. When she finally stepped into the front room, she carried a wide wooden tray laden with food. Steam curled from the stew bowls. The bread, freshly sliced, still let out its rich, yeasty scent. She set it down without a word. Reinhardt stood and met her at the tray. He didn't speak softly, like a boy would. He spoke plainly, directly, like a man would.

"Mother," he said. "Could you bring us another round of beer?"

She looked up at him, the faintest flicker of something behind her eyes. Weariness, pride, and perhaps grief she wasn't ready to wear on her face. She nodded once.

"I'll get them."

Reinhardt held her gaze for a second longer, then gently turned back to the table. Elias and Kasper had already begun spooning the stew into their mouths with quiet reverence, like men who hadn't eaten hot food in days. They didn't speak, but the gratitude was visible in the way their shoulders loosened, the way their hands steadied. Annika returned moments later with three more bottles. She set them down, her hands as steady as ever. As she turned to leave, Reinhardt spoke again, this time quieter but not uncertain.

"Thank you."

She paused at the doorway, a beat. Then...

"Your uncle always said you'd carry more than your own weight."

Then she was gone, retreating to the back of the house. Likely to cry or maybe to pray. The three men sat together, not yet speaking. Not needing to. Outside, the wind moved gently through the tall grass. In the stone shed, Gerhardt remained with his brother. In the house, the next generation of men ate quietly, drank slowly, and kept the fire lit.

The meal passed slowly. Forks scraped gently against the bowls, the only sound aside from the quiet crackle of the hearth. No one filled the silence, not out of awkwardness but respect. The house itself seemed to understand that something sacred was underway. Reinhardt leaned back in his chair, half-finished beer in hand, the other resting on the table. His eyes stared not at his companions but into the past, into the long corridor of memory where his uncle still lived. He cleared his throat once, softly.

"He wouldn't want us brooding like this," he said, almost to himself. "Not forever."

Elias and Kasper looked up, attentive but not intrusive. Reinhardt gave a faint smile, tired but real.

"I remember once," he said, "when I was maybe six or seven, Ludwig dared me to play a trick on Father."

He chuckled lightly, the memory surfacing like a ripple breaking through the grief.

"He handed me this little rodent. It was dead and stiff, probably something a barn cat left behind. He told me to leave it behind one of Father's bookshelf panels. Said it'd be funny. I was young. Of course I did it."

Kasper blinked, caught between surprise and amusement.

"Father found it a few days later. He nearly had a heart attack." Reinhardt smirked. "He was shouting, furious even, swore it was some omen or pestilence or sabotage. He stormed through the whole house yelling about vermin and hygiene like he was giving orders in a trench."

"Ludwig didn't laugh," Reinhardt added after a pause. "Not then. He just stood up, looked Father in the eye, and said, 'I told the boy to do it.'"

He tapped his finger against the side of his beer bottle.

"He never let me take the fall alone."

They all sat in silence again for a moment. This time it was lighter, less like mourning, more like remembrance. The smile on Reinhardt's face faded into thought. He stared into the firelight now, voice softer.

"He was a lonely man."

Neither Elias nor Kasper interrupted.

"After he left the army, he settled here with us, here on Delumina. It was one of the early settlement waves. Third or fourth, I think, after the Taurosplasmy finished breaking down the upper atmosphere and allowed life to blossom."

He nodded to himself.

"Delumina was just a name then. Red sky, hard soil. No crops worth a damn yet. But we had a claim, and the promise of land. That was enough."

He let out a quiet breath.

"He married a woman. Sophia. Sweet voice. Hair the color of sunlight on river mud. She was pregnant before the first harvest came in. They named the boy Joachim."

His voice caught slightly, but he pressed on.

"They both died. Same night. She was hemorrhaging by the time the midwife got here. We didn't even have a proper clinic then. Just an old cold room with a cot."

He swallowed hard.

"He buried them both behind the east tree line, the place where the barley won't grow."

The silence that followed was heavy, but reverent.

"He never remarried," Reinhardt said. "I think part of him was buried with them. But he stayed. Raised me like I was his own. Pulled me aside when Father got too harsh. Drilled me on the MG. Took me hunting. Taught me when to speak, and when not to."

Reinhardt looked up at them.

"He was a better father to me than I probably deserved."

Elias nodded slowly, eyes misted. Kasper raised his beer just slightly, no toast or clink, just acknowledgment. Reinhardt, though his jaw remained clenched and his heart heavy, allowed himself the first moment of peace since the call went out yesterday. The bowls were scraped clean, the bread long gone. Only the last remnants of broth and a few beer bottles remained on the table. The warmth from the food had spread through their limbs, but not enough to ward off the weight in their chests. Elias was the first to rise.

"I should go," he said quietly, rolling down his sleeves. "My mother... she'll be waiting by the road, probably fearing the worst."

Kasper nodded in agreement, pushing back his chair. "Mine too. And my little sister gets nightmares when I don't come back right away."

They both looked at Reinhardt, not sheepishly but with the solemn look of men who know their place and their duties. Reinhardt stood with them, slow and steady. His shoulders no longer carried the same tension. Something in him had shifted, grief still deep but now anchored with meaning. He walked with them to the front door, stepping back into his boots with quiet movements. The morning light outside had grown stronger, casting long, gold-edged shadows across the hills and blackened fields beyond. At the threshold, Reinhardt turned and faced them. He looked at Elias first, then Kasper. No words came at first but then he stepped forward and wrapped each of them in a firm, sincere embrace. Not the awkward clutch of boys pretending to be men. This was the quiet, respectful hug of comrades; brothers by blood earned, not born. When he pulled back, he met their eyes squarely.

"Thank you," he said. "For the company, carrying him and standing beside me."

Neither man replied right away. Elias gave a soft nod, his lips tight, emotion barely contained. Kasper clapped Reinhardt lightly on the shoulder.

"You stood beside us first," he said.

And with that, the two men stepped off the porch and made their way down the dirt path, rifles slung and heads held high. Reinhardt stood at the doorway, watching them shrink into the distance, back to their own homes and families. Back to the world they had fought to keep. He stood there for a while, alone now. But not lonely. The MG was still on the rack inside. His uncle's body was still in the shed. The sun, now fully risen, cast its light across the scorched fields of Delumina. The front door creaked shut behind him. Reinhardt walked across the quiet house, past the empty bowls and cooling bottles, past the hearth where the last embers were dying low. He moved with purpose now, not just out of mourning, but responsibility. In the side room near the pantry, what once served as a storeroom and now doubled as a communications nook, sat the family's field radio. A durable, iron-framed unit bolted to an old butcher's block that patched into the wider militia grid. Ludwig had maintained it obsessively, ensuring it worked even when the wind howled or the relay towers flickered under storm surge.

Reinhardt sat, adjusted the tuning dial, and keyed the mic, a static crackle answered.

"Militia Net, this is Jaeger Homestead, call sign Delta-88 Over."

A brief pause. Then a reply came through, grainy but clear.

"Copy, Delta-88. This is Militia Central. Send your traffic."

Reinhardt took a breath, held the mic steady.

"Requesting formal burial honors for one confirmed fallen, Delta-2. Repeat, Delta-2 had fallen in action during operations pertaining to the Wessel farmstead at grid six-four-seven."

He paused only a beat.

"Request full honors for interment on the Jäger homestead, burial detail, flag, and rites. I will provide the body and dig the grave myself. Requesting the earliest available day."

The silence that followed was short, but weighty. Then the voice returned but slightly different now, respectful and measured.

"Copy that, Delta-88. Confirmed, Delta-2 as fallen. We have his service record on file. Honors approved."

Reinhardt exhaled slowly through his nose.

"Date?"

A pause then the sound of typing and low chatter in the background. Then...

"The earliest window is the day after tomorrow at twelve-hundred hours. Dispatching two-man honor guard and chaplain team from Militia District East. Confirm receiving."

Reinhardt pressed the mic again.

"Received and acknowledged. We'll be ready. Delta-88, out."

He released the key. The silence of the house returned, but it was no longer hollow.

Reinhardt stood slowly. The mic hung limp beside the radio now. He looked toward the door leading back outside, to the shed. The rite was set. Ludwig would be buried as a soldier, not forgotten or lost in smoke. This gave Reinhardt one more day to prepare. The house felt heavier after the call, but not in the same way. Reinhardt stepped away from the radio, shoulders set with quiet purpose. He moved through the doorway and onto the porch, blinking against the noonday light. The sky over Delumina was clear, a soft blue stretching endlessly above the hills. Somewhere in the grass, insects hummed. Life went on, indifferent. He walked across the yard, past the clothesline, past the worn boots still drying near the wall. His steps slowed as he approached the stone shed. The door was slightly ajar. He didn't knock. Inside, the light was dim as only a single shaft of sun cutting through a high-set window, spilling down onto the still body of Ludwig, laid out clean and composed, arms folded over his chest. The poncho had been adjusted. A cloth now rested over the ruined side of his face. Gerhardt sat on a low stool beside the table, elbows on his knees, hands clasped loosely. He didn't move when Reinhardt entered. He hadn't cried, but his face looked carved from stone like it was weathered, immovable, and cracked in places that would never fully heal. Reinhardt knelt beside him, slow and steady. He didn't speak right away. He simply placed a hand on his father's shoulder. They sat like that for a moment as father and son, alone with the dead.

Then Reinhardt said softly. "I called it in."

Gerhardt turned his head just enough to meet his son's eyes. Reinhardt continued.

"They'll give him full honors with a burial team, flag, and rites. The day after tomorrow at noon."

He paused, voice firm.

"We'll bury him next to Sophia and Joachim."

Gerhardt's hands clenched slightly.

Reinhardt added, gentler now. "I'll dig it myself. Unless you'd rather..."

Gerhardt shook his head.

"No." His voice was rough but clear. "He's your uncle but he was my brother. We'll dig it together."

Reinhardt nodded once. The two men sat in the silence again. Outside, the breeze moved softly through the trees near the east tree line, the place where barley never grew. The place where three now would rest, together.

The silence between them lingered a moment longer, then passed like a shadow at dusk. Gerhardt stood slowly with stiff joints and heavy shoulders. Reinhardt rose beside him. They didn't speak again. Together they stepped out of the shed, letting the door fall shut behind them with a muted thud. The air was still warm. A few birds flitted through the tree line. Life moved on, unaware.

They walked side by side to the old equipment shed near the edge of the main barn. Inside, the air smelled of oil, leather, and earth. Rows of tools lined the wall. Spades, picks and post-hole diggers, all kept sharp by Ludwig's hands over the years. Reinhardt reached for a shovel with a hickory shaft worn smooth by time. Gerhardt took the heavier spade, the one used for trenching drainage ditches and winter graves. No words were exchanged, only nods.

They made their way past the eastern fence line, the grass taller here, where the plow never touched. Just beyond the last row of fence posts, under a gentle hill sloping toward the old riverbed, the earth had been turned only twice before. Two small wooden markers stood there, weathered and half-covered by weeds.

Sophia. Joachim.

Gerhardt paused, staring at them. He set the spade down, knelt, and brushed the moss from Sophia's name. His fingers lingered there, just once. Then he stood, and the work began. They measured with their eyes, no tape or rope, only instinct and memory. They staked out the third grave by feel. One shovel plunged into the earth, then another. The ground gave way slowly, stubborn in places but softer in others. The sun arced overhead, casting long shadows behind them as sweat began to form beneath their collars. Reinhardt worked in silence, hands steady but with measured breath. Gerhardt's spade cut deep, his body moving like a man who knew grief had no shortcut, only work. As the hole grew deeper, the two men labored not as father and son, not just as kin of the dead, but as the living, fulfilling the final duty owed to a man they both had loved.

Chapter 6

The road to the schoolhouse wound through golden fields still heavy with dew. Reinhardt walked alone, boots crunching softly against the packed dirt path. The morning sun rose behind the low hills, casting long rays through the barley and wild grass that shimmered under the breeze. Far off, a group of white-breasted crows circled lazily near a thresher barn. Somewhere nearby, a windmill creaked in rhythm with the land. He said nothing. There was no one to hear, but as he walked a small, fleeting smile touched the edge of his lips.

Delumina.

This world, their world, was hard-won. Every tree, every stone, every acre of tilled earth had been claimed by sweat and rifle. Now, after the bloodshed, it stood in the morning light with a kind of grace. Quiet and clean, the sort of peace only men who'd fought could truly recognize. He walked past the old orchard where the militia had trained last summer and past the community bell that was rung at births, at harvest, and, sometimes, at war.

This is the place Ludwig died for..This is what the men bled to protect..And this is where he returns, still standing.

As the schoolhouse came into view with whitewashed stone, arched windows, and a Confederation banner swaying from the flagpole. Reinhardt slowed his step only slightly. A few boys were already milling about near the entrance, laughing, slapping shoulders, and pretending the world hadn't changed. He approached, eyes steady, posture upright, with book satchel slung across his back like a rucksack. From the side, Tomas and Jules broke from a small crowd and walked toward him. Tomas was first to speak, his voice half-greeting and half-curious.

"Reinhardt! You weren't in class yesterday, where'd you vanish off to?"

Matthias grinned, elbowing him lightly. "Didn't think you could even talk your way out of an inspection day."

Reinhardt stopped a few paces from them. He didn't answer right away. He just looked at them, really looked. They were good boys. Loyal, sharp, and still untouched in that subtle way you could now see if you'd stood at the edge of a body pit. His expression didn't harden. It didn't gloat. It simply changed, matured behind the eyes. He gave them a knowing look, calm and sincere. The kind that said, "You'll understand one day."

Tomas blinked, the smile on his face fading a little, unsure now. Jules caught on just a second later. Neither asked again. The bell rang overhead, a single deep tone as a summons. Reinhardt nodded once, and they turned together toward the front steps of the schoolhouse.

.The classroom was already filling when Reinhardt stepped through the door. Old timber beams ran overhead, casting long shadows across rows of worn desks. Sunlight slanted in through open windows, catching dust in the air. At the front of the room hung the banner of the Confederation, a reminder of order, sacrifice, and destiny. The boys were already seated. Some whispered quietly, others scratched away at notes or diagrams. A few heads turned as Reinhardt entered, conversations fading to murmurs. He didn't speak. He didn't scan the room for familiar faces. He simply walked with quiet, measured purpose to his usual desk in the third row and the left side. His satchel was set down, and took his seat with his back straight, hands folded, and eyes set toward the front of the room. There was no awkwardness in him anymore. No boyish shifting or nervous glances. He moved like a man who had crossed fire and returned intact.

Unbeknownst to him, Herr Brandt was already watching. He stood at the front of the room. The same man who had led the militia element two mornings prior was now, once again, in his teacher's coat. The black fabric fit him just as well as the field harness had. His posture hadn't changed, nor had his eyes. They were the eyes of a man who remembered everything with every name, every shot fired, and every man who stood and every man who fell.

Now he watched Reinhardt enter his classroom the same way he had watched him on the battlefield. No salute or announcement but Brandt saw it clearly. He came back changed. The class began to quiet as Brandt stepped forward. Chalk in hand, boots sharp on the floorboards, he faced the blackboard. Before turning, his eyes settled once more on Reinhardt. Not with pride but with softness and recognition. A single nod came as almost imperceptible. Not for the classroom but rather just for one of his own. Then the chalk tapped the board.

"Page seventy-four," Herr Brandt said, his voice clear.

"Civic Honor and the Line of Fire."

Herr Brandt wrote with the same precision as he commanded, measured and unflinching.

"The state is not sustained by words," he said, his voice clear, but not loud. "It is not preserved by good feelings, nor defended by memory alone. It endures only through action, right conscious action, by those willing to bear its burden."

He turned and faced the class.

"Civic honor is not pride in your soil, or even love of it. It is stewardship. The understanding that what you have was bought for you and what you pass on must be bought again. The price is blood, struggle, and sacrifice. Just as Taurosplasmy is the method to seed new worlds, the citizen-soldier is the one who defends the community with blood, whether his own or that of the enemy. Every man is a soldier of the state, whether he is a farmer, shop-keeper, or a professional soldier of the Confederation."

A few boys shifted in their seats. One scribbled notes furiously, while others watched in silence. In the third row, Reinhardt sat still, hands folded, eyes forward. He hadn't moved since the lesson began. There was no attempt to hide the faint red around his knuckles, or the soil still lingering beneath his nails. His uniform sleeves were ironed, but his boots were still dusty from the march. Brandt's gaze swept the room.

"Young men of the Confederation, your ancestors carved fields into a hostile world. They gave you peace, not as a gift, but as a responsibility. What will you do when peace is broken? When the line of fire reaches your village? Your farm? Your brother's bed?"

The room was quiet. Then, from near the back, a hand rose hesitantly. It was Erik, one of the younger students. He is fourteen pale, slight, and thoughtful. He spoke softly, but everyone heard him.

"Herr Brandt... was it true? The fighting, I mean. About the Red Twilight camp. Did it really happen?"

A brief silence followed. A few boys glanced toward Reinhardt, but he didn't move. Didn't blink. Brandt stood still, chalk still in his hand. He didn't answer immediately. When he did, his voice was softer but firmer.

"When men fight in the name of order, their deeds don't become stories.

They become duties fulfilled. That is all you need to know."

Another pause. Then a boy near Erik who is older, not cruel but careless, murmured under his breath. "He was there, so I heard."

Reinhardt didn't react. He kept his hands still, gaze fixed on the board but there was a tension now in the room, like the air had thickened. Herr Brandt set the chalk down and looked across the room. His eyes settled on no one in particular.

"No one owes you their wounds."

His voice was quiet now.

"And no man must speak of what he did before he understands it."

That silence returned, heavier this time. Herr Brandt stepped back behind the lectern.

"Open to page seventy-seven. Read the section on volunteer militias and the role of civil defense during the early settlements. We will discuss the Wessel Accord and the price of internal sovereignty."

Pages were turned and pens scratched. Reinhardt finally reached for his book. The room rustled as boys flipped to page seventy-seven, the heading printed in bold block script:

The Wessel Accord and the Doctrine of Communal Defense

Herr Brandt let the silence linger just long enough for the text to settle in their minds before he spoke again, this time without the chalk and his hands clasped behind his back like an officer before a field map.

"The Wessel Accord," he began, "was ratified one generation after the first successful colonial landings on Delumina. Named for Horst Wessel, the poet-warrior who gave his life in the streets of a broken Europe, it codified the sacred obligation of every colonist to take up arms in defense of our civilization."

No one interrupted him now, even the younger boys leaned forward with idle pens.

"Where the Army, Navy, or ESS cannot respond with immediacy be it due to distance, weather, communication failure, or escalation lag then the militia becomes the sovereign instrument of resistance. Its legitimacy is not provisional. It is sacred."

He let that hang in the air.

"Under the Accord, Militia HQ on any settled world is granted full authority to muster, train, and mobilize men in defense of European sovereignty. This includes the right to conduct reconnaissance, defensive action, retaliatory strike, or preemptive suppression of insurgent threats."

Reinhardt remained still, but his jaw set slightly at the words. Brandt continued.

"Every citizen-settler household has the obligation to retain arms appropriate for defense such as semi-automatic rifles, battle carbines, light machine guns, ammunition, field radios, and even anti-armor or anti-air weapons at the militia armory level."

He scanned the room.

"But with rights come obligations."

He turned back toward the chalkboard, tapping the underlined title once with a fingertip.

"The militia must drill regularly, maintain its arms, and answer the call to muster at any hour. Each man must know his role, his unit, and his place in the line. Those who shirk this are not civilians. They are liabilities."

A silence fell over the classroom like snowfall. Then Brandt's voice lowered but retained the usual firm tone.

"If the threat grows beyond the capacity of the local militia, the Wessel Accord permits immediate escalation. The militia may be folded into a larger defensive apparatus, formed into divisions, regiments, or battalion-level Volkssturm units. These may be placed under direct command of the Pan-European Army in the event of war or mass insurrection."

He returned to the lectern, fingers lightly touching its edge.

"But you must understand this: no world is secure unless its own sons are willing to die for it first. No law, no fleet, no satellite can save people who refuse to bleed for their soil."

No one spoke, but Brandt looked out over the class once more.

"That is the price of civilization among the stars. That is the Wessel Accord. You will be tested on it. But more importantly, one day, you will be measured by it."

The bell rang a moment later, long and low. Boys began to pack up slowly, heads bowed in thought. Reinhardt rose without haste, sliding his chair back and lifting his satchel over one shoulder. He made for the door without a word but Herr Brandt watched him as he left. No longer a student, but as a man who had already passed his first measure. The forum sat in the heart of the school grounds. Circular, stone-paved, ringed by benches and shaded by young oaks that had been planted during the colony's early years. It was a place for midday meals, study, and quiet debate. Reinhardt moved to the far side, where the shade was thinner and the breeze touched the skin. He sat alone. From his satchel he retrieved a small tin of stew that had cooled from the morning, but packed tightly. He placed it on the heating plate bolted to the stone bench and ignited it with a thumbpress. A faint hiss and soft orange glow came to life beneath the base. While it warmed, he poured a packet of instant coffee into a battered metal cup, added water from his flask, and set it beside the stew. The scent rose slowly as the stew contained onions, root vegetables, black pepper, boiled meat and marrow. His mother had made it with care. He dipped a piece of bread into the edge of the stew and tore off a bite as the coffee reached temp. He took a slow sip, exhaled, and said nothing. The sun was warm. The wind carried no smell of gunpowder.

He had nearly finished the bread when he heard footsteps. Jules and Tomas approached, a little hesitant, but not unsure. They carried their own mess kits and thermos flasks, and sat a few feet from him. Not too close, but close enough to show they were with him.

"Hey," Jules said, a little softer than usual.

Tomas gave a short nod. “Mind if we sit?”

Reinhardt glanced up from his cup, nodded once. “Go ahead.”

They sat, unpacked their food in silence. A moment passed. Jules was the first to speak again, voice quieter.

“How are you holding up?”

Reinhardt looked down at the last of his stew, then took a final sip of the now-cooling coffee.

“Fine.” A pause. “Or as fine as I can be.”

The other two nodded slowly. Neither of them forced the silence to move faster than it had to. Then Tomas leaned forward, elbows on knees.

“You were in it, weren’t you, the militia action? That’s why you weren’t at school yesterday.”

Reinhardt stared at the trees for a moment. Then he nodded. Tomas didn’t press, but the question hung in the air. Reinhardt set his cup down carefully.

“Herr Brandt led the column. It started after the Wessel farmstead burned.”

Jules looked up sharply. “They really burned it?”

Reinhardt nodded. “We only found Herr Wessel. The rest of the family was gone. No sign. No bodies. Just ash.”

The quiet became heavier.

“We struck their main camp,” Reinhardt continued. “It was believed to be the local command cell for the Red Twilight, maybe two dozen fighters. A couple of our classmates and a couple girls from the girl’s school were among the dead. All of the insurrectionists were killed in the assault or executed right after combat was over.”

Jules exhaled sharply. “That’s what the older boys were saying. That it was the real thing.”

Reinhardt didn’t confirm or deny. He just looked them both in the eye and said, calmly, “It was.”

Tomas shifted on the bench. “They said... two militia died. Is that true?”

Reinhardt nodded once, slower this time.

“Herr Schmidt, the pub owner, was in the second fireteam.”

Then he paused, looked down at his empty cup, and said,“The other was my uncle.”

The words fell like a slow stone into water, neither boy said anything right away.

Jules swallowed. “The funeral?”

“Tomorrow,” Reinhardt said. “Noon. At my family’s farmstead.”

He didn’t say more. He didn’t have to. Tomas bowed his head slightly. Jules stared at his flask. All three sat in silence again, but not broken. The wind stirred the leaves above them. The sun warmed their backs. And the future sat waiting just beyond the edge of the school grounds, where duty would one day call them all.

Chapter 7

Reinhardt woke before the sun had cleared the hills. The house was quiet, no birdsong yet or the sound of distant engines in the fields, but the stillness of a day that already carried more weight than sound. He dressed in silence. His clothes were clean and pressed. His boots polished the night before. A black armband marked his right sleeve, pulled taut against the muscle beneath. He didn't eat because he didn't feel hungry. By the time he stepped outside, his father was already in the yard. Gerhardt stood beside the casket, it was simple and clean in its rigidity. He had built it himself in the hours before dawn, working by lantern-light with the same tools his brother once used to cut fence posts and repair the barn roof. It was made of pine, planed smooth, and joined tight. No decoration or unnecessary flourishes, just quiet craftsmanship and care.

Reinhardt walked over, joining him without a word. Together, they lifted Ludwig, still wrapped in the burial shroud, arms crossed over his chest and laid him gently into the casket. The fabric over his face shifted slightly. For a moment, Reinhardt hesitated. He reached forward, and with a slow, deliberate motion, pulled the cloth back. The wound was there but covered cleanly with gauze and care. The rest of Ludwig's face was untouched, pale, and still. The lines of sorrow, laughter and storms are all at rest now. They had decided on a closed casket. Not because of shame, but because they knew Ludwig wouldn't have wanted to be remembered broken. He had been struck in the face, irrevocably hard and sudden. There was no need to let that be the last memory. Still, this one look mattered.

Gerhardt bent forward, cupped the side of his brother's head, and kissed his forehead, a gesture that was old, older than anything written in books. Reinhardt leaned down, pressing his forehead to Ludwig's chest, just above the heart. He stayed there for a moment, long enough for the silence to say what words couldn't. A single tear welled in the corner of his eye and slipped free, leaving no shame behind it. Then, softly, he whispered, "Goodbye."

They pulled the cloth back into place, lifted the lid, and placed it gently over the casket. Together, they picked up the hammer and drove the nails in, not as punishment, not as ending, but as completion. Each strike was a heartbeat. Each strike said, "He lived. He fought. He is ours."

When it was done, they stepped back and left Ludwig alone, for the last time.

The sun was fully risen now when they stepped back into the house. Annika was already preparing the hearth room for guests. The door creaked open more than once with neighbors, militia men, and kin arriving in small groups. No one spoke loudly. No one lingered in greeting. They knew what this day was.

At 1100 hours, the active militia detail arrived. Two men in full uniform with rifles slung, boots dusted, faces stern. One wore a black armband like Reinhardt's. The other carried a folded Confederation banner in a ceremonial case. Reinhardt stepped forward, greeted them with a nod and salute. They returned the salute, in the knightly fashion with the finger to the brow, palm downward

"He's ready," he said. "The casket is behind the barn, under the stone shed. The grave is just past the east tree line."

The senior of the two nodded once. "Understood, will we have help lowering?"

"Yes," Reinhardt said. "I'll carry."

The younger militiaman stepped forward, unrolling a length of black rope from a canvas satchel.

"We'll secure it beneath," he said. "Four to carry. Two to lower. With your help, it'll go clean."

Reinhardt nodded. He didn't look back at the house. There was still one more duty to fulfill.

.The funeral began just before noon. The sun sat high and still in the sky, casting sharp, clean light over the land Ludwig had once defended with his hands and rifle. There was no wind now, only the stillness of a world holding its breath. From the farmhouse to the east tree line, a quiet procession formed. Neighbors, kinsmen, local militia, the village smith, two boys from school and a dozen or more settlers with sun-browned faces and solemn eyes. None wore black uniforms, just the earth-colored garments of working men and women, with black bands on their sleeves, and reverence in their step.

At the rear of the house, six men stood beside the casket beneath the stone shed. Reinhardt, Gerhardt, Herr Brandt, The two militia guards and a man Reinhardt didn't know well, Wilhelm. He is older, gray at the temples, and once a soldier beside Ludwig in the German Army, before they left the old world behind. They stood in silence for a breath. Then Wilhelm stepped forward and unfurled a folded banner from a sealed case. A deep crimson cloth, edged with silver thread, bearing the old unit markings of Germanic runes, oak leaves, and a number long faded into memory. Ludwig had kept it preserved all these years. Without a word, they laid the banner across the casket, smoothing it with care.

Then, together, they gripped the rope-handles fastened along the side. They lifted him, not as pallbearers, but as comrades. The movement was slow, exact, and sacred. The pine casket rose like something weightless beneath their touch, though each man bore its true weight in his chest. They began the walk. The path to the gravesite, through tall grass and barley, had been trodden smooth by the many feet of mourners. Lining either side stood the people of Delumina with their heads bowed, hands clasped, rifles slung across backs. Children stood quietly beside their mothers. Old men doffed their caps. As the six passed with the casket, the people fell in behind, forming a silent column of witnesses. Reinhardt walked at the front left corner. He kept his pace even, his posture straight. Every footstep felt like it moved through eternity.

They reached the east tree line, the place where Sophia and Joachim already rested beneath the soil. There, the casket was set down gently beside the open grave. A moment of breath. A flicker of sun through the trees. Then the local preacher stepped forward. His coat was simple, his collar unadorned. He opened a leather-bound book, cleared his throat, and spoke in Hochdeutsche, the pure, ancestral German tongue.

“In the name of the Lord who binds the world in order and the sun in its course, we gather not to mourn alone, but to remember what has been lived and given. A man does not belong to the state alone. He belongs to his people, his family, his land and in serving them, he becomes eternal.”

“Ludwig Jäger gave it all. Not for medals. Not for legacy. But for love of this place, these fields, this soil, and the lives that grow from it.”

“Let the earth receive him as a son. Let memory preserve him as a brother. Let his death remind the living, you must never yield.”

He closed the book. Bowed his head. The wind stirred slightly through the barley. The two militiamen stepped forward. They took hold of the black ropes, now looped beneath the casket. One on each side. They lowered Ludwig down with slow, perfect control, no haste or fumbling. The moment the casket touched bottom, they stood upright, turned sharply to face the grave, and raised their right arms in the Roman salute. The air stood still. Then, one by one, every man in attendance raised his arm as well.

Farmers, officers, students, smiths, and even old Wilhelm, whose arm shook slightly with age, raised it in full. Only after the salute had been held in silence did the old soldier step forward. Wilhelm stood alone by the grave, his voice soft, cracked by time but steady.

And he began to sing...

"Ich hatt' einen Kameraden.... Einen bessern findst du nicht..."

The words were old. Older than war. They had been sung in trenches, in forests, in ruined cities, and now on a colony world across the stars. Reinhardt had heard the song before, at ceremonies, in old recordings, at the end of the school day, and even in passing at the village square. Now, standing above the grave of his uncle, he understood it for the first time. A tear, just one, slipped down his cheek. He didn't wipe it away. Beside him, Gerhardt dropped to his knees. His hands clenched into the earth, shoulders shaking. He began to weep, not loudly or out of weakness, but like a man breaking open beneath the weight of love and loss. Reinhardt didn't speak. He didn't move. He stood beside his father, his hand resting lightly on his shoulder, and watched the final rites of a man who had been more than uncle, more than warrior. He had been the best of them.

The song ended, fading into silence. Only the sound of the wind remained, brushing softly through the tall grass and rustling the leaves above the graves. The militiamen stepped forward once more, no longer as bearers of weight, but as custodians of memory. One of them carried a cloth-wrapped object in his arms. With slow, deliberate motion, he unwrapped it, revealing a ceremonial flag, the banner of the Pan-European Confederation.

Before presenting it, they began to fold it, nine times. Each fold was slow, and reverent. The first fold, longways, symbolizes the unity of Europe across borders, blood, and planets. The second, again longways, represents discipline, and the narrowing of one's life to service. The third through fifth, into thirds across, signifying soil, spirit, and struggle. The final four folds compacted the flag into a perfect, symmetrical square, like a foundation stone. Nine folds, one for each principle etched into the old soldier's code. When they finished, the banner no longer waved. It rested, compact, unyielding and eternal. The senior militiaman turned and stepped toward Gerhardt, still kneeling beside the grave. He knelt beside him and extended the folded banner with both hands. His voice was soft, but heard by all.

"This flag does not belong to the dead. It belongs to those who carry their memory.. Your brother died with his oath unbroken. This is his stone. Now it rests in your house."

Gerhardt looked at the banner through red-rimmed eyes. He stared at it, not in rejection, but in grief. His hands trembled. He reached out, then pulled back. He stood slowly, shoulders heaving.

"He raised that boy like his own," he said hoarsely, voice breaking. "Trained him and spoke to him like a son."

He turned to Reinhardt, who was still standing beside the grave, face solemn and hands folded at the small of his back. Gerhardt placed a hand on his shoulder.

"He's yours now."

And with a gentle push, he stepped back. The militiaman looked at Reinhardt. He stepped forward. His hands were steady. He received the ninefold banner in silence, holding it close against his chest. It was heavier than it looked, not in mass, but in meaning. He looked down at the square of cloth, then to the grave, then to the tree line beyond. In that moment, something passed from one generation to the next.

Chapter 8

The grave still lingered in the corner of his mind but Reinhardt did not linger. The morning after the funeral, he rose before the sun. The air smelled of dew, rust and pine dust, the kind of smell Ludwig used to call "the smell of a world worth dying for." He pulled on his boots, cinched the belt over his tunic, and stepped out into the barn shed that doubled as the militia's local field station. He carried his STG-91 and the MG-82. It was a humble thing with a concrete floor, wooden racks, and an old steel cabinet with a reinforced lockbox welded into one side. A rack of rifles stood lined up against the far wall, bolt-actions and a few semi-autos still smeared faintly with bore grease. Ammunition crates were stacked neatly along the rear with some factory stamped, others plainly reloaded. Reinhardt stood at the threshold for a moment, clipboard in hand. His pen clicked once. He began.

"Radio equipment..." he muttered under his breath. He walked to the leftmost bench where Ludwig had always kept the comms gear, the base station, backup batteries, signal map, and call-frequency register. He flipped the power switch and watched the indicator blink green. Good, still functional. He jotted notes in tight handwriting. He moved down the line and saw antenna cables coiled and bagged, signal flares accounted for, and the emergency field radio packed and sealed. The codebook was still beneath the panel drawer, wrapped in a dry cloth.

"Firearms..." he turned, walking across the concrete. One by one, he checked the weapons.

Six working rifles, four chambered in 6.5mm and two older 8mm holdovers. All barrels are clean. All bolts oiled. One was missing its rear sight. He noted that. "Request replacement or local repair."

The two shotguns were intact. One had a cracked stock, the other loose action screws. Still functional, but borderline. The militia had no dedicated gunsmith as Ludwig had done most of the patchwork with tools and patience. Reinhardt traced a finger across the stock of the second shotgun, then nodded slowly. "Reinforce. Keep in rotation."

He opened the ammo crates next. The inventory was uneven, dozens of 7.5mm rounds but only one partial box of 8mm. He counted by hand, lips moving in quiet calculation. It startled him how they were almost out of 8mm, the most crucial of all rounds since it was the ammunition for the MG-82. Once his tally was completed he would need to call up Militia HQ to get an immediate resupply.

He clicked the pen again and noted his tallies of 6.5mm full metal jacket: 460 rounds, 6.5mm soft point: 122 rounds, 8mm Mauser: 300 rounds, 12-gauge buckshot: 66 shells, Signal flares (white): 3, Signal flares (red): 1, Smoke grenades (green): 2, Ration packs (emergency): 5, and Medical kits (partial): 2.

He paused over the medical kits. Both were lacking proper clotting agents. Just gauze, bandage tape, and antiseptic. Reinhardt circled them on the form and marked them in red: URGENT REPLACEMENT NEEDED. He moved to the back table, where a drawer held the ledger, a proper bound book in which Ludwig had meticulously written every report, order, and call sign for the last six years. Reinhardt ran his hand over the leather cover and opened to the most recent entry.

"Delta-2, last report submitted 7 July. Eastern patrol route unremarkable. Ammunition log update submitted. Inventory complete pending resupply."

The line ended there. Reinhardt flipped to the next empty page. Slowly, he raised his pen and began to write.

"14 July. Delta-2: Fallen in defense of Wessel homestead. Duties assumed by Delta-88, acting radio chief and quartermaster. Inventory underway. Full resupply request pending."

He wrote it cleanly. No fanfare. Just the truth. After finishing the log, he rose and scanned the room one last time. It looked the same. But it wasn't. He wasn't just the boy who helped reload boxes anymore. He was the man who would keep this station running. The man who would answer the call and he would do it in his uncle's stead.

.Reinhardt sat before the radio set in the field shed, the worn headset resting around his neck, the main transmitter unit humming faintly. He reached forward, fingers steady, and turned the frequency dial until he locked in the militia net. Static buzzed, then cleared. He took the microphone in hand, thumb hovering over the transmit key. He pressed down the key.

"Militia HQ, this is Delta-88, Jäger homestead relay," he said, voice firm but low. "Assuming duties in place of Delta-2, fallen in action. Requesting immediate resupply of 8mm Mauser. Majority of stock was expended during militia action on Wessel farmstead. Repeat, requesting 8mm resupply, as many crates as can be spared."

He released the key, static returned and silence followed. Reinhardt waited, eyes focused on the indicator needle. He gave it ten full seconds, then keyed again.

"Militia HQ, Delta-88 repeating request. Do you copy?"

A burst of static flickered in his earpiece, then a clipped voice came through, half-buried in crosstalk.

"...Delta-88, acknowledged... standby. HQ receiving high traffic, over."

Reinhardt straightened. He adjusted the gain slightly, trying to isolate the channel. The net was flooded with clipped voices, overlapping coordinates, phrases like "sector breach" and "civilian report confirmed." There was tension in the airwaves.

He keyed again, carefully.

"Understood. Standing by, HQ. Delta-88 out."

He set the mic down gently, then folded his hands. His eyes narrowed slightly. Something was moving, whether just administrative chaos from the aftermath of the Wessel raid or signs of a deeper mobilization, he wasn't certain, but the militia wasn't idle, not anymore.

Reinhardt sat still, the crackle of the militia net now a storm in his ears. Broken words. Misaligned frequencies. Voices overlapping like distant ghosts, some clear and cold in their urgency, others near-incomprehensible shouts, gasps, and clipped orders swallowed by static. It was chaos and Reinhardt had never heard the net like this. The militia radio, which once sounded of drills, dispatch requests, or slow, steady rural reports, now roared with unfiltered tension. He listened. Not with panic, he'd already learned that lesson, but with the tight stillness of a man bracing for the wind before it breaks the glass. His hand hovered near the tuning dial, trying to parse clean signals from the rest. Snatches came through:

"...possible breach headed south... no confirmation on command relay...."

"...Delta-Twelve responded, but the fireteam's down one, we... static... retreat..."

"...children evacuated from Westhold district, request escort..."

Then, suddenly, the net cleared. A commanding voice, louder and firmer than the rest, cut through with full channel priority override.

"All friendly assets, all friendly assets collapse to local bastions. A state of emergency is declared. I repeat, a state of emergency is declared. Neue Frankfurt Airport was seized within the hour by enemy forces. All militia elements are activated under the Wessel Accord."

The words struck like a slow, deliberate hammer. Reinhardt's jaw tightened. His chest rose once. Then again. He reached forward, turned down the volume, and rested his hands on the edge of the radio. He did not move for a moment. The war had come to them. Delumina, his world, his home, the soil Ludwig had died to protect, was no longer a sanctuary. The enemy was here, inside the gates. The Red Twilight or something else entirely... it didn't matter now. The Wessel Accord was no longer theory. No longer drill. It was the law and Reinhardt Jäger, of the Jäger homestead, was now an active node in the defense of the entire colony. He stood. There was work to do.

.The moment the call ended, Reinhardt was already moving. He burst through the back door of the farmhouse, boots heavy on the floorboards. His father looked up from the table, brow furrowed. His mother paused, dish in hand. Reinhardt's voice was low but firm, his tone the same one Ludwig had once used after a militia drill. "Stay here, both of you. Lock the doors. Don't leave the property unless ordered by Militia command."

His father stood halfway, confused, ready to object.

Reinhardt cut him off. "State of emergency. Wessel Accord is active. Neue Frankfurt's airport has fallen."

A silence hung, brief and grave. His mother's hand went to her mouth. Gerhardt sat down, slowly, the meaning hitting him but Reinhardt was already gone.

He sprinted toward the shed. The rifle was already in his hands, the MG-82 slung over his back. As he reached the shed, he threw open the creaking metal doors to reveal the machine that had carried Ludwig through storms, patrols, and countless drills, the motorcycle. An old, growling piece of Italian manufacture, half rust and half roar, but dependable. He crouched, running checks like muscle memory. Tires. Chain. Brakes. Fuel. Good enough. He wheeled it out with a grunt and gunned it briefly to life before easing off the throttle. Back to the shed. His boots scraped on concrete as he grabbed the field satchel, spare belts for the MG, an oilcloth-wrapped toolkit, and two additional magazines for his STG-91. A trench spade. A ration tin. Two canteens. All of it was thrown into the sidecar or lashed to the frame. The MG-82 was mounted next, clicked into place on the reinforced pintle welded years ago by Ludwig himself. He remembered holding the rivet for him. Now he locked the feed arm, checked the belt, and gave it one last confirming tug. The rifle went cross-slung over his chest. The final item, the handheld radio from the farmhouse, slipped into the outer pouch of his rucksack, antenna extended, and net already active.

Crackling voices. Commands half-cut.

"...need reinforcements at..."

"...Hussar-2 report... unknown number of hostiles..."

"...civilian convoy ambushed on the East Line Road..."

No time to sort the mess. Reinhardt didn't look back, wave or say goodbye. He kickstarted the motorcycle, felt the engine stutter and catch, and throttled it back toward the road. The wind bit as he accelerated, the hum of the radio mixing with the growing howl of the engine and the distant thunder of war. He was no longer just Reinhardt. He was Delta-88 and the bastion would hold.

.The wind knifed through his jacket as Reinhardt roared down the gravel-blown country road, the old motorcycle snarling beneath him like a wolf given purpose. Dust kicked up behind his tires in long gray plumes. The sidecar rattled with every bump, the MG-82 bouncing lightly against its mount, the ammo belt fluttering like a battle flag. To his left, a family stood frozen on their porch, shaded beneath a slate-tiled roof, watching the northern horizon. The father had a pair of binoculars. The mother clutched her children. Reinhardt didn't slow.

Further ahead, a trader's truck veered into a ditch, overloaded with furniture, sacks, and panicked faces. He swerved past it, barely glancing at the chaos. His eyes were forward, locked on the black line of Neue Frankfurt's southern skyline rising over the next ridge. Crackling voices fought for dominance on the handheld radio. Nothing was clear. Whole messages stepped over each other. Callsigns repeated. Screams. Static. Echoes of emergency orders, some authentic, others likely ghosts. Reinhardt grit his teeth, leaned forward slightly to lessen the drag, and turned the dial. One channel. Then another. Then another. Still nothing.

He pulled the motorcycle off the road just past a hedgerow, engine idling as he thumbed the knob again, carefully scanning for clarity amid the storm. Finally, one voice punched through the mess like a thunderclap.

"...This is Colonel Brandt, Militia Command, 5th Battalion... All Delta, Bravo, and Echo elements muster at the south side of Neue Frankfurt...repeat, muster at Militia HQ. Emergency protocols active. No exceptions. Wessel Accord is binding... no further instructions needed."

Reinhardt froze. Colonel. So Brandt had been given field command. He didn't reply. That wasn't his place, not as a Delta. He was a line rifleman, maybe a fireteam leader at most. Sending acknowledgment would only jam the net further. This was wartime radio now. Only officers and emergency transmissions had the right to speak. He let go of the mic. Adjusted the frequency knob just enough to lock it in. Then he kicked the bike into gear and peeled away from the tree line, dirt flaring behind him, the black spires of Neue Frankfurt growing closer by the second.

Reinhardt slowed the motorcycle as he approached the makeshift checkpoint on the southern outskirts of Neue Frankfurt. A burned-out civilian hauler had been dragged across one lane of the road, turned broadside to serve as a barrier. Sandbags, wire, and scavenged corrugated steel sheets braced the perimeter. A squad of militia, some in uniform with others in work clothes with armbands and rifles, stood ready. A mounted machine gun tracked him from behind a stack of crates as he neared. A young soldier with soot on his face stepped into the road and raised his hand. Reinhardt throttled down and coasted to a halt.

"State your name and intent," the man called out, his voice taut but not aggressive.

"Reinhardt Jäger," he answered quickly, removing his helmet. "Militia. Reporting to Colonel Brandt with Fifth Battalion."

The militiaman looked him over. His eyes passed over the MG-82, the old motorcycle, the dirt on his jacket, and finally landed on the rifle slung over his chest. He nodded.

"You know where you're going?"

"Southside HQ, corner of Grenzerstraße and Aschheim. I know it."

"Good, but be quick. Things are moving fast. Stick to the right lanes once you cross into the city. Avoid bottlenecks. Keep your eyes open, Red Twilight's not just in uniforms."

Reinhardt gave a short nod of gratitude. "Understood."

The checkpoint soldier waved him through, and the sandbag line opened just enough for the motorcycle to slip between. Beyond the barricade, the city was chaotic. Smoke hung over the rooftops like a shroud. People scrambled across intersections, some on foot, some in overloaded trucks, others dragging carts or carrying children. Old men with hunting rifles stood guard on stoops. A mother and son pressed flat against a brick wall as a militia jeep sped past, tires screeching. Reinhardt wove through it all with precision. Every second counted now. The streets narrowed and twisted. Holo-signs flickered. The Confederation banners on the lampposts flapped wildly in the growing wind. Sirens wailed far off toward the airport, where smoke rose in thick black plumes.

This wasn't a drill. It wasn't even a raid. This was war, and it had found Delumina. Reinhardt leaned into a turn and accelerated past the remnants of a barricade knocked over by a fleeing vehicle. He could see the southside command post now, its arched windows shuttered, its front steps crowded with armed men receiving orders, checking gear, and preparing to fight. He didn't hesitate. He throttled forward, gripping the handlebars tight, ready to report for duty.

Reinhardt pulled the motorcycle up near the entrance of the southside Militia HQ. The courtyard was filled with men, militiamen, some still in farm gear, others in partial uniforms, all armed. Weapons were being handed out, crates were being opened, and the air was thick with shouted orders and the scent of oil and exhaust.

He killed the engine and stepped off. The MG-82 in the sidecar was locked and ready. Slinging his STG-91 back over his shoulder, he moved toward the door, scanning the flow of men and gear. A young officer in militia field greys was standing by the entrance, clipboard in hand and headset on. Reinhardt approached him.

"Name and unit?" the officer barked, not looking up.

"Reinhardt Jäger, reporting in from the Jäger homestead."

The officer finally looked up, eyes narrowing as he scanned Reinhardt's face.

"You're the nephew of Ludwig Jäger?"

"Yes. He fell in the Wessel farmstead engagement. I'm taking his place."

The officer nodded, the recognition clear now.

"Good. We need every man who can shoot and think. The Fifth Battalion is forming up outside, but Colonel Brandt will be speaking to platoon and company leads soon. You're not on the officer list, so find your squad lead. Bravo Company is light but you'll likely slot in there."

"Jawohl," Reinhardt said crisply, snapping a Roman salute before turning on his heel.

He stepped into the warm, humming chaos of the staging yard. The MG-82 was still locked in the sidecar. He unlatched it, slung it up onto his shoulder, and secured the ammo belts into his satchel. The weight was familiar, grounding. He made his way across the yard where militiamen were forming into rough squads and platoons, many still receiving their assignments. He cut through the crowd, asking around as he moved.

"Which unit's Bravo Company?"

A corporal glanced up from where he was oiling a bolt.

"Down the far row. You'll see 'em. Sparse turnout."

Reinhardt nodded his thanks and moved on. He found them arrayed loosely near a fuel truck, men sitting on crates or standing at ease. Some still wore civilian coats over their uniforms, roughly sixty men, half-strength at best. A few were smoking. Others were checking straps and sights. The company commander, the XO, and the First Sergeant were huddled around a portable table with the other platoon leaders, going over the operation map. Reinhardt approached a group near the edge, rifle over his shoulder, MG-82 in hand.

"Which squad takes the MG?"

A man with a broad face and buzzed hair looked him over, then pointed with his chin.

"Weapons squad, First Platoon. Sergeant Voss runs it. He's over there."

Reinhardt followed the gesture and saw him, an older man maybe sixty with thick gray stubble and a cigar clenched between his teeth. He wore an old-pattern militia jacket, sleeves rolled to the forearms, and a scar down his left temple. He was methodically inspecting a belt of grenades when Reinhardt stepped up.

"Sergeant Voss?" Reinhardt asked.

The old man didn't look up immediately, just tugged on the belt pouch and gave it a nod of approval.

"Depends who's asking."

"Reinhardt Jäger, Delta-88, reporting in. I've been assigned to the weapons squad."

That made Voss look up. His eyes were hard, clear, and assessing.

"You the one from the Wessel fight? The boy whose uncle bought it?"

Reinhardt gave a short nod. "Yes, sir."

Voss chewed the corner of his cigar.

"Well, hell. That makes you my new MG. Good, we need the firepower. You got belts?"

"Three with me. I'll need resupply."

"You'll get it when we all do. For now, find a seat and make sure that weapon's spotless. We'll be moving during the night."

Reinhardt didn't argue. He stepped aside, laid the MG-82 across his lap, and began checking every part, every screw, every feed pawl with careful precision. Around him, the scattered remnants of Bravo Company were slowly forming into a fighting unit again. Reinhardt finished wiping the feed tray and slapped the cover closed on the MG-82. The weapon was clean. He was ready. The old sergeant, Voss, leaned down beside him, eyes scanning the company perimeter.

"Alright, listen up," he said, voice low and gravelly. "Bravo's not going in. We're not the hammer. We're the wall. Support-by-fire line. We hold ground and make noise."

He jabbed a thumb toward the rear of the staging area where a handful of trucks were being hastily refueled.

"Mortar section's getting set up with those trucks and trailers. 120mm tubes pulled by rust buckets. Ammo's light, so make it count. Our job is to protect those tubes. If they go down, we have nothing to stop them pushing into city limits."

Someone asked, "What about support? Do we get any help?"

Voss spat into the dirt.

"Regimental HQ's got a pair of hundred millimeter howitzers, but only one works and she's missing a firing pin more often than not. Ammunition's scarce. That's the truth."

He paused and scratched at the back of his neck.

"Army, Navy, and ESS requests already went up the minute the state of emergency was declared. Until they get here? We hold. That airport's lost, but if they break out of it and reach the rural belts, we're finished."

He looked over the line.

"That's all you need to know. Watch your sectors. Keep the mortars firing. If we're lucky, those bastards stay penned in. If not..."

He didn't finish the sentence. He didn't have to. Voss moved off to check the rest of the squad, barking orders, straightening formations, and tightening the perimeter as the sun climbed higher. Reinhardt loaded his first belt into the MG-82 and took a deep breath.

The order came quietly, almost too quietly for what it meant, pre-dawn movement. Bravo Company was to reposition under cover of darkness, escorting and guarding the battalion's mortar section as it established fire positions southeast of the airport. Every man moved with hushed urgency, whispering final checks and adjusting straps and slings. Engines were kept off until the last possible moment. Trucks and motorcycles lined up like ghosts in the dim light, men silhouetted by their gear, packs heavy and weapons loaded.

Reinhardt felt the chill creep down his collar as he stood beside the mounted MG-82. The street smelled of cordite, oil, and dew-damp dust. Somewhere nearby, a baby cried inside a shuttered home, then fell silent. Orders passed from squad leaders to fire teams like wind through leaves. "Mount up. One minute."

The convoy rolled forward, slowly at first, wheels crunching over debris and old leaves. They moved through alleys and service roads to avoid open boulevards, cutting through the shattered veins of the city like blood in old arteries. Streetlights were off. Only the headlights of lead vehicles and occasional muzzle flashes in the far distance gave hints of where they were, or where the enemy was. Reinhardt didn't speak. He just kept his hands tight on the grip of the MG and his ears open to the distant bursts echoing from the north. Somewhere up ahead, someone cursed as a truck struck a pothole. One of the mortar crews shouted a warning about spilled shells, then righted the crate.

By the time they reached the edge of the assigned fire line the horizon was beginning to pale with the first sign of morning. The mortar crews jumped down and began setting up quickly, unlimbering the 120mm tubes and preparing the baseplates. The trailers were light and aged, but still functional. The men worked fast, quiet, but confident.

Bravo Company moved in a loose semicircle around the mortar site, digging in along shallow depressions and natural rises in the ground. There was no fortification, just dirt, sandbags, and old-fashioned sweat. Reinhardt's section was placed just left of the main line, his MG given clear fields of fire toward a small industrial complex about four hundred meters out, likely enemy-held.

The platoon sergeant pointed to a spot beside a scorched delivery truck. "You cover that approach. If they try to flank the tubes, you open up and don't stop 'til I tell you."

Reinhardt just nodded, then set to work. The MG-82 was mounted low against the bipod, the ammunition belt linked and ready. He lay prone behind it, sighting down the barrel. The position was imperfect, no overhead cover or armor, but it was his. Behind him, the mortars were set into place. The gunners tested elevations, murmured calculations. Radios buzzed quietly as coordinates were passed from command. The whole battalion was holding its breath. The sun wasn't up yet but the war was.

The low murmur of final coordinates crackled over the radio net. Reinhardt heard it even without leaning in as Alpha, Charlie, and Delta Companies were advancing. A sweep toward the outer fringe of Neue Frankfurt Airport, the initial push to retake the perimeter. Then the word came over comms, cutting through the tension like a blade.

"FEUER!"

The entire mortar section answered in perfect harmony.

THUNK. THUNK. THUNK.

Three thunderous launches in quick succession. The air behind the tubes shimmered with the heat of ignition as the first volley arced into the dim sky, disappearing like meteors in reverse up into gray and blue, down into the unknown.

Seconds passed then came the second volley.

THUNK. THUNK. THUNK.

The gunners worked with brutal rhythm. Sweating men shouting elevation numbers and adjustments, loading fresh rounds, slapping the tubes like the throats of great iron drums. Each shell vanished into the misty sky, bound for enemy positions buried somewhere in the maze of hangars and terminals. Reinhardt hugged the earth, feeling each concussion in his chest. His MG was silent but alive, an extension of his nerves as he waited. His eyes scanned the tree line and distant rooftops, ready for retaliation. The last of the initial five volleys thundered skyward.

Then came the next order: "Shift fire to creeping fire, 100m north."

Another three shells loaded and sent. The fire mission wasn't stopping, it was evolving. They were carving a path ahead of the assault companies, softening entrenched positions, buying seconds of survival for every man clearing rooms and alleys. To Reinhardt's left, a young mortar assistant knelt, arms wrapped around a crate of shells, his face pale with strain. He looked up at the sky, then toward the city. The tubes boomed again.

The sky was gray with smoke and the smell of ammonium and churned earth. Bravo Company had been in place for nearly an hour. The mortars behind them had worked without pause, each fire mission called down like thunder upon the edges of the airport complex. Reinhardt had counted each volley at first, but after the twelfth he lost track, only registering the rhythm in his bones. Fire, reload, fire. The high crack of the bipods bucking against the soil then another. Some of the men had grown used to the sound. Others flinched each time. Reinhardt didn't flinch. He just waited, eyeing the fields through the sights of his MG-82, watching for anything be it movement, muzzle flashes, or anything that looked like the enemy punching out of the smoke.

Then the radio flared. Not scattered chatter this time, not confused updates from squads in contact. This was sharp and directed.

"Bravo Actual, this is Battalion. Be advised, fragmentary order incoming. Stand by."

Reinhardt looked back toward the company commander, who already had his headset pressed against his ear, listening. A moment passed. Then he signaled for platoon leaders and sergeants. Quiet intensity followed. The murmuring in the company fell to silence as leaders closed in around the CO. They nodded grimly, no arguments. Sergeant Voss came walking fast, voice raised just enough.

"All squads, rally in column. The mortar section is packing up and we're moving up to support the assault. Reinforcements needed."

Reinhardt glanced at the mortars. The crews had already begun pulling pins, folding legs, slapping canvas over the tubes. Ammo crates were getting stacked into trailers by hand, rushed and silent. He slung the MG-82, adjusted the side-mounted belt box, and fell in line as his squad took shape, still ragged, still understrength, but moving. Boots over churned dirt, past shell-scarred trees and the old transport trucks that bore the 120mm mortars now being hauled south. As Bravo moved forward, the old support by fire position emptied. Behind them, the thunder finally ceased. Ahead, a different thunder waited, one closer and more personal.

Bravo Company moved like a shadow through Neue Frankfurt, weapons shouldered, and eyes scanning windows, doorframes, as well as rooftops. They were roughly two miles out now, over four klicks, from the outer perimeter of the airport. No time for wide flanking movements. This was a hasty push, and every man knew it.

First Platoon held the left, threading through ruined apartment blocks and half-demolished parks, the red sun barely peeking through the smoke overhead. Second Platoon pressed the center line, cutting across intersections and small boulevards, hugging vehicles and low brick walls. Third Platoon kept the right, skirting alleys and fences, covering open-air cafés and office lots that had long since been stripped to concrete bones. Reinhardt moved near the rear, beside Sergeant Voss, the weapons squad leader. That term felt hollow now. There was no squad. Just him, the MG-82, and whatever belt-fed fury he could still muster. No assistant gunner. No tripod. No shield. Just his trigger finger and the belt box strapped to his hip.

"You good?" Voss asked, voice quiet but cutting through the morning tension.

Reinhardt gave a single nod, eyes alert. "Loaded and ready."

"Good, you're fire superiority. Keep your eyes open."

They followed just behind Second Squad, keeping tight to the ruins of what had once been a tram station. Burnt steel ribs jutted into the air. The city still smoldered in places. Trash fires, flares, scorched-out utility lines crackling with intermittent static. Power was dead in this sector. All signals went through line-of-sight relays or the militia net, which crackled every few minutes with updates from the battalion.

They crossed danger areas fast. Parks were sprinted across in bounding movements, rifles covering the treelines. Streets were darted over two men at a time, scouts scanning for movement between the shattered glass and flickering neon signs still dimly glowing from battery backups.

Each time, Reinhardt covered them. The MG-82 felt heavier now, not from the weight but from responsibility. They were closing in on the first ring of outer airport control, warehouses, radar towers, and fuel depots. But so far... no shots. No contact. Uneasy silence and that kind of silence always meant something worse.

Bravo Company reached the perimeter of the airport just before noon. Smoke curled upward from the cracked runways and splintered hangars, the long skeletal shapes of transport aircraft lying motionless as some shredded by fire, others still burning. Flames licked along the fuselage of one large planetary hauler, its tail snapped and buried in a hangar roof. Another lay on its side, fuselage buckled like a crushed can.

Reinhardt crouched low beside a concrete barrier, scanning the airfield. He could feel the tension in the air, like a taut string waiting to snap. Then came the familiar thunk-thunk-thunk behind him, followed by the screech of steel overhead. The 120mm mortars were back online.

He looked up just as the first wave of shells cut the sky, whispering their deadly chorus. Impact. Impact. Impact. Three brilliant geysers of flame and debris erupted on the far end of the airport, just past the southern hangars. The ground shook faintly under his boots. Another volley followed. Then another.

Sergeant Voss barked orders. Bravo Company spread out quickly in a hasty perimeter, weapons oriented outward toward the airport, eyes on the skyline. Reinhardt settled behind a piece of cover near what had once been a small cargo checkpoint. He trained the MG-82 outward, finger resting lightly on the trigger. One belt in. Two more in his pack. He was ready. Off to the west, he caught movement, friendly uniforms massing. Trucks, light utility vehicles, and a few makeshift armored transports bearing the green armbands of the Militia. That was 2nd Battalion's reserve elements forming up, half a kilometer out and fanning along the slope of a rail embankment. They were getting ready for something. Then the call came over the radio. A shift in tone. Urgent. Clipped.

"All elements, be advised, all 2nd and 5th Battalion frontline companies are ordered to pull back from forward positions immediately. I repeat, pull back immediately. Regroup at Rally Point Echo and prepare for containment posture."

Reinhardt blinked, stunned for a moment.

"We're pulling back?" someone muttered beside him.

He adjusted the dials on his radio, making sure it wasn't interference or some delayed message. No, the net was buzzing now, layered with chatter and acknowledgments from company and platoon-level commanders. Reinhardt looked up just in time to see the distant mortar crews frantically loading their gear. The trailers were being hitched to the trucks. They were pulling out. He swallowed hard. They were giving up the airport.

Reinhardt remained low, pressed behind a shattered wall, the MG-82 angled across the rubble in front of him. The order to fall back was still echoing through the battalion net but Bravo hadn't moved. Not yet then he saw why.

Across the open stretch beyond the terminal, past the control tower's blackened stump and the field of gutted transports, they came. At first it was just two men, one limping and half-carried by the other, blood soaking his sleeve and chest. Then came three more, one dragging a stretcher that wasn't quite long enough, the man atop it barely conscious, jaw slack and head bouncing with every jolt. Then more. The slope of the airport was a river of broken men. Their uniforms were shredded, arms bandaged in bloodied tourniquets, faces blackened with smoke and dust. Some clutched weapons with cracked stocks and empty magazines; others had lost theirs entirely. A few walked like aimless spirits, silent, eyes forward, mouths open but making no sound. One collapsed right at the base of the embankment, screaming for his mother before a medic reached him.

A man stumbled past with no helmet and half his face torn open, the other half grimacing in silent agony. A medic followed behind, holding his jaw shut with one hand, muttering "You're alright, you're alright," over and over, even though they both knew it wasn't true.

The backflow of the dead and dying did not stop. Reinhardt gritted his teeth, his jaw clenching harder with each passing minute. He watched as a two-man MG team limped by with no ammo or assistant gunner. The belt had clearly run dry mid-fight. The barrel was scorched red. One of them, eyes glazed, dropped the MG-17, the updated version of the MG-82, right on the pavement and kept walking without saying a word. Reinhardt was on it in an instant.

He slung his MG-82 over his shoulder, scooped up the abandoned MG-17, checked the chamber and tossed it into the sidecar of a burned-out militia motorcycle just behind his cover. The barrel was usable, but warped from overuse. He stripped it fast and left the housing open, knowing he'd have to scavenge more.

Another group passed, this one dragging crates of 8mm Mauser and two spare barrels. The rear man had a shattered collarbone and could barely hold on. Reinhardt ran over and caught the crate before it fell.

"You need these?" he asked sharply.

The man didn't answer. He just looked at him with a silent, hollow face then nodded once and moved on, gripping his arm like it might fall off. Reinhardt stacked the fresh barrels and crate of 8mm beside the MG-17. He was starting to build a small arsenal. Another ammo belt came loose from a pack tossed aside by a retreating man, Reinhardt snatched it, unrolled it, and began feeding it into the MG-82's box.

He paused and looked up again. A stretcher passed. This time, whoever was on it wasn't moving. The man on it was still, eyes staring upward, the entire right side of his ribcage caved in. His boot was gone, foot hanging by sinew. A bloody field jacket had been tucked over his head, but the outline of his collapsed skull was still visible through the fabric. The bearers said nothing. They just carried him past in silence.

Another came crawling. No one carried him. No one could. His legs were gone at the knees, just ragged stumps wrapped in belts and soaked rags. He was using his elbows to drag himself forward. Reinhardt watched him go, stunned.

Reinhardt sat near the perimeter wall of a charred outbuilding, his arms resting over his knees. Around him lay what had become his own small arsenal: several bandoliers of 8mm rounds, two spare MG-82 barrels, and his STG-91 slung across his back. A few loaded magazines sat on his lap. None of it felt like excess. It was insurance, tools for the hours to come.

Nearby, Sergeant Voss paced quietly, occasionally glancing out toward the smoldering airfield. Across the cracked tarmac and wrecked civilian transport planes, no enemy movement could be seen, yet.

A new set of engines rumbled behind them. Colonel Brandt had arrived with what remained of the 5th Battalion's headquarters company. Their vehicles were dusty, armor-scratched and bearing scorch marks. Men offloaded quickly, establishing a tight 360° security around a battered command truck now serving as the forward HQ. A long whip antenna rose from the roof, crackling with bursts of static and scrambled voices. Brandt stepped out, helmet tucked under his arm, face streaked with grime and exhaustion. Despite it all, he radiated will, implacable and focused. He barely acknowledged the salutes as he moved to the vehicle's comms station, slapping the side panel.

"Still no goddamn connection to Delumina Station?" he barked.

One of the militia techs inside responded, "We're trying all channels. Something is jamming wide-band, or they're bottlenecked."

Brandt grimaced and turned, spotting Reinhardt nearby.

"You," he called, walking over. "Get up."

Reinhardt stood, slinging the STG-91 back over his chest.

"You got a working handset?"

"Yes, sir."

"Keep it tuned to Battalion net and Orbital relay channel three. If you hear anything from Delumina Station, especially Navy or ESS, I want to know it before the bastards across the tarmac do."

"Understood."

Brandt lingered, then added in a lower voice, "If the Navy or the ESS respond, they'll be the first to act. The Army won't reach us in time, most of their deployments are locked in-system or on the Terran bastions."

Reinhardt nodded, and Brandt moved off again, already shouting for a sitrep from the mortar section. The crackle of Reinhardt's radio never ceased. No confirmations. No reinforcements. The haze of mortar smoke and burning aviation fuel hung low over Neue Frankfurt's ruined southern district. Reinhardt sat crouched behind the second-floor parapet of a half-demolished warehouse, his radio set crackling uselessly in his ear.

He glanced up. There it was, Delumina Station, the orbital station. A silver sliver against the midday sky, its lights faint but steady. He could see it with his own eyes. So why couldn't he hear them? He tapped the mic again. Nothing but background static and ghost-chatter from friendly ground elements. Too many buildings, too much interference. It could be jamming or maybe worse.

Reinhardt sighed through his nose. Then stood. He slung his STG-91, grabbed the MG-82 by its carry handle, clipped a bandolier of 8mm to his chest, and slung the portable radio over his shoulder. A coil of cabling and a longer whip antenna clattered gently against his belt as he moved. He stepped past other militiamen taking cover behind sandbags, climbed the interior stairwell of the warehouse, and forced open the access hatch to the roof.

The wind met him first. Cold. Clean. Above the fires, above the shouting. Reinhardt crawled low across the flat, blackened rooftop. His silhouette kept tight against the lip of the structure, rifle beside him, he pulled the radio kit from his back and unfurled the extra antenna. It clacked into place as he extended it upward, fastening it to a bent rebar spine jutting from a broken roof beam. He keyed the mic.

"Delumina Station, this is Delta-88, Delumina militia element under 5th Volkssturm Battalion. Requesting immediate confirmation of transmission. We are actively engaged against an occupying force at the planetary airport. I say again, do you read? Over."

A pause. Static. Then a garbled tone. A faint crackle. Like the edge of a voice just beyond reach.

"Delumina Station, this is Delta-88, do you read?"

He stood slowly, extending the antenna slightly higher. The sky remained quiet. He stared at the stars orbiting overhead. The station passed slowly westward, its comm relays facing the horizon. Reinhardt gritted his teeth, pressed the transmit key one more time.

"To any Confederation assets monitoring this channel... We are under siege. This is Delta-88 at Neue Frankfurt airport containment line. We are holding the line. Requesting reinforcements. Over."

The wind carried his words into silence. He lowered the mic as he looked out over the airport. Fires still burned in the hangars. Somewhere, gunfire echoed in the distance. But here, at this moment only wind, smoke, and the great sky above. He knelt beside the MG-82, checked the feed tray, locked in a new belt, and waited.

The antenna clicked faintly as Reinhardt adjusted the tuner again, trying to isolate the fluttering signal he had heard moments ago. Most of the militia channels were clogged with panicked cross-talk or garbled orders, but this one was different but clearer, higher-pitched, and coming from above. Static cracked once more, then broke into a clipped, mechanical voice. His breath caught.

"This is an automated emergency broadcast from Delumina Orbital Station. Control of the station has been compromised. Repeat, control compromised. Personnel compromised. Do not attempt docking. Do not transmit sensitive data. This station is in a state of emergency. Mayday. Mayday. Mayday."

The message repeated every thirty seconds in rotating languages such as German, Gaelic, English, French and even Russian. At the end of each loop, a timestamp blinked on the receiver. Timestamp: 0605 hours. Reinhardt checked his watch. It was 1212 now. Six hours ago. That was before the ground assault had even begun in earnest. Before Bravo Company had taken up its defensive line. Before the battalion's first mortar tube had fired. His stomach tightened. They had already seized the station before we even mobilized our counterattack. He didn't key his mic. He didn't report it over the battalion net. If that message went live across militia comms, morale would fracture within minutes. There would be panic, second-guessing, and collapse. No, this had to go to Brandt directly. Reinhardt keyed the radio on the battalion net to request the Colonel meet him on the rooftop. Colonel Brandt ascended the final ladder rung with a grunt, pulled himself up onto the rooftop, and walked toward Reinhardt's makeshift comms station.

"What is it, Jäger?

Reinhardt didn't answer right away. He crouched next to the set, keyed up the recording, and let the Colonel hear it for himself. The voice repeated:

"Control of the station has been compromised. Personnel compromised. Mayday. Mayday."

Brandt said nothing at first. His eyes fixed on the timestamp. His jaw flexed as he processed it. Reinhardt finally spoke, low and measured. "They took it six hours ago, sir. Before we even reached the airport."

Brandt gave a single slow nod. "Did you report this on the battalion net?"

"No, sir."

"Good," Brandt said flatly. "If the boys hear this, they'll think we've already lost."

He looked up at the sky. There, above the haze of smoke and clouds, Delumina Station glinted like a tiny silver nail hammered into the heavens.

"You did the right thing," he added. "Keep trying to raise someone up there. Anything that isn't automated. If they've got survivors, I want them to talk."

Reinhardt nodded. "Understood."

Brandt turned to go, then paused. "If this is true... the next wave won't come from down here."

He didn't explain. He didn't need to. Reinhardt already knew what he meant. Reinhardt lay prone against the sun-warmed concrete of the rooftop, his MG-82 resting on its bipod, barrel angled just low enough to cover the outer edge of the airport perimeter. Smoke still drifted from the husks of grounded aircraft, civilian transport shuttles, freighters, even a few private orbital hoppers, all half-buried in rubble, some flickering with dying fire.

He pulled his field cap lower over his brow, squinting into the shimmering distance. Nothing moved. The militia line, thin and disorganized, was fanned out in a shallow crescent around the southern perimeter. The rest of Bravo Company was dug in below him, using broken vehicles and fencing as cover, watching and waiting. The quiet wasn't comforting. He had seen too many sudden storms follow moments like these.

Reinhardt leaned over and turned the radio dial with a gentle hand, listening through the headset. The militia net had calmed somewhat, with occasional call-and-response pings between platoon elements. No word yet on reinforcements. No word on counterattack. He adjusted the antenna position. A crackle of encrypted static flared briefly on one of the orbital bands, then faded. He stayed on it, just in case. Whatever was transmitting from Delumina Station was buried under layers of interference, or encryption, or both. His eyes went back to the airport to watch the edges.

That was something his uncle always said. The center will always seem calm but watch the sides. That's where they'll try to break. Reinhardt was watching. His MG-82 had a clear field of fire along the southern tarmac and taxiway lanes. Anyone charging out would find themselves in a lethal cone of lead.

His finger brushed the safety. He let out a slow breath, nothing yet. He could feel it. The stillness before impact. The breathing space before the next scream of chaos. His ears tuned to the silence like a predator's, filtering out the wind, the chatter, and the idle rustle of uniforms down below. He could feel their next move was coming. When it did, he'd be ready.

It began with a flicker. Reinhardt's eye caught the movement just past the smoke curtain drifting from the wrecked aircraft, three shadows darting low across the runway with no set formation. Then another group, crawling through the gaps between debris and fencing like vermin under broken light. Contact, his hands moved without thinking. He keyed his headset and pushed the transmit switch. "Delta-88 reporting movement at the airport perimeter. Multiple contacts. This is a probe."

He glanced left, dust rose sharply from an alley past the main line. His blood went cold.

"They're flanking. Repeat, flanking maneuver left of Bravo Company's forward line. Estimated to be squad strength."

Then the first shot cracked, not his, a sharp report from a friendly rifleman down the slope. The quiet shattered. Reinhardt pressed the stock of the MG-82 into his shoulder and swung to meet the movement. His finger depressed the trigger. The gun barked to life, loud and violent as the barrel spat fire. Muzzle flash lit the rooftop as he dragged his fire across the field. Brass casings rattled over the rooftop edge. Two enemy shapes folded mid-run. Another dove behind cover but not fast enough. Reinhardt stitched the concrete where it landed.

"Contact front, contact front!" came voices over comms. Platoons were waking up, opening fire. The sudden rattle of rifles joined the thunder of the machine gun. From the street below, Sergeant Voss was shouting orders, trying to shift men to cover the left flank.

"Reinhardt, give us another belt!" someone called from below.

"Already on it," Reinhardt growled, slamming a fresh belt into place.

He sighted again. More shapes emerged, this time they moved with coordination as short rushes, covering one another. They were testing, measuring the militia's readiness and trying to punch through. A burst of fire crackled from a rooftop farther left. Friendly tracer rounds lit the air red-orange. Grenades went off near a vehicle wreck, sending smoke and debris high into the air. Reinhardt kept up the rhythm as twelve-round bursts, then another and another, sweeping fire across the insurgents' point of advance. He keyed the battalion net again, breathing hard.

"Delta-88, Bravo line engaged. Left flank holding for now. Recommend 2nd Platoon shift two squads to reinforce. Requesting mortar fire..."

There was no panic in his voice, only urgency. This was what Ludwig had trained him for. This was why he had stayed behind on the farmstead, learning the old ways of war. He fed another belt, reset his position, and brought the gun back up. He wouldn't let them through. The barrel smoked. Reinhardt's shoulders ached from the recoil and weight. He slammed open the feed cover, yanked the empty belt out, and shoved in another. The MG-82 roared again, spitting fire across the runway's jagged edge. Second belt, halfway gone. The insurgents were testing every inch now with bursts from the fence line, skirmishers darting between burning cargo crates, and muzzle flashes winking like fireflies. But every time they pushed, Reinhardt answered with precision and brutality.

By the time he reached the end of his third belt, the feed tray was hot enough to blister flesh. His gloves smoked faintly as he locked the weapon open, panting. He keyed his mic.

"Delta-88 to any Bravo element, I'm black on MG belts. Repeat, I need ammo now."

Silence for a moment. Gunfire roared below. "On it! Coming up!"

Footsteps on metal. Boots scraping against the narrow rooftop ladder. Reinhardt turned his head just in time to see a familiar, sweating face pull over the ledge. It was Kasper.

"Hell of a view up here," Kasper muttered, dropping two ammo cans and a spare barrel beside Reinhardt. "Didn't know you were Bravo."

"I didn't know you were," Reinhardt said, managing a grin through grit. "Good to see you, though."

Kasper handed him the fresh belts, chest still rising and falling fast. "You already went through three?"

"They keep coming," Reinhardt said, reloading with muscle memory. "Flank's barely holding."

Kasper crouched beside him, rifle at the ready, eyes scanning the burning perimeter. "Then let's make sure it doesn't fall."

Reinhardt swapped barrels quickly, locking the new one into place with a satisfying twist. The fresh belt snapped in behind it. He looked out across the field and opened fire once more. The enemy wanted through. They were going to learn it would cost them everything. As Reinhardt laid down fresh bursts, his ears tuned to the rhythmic blasts of the MG, but his eyes were drawn to the battlefield below and what he saw wasn't just chaos. It was movement, adjustment and lines flexing. Bravo Company's center had begun to compress, drawing its second platoon back twenty meters to form a tighter arc around the mortars, who themselves had repositioned again behind the tree line and were now firing on new azimuths. Their fire was slower, more deliberate now, and conserving what few remaining rounds they had.

To the left, 1st Platoon pulled back to anchor against a partially collapsed fuel depot, using it as hard cover. They stacked sandbags from broken cargo pallets, even as rifle fire snapped overhead. A pair of wounded were dragged behind cover by the last remaining medic.

The Third Platoon on the right wasn't so lucky. Their flank had been stretched thin, and now a team of runners, likely pulled from reserve company staff, were reinforcing them with ammunition, but no fresh bodies. Smoke grenades popped to obscure enemy vision as they withdrew to a tighter wedge near a burned-out transit bus.

Across the battalion net, voices called out in clipped, combat-fatigued German.

"Bravo-33, reposition behind the customs building, hold that corner or we're rolled."

"1st platoon's line has broken on the east taxiway. We need re-tasked fire support now."

"Bravo Company reports five fallen, seventeen wounded, still holding."

From the rooftop, Reinhardt saw Colonel Brandt step into the open near the HQ truck, unflinching despite incoming fire. He was shouting something to the forward artillery liaison. Behind him, runners carried sealed field reports and status slates back and forth. The battalion was stretched to its breaking point but still breathing, still alive. Reinhardt keyed his mic again, pausing only to scan the next line of movement along the fence.

"Delta-88 reporting that the enemy is still probing on the southern fence line. No breakthrough yet. Flank is stable, for now."

A pause. Then the battalion reply, calm but firm:

"Copy, Delta-88. Hold position. Reinforcements are en route, estimated time unknown. You hold that MG as long as you can."

Reinhardt looked at Kasper. "You hear that?"

Kasper nodded, jaw tight.

"We hold."

The barrel was red and steaming. Reinhardt could smell the burnt lubricant and scorched dust as he twisted it free with practiced hands. The replacement clicked in with a hiss as the cooler metal met the still-warm receiver. He locked it down, slapped a fresh belt into place, and racked the charging handle with a snap of resolve. Kasper stood off to the side, catching his breath, sweat streaking the soot on his face.

"Get me more belts," Reinhardt ordered, his voice low but urgent.

Kasper nodded and slipped back down the stairwell, boots thudding against the concrete as he vanished into the dark. Alone again on the rooftop, Reinhardt let himself think, not long, just enough for a single thought to wedge in. Where were the 1st, 3rd, or 4th Battalions? If 2nd and 5th had already been committed, mauled, and still the others hadn't arrived, then either something was deeply wrong behind the lines, or the entirety of the Volkssturm Regiment had been fractured. Maybe we're all that's left on this side of the river. He didn't voice it. Not over the radio. Not even to Kasper. That kind of thought was a sickness, contagious, and fatal to morale. So he pressed it down into his gut like old iron.

He checked the feed tray. The belt was seated. Cover down. The radio on his hip cracked with static, but no clear signal. Just fragments. More wounded were pulled from the airport perimeter. One squad overrun near the southern terminal.

Mortars repositioning again. Reinhardt exhaled slowly, braced his elbows on the sandbagged ledge, and scanned his sector. Smoke still drifted from the airport, orange flames licking at the underbellies of ruined transports. He shifted the MG's sights toward the northeast fence line, just in case the enemy decided to try again. He waited for Kasper. Waited for orders. Waited for the next shot to fire. All the while he listened, both to the net and to the silence between transmissions. Kasper reappeared, faster than Reinhardt expected. He was panting, flushed, two fresh belts slung over his shoulders and a third clutched in his hands.

"Speak of the devil," Reinhardt muttered under his breath as he remained prone waiting to receive the ammo. He gave Kasper a nod of gratitude, helping unload the belts beside the gun.

"Good work."

"Didn't think I'd be sprinting ammo up rooftops today," Kasper said between gasps.

Reinhardt gave a dry chuckle. "None of us thought any of this would happen."

Just then, the radio on Reinhardt's hip crackled to life, not with more panicked chatter or casualty reports, but a calm, firm voice punching through the static.

"This is Colonel Ternes of the First Battalion. To Colonel Brandt, be advised, we are en route from the eastern bypass. Expect arrival in thirty minutes. We're bringing three full companies with support weapons. Hold the line."

Reinhardt's eyes widened slightly. He quickly turned the volume up and looked over the sandbags toward Colonel Brandt's position across the courtyard. The man's hand was already to his headset, acknowledging the call. A few nearby officers were motioning to their men, news was spreading. For the first time since this chaos began, a current of hope stirred beneath the weight of exhaustion and blood.

Reinhardt looked over at Kasper. "First Battalion's coming."

Kasper blinked. "Reinforcements?"

Reinhardt nodded, a flicker of relief crossing his face. "Three companies. Heavy weapons too."

Kasper sat down beside the spare belts and let out a long breath, almost a laugh. "Finally."

The tension didn't break, not entirely, but something in the air shifted. The silence wasn't just waiting now. It was bracing and preparing. The line would hold and maybe now, just maybe, they'd push forward. Reinhardt slapped the fresh belt into the MG-82, locking it into place with practiced force. The bolt slid forward with a mechanical clack. Then he heard it, an unmistakable thump-thump-thump in the distance incoming, not from the enemy, mortars. He ducked instinctively, but seconds later, the shells screamed overhead and crashed into the airport tarmac beyond. A wave of fire and smoke erupted, followed by another and another. The intervals grew shorter, with precision and tempo.

Reinhardt's pulse jumped, not from fear, but recognition. That wasn't the 5th Battalion's ragged section. That was the 1st Battalion's mortar battery. He knew the difference with their tighter spread and cleaner fire control. He stole a glance skyward and then down the line, watching the tarmac being pounded into smoking craters. The Red Twilight assault faltered. Men were scrambling, diving for cover, and their flanking attempt dissolved under steel and shrapnel.

He keyed his radio and muttered to Kasper, "That's First Battalion, active-duty militia."

Kasper nodded, his face pale but steady. Reinhardt continued, "5th is the home guard of old men and farm boys like us. But 1st? That's the hammer."

Out on the left flank he saw them, dark silhouettes weaving between structures and bounding toward the containment line. Their discipline was evident even from this distance. It was controlled, aggressive, and deliberate. As they pushed up, Bravo Company's line steadied further. The enemy began to break contact in pockets, their momentum collapsing under the dual pressure of plunging fire and closing steel. Reinhardt stayed behind his gun, adjusting his aim, watching and waiting. The worst might not be over but they weren't alone anymore. They had teeth now.

The last of the mortar shells landed with a dull thunderclap, kicking up smoke and debris over the shattered edge of the airport tarmac. The return fire had gone silent. No more movement across the wire. The line, for now, held firm. Reinhardt took a long breath, shoulders easing slightly as he released the MG-82. The weapon sat loaded and ready, but no more rounds were needed, at least for the moment. Around him, the other militiamen slowly stood, shifting from braced defense to cautious vigilance.

He tilted his head upward, peering through the smoke-tinted sky. There it was. Delumina Station, bright and constant, a cold sentinel hung above the world. Something else caught his eye. Just to the left of the station, relative to his position, two small dark shapes floated against the backdrop of the stars. Not stars or debris, Vessels. He blinked, unsure at first if the fatigue was playing tricks on his eyes. They weren't blinking or drifting. They were too symmetrical, intentional. He narrowed his gaze, trying to discern any detail, but the altitude and distance gave him no clues.

He lowered his head slowly, a creeping uncertainty settling into his gut. Something was wrong up there. He turned back to the radio beside him, adjusting the dial, twisting the gain knob, hoping to catch a fragment of comms. The static hissed and popped, a garbled fragment coming through, indistinct. He leaned in closer, hunched low beside the MG. Behind him, the lines were holding. Men spoke softly, moved supplies, and checked wounded. The tension had eased. Reinhardt knew better than to take that as comfort. He listened and watched the sky.

Reinhardt squinted through the haze above the tarmac, his eyes fixed not on the smoke or the fading sun but on the orbit above. There hung Delumina Station, a silent crown in the sky, still flanked by the two foreign silhouettes. He couldn't tell what class or configuration, but the glint of engine flares and hull markings betrayed their nature, warships. He reached instinctively for the radio, but before he could even key the mic, the air cracked.

The unmistakable rhythm of naval autocannons lit up the night. Streaks of fire raked across the northern sector of the airport, followed by the long, low whine and roar of guided rockets descending in tight succession. Explosions erupted across the perimeter. The earth trembled under him. He ducked slightly, instinctively lowering his profile on the roof as comms came alive.

“All elements, be advised, Delumina Station has been retaken by Naval and ESS forces. I repeat, Delumina Station is secure! Friendly forces are now engaging the enemy strongpoints at the airport. Hold fire unless coordinated!”

There was a beat of silence, then cheers erupted down the line. Reinhardt didn’t cheer. He just exhaled. He stayed prone, face close to the warm metal of the MG-82, eyes scanning the chaos. The air above the airport trembled with the approach of Valkyra gunships, sleek, twin-rotored silhouettes slicing through the overcast sky, painted a grim black with twin Sieg runes etched on their side panels. The Valkyra moved with brutal grace. Reinhardt caught the glint of their underbelly autocannons, scanning and locking onto targets even before the hatch opened. Then came the descent. With a heavy thunk and a hiss of pressure release, the bay door yawned open mid-hover. Inside, black-armored ESS shock troops stood rowed like statues of war. Each one was clad in matte black ceramic power armor, their helmets expressionless, and eyes glowing a dull red. From the base of their spines, thick grav-cables snapped to life, tethered into reinforced armor mounts along the backplate.

One by one, they stepped from the bay and dropped. The grav-cables whined with power, arresting their fall just enough to keep them from slamming into the concrete below. It was not a rappel. It was a controlled plunge. The cables guided each descent with terrifying speed, then disengaged in a blur of motion the moment boots met earth. Each landing was heavy, deliberate, and final. 50 meters. Five seconds. No margin for error. The ESS troopers immediately fanned out, weapons at the ready. Knee braces hissed as they dropped into low positions, sweeping the terminal edge. Shoulder-mounted sensors rotated on micro-motors, painting the wreckage with infrared and motion signatures. The air shimmered around them as their suits’ cooling systems hissed against the heat of descent.

Reinhardt, still prone behind his MG, couldn’t help but stare. He had seen action. He had held the line, but this was different. This was the storm made flesh. More Valkyra gunships swept in with more shock troops. Each one descended like a hammer from the heavens, guided by tech older than the Delumina colony and trained in nothing but rapid, lethal execution. The black-armored ESS men didn’t shout. They didn’t chant. They moved and that was enough. The insurgents had taken the airport and now Europe had come to take it back.

"Delta-88. Enemy positions along the northeastern apron are under precision strike. Multiple secondary detonations. ESS elements confirmed on the ground."

No reply came, none was needed. He kept watching. The station above remained visible, an eerie reminder of just how quickly the world had changed. Delumina Station, a jewel of civilian commerce and orbital supply, had become a battlefield and was now under Confederation control again. But the fact it had been taken at all... that haunted him. He could still hear the emergency broadcast's timestamp echo in his mind, six hours ago. Whatever this insurgency was, it wasn't just bandits or rioters. This was war and it was just beginning.

Seconds later, the second wave arrived with the Naval Infantry. Lighter armed, lighter armored, and without the same air of divine terror the ESS inspired but elite nonetheless. They fast-roped from drop-rigged tilt-rotors, some descending on grav-assisted tethers of their own, others using reinforced rope systems that bit deep into gloves and gauntlets. They moved with the confidence of men who had stormed ports, dockyards, and refinery outposts across the Confederation's worlds.

Where the ESS cleared the first bastions and ruptured enemy strongpoints in a flash of violence, the Naval Infantry swept in behind them by taking cover, setting up temporary fire bases, and binding the chaos into a coherent front. The contrast was striking, one force moved like living thunder and the other like a disciplined tide, but both bore the black sun of the Confederation. Reinhardt watched from the rooftop, MG-82 beside him, awe rising in his throat like a suppressed war cry. For the first time since the Wessel raid, the tide of war no longer felt like a desperate holding action. This was vengeance, precision, and sovereignty made manifest.

Chapter 9

The last of the shots echoed off into stillness. The crack of rifles and stomp of boots gave way to quiet murmurs and the scrape of gear. Bravo Company, what remained of it, filtered down from their scattered positions along the rooftops and rubble-strewn avenues. Reinhardt and Kasper dismounted from their perch, boots crunching glass as they made their way back to the company. In the streets adjacent to the smoldering airport, the scene was surreal, war-worn men catching their breath beside burning machines and spent brass. Some lit cigarettes with shaking fingers. Others popped open warm beer bottles scavenged from the rearward supply trucks, not out of celebration, but as tribute to the living and the dead. It was not joy, only survival. Reinhardt and Kasper accepted both offerings with a quiet "danke." The cigarette steadied his hand more than the beer did. He took a long pull, then exhaled slowly into the post-battle haze as his MG rested beside him like a trusted hound.

A few men still watched the skyline, rifles slung but ready. Most sat in loose clusters, backs against walls, helmets off, steam rising from sweat-drenched heads. It was the first real moment of calm since the sun had risen or perhaps since the state of emergency had been declared. Time had lost meaning in the violence. Colonel Brandt was already in motion, linking up with the battalion commander from 1st Battalion, an older man with a clean-shaven jaw and the weary stiffness of someone who had seen one too many battles. Their conversation was hushed but firm, words too far off to hear. Orders would come soon. Reinhardt didn't care for now.

Then the sky stirred again. A Valkyra swept down, engines howling as it descended in controlled fashion just outside the perimeter. Two other vessels followed, one marked by naval insignia, the other dull and less ornate, bearing symbols Reinhardt didn't immediately recognize. Army maybe, a liaison force perhaps, hard to say. The three ships set down with practiced precision. Hatches hissed and opened.

Out they came, officers in dark uniforms, grey coats and visor caps. Some bore the lean look of ESS, others had the squared posture of naval command, and the last group was something different altogether, subtler, less adorned, but alert. Reinhardt didn't move. He stood quietly, cigarette between two fingers, beer in his other hand. His MG-82 leaned against his leg. Kasper was beside him. They didn't speak. They didn't need to.

The Valkyra's engines were still ticking with heat when the grey-uniformed ESS commander approached the two senior militia officers near the edge of the defensive perimeter. Even in the darkness Reinhardt could see the twin thunderbolts on the officer's right collar. Colonel Brandt stood tall despite his exhaustion, and the way he greeted the newcomer with a firm handshake and a shared look of old comradeship made it clear they had fought together before, likely long ago. Brandt was no stranger to the grey uniform himself.

From where he stood near the curb, Reinhardt watched silently, flicking the ash off his cigarette. The last of the sun dipped behind the smoking airport as boots crunched gravel behind him. He turned just enough to see a man in a pressed uniform approach. He was older, stocky, and clean cut.

The man came to a stop, hands on his belt. "You Jäger?"

Reinhardt stood up straighter, coming to a tired but disciplined parade rest. "Yes, Sergeant."

The man gave a single nod. "Schaffer. Retention NCO for 1st Battalion." He hesitated just long enough to glance at the MG at Reinhardt's feet. "I heard about what you did. Hell of a thing. What happened to your uncle, I'm sorry."

Reinhardt's jaw tightened slightly, but he gave a respectful nod. "Danke."

Schaffer shifted his weight. "Look, I won't dance around it. You've got what it takes. Your officers saw it, our officers saw it. You held that flank alone for a stretch, and that's no small feat, especially for a young man fresh off the homestead."

Reinhardt didn't speak. He didn't need to. His silence wasn't pride, it was perspective. He remembered the flinch of rounds past his ears, the stink of blood, and the heat of the barrel he'd tossed aside like a spent matchstick. He thought of how close they'd been to breaking before 1st Battalion's mortars started falling and how only the ESS and Navy made survival possible. It wasn't glory he felt, it was reality.

Schaffer noticed the distant look in his eyes. "Not trying to butter you up, Jäger. Just saying what's true. You've got potential. We need men like you on

Delumina, full-time. Not just weekend drills and muster calls."

Reinhardt took a long drag from his cigarette. "I'll consider it."

"That's all I ask," the sergeant replied, pulling a folded paper from his field pocket. "Perks are real. Full pay, Delumina station posting if you qualify, options for advanced training. Housing assistance, even marriage priority if you stick with it long enough. Could do a lot worse."

He handed Reinhardt the paper. Reinhardt took it, nodded again, and tucked it into his chest pocket without unfolding it.

"I'll check back later," Schaffer said, starting to walk off. "You've earned your beer. Hell, maybe a whole crate."

Reinhardt allowed himself a dry smile as the sergeant faded into the bustle of uniforms and shadows. He looked again to where the ESS commander and Colonel Brandt spoke, then up toward Delumina station, where two ships still lingered, silent in orbit like watchful eyes.

As soon as Reinhardt lowered his eyes from the faint glow of Delumina Station, he caught sight of something unexpected, both Colonel Brandt and the ESS officer were staring directly at him. There was no gesture, no salute, not even a nod. Just a single shared look, a momentary mark of recognition. They turned away just as quickly, returning to their conversation. Reinhardt wasn't sure what it meant, but the feeling stuck.

He took a long sip from his beer, the bitter taste warming his gut more than his soul. The smoke from his cigarette curled lazily toward the cooling sky. Then came another figure. Unlike the others, this one wasn't a militiaman. The uniform was a different cut entirely made of cleaner, grayer, and heavier fabric. A small eagle over the breast, and a black stripe down the trousers. He carried himself like a man used to giving orders and rarely repeating them, an officer.

"Reinhardt Jäger?" the man asked, his voice formal but not cold.

Reinhardt stood again, slower this time, more out of reflex than discipline. "Yes, sir."

The officer extended a hand. "Hauptmann Wilhelm Kraus. Liaison for Heerkommando Süd, attached to the Delumina sector. I've heard your name already, several times tonight."

Reinhardt hesitated, then shook his hand. "I didn't do anything special."

"On the contrary," Kraus said, glancing over Reinhardt's MG and then the street where Bravo Company lounged in smoky clusters, "you recognized the orbital situation before anyone else did. You stayed on the gun and kept your head. That alone sets you apart."

Reinhardt said nothing.

Kraus raised an eyebrow. "You're German, aren't you?"

"Yes," Reinhardt replied. "Born in Lower Saxony, on the outskirts of Hanover. My father emigrated when I was still young."

Kraus nodded, visibly pleased. "Good. Then you'll understand what I'm about to say. Germany still breeds men of grit, of instinct. There are those of us who still see that as the most sacred inheritance we have."

He let that linger, watching Reinhardt's expression.

"Have you ever considered joining the Army?" Kraus continued. "Proper Army, not militia."

"I've considered it," Reinhardt admitted. "My uncle was in the German army before we settled here on Delumina. He really wanted me to."

He paused, then stepped slightly closer.

"I'm not offering you a post, not yet. If the time comes and if you want training, real field command preparation, not just holding the line with rusted gear and hand-me-down doctrine. You come find me. The Deutsches Heer could use you. We'll need your kind more than ever before this is over."

He handed Reinhardt a slip of paper, much like the one Sergeant Schaffer had. This one was more formal, black ink on high-quality parchment with a wax-sealed crest of the German Army. Kraus gave a respectful incline of the head, then turned and left as silently as he had come. Reinhardt looked down at the paper for a long moment. He didn't open it. Reinhardt had barely settled back onto the curb when Kasper walked over, still holding his half-drunk beer. He smirked and kicked a pebble near Reinhardt's boot.

"Well, well, look at you. First the sergeant, then some greycoat from the Army... What's next, the High Priest of Sol himself?"

Reinhardt gave him a look.

Kasper took a swig and chuckled. "Come on, hero. Don't tell me you're not loving the attention."

Reinhardt snorted and muttered, "I'd rather be back on the gun."

"Yeah, yeah," Kasper said, "I'll be sure to tell the history books you were humble about it."

Before Reinhardt could respond, another figure emerged from the direction of the Valkyra. This one with a naval cut uniform, dark blue with silver trim, not too formal, but crisp. A petty officer, judging by the tabs. Broad-shouldered, clean-shaven, and moving with the confidence of someone used to steel decks and tight bulkheads.

"Reinhardt Jäger?" the petty officer asked.

Reinhardt stood, stifling a sigh. "Yes, sir."

The sailor gave a respectful nod, but no hand extended. "Petty Officer August Vella, Recruitment Liaison, Neue Frankfurt Naval Command. I'm not going to waste your time."

Reinhardt kept his face still.

Vella continued. "You've got options including scouts, Taurosplasmy crews, Naval Infantry, or flight track, if you pass screening. Even suborbital pilot training if you show the aptitude."

"I haven't decided anything," Reinhardt said flatly.

"Didn't ask you to," Vella replied. "I'm just telling you the door's open. You've proven yourself. That's all it takes sometimes."

He reached into a side pouch and produced a simple metal chit, brushed steel with a serial code etched into it.

"This has my signature. Bring it to the southern docks when you're ready. Doesn't expire."

He handed it over, then gave a curt nod and walked off. Reinhardt turned the chit over in his fingers.

Kasper leaned in. "That one didn't even try to butter you up, navy types never do. They just assume you want to live in a tin can."

Reinhardt cracked a faint smile but said nothing. The beer was warm now. The cigarette half-smoked. The MG-82 rested beside him like a sleeping dog, barrel cool again.

Chapter

10

The morning bell rang with sharp clarity, echoing down the polished stone halls of Neue Frankfurt Secondary Academy. Sunlight streamed through the high windows, clean and golden. The fighting was over, at least for now, but the aftershocks lingered in every step, in every face. Reinhardt Jäger walked alone, boots thudding softly, the school uniform pressed but worn at the seams. He had just turned seventeen. Old enough to enlist, and everyone knew it. Some already had.

There were fewer boys in his class now. Some had joined the regular militia and been posted elsewhere. Others lay buried in soil still dark from the shelling. A couple, he'd heard, were in hospital wards missing pieces of themselves.

He reached Room 104 and paused at the threshold. The door was open. Inside, desks were spaced as before, precise rows like soldiers in parade formation, but the atmosphere had shifted. Herr Brandt stood at the front, arms behind his back. No longer in the field grey of command, but in the dark brown instructor's coat again. The black-and-white insignia of the ESS still gleamed at his collar, but his eyes were more tired than before. Their eyes met briefly. Brandt gave the smallest of nods. Reinhardt returned it.

He stepped into the classroom, his satchel slung tight. A few heads turned to greet him, others didn't. The silence was heavy. He took his seat.

One of the boys beside him leaned over. "Heard about the MG. Heard you saved the flank."

Reinhardt didn't answer. He pulled out his pen and notebook and looked straight ahead. Brandt cleared his throat and the class settled.

"Boys," he began, "this semester, we will continue where we left off: Federal History, Volume II: the Age of Unification. I suspect many of you now understand history a little more than before. Not just as words on a page, but as something lived."

His eyes flicked toward Reinhardt, then away. Outside the window, the sky was clear. Delumina station was no longer visible by day, but everyone knew it was up there still, scarred but sovereign again. The lesson began. Reinhardt cared about the lesson, but found comfort in looking at the trees bending in the wind and the occasional song bird. The lesson ended and the boys began to file out. Reinhardt stood, gathered his items, and decided to approach the front desk.

Herr Brandt glanced up from the stack of lesson materials he was gathering, his expression unreadable for a moment. He studied Reinhardt, not as a student, but as a comrade, one of the few in that room who had seen the line hold, and nearly break. Reinhardt asked, "who was the ESS officer you spoke to after the battle?"

He gave a slight nod, then turned and reached into the drawer of his desk. He pulled out a thin folder, mostly blank, save for the emblem of the ESS in the top corner. Sliding it toward Reinhardt, he spoke in a low tone, meant only for the two of them.

"Major Albrecht Weiss," he said. "3rd Assault Brigade of the Wiking Division, one of the original divisions from before the expansion. He fought in the Sirius Insurrection and the Arcadia Reclamation. Decorated. Efficient."

Brandt met Reinhardt's eyes. "And a man I trust."

Reinhardt nodded slowly, his fingers tightening slightly on the strap of his satchel. "He looked at me."

"He did more than that," Brandt replied. "He marked you."

Reinhardt shifted uncomfortably, unsure what to say.

Brandt's tone softened slightly. "You held the line when it would've broken. That's not nothing. The ESS notices things like that."

Reinhardt looked down at the folder. "Is this for me?"

"No," Brandt said. "Not officially. But if you're serious, I'll vouch for you. ESS doesn't take just anyone, you know that. You're not just anyone anymore."

Reinhardt took a breath. "I'm thinking about it."

Brandt gave the faintest smile. "Then keep thinking. Just don't take too long."

He closed the drawer. The room was nearly empty now. Only the hum of overhead lights and the distant murmur of younger students in nearby corridors remained. Reinhardt looked out the window again, at the swaying trees, the open sky, and the hidden orbit of Delumina.

"Thank you, sir," he said finally.

Brandt simply nodded. As Reinhardt turned to leave he paused, reaching into his satchel. Wordlessly, he laid two folded slips of paper and the chip from the Navy on Herr Brandt's desk, one marked with the crest of the Army, another bearing the anchor-and-star of the Navy, and the third sealed with the militia's triskelion.

Brandt raised an eyebrow and gave a short exhale through his nose, half chuckle, half sigh.

"So they've all come calling," he said quietly, tapping a finger on the ESS folder. "Makes sense, they see what I see."

Reinhardt gave a small shrug, but said nothing. Brandt didn't need him to. "Just remember," he added, looking up at the boy who was now a man, "the branch you choose won't change who you are, it will determine the kind of man you become."

Reinhardt met his gaze with a steady nod. Then, without another word, he turned and left the classroom with the papers folded neatly under his arm, the weight of choice resting across his shoulders. The sunlight was soft that morning, filtered through the high columns of the school forum as Reinhardt sat alone at a stone table near the edge. The long shadow of the flagpole cut across the square tiles like a spear. He poured himself a small cup of coffee from a battered thermos and slowly buttered a slice of crusty black bread absently, with one hand, while the other rested atop the folded papers.

Three folders and a metal chit, each bearing the seal of a service branch. The stark thunderbolts of the ESS, the triskelion of the militia, the grey-green oak leaves of the Heer and finally, a navy-blue chit, creased from being in his coat pocket too long, stamped with the crescent-and-anchor of the Confederation's fleet. He took a sip of the coffee, bitter but warm, and tried to weigh the future. Then came the sound of very familiar, friendly voices.

"Would you look at him," said Kasper with a grin. "Breakfast like a Kaiser."

"More like a condemned man's last meal," Tomas added, half-joking as they approached.

"Cut the man some slack," said Jules, shouldering his satchel as he sat down across from Reinhardt. "He's got half the Confederation trying to sign him."

Elias arrived last, slower, his left arm in a rigid white cast slung at his chest. He nodded once and took a seat, setting down his own satchel with a gentle thump.

Reinhardt looked up at them all and gestured to the thermos. "Coffee?"

They nodded, and he passed around the tin mugs. Kasper took his and leaned in, peering at the documents laid out before Reinhardt like sacred relics. "So, any idea which banner you're going to bleed under yet?"

Reinhardt didn't answer immediately. He tore off another bite of bread, chewing slowly. Then he looked down at the folders again.

"Not yet," he said. "But whichever one it is... it won't be the easy path."

Jules sipped his coffee, thoughtful. "None of them are."

Elias spoke next, voice a little hoarse. "What matters is who you fight beside, not just what colors are on your uniform."

Reinhardt gave a slow nod. The papers would wait. For now, the sky was clear, the coffee warm, and his brothers were here. That was enough. Tomas leaned back on the bench, one leg crossed over the other as he held his coffee. "I think I'll stay," he said, glancing up at the sunlit buildings beyond the forum. "Delumina's still raw, still growing. There's good work for a stonemason, maybe even a builder. It's honest work and clean."

Jules nodded beside him. "I've thought the same. My father's been offered a plot outside the southern ring, cropland. He asked me to help him run it. Feels right, staying where the land still needs shaping."

Reinhardt gave a faint smile at that, both of them had always leaned toward earth and stone more than fire and steel.

Elias flexed the fingers of his good hand, his other still bound in a cast. "I don't know," he said. "I don't have the patience for farming. I've thought about joining the active militia. Not the best pay, but... it feels right. After what happened at the airport, I can't just pretend none of it matters."

Reinhardt looked to his side. Kasper was silent, stirring his coffee absently with his finger. He hadn't touched the folders. His eyes wandered now and then, settling on the ESS crest before flicking away again.

"What about you, Kasper?" Reinhardt finally asked.

Kasper paused. His eyes met Reinhardt's for a moment longer than usual, then dropped to the table.

"I'm not sure," he said quietly. "The city feels smaller now, after what we've seen. I don't know what I'm built for. I keep thinking... maybe I'll just follow your lead."

Reinhardt arched his brow. "You'd really let me decide that for you?"

Kasper shrugged. "You found the signal. You held the line. They all came to you. Whatever you choose, it'll mean something. That's more than most get."

There was a stillness for a moment, the hum of wind through the forum arches, the echo of birds in the distance. Then Reinhardt nodded slowly, accepting the weight that was quietly settling over his shoulders. Reinhardt leaned forward, elbows resting on the table as he looked at Kasper. The folders sat between them like heavy stones, each one marked with the seal of a different fate.

"If you were in my place," he asked, voice quiet but firm, "what would you choose?"

Kasper blinked, clearly caught off guard. He straightened in his seat, eyes searching Reinhardt's face for sincerity, then he nodded, lips parting slightly in a moment of stunned warmth. It meant something, being asked, being trusted. His gaze fell to the folders, fingers brushing across them until they landed on the black one marked with the twin Sieg runes of the ESS. He tapped it once, deliberate.

"I still remember the sound," Kasper said, voice low. "The way those Valkyra gunships dropped in, and the grav cables slicing through the smoke. It was like the gods had descended. Everyone else fought hard, sure, but they were different, focused and unshakable. When they hit the ground, I knew the fight was over."

He looked back up at Reinhardt, eyes steady now. "If it were me... I'd want to be one of them. Not just because they won, but because they didn't hesitate. They knew who they were. That's the kind of man I want to be."

Reinhardt didn't respond immediately. He just looked at the folder, at the white sigils and path it promised. Then he met Kasper's eyes again, and there was a subtle nod between them, not of agreement or decision, but of mutual respect.

Reinhardt stood, slow and deliberate. The others went quiet, watching him. He gathered the folders from the militia, the army, and the chit from the navy, tucking them neatly under his arm. There was no speech, no explanation. He walked a short distance to a nearby trash bin tucked beneath a concrete column. One by one he dropped the items in, each landing with a soft, final thud. There was no anger in his movements, no disdain. Just a calm, reverent certainty, like a man placing stones on a grave. A quiet farewell to lives he would not live. He turned back toward the table, meeting Kasper's eyes.

"Are you seventeen?" he asked plainly.

Kasper blinked, then nodded. "Yeah, just turned."

Reinhardt gave a quiet grunt of acknowledgement, stepping back toward the table. Reinhardt took a sip from his cooling coffee, eyes steady on Kasper.

He said, voice low but firm, "we'll head to the ESS liaison office in Neue Frankfurt."

Kasper's brows lifted, a spark lighting behind his tired eyes. "You mean it?"

Reinhardt gave a single nod. "If you're up for it."

Kasper didn't smile, not quite, but the grin was in his voice. "I've been ready since the Valkyras came down."

Reinhardt looked out toward the city in the distance. The day was already moving, the sun catching on the rooftops and glinting off the windows of a world that was changing beneath their feet.

"Then let's go."

The bell for midday classes hadn't rung yet. Reinhardt stood from the stone bench beneath the trees in the school forum, leaving behind the half-empty coffee cup and the crumb-dusted napkin from his buttered bread. Without a word, Kasper stood with him. They walked in step toward the tram station at the edge of the school grounds, past students still finishing their lunch, a few of whom glanced their way with curiosity. Tomas and Matthias called something after them, but Reinhardt didn't respond. Elias simply gave a knowing nod.

The tram arrived within minutes. It was clean, white, and marked with the crest of the Confederation. As it glided to a stop, Reinhardt and Kasper stepped aboard in silence. The doors hissed closed behind them, and the tram pulled away from the Academy grounds, beginning the quiet descent toward the city below. Neue Frankfurt lay spread out beneath a pale afternoon sky. The scars of battle were still present, shattered windows patched with plasteel, scorch marks along the edges of buildings, and craters in old intersections. Cleanup crews were working in every district, and the air smelled of dust and concrete, not smoke and burning fuel. The airport in the distance was no longer burning. Aircraft wreckage had been pushed aside. And the skies were calm. The tram hissed again as it came to a stop near the civic plaza. Reinhardt and Kasper dismounted, walking with quiet purpose down a narrow side street. They passed a bakery with fresh bread in the window, a tailor's shop with blue and khaki uniforms on display, and a statue of Europa embracing the eagle, her foot upon the serpent. Finally, they turned the last corner.

There it was, small, nondescript, but unmistakable. A rectangular two-story building faced the street standing white stone walls, reinforced windows and a single banner flying high above it, catching the wind. Black field. Twin white Sieg runes gleaming in the midday light, the banner of the ESS. Reinhardt and Kasper stopped several paces from the door. For a moment, they simply looked up. No music, crowds or fanfare as the two young men staring at the symbol of the force that had descended from the heavens and turned the tide.

Kasper's voice was quiet. "Still want to do this?"

Reinhardt didn't speak. He just stepped forward and opened the door. The air inside was cooler, cleaner. White tile floors, gunmetal gray desks. A waiting area with stiff chairs and a water dispenser. Behind the desk sat a man in field-grey, his uniform crisp, clean, and his hair close-cropped. The Sieg runes were stitched onto his collar, and the eagle of the Confederation was pinned above his heart.

The man looked up. He wasn't smiling, but neither was he scowling. His face was calm, almost serene. Older than them, but not by much, perhaps mid-twenties, a soldier's build, cold eyes that had seen fire, but steady hands that did not tremble.

"What are you two doing out of school?" he asked, not unkindly, but with clear expectation.

Reinhardt stepped forward and placed the folder from Herr Brandt on the desk.

"We've come to enlist."

The ESS man looked down at the folder. Then up at the banner outside, still visible through the window behind them. Then back to the boys.

"You're in the right place."

The Scharführer behind the desk reached beneath the counter and retrieved two clipboards, each stacked with several crisp folders bound in black. With practiced hands, he split the stack in two and slid one set toward Reinhardt, the other to Kasper.

"These three folders are your enlistment intake," he said evenly, tapping the top sheet with a gloved finger. "The first is a basic mental aptitude test. Second is your criminal, educational, and family history. The third is your medical and physical readiness form."

He tapped the third form again. "We don't have an examining physician on-site, so for this one, you'll take it to the civic clinic two blocks south. Military forms get triaged faster, as long as they're not swamped, you should receive priority service. Understood?"

Both young men nodded. Reinhardt took the packet with both hands, standing tall. Kasper followed suit. There was a quiet reverence in the way they handled the documents like soldiers lifting swords for the first time.

The Scharführer gave a single nod and motioned toward the waiting area. "Chairs are there. Pens on the table. Don't rush. Print legibly."

They stepped away from the desk and lowered themselves into the black synthetic chairs beside the reinforced window. A gentle breeze stirred the ESS banner outside. Neither boy spoke as they opened the first folder. The aptitude test was simple enough. It contained portions testing pattern recognition, historical logic, spatial awareness, and a few riddles designed to assess reasoning under pressure. It wasn't difficult for Reinhardt. He finished each page slowly but with purpose, recalling how similar drills had once been part of Herr Brandt's teaching. Beside him, Kasper seemed to fumble at first, scratching behind his ear or staring too long at a particular question, but eventually he found his rhythm. They worked in companionable silence.

The second folder was more intimate. Name, birthdate, colony of residence. Parents. Siblings. Any criminal history. Known vices. Confessions of ideological subversion, voluntary or witnessed. Reinhardt filled it out steadily, feeling a strange weight as he did so. This wasn't a school form. It was a full accounting of who he was.

When they were done, they both reviewed their packets. Neither spoke, but both looked slightly more serious now, perhaps from the personal nature of the forms. They stood together and walked to the desk.

The Scharführer looked up from a terminal where he had been reviewing deployment rosters.

"We're finished," Reinhardt said simply.

The NCO accepted the completed forms and leafed through the pages briefly, scanning for errors or omissions. Apparently satisfied, he nodded and handed back the third folder, the medical and physical form.

"The clinic is southbound. It's a white building, Confederation seal over the entrance. Let them know you're ESS candidates. They'll flag it. Bring back your signed fitness reports when you're done. If all's in order, we'll start processing by tomorrow. As a reminder, if you didn't know, which some aren't aware, ESS enlistment is a twenty year oath. You are free to back out anytime before your official enlistment upon completion of your basic training. Keep that in mind."

Kasper tucked his clipboard under his arm. Reinhardt held the folder flat in his hand. They both understood the seriousness of this. As they exited into the sunlight once more, the ESS banner above the office door snapped sharply in the wind.

The short walk to the clinic was quiet. A few mag-trams whined gently down the boulevard, and a reconstruction crew across the street worked in silence save for the occasional clang of rebar or hiss of welders. The worst of the post-battle chaos had passed, and now the city felt like a place cautiously exhaling. The clinic was, as the Scharführer said, two blocks south, a tall white building with polished siding and the black sunwheel of the Confederation stamped above the reinforced glass doors. Reinhardt pushed the door open, holding it for Kasper. Inside, the air was cool and clean, with the faint smell of antiseptic and flowers.

The two walked toward the reception desk and stopped short.

Behind the counter sat a nurse unlike any they had expected. She was striking, pale as winter milk, with jet black hair in a tight bun and piercing, almost surreal blue eyes that locked onto them as they approached. Her uniform was neat and professional, a soft navy color with a gold-trimmed caduceus pin at her collar. Her smile was warm, too warm for the sterile surroundings.

"Well now," she said in a lilting, unmistakably Irish accent, her voice somewhere between silk and song, "you two look a bit lost. Or are you just shy?"

Reinhardt blinked. Kasper stood motionless, mouth slightly parted, before clearing his throat.

"Uh... ma'am... We're... We're ESS candidates," he managed, adjusting the folder under his arm. "We're here for our medical screening."

"Ah, that explains the nervous energy," she replied, amused. "First timers, are ye?"

She extended her hand across the desk. Reinhardt, almost too slow to react, passed over his clipboard. Kasper followed, still visibly stunned. She scanned the forms briefly, then tapped on her console with brisk efficiency.

"Right, both of you are already flagged in the ESS system," she said, nodding to herself. "No wait today. You're lucky, it's usually packed this time of day."

She glanced up again and caught both their eyes at once. "Don't worry, we'll take good care of you."

Reinhardt felt a flush creeping into his ears. Kasper nodded stiffly.

"Names?"

"Reinhardt Jäger," he replied, still trying not to stare.

"Kasper Engel," the other added.

"Well then, Reinhardt and Kasper," she said with a mischievous little smile, "you can take a seat right over there. Doctor Malinowski will call you shortly. Don't worry, it's not the army. We don't use blunt instruments."

That earned the faintest smile from Reinhardt. As they turned to sit in the waiting area, Kasper leaned over and whispered, "She's not real. There's no way she's real."

Reinhardt grunted, still red around the ears. "If I fail this medical test it'll be from high blood pressure."

They sat in silence for a moment, the low murmur of clinic machines surrounding them, until the nurse called out cheerily, "Next!"

Both boys stood up sharply at the nurse's call, suddenly all nerves and forward momentum. Their boots thudded against the polished floor as they followed the assistant deeper into the clinic. At the branching hallway, the nurse pointed to two separate exam rooms.

"You in there," she said, gesturing to Reinhardt. "And you, love, right next door."

Reinhardt gave Kasper a small nod before stepping inside. The room was sterile and brightly lit, with a paper-covered medical bed, a sink, a tall scale, and a couple of clinical posters about muscle groups and common injuries. The nurse handed him a folded paper gown.

"Down to your underwear," she said with practiced ease. "Doctor will be in shortly."

She drew the curtain and closed the door behind her. Reinhardt hesitated for a moment, glanced around, and began to undress. He folded his shirt, boots, and trousers into a neat pile on the chair and then sat on the edge of the bed, bare-legged, feeling the crinkle of paper beneath him. He waited. Maybe they took Kasper first, he figured. That'd explain the delay.

Then the door opened. A tall, gaunt man in his late sixties stepped in wearing a long white coat, circular glasses, and a stone-flat expression. His face was lined, his hair silver, and his accent, when he spoke, marked him clearly as Slavic. Polish or Belarusian, maybe.

He didn't greet Reinhardt right away. He simply closed the door, stepped forward, and pulled the curtain aside in one motion. His eyes swept Reinhardt once, clinically, before he sat in the rolling chair and began thumbing through the forms.

"Name. Reinhardt Jäger, yes?" the doctor said without looking up.

"Yes, sir."

"Do you have medical history?"

"No, nothing serious."

"Any operations?"

"No, sir."

"Blood type?"

"O positive," Reinhardt said, hoping he remembered correctly.

The doctor grunted and made a note with a thin stylus. "Good. Up. Scale."

Reinhardt stood and stepped onto the medical scale, the floor cool beneath his socks. The doctor adjusted the counterweights with precise movements, his lips pressed together.

"Seventy-eight kilos. One-eighty-four centimeters. Sit," he ordered.

Reinhardt returned to the bed. The doctor glanced at him, then began the inspection checking limbs, posture, and visible musculature.

"You are not obese. Strong build. Body fat within threshold," the doctor noted. "Now movement. Stand. Squat."

Reinhardt squatted.

"Again. Deeper."

He obeyed.

"Touch your toes."

He bent forward until his fingers brushed the tile.

"Duck walk."

Reinhardt suppressed a sigh and did the awkward squat-walk across the room. The doctor watched him with unreadable eyes.

"Pushups. Ten. Good form."

Reinhardt dropped and pumped out ten without pausing. His body moved with practiced ease, the kind you get from work and a soldier's upbringing, not vanity. The doctor nodded faintly and jotted a few more notes.

"You will pass fitness. I still need a heart rate, eyes, ears, reflexes, then blood samples. No complaints?"

"No, sir."

"Good. Sit. We finish quickly."

The doctor stood and retrieved a small cart of equipment, beginning the second half of the exam. Reinhardt, for all his nerves walking in, now just wanted it done. Not out of embarrassment. He just hated waiting. The doctor moved with quiet efficiency. He wrapped the blood pressure cuff around Reinhardt's arm and inflated it with steady squeezes of the bulb. "Breathe normally," he muttered, listening with his stethoscope. After a moment, he released the pressure with a soft hiss and made a note.

"Resting heart rate... satisfactory."

He checked Reinhardt's ears with a penlight, tapped his knees with the rubber reflex hammer, shone the light into each eye, and watched how his pupils reacted.

"All standard. Now the blood."

From the tray, he produced a slim, sealed kit and drew a small vial of Reinhardt's blood with practiced ease. The vial clicked into a labeled rack. Then the doctor sat back and glanced at the file again. Instead of putting it away, however, he folded his hands and looked at Reinhardt over the rims of his glasses.

"Tell me," he said in a quieter tone, "do you sleep well after combat?"

Reinhardt blinked. The question came like a jab to the ribs.

"I... don't know yet. I think so."

"No dreams? Or any worth remembering?"

"There are dreams," Reinhardt admitted, voice steady. "Nothing that wakes me up."

The doctor gave a slow nod, then tilted his head.

"What do you think of birds?"

"...Birds?"

"Yes. Birds."

Reinhardt narrowed his eyes slightly, uncertain. "They make the world feel alive again."

"Good. And trees?"

"...They calm me down."

"Would you consider yourself more quick to anger, or slow to act?"

"Depends," Reinhardt said after a breath. "If I need to move, I move. If not, I think."

"Hm."

The doctor scratched a few words into the margin. His face betrayed nothing.

"Have you ever heard voices that weren't there?"

"No."

"Ever believed someone was watching you, even if you were alone?"

"Not outside of a warzone."

A faint crack of a smile touched the old man's lips, just briefly.

"Very well. Final question. Why are you here?"

Reinhardt thought of that. The real answer wasn't a slogan. It wasn't something printed on a brochure.

"...Because I saw what happens when you don't act fast enough, because the ESS acted. I won't forget that."

The doctor nodded once. He stood, collected the chart, and placed it into a plastic slot by the door.

"You pass. A nurse will come to finish paperwork. You may dress."

Without another word, he stepped out, the door closing softly behind him. Reinhardt sat still for a moment longer, staring at the spot the doctor had stood. That hadn't just been a physical. It had been an unspoken trial of character. Reinhardt had just pulled his boots on when the door opened again. It wasn't the old doctor, it was her. The Irish nurse from the front desk. Black hair pinned back neatly, piercing blue eyes that seemed to shine with candlelight, clipboard in hand. She shut the door behind her and offered a brief smile.

"All finished, are we?"

"I think so. The doctor said I passed."

"Did he now?" she said, stepping forward with a faint smirk as she flipped through the file. "Well, let's not get ahead of ourselves. There's a bit more to do."

Reinhardt straightened slightly, shoulders tensing out of instinct. He said nothing. She looked up from the clipboard. "This won't take long. Just a few questions. Relax."

He gave a faint nod and sat back down on the exam bed. She clicked her pen.

"Do you live with both of your parents?"

"I live with my father and mother."

"Do you have siblings?"

"No, I am an only child."

She scratched the answer down. Then, without looking up, "What would you do if you found a broken animal on the side of the road?"

"...What kind of animal?" Reinhardt asks, inquisitively,

"It doesn't matter."

Reinhardt paused, brow furrowing. "If it could be saved, I'd carry it. If not... I'd make sure it didn't suffer."

Her pen moved silently.

"What does it mean to be in love?"

That one caught him off guard. "I... think it means recognizing someone else is worth more than yourself. That you'd die before letting them suffer."

She met his eyes for a moment. No smile. Just silence.

"And if you woke up in a box? No light. No air. No door. How would you feel?"

"Alive," he said without pause. "Which means there's still a way out."

Her pen stopped. She looked at him again, this time with the faintest tilt of her head.

"...All right then."

She closed the clipboard gently and slid it under her arm. "That's everything. Get dressed. You'll both be contacted after processing."

She moved to the door, opened it halfway, then paused.

"One last thing, Reinhardt Jäger."

He looked up.

"I was told to watch for hesitation. You didn't show any. You are free to go."

And then she was gone, the door shutting behind her with the same quiet finality. Reinhardt adjusted his shirt collar as he walked down the hallway, trying not to look like he was in a rush. The door clicked shut behind him, muffling the faint echo of footsteps and hushed conversation. His boots echoed lightly against the clean tile floor until he reached the waiting room. A different nurse stood behind the reception counter now. She is older, hair in a tight braid, and a crisp uniform. Reinhardt stepped up and asked quietly, "Is there anything else you need from me?"

She glanced at the file in her hand, cross-checked something on her screen, then shook her head. "No, Mr. Jäger. You're all set. You'll be notified of the results through the ESS liaison office."

He nodded in thanks, then turned, his eyes locking with Kasper's. Kasper sat in the corner, his posture casual, legs stretched out slightly, hands folded over his stomach. He perked up as Reinhardt approached. Reinhardt lowered himself into the seat next to him, exhaling through his nose.

"Well?" he asked.

Kasper smirked. "Well, they didn't throw me out. So I'll call that a win."

"You pass?" Reinhardt asked.

"They didn't say, not directly. But I think so."

Reinhardt leaned back slightly, staring at the ceiling for a breath.

Kasper glanced over. "And you?"

"I think I did alright. Questions were... strange, not bad, just specific."

Kasper nodded. "Same."

They sat in silence for a moment, the waiting room quiet save for the low hum of fluorescent lights and the occasional rustle of paper from behind the counter. Reinhardt looked sideways. "Still up for this?"

Kasper gave a small grin. "I told you before. You lead, I follow."

.Reinhardt and Kasper stepped back inside the ESS office, the sharp sunlight casting long shadows across the tile floor. The Scharführer behind the desk looked up from a thick stack of paperwork, his expression unchanged. He remained disciplined, unreadable, but not unkind. Reinhardt approached with the folders under one arm. "We've completed our packets and had the physicals done."

Kasper chimed in, "Just wanted to ask, when should we expect to hear back?"

The Scharführer stood and accepted the paperwork. He leafed through the first few pages quickly, eyes scanning for any glaring omissions. Then he nodded.

"If all checks out, return here tomorrow. Early, if you can. Your paperwork will be submitted to headquarters by this evening. If no complications arise, your orders will be cut by morning." He looked between the two of them. "You'll be officially enlisted."

A quiet silence passed between the two boys. Reinhardt's jaw tensed slightly with anticipation, and Kasper's grin was hard to suppress.

"Understood," Reinhardt said.

"Danke, Scharführer," Kasper added.

They both gave a small nod, then turned and exited into the warm afternoon air. Outside, the wind blew steadily through the clean, recovering streets of Neue

Frankfurt. Construction scaffolding still clung to a few buildings, and every now and then a utility drone buzzed past overhead. But there were no sirens. No gunfire. No smoke. Just the slow, steady murmur of a city healing.

Reinhardt paused at the base of the office steps.

"I think we ought to eat," he said. "Something decent."

"Celebratory meal?" Kasper raised a brow. "Are you buying?"

"I might," Reinhardt said, thinking. "I know a place."

Kasper followed close behind as Reinhardt took a turn down a quieter street, more residential than commercial, the Schmidtt pub. It had come back to Reinhardt in a moment of quiet reflection. During the last militia operation at Wessel Farmstead, one of the men who had died was his business. A homey place, more for locals than soldiers. They found it still standing. Its whitewashed stone walls were intact, and the green shutters flanking the windows were freshly painted, though the flag out front hung at half-mast. The lights inside glowed soft yellow behind the glass. When they stepped through the door, a gentle hush fell over the few patrons already seated. It wasn't a tense silence, just the natural quiet that fell when newcomers entered a place where regulars kept to themselves.

Behind the counter stood a young man in his early twenties, wiping a glass with a towel. He looked up, and though his face was clean-shaven and youthful, his eyes were tired. A pale scar ran along his jaw. He didn't smile, but there was recognition behind his gaze, Franz Schmidt. He didn't need to say anything. His presence behind the bar said enough, his father was gone, and now it was his duty to hold the line.

Reinhardt stepped forward.

"Herr Schmidt?"

"Franz is fine," he said, his voice quiet but steady. "What can I get you two?"

Reinhardt took a breath. "Whatever's hot and hearty. And beer. Two."

Franz gave a simple nod. "Coming right up."

As Franz turned away, Reinhardt and Kasper took a seat at the bar. The old place still smelled of roast meat and woodsmoke. A tin radio played faint music in the background. Everything felt... real. Grounded. They didn't speak at first. And they didn't need to. Franz returned shortly, setting two heavy pint glasses on the table with a solid clink. The beer was deep amber, almost bronze, with a thick white head that slowly settled. Reinhardt stared at the pint for a moment, watching the foam swirl and fall. Then, without a word, he rose to his feet.

The pub wasn't crowded, just a few scattered workers, militia men, and locals. All eyes gradually turned toward the young man standing by the table, pint in hand, the light from the overhead lamps glinting off his glass and the faint edge of the dog tag chain around his neck. He lifted the pint high, voice clear and steady.

"To the fallen," Reinhardt began. "To Herr Schmidt. To my uncle Ludwig. To the boys of Bravo Company. And to all those who gave their lives for Delumina, for the farms, the station, and the air above us."

He looked over at Kasper, who was already raising his pint beside him.

Reinhardt's voice rang fuller now. "To those who didn't run. To those who stood their ground when the world came crashing down."

He raised the glass a little higher.

"We toast! Prost!"

A few in the bar echoed him: "Prost!" One old militiaman thumped his hand on the table. Another simply nodded, his own glass raised halfway in quiet respect. Reinhardt and Kasper drank deep, the beer cold and bold, bitter with just a hint of smoke.

Reinhardt sat back down slowly. "To the next life," he muttered softly. "Or the next fight."

Kasper clinked his glass lightly against Reinhardt's. "Hopefully both."

Reinhardt and Kasper finished the last of their meal in silence. The warmth of the beer and food had settled into them. There was no need to say much, what was left unspoken between them was understood. When they were done,

Reinhardt stood first, dropping a few folded bills beside the empty pints. "That's for Herr Schmidt," he said. "And for Franz."

Kasper nodded, and the two stepped out into the cooling air of early evening. They walked together, boots soft against the stone-paved street, toward the tram stop. The city felt quieter now. Its breath finally slowed after days of chaos. As they waited, Reinhardt watched the orange sun dip low behind the hills, casting long shadows over the shattered skyline. The tram arrived with a low hum, and they boarded wordlessly. The ride back was short and mostly quiet, save for the occasional rattle of the track and the distant cry of birds overhead. When they arrived at the stop nearest the school, the two stood.

Reinhardt turned. "Tomorrow then?"

Kasper gave a tired but genuine smile. "Tomorrow."

They clasped arms briefly, then parted with Reinhardt heading south, Kasper east, their silhouettes peeling away in different directions under the darkening sky. When Reinhardt reached home, he opened the door quietly and stepped inside. The warmth of the hearth met him, along with the smell of cooked potatoes and meat gone cold. His mother turned first, face taut with quiet disappointment. His father sat in his usual chair, arms folded across his chest.

"You missed dinner," his mother said, not raising her voice but not needing to.

"You skipped school," his father added flatly.

Reinhardt said nothing at first. He stood in the doorway, the scent of beer still faint on his breath, the weight of the day's decisions pressing on his shoulders.

"I know," he finally said. "But it was important."

His father stood up slowly from the chair, arms still crossed. The man's jaw was tight, his eyes searching. His mother hovered behind him, hands wringing the hem of her apron.

"You're seventeen," his father said. "That means you're still under this roof, under our responsibility. You skipped school, Reinhardt."

"I didn't skip," Reinhardt said, setting his pack down by the door. "I went to the ESS office."

His father raised a brow. "That's supposed to excuse it?"

Reinhardt didn't flinch. "It's not an excuse. It's a fact. I went to enlist."

Silence followed, only the quiet creak of the old house answered for a moment. His mother's face shifted from frustration to worry. "Enlist? Without even speaking to us first?"

"You want me to act like a man," Reinhardt said, voice low but steady. "But you speak to me like I'm still a boy. I fought at the airport. I held the line. I watched men die. I didn't run. I didn't hide behind school walls when our home was under siege."

His father's mouth opened, but Reinhardt pressed on.

"I didn't throw my life away. I chose what I wanted to do with it. The ESS gave me the chance to step forward. I took it."

He straightened his posture, eyes locked with his father's. "I'm not asking for permission. I'm telling you what I've done."

For a long moment, the room remained still. The hearth crackled behind them, soft and rhythmic. His mother looked down. His father looked older than he had a moment before.

"You could have told us," his father finally muttered.

Reinhardt nodded once. "Now I have."

No more was said. He picked up his pack and walked past them both, heading to his room. There would be no more debates. The boy had died at the airport; what returned was a man.

Chapter

II

Reinhardt woke before the sun. He didn't linger in bed or wait for the warmth to pull him out of sleep. He sat up with purpose, the weight of yesterday's decisions still resting on his shoulders but no longer heavy. He had already made peace with the path ahead. He washed quickly at the basin, ran wet fingers through his hair, then slid on a clean undershirt, a soft grey work jacket, and his boots. The house was silent but not asleep. Downstairs, he could hear the soft shuffle of feet and the clink of utensils, the familiar rhythm of his parents beginning their morning. He descended the wooden stairs and stepped into the kitchen, where the smell of bread and black coffee lingered. His mother was standing at the stove, stirring something gently in a pot. His father sat at the table, glancing over the small town paper, its pages half-folded and barely read. Reinhardt offered a calm, steady greeting.

"Guten Morgen."

Both parents turned to look at him. There was no tension this time, just the recognition of a rhythm changed.

His mother gave a small nod. "Coffee's fresh."

His father gave a grunt, less of annoyance more of acknowledgment. Something in his eyes had shifted. The boy who had once been scolded for tracking mud across the floor now stood upright, composed, and unreadable, a man. Reinhardt poured himself a cup and joined them, the quiet between them no longer strained, but simply quiet. He took a sip, exhaled through his nose, and looked out the window. Today, they will return to the ESS office. Today, it will be official. Reinhardt stood from the table and slung his jacket across his shoulders.

"I'll be back later," he said simply, setting down his cup. "I am not leaving yet. I need to stop by the school and run some other errands."

His parents looked up, but said nothing. They had already spoken their last protest the night before. Now came the quiet parting, the one between boyhood and the road ahead. He stepped out into the morning air. The wind was light, brushing softly through the hedges along the path. Reinhardt walked with steady purpose, taking the familiar trail past the old trees, the worn cobblestones, and toward the school that had shaped much of his young years. The distant bell had not yet rung, the first period was still ahead.

He arrived at the building and climbed the steps without hesitation. The halls were empty, quiet save for the ticking of a hallway clock and the subtle creak of floorboards beneath his boots. He found the door to Herr Brandt's office slightly ajar. He knocked twice.

"Come," the voice called, deep and certain.

Reinhardt opened the door to find Herr Brandt seated at his desk, spectacles low on his nose, a worn book resting in his calloused hands, Leon Degrelle's Eastern Front.

The teacher looked up. "Ah, Jäger."

Reinhardt stepped in and stood before the desk, not at attention but still straight-backed.

"I wanted to tell you myself," he said. "I'm enlisting with the ESS. I'll be missing class today, and depending on the paperwork... maybe all the rest. I'll bring a copy of my orders once they're issued. Then I'll be officially released."

Brandt closed the book slowly, the creased pages resting under one palm. He looked at Reinhardt for a long moment, through him almost.

Then he gave a nod. "Understood."

There was no lecture, no overdrawn speech, but Brandt added, voice low. "You know what they'll expect of you. What it means. Don't go into this thinking they want recruits. They're looking for wolves."

Reinhardt met his eyes.

"I know," he said simply.

Brandt's mouth flicked into the barest hint of a smile. "Then go, make the ancestors proud."

Reinhardt turned and left the room, the door whispering closed behind him. The wind carried the scent of earth and old leaves as Reinhardt walked from the school grounds toward the tram station. Each step felt weightier than the last, not because of hesitation, but because of certainty. He wasn't running anymore, not from questions, not from the future. His course was set. A quiet pride welled in his chest. Not the loud, boastful kind, the type born of shouting slogans or rattling a saber, but something deeper, older. This wasn't about glory. It wasn't even about vengeance, though his uncle's memory stirred beneath the surface. It was about proving something to himself, that he could stand among men and not falter.

When the call came, he answered. He turned a corner and saw the station ahead. The steel-and-glass shelter stood like a sentry against the morning chill, its bench half-occupied by a familiar figure, Kasper. He was sitting hunched forward, elbows on knees, fiddling with the zipper of his coat. When he noticed Reinhardt, he straightened and offered a short wave.

"You made it," Kasper said, standing.

Reinhardt nodded. "Of course."

They stood together in silence for a moment. Two young men, no longer boys, waiting not just for the tram but for the rest of their lives to begin. The track hummed in the distance. Their ride was coming.

The tram hissed to a stop at the edge of Neue Frankfurt, and the boys stepped off in unison. Reinhardt and Kasper crossed the narrow street, boots clicking against the cobbles. Ahead stood the ESS liaison office, small but unyielding, the black banner with its twin white Sieg runes snapping crisply in the breeze. The same banner they had stood before just days earlier. They pushed the door open. The Scharführer behind the front desk glanced up from his paperwork. Reinhardt stepped forward, standing at respectful attention.

"Sir," he said plainly, "have our orders been cut?"

The Scharführer gave them a quick once-over and then cracked the faintest smirk of approval, pride, or even amusement. He pulled a pair of folders from a metal tray beside him and set them on the desk.

"Jäger. Engel. You're official now," he said. "Orders signed this morning. You're no longer candidates. As of today, you're enlisted cadets of the Europaisch Schutzstaffel.

Reinhardt exhaled through his nose. Kasper blinked hard. The Scharführer handed each of them their orders and continued, "Report here at 0600 tomorrow for your transit briefing. Until then, get your affairs in order."

Reinhardt took the folder. Not heavy in weight but in meaning. A clean document. A seal. A future.

Kasper looked at him, then back to the desk. "Understood, Scharführer."

They turned to go, stepping out once more beneath the banner. The first stop on their way back through the city was the local militia headquarters, a squat concrete structure still ringed with sandbags and razor wire. The flag of the Delumina Militia fluttered atop the pole, but even it seemed to acknowledge the shifting tides. Reinhardt and Kasper entered together, boots echoing in the dim corridor. Inside, the air smelled of oil, paper, and dust, the scent of a citizen force built on necessity, not permanence. They approached the front desk where a duty clerk, a wiry man in his forties with the deep-set eyes of an overworked reservist, glanced up at them.

Reinhardt set his ESS orders down gently. "We're here to be formally released from militia rolls," he said. "Effective today."

The man took the folders, scanning them without comment at first. He gave a slow nod, opened a battered ledger, and scribbled something in the margins before stamping their orders with an official seal of release.

"You'll need to surrender your militia tags," he said flatly.

Kasper unsnapped his from his belt and set them down. Reinhardt did the same, running his thumb over the worn steel one last time before letting it rest atop the counter.

The clerk scooped the tags into a tray without ceremony. "You're clear. You'll be listed as discharged for voluntary Confederation military enlistment."

There was no congratulations, or speech, just a final nod. They stepped outside into the morning wind. For the first time, they no longer belonged to the farms, nor to the streets of Delumina, nor even to the planet's militia. They belonged to the Confederation now.

Reinhardt adjusted his collar. "One more night," he said quietly.

Kasper nodded, watching a freight truck roll past, its tires humming against the road.

"One more night," he echoed.

Reinhardt and Kasper made one last detour before returning home. The school loomed ahead, quiet in the late afternoon sun. Students still filled the classrooms, unaware or unconcerned with the quiet ritual about to unfold. They stepped inside through the front hall. It smelled of chalk and waxed floors, of long hours spent in formation and lectures on duty, history, and faith. They turned left at the main corridor and approached the principal's office, a solid wooden door with brass lettering: Oberlehrer Helmut Krämer, Rektor.

Reinhardt knocked twice. A pause, then a voice from inside: "Come in."

They entered together. Principal Krämer looked up from a sheaf of paper on his desk. He was a stern but fair man, with iron-gray hair combed neatly and a ribbon of commendation from the Confederation pinned just above his heart. Reinhardt stepped forward and laid the folder on the desk.

"Our orders, sir," he said. "We've been accepted into the ESS. As of this afternoon, we are no longer students."

Kasper followed, placing his own folder beside Reinhardt's. The principal adjusted his glasses and flipped through the documents. He read in silence for a moment, then closed the folders and folded his hands.

"You boys made your decision. Not lightly, I imagine."

"No, sir," Reinhardt said.

Krämer gave a single nod, not approval or judgment, just acknowledgment. "I'll notify the registrar. You'll be listed as honorably released under military orders. Your records will reflect that."

He stood and extended his hand first to Reinhardt, then to Kasper. "Whatever happens next... return better than you left."

Reinhardt shook his hand. "Yes, sir."

Kasper followed. "We'll make the school and Delumina proud."

"I hope so," Krämer said quietly, and sat back down.

The two boys stepped out into the hallway. The door clicked softly shut behind them. The sun had just begun to dip beyond the rooftops of Neue Frankfurt, casting long shadows across the empty sports field and chapel roof.

The chapel was silent as a tomb, yet warm with the weight of centuries carried across stars. Reinhardt and Kasper stepped through its tall oaken doors, the ancient hinges groaning softly as they entered. The air smelled of old incense, of dust, of sanctity preserved across worlds. Above, stained glass windows filtered the waning sunlight into shifting pools of amber and red across the polished floor. The chapel was divided, not in conflict, in reverence. One side bore the crucifix, candles flickering before statues of martyrs and saints.

The other, older side, was carved in stone and wood, a circle of altars dedicated to the old gods of Europe: Donar, Wodan, Týr, Freyja, and at the center, facing east, the golden embodiment of Sol. Reinhardt turned toward that altar, drawn not out of obligation, but instinct. The image of Sol, radiant and armored with his rays cast like spears, seemed to shimmer even in the dim light. A thin shaft of golden sun, refracted through the upper window, struck the altar squarely. It was late afternoon, Sol's hour. He knelt slowly. He bowed his head, one hand clenched against his chest. The other rested open on his knee.

"Sol... Lord of Light, of Order, of the Path Forward..." he whispered silently, the words forming not in his mouth, but in his heart. "You watched over me on the farm. You watched over me in the smoke. You lifted me from despair and showed me the way. I will serve with strength, I will hold the line, I will never turn from the path. Shine through me, that I may burn away all darkness."

He remained still for a moment longer. Then Reinhardt rose, no longer in prayer, but in calm. A boy made harder. A man on the edge of becoming. He stepped out quietly, the doors creaking shut behind him, and stood under the archway, watching as the shadows stretched long across the school grounds. A few minutes passed and Kasper emerged not long after, his own confession done in the Christian half of the chapel, face thoughtful but clear. He didn't speak right away, and neither did Reinhardt. They simply nodded to one another. That was enough. Then they departed, each walking the familiar road home for one last quiet night beneath the stars.

Reinhardt walked the winding path back to his family's homestead with the orders packet tucked under his arm, the weight of it far greater than its paper suggested. The sun was dipping low now, casting long bands of gold across the fields. The soil smelled rich, the stalks of late barley swaying gently in the breeze. It was the same road he had taken all his life. Not once had it ever felt so final.

The farmhouse came into view. Warm lamplight flickered through the windows. The scent of roasted root vegetables and stewed meat wafted in the air. He stepped through. the door quietly and slid off his boots at the threshold, as he had been taught since he could walk. His mother turned from the hearth. She didn't speak at first. She simply looked at him, at his clothes still dusty from travel, at the packet in his hand, and the subtle change in the way he carried himself.

"Dinner's ready," she said softly, motioning toward the table. She placed a plate down at his usual spot, simple, fair, but hearty. Meat, potatoes, cabbage, the food of soil and sun.

He sat. Nodded. "Danke."

His father sat across from him but kept his eyes on his plate. He was a man of the land, not given to speeches, and not quick to forgive a son for choosing war over furrows. Even he understood that the world was no longer what it had once been. They ate in silence, the sound of cutlery soft and slow. His mother reached across and laid a hand gently over his, her fingers calloused from years of work. She did not smile, but she held his gaze.

"You're still our son," she said. "That doesn't change."

"I know," Reinhardt answered quietly. "But I am... something else now."

The words didn't cause a stir. His father only nodded once, firm and resigned. They would never fully understand, but they didn't need to. He had seen fire fall from the heavens. He had pulled wounded comrades into cover. He had watched men twice his age falter while he stood firm. He had seen the banner of the confederation ripple in the smoke. He had chosen his road. He finished his meal slowly, savoring each bite. It might be the last time he tasted home for a long while. When he stood, he looked at both of them. "I'll be leaving in the morning."

No one stopped him. There was nothing more to say. Reinhardt didn't sleep long, but he didn't need to. He awoke with a calm sense of purpose, the kind that felt like the hush before a great march. The sky was still gray when he stood and dressed. He moved through his room quietly, packing only what mattered. A clean shirt, spare underclothes, a canteen, and the same steel knife his uncle had once carried in the border forests. Then he reached for the drawer at the foot of his bed, two banners lay folded inside.

One was deep crimson and black, edged in iron gray, the old Prussian-style banner from home, with the hooked-cross bold in the center, its lines sharp and proud. A memory of old blood and steel. The other was white and cobalt, with the golden sunburst of the Pan-European Confederation at its heart, like the one they'd draped over Ludwig's casket. Both were sacred. He took them both. Carefully folding them, he placed them deep in his pack beneath the rest, the red and the white, the old world and the new.

When he descended the stairs, the first hints of sunrise colored the windows. His parents were already awake. His mother had prepared a plate of buttered bread, a slice of cheese, and strong black coffee. She didn't speak as he sat. There was no need to. This wasn't a farewell of tears. She had raised a man. He ate quietly, hands steady. When he stood, she stepped forward first, pulling him into a firm embrace. She said nothing for several seconds, then whispered, "Wherever they send you... remember who you are."

He nodded. "I will."

His father stood next, silent and tall. They clasped forearms, man to man. His father's grip was firm. "Bring no shame to the name Jäger."

"Never," Reinhardt answered.

Without another word, he slung his pack over his shoulder, stepped to the door, and opened it after sliding on his boots. Outside, the sky was beginning to break, pale sunlight cresting over the eastern hills. The wind whispered through the barley like the breath of the gods. He stepped out, boots crunching the frost, and shut the door behind him. Two banners, two names, one path. Before him, the dawn of a harder, holier life.

With due haste, Reinhardt made it to the tram station, his pack slung across his shoulder, boots wet from the morning dew. He had no time to stop by the school or bid farewell to old classrooms, or even to see Herr Brandt one last time. He told himself there would be time for that later, though part of him doubted it. But as the station came into view, a surprise awaited him. Kasper was already there, leaning against the steel post of the schedule board, hands in his pockets, his own pack at his feet. He stood upright when he saw Reinhardt, giving him a firm nod. What Reinhardt hadn't expected was who stood beside him. Tomas, Jules, Elias and a handful of other boys from school and the militia stood in a loose half-circle, waiting in the pale golden light of morning.

"About time," Kasper said with a half-smile.

Reinhardt looked around at the familiar faces, momentarily unsure of what to say.

"You didn't think we'd let you go off without seeing you off, did you?" Tomas asked, clapping him on the shoulder.

Elias grinned, though the gesture looked tired. "Not every day someone marches off to join the black sun."

Reinhardt looked at them all, one by one. For a moment, his throat tightened, not with sadness but with an odd, powerful sense of brotherhood.

"I thought you lot had fields to tend to," he finally said.

Jules shrugged. "They'll wait."

The tram's low hum became audible in the distance, still a few minutes off. There was a moment of quiet among them, not awkward but reverent. The kind of silence that follows shared fire and battle. They had all bled on the same soil for Delumina. Reinhardt adjusted the weight of his pack and looked toward the horizon. "You've got your place," he said. "Now I'm going to find mine."

"You already found it," Tomas said. "You're just walking into it now."

They stood together in a quiet ring, the breeze tugging lightly at jackets and loose hair. The scent of morning dew still clung to the soil, mixing faintly with the metallic smell of the tracks. The boys spoke of old times , of classroom pranks, hard winters, and the first time they fired a rifle. Tomas brought up the time Reinhardt had climbed the old water tower on a dare and hung a Prussian banner from the top, "like some sort of war hero."

"You nearly broke your damn neck," Jules chuckled.

They laughed in the way young men do when they know they won't laugh like this again for a long while. Reinhardt looked at each of them, memorizing the faces, flushed with youth, touched by smoke and grief, yet still shining with something resilient. These were not boys anymore, not after Wessel Farm or the airport. The distant low whine of the tram became louder. They all fell silent. One by one, the young men extended their hands. Reinhardt gripped each firmly, starting with Tomas, then Jules, Elias, and even some of the quieter ones he hadn't expected to see. Each handshake lingered just a second longer than usual. The kind that says live well.

Kasper followed behind him, exchanging his own nods and farewells. When the tram finally hissed to a stop, the doors sliding open, Reinhardt gave one last look at them, his brothers of boyhood and war. He and Kasper stepped aboard. Then it happened. Silent, like a ritual too sacred for words, every one of them raised their right arm in the Roman salute, a still, timeless gesture.

Reinhardt and Kasper turned toward them, stood at attention, and returned it with unflinching pride, a final sign of loyalty and parting. The doors closed. The tram jolted gently, then glided forward down the track, carrying them toward their future. Neither of them spoke for a long while. The silence was not empty, it was full.

The small ESS liaison office, quiet and unassuming, became the gateway to everything that came next. Reinhardt and Kasper stood at the edge of the waiting room, orders in hand, and packs on their backs. The man assigned to escort them, a wiry noncommissioned officer in a plain Field-grey ESS field jacket, nodded for them to follow him into the utility groundcar. The drive was short, and mostly silent. No final parting words were spoken or joking. The faint electric hum of the motor and the gleam of the freshly repaired road beneath the wheels was all that was audible. Halfway through, the man keyed his radio.

"Delumina tower, this is Delumina ESS Liaison. Any remaining outbound traffic to the station?"

A pause.

"Liaison, one Valkyra prepping final departure, manifest space open. Recommend rapid insertion."

The man smirked faintly, then turned to them. "That's your bird."

They crested a slight hill near the edge of the perimeter fencing. There it was, the Valkyra, black and monolithic, just finished its final pre-flight checks. The rotors angled into launch position with a mechanical screech and hiss. Steam vented from beneath the belly. A ground crewman waved them forward. The ESS man threw the vehicle into park and turned to the boys. For the first time, he smiled.

"Godspeed."

Reinhardt and Kasper didn't waste time. They broke into a sprint, boots pounding the tarmac. The rear ramp of the Valkyra remained down, and the crew chief waved them aboard. Inside, seated and already secured, were four ESS soldiers clad in the matte-black ceramic power armor of the Shock Korps. Their visors glinted, impassive. Their presence was gravitational, like statues of gods strapped into the hull. The air stank faintly of oil, ozone, and metal, no one spoke. A crewman grabbed them by the shoulders and guided them into the last two seats, facing the armored fireteam. A third seat remained empty between them. It was only then that Reinhardt noticed the four troopers across from them were all watching. One of them, helmet still on, gave a tiny nod. The oxygen masks were brought down and clipped over their faces. Filters hissed. The internal headset activated with a soft chime. For the first time, Reinhardt heard the pilots' voices and they had a tone of being stoic, professional, and distant.

"Black Lance, tower clearance granted. Vector 115, ascend pattern 7."

Straps tightened across their chests. The ground crew gave them the double thumbs-up. Reinhardt responded with a quick nod. The crew chief raised his hand, circle motion, then slammed his palm down. The ramp lifted shut. The cabin grew darker. The engines roared to full power. Reinhardt felt the vibration in his bones. The Valkyra rose, hovering a moment, then tilted nose-up and punched through the lower atmosphere. He gripped the side rail and cast one last glance at the soldiers across from him. This wasn't a ride. This was an ascent.

As the Valkyra rocketed up from the tree-thick valleys of Delumina, Reinhardt could feel the shift, gravity thinning, the hum of the engines deepening, resonance building in the frame like a chant held between iron lungs. Through the viewport, the sky had turned from burnt amber to violet-black. Then came the voice of the flight-sergeant. "Brace. Skyhook engagement in five."

Reinhardt and Kasper locked in. Outside, the Sky Chariot descended. It is a massive, cruciform vessel shaped like a descending sword, hovering at the edge of the atmosphere. It was not a shuttle, not a carrier, but something in between, a vessel built only for retrieval, clad in ablative tiles and layered grav-tethers. The Valkyra surged upward on its final chemical pulse, then coasted silently toward alignment. The Skyhook armature, trailing out from the Chariot's underbelly like a silver tendon, locked onto their frame with a magnetic slam. Cables hissed, clamps engaged, and the acceleration that followed wasn't propulsion. It was extraction, like being pulled up by the gods.

"Skyhook locked. Chariot's taking us home," the sergeant said. "We're off this rock."

As the atmospheric haze fell behind them and the stars turned cold and white, Reinhardt looked to Kasper and understood the symbolism. To descend is war; to rise is grace. No man ascends alone. Only the Sky Chariot brings you back.

The black gunship bucked slightly as it hit upper air turbulence, then smoothed out into the gentle float of zero gravity.

The pilot's voice echoed in their headset. "Black Lance on approach. Docking ring Three. Prepare for internal gravity adjustment."

The shift was subtle, a hum, a slow tilt, then a faint thump as magnetic clamps engaged. The Valkyra was docked. The cabin lights shifted from red to green. The rear ramp dropped with a mechanical hiss. Pressure equalized, and the air crew stepped aboard. One by one, they unstrapped the seated soldiers. When they reached Reinhardt and Kasper, they were brisk but respectful. They followed the others down the ramp and into the cavernous bay of Delumina Station's hangar three. The air smelled recycled but clean. The lights were bright, white-blue. Tech crews moved with purpose across the polished floor, directing arrivals and loading cargo.

A man in an ESS flight jacket and white gloves stood with a clipboard. Reinhardt approached. "Sir, cadets. Reporting inbound for transfer."

The man looked up, nodded. "Right on time. Your bird's prepped."

He pointed across the hangar to a smaller craft, a sleek, silver-gray personnel transport. Far less aggressive than the Valkyra, but fast and ready.

"That one will take you home," the man added.

Reinhardt furrowed his brow slightly. "Home?"

The officer smirked. "You'll see."

Chapter 12

The interior of the passenger vessel was unlike anything Reinhardt had ever seen. Wide and clean, softly lit with blue-white ambient panels along the curved ceiling. Polished alloy bulkheads. Softly humming floors. This wasn't a gunship, a transport, or a freight hauler. It was a craft designed for long-haul movement, not just of personnel, but of future servants of the Confederation. As they stepped aboard, a pair of automated mechanisms gently took their duffel bags, scanning and tagging them with precise alphanumeric labels. Their manifests flickered on a side monitor, ESS Cadets: JÄGER, R. / ENGEL, K. — Destination: Heilige Terra (Holy Terra), Confederation Core. Waiting near the forward cabin was a woman. She was striking, elegant, and professional. Her dark hair was swept back in a clean bun, and her uniform bore the insignia of Confederation's long-haul civilian transport corps. A stylized winged sun over crossed fasces sat on her shoulder tab. Her name badge read: CHLOE — STEWARDESS. She greeted them both with a slight, practiced smile. Her voice carried the soft musicality of the Hellenic people.

"Welcome aboard, cadets. My name is Chloe, and I'll be assisting you during transit. We're set to depart in just under an hour. Until then, feel free to get comfortable, seating is open in the forward passenger cabin. Refreshments are available at the front console."

They walked forward, boots softly hitting the quiet floor as they entered the seating compartment. It reminded Reinhardt more of a lounge than a military transport with cushioned seats, small tables, and individual lights. The windows were wide by spacecraft standards, allowing an unbroken view of the stars. Reinhardt and Kasper took seats near the port side. The stewardess followed shortly, holding a silver tray with simple drinks including tea, mineral water, and small ration biscuits.

"Would you like anything before departure?" she asked, standing with gentle poise.

"Water, please," Reinhardt said.

"Same," Kasper added, glancing around the cabin.

Chloe served them with quiet grace, then moved on, checking displays near the front of the vessel. They drank in silence for a moment, letting it all settle in. This was the threshold. Journeys across the Confederation could last days or even weeks, depending on alignment, rotation, and speed, from the far side of Europa's frontier to the heart of her memory. But this one, this one would take them home. To Earth.

.The cockpit doors slid open with a soft mechanical hiss. Two figures entered, both in dark gray flight suits trimmed with blue piping and the insignia of the Confederation's interstellar transport command. The pilot, a lean man with sharp cheekbones and silvering hair, nodded briefly toward the cabin. His co-pilot, a younger woman with olive skin and data-glasses across one eye, offered the stewardess a polite smile before stepping into the cockpit. Neither said a word to the passengers. Instead, they moved with ritual precision, taking their seats behind the sealed glass bulkhead. A quiet flurry of switch-flips and touchscreen gestures followed including pre-flight checks, environmental scans, magnetic clamp disengagement, and navigational stabilization. The hum of the ship's core deepened slightly. A chime echoed through the cabin.

"Attention passengers," came the pilot's voice over the cabin intercom, crisp and restrained. This is Flight Aethur-719, bound for Terra. I'm Pilot Doran, joined by Co-Pilot Laska. You are aboard the Confederation vessel Eos Callista. We will be making two brief stops at Visegrad station in the Tau Ceti system and at the military transfer node of Neue Swabia station in the Alpha Mensae system, before making the final approach to Terra orbit via the Sol Lance. Estimated total transit time is five standard days, but the trip will feel much faster than that. Please remain seated during the initial departure. You may remove your grav-harness after clearance from the crew. Temporal shielding is active. We are going for a full-synch intersystem transition."

The comms cut with a soft click. The stewardess, Chloe, passed once more through the cabin to check their seats. She gave a small nod to both Reinhardt and Kasper. Then the engines activated. No roar, just a low, expanding resonance, like the deep tone of a mountain shifting in its sleep. The floor beneath them pulsed faintly. The Eos Callista lifted smoothly from the hangar deck of Delumina

Station, pivoted nose-first into the blackness of space, and slowly began its glide toward the system's heart. Reinhardt stared out the window, watching as the station receded behind them, a gray cruciform silhouette shrinking against the sea of stars. Ahead, Epsilon Eridani burned. Delumina's star was young by cosmic standards as a yellow-orange flame set in the dark, slightly wilder than Sol. Sunspots churned visibly across its surface, and long loops of plasma arced outward in slow spirals of coronal heat. Even from this distance, its light carried weight.

Kasper leaned forward slightly. "Why are we heading toward it?"

Reinhardt answered without looking away. "The Lance needs the star. Without the pull, it can't activate."

Kasper blinked. "I thought it pushed us."

Reinhardt shook his head. "No, the Aetheric Lance doesn't push, it collapses space in front of us. Think of it like... latching onto the gravity well of the star, and pulling a tunnel through space-time, anchored by that energy."

Kasper frowned. "So we surf the sun?"

"Kind of," Reinhardt replied. "The sun's core gives off more than heat or radiation. It produces resonance patterns, frequencies the Lance engine can lock onto. Once aligned, the engine amplifies that energy into a directional wave that folds space ahead of the ship. We're not flying faster than light. We're folding the distance between here and there."

"Huh." Kasper leaned back. "And what keeps us from showing up in the year 4000?"

Reinhardt smirked faintly. "The Aetheric Shield. It's a phase-mirror field. It syncs our vessel's local time to Confederation sidereal standard, the same temporal signature as Earth, called Terra Standard Time. Without it, we might exit the Lance corridor hundreds of years later than we left."

“Has that ever happened?”

“Once, early on,” Reinhardt said quietly. “They say a scout ship from Tau Ceti arrived in Sol system with no crew left alive. They’d been in the corridor for six thousand years.”

Kasper’s face paled slightly. “And we trust this system?”

“We have to,” Reinhardt said, tapping the side of the hull with his knuckles. “It’s not a matter of trust. It’s a matter of civilization. Without the Lance and Shield, the stars are just empty.”

The ship banked slowly toward the inner system. Delumina’s sun began to grow in the viewport from a star to a blazing disk. Reinhardt looked toward it, unblinking. Sol may still shine in the night sky but every world now turns to a nearer fire.

Reinhardt unbuckled his seat harness and stood. The quiet hum of the ship filled the cabin as it coasted toward Delumina’s sun, the engines in low-burn. He walked past Kasper, who was still half-lounged in his seat, and made his way toward the back of the passenger compartment.

There, bolted into the wall near the steward’s terminal, was a small library. Simple, elegant. No propaganda posters. Just a clean metal shelf with leather-bound and polymer-backed titles including Confederation classics, memoirs, philosophical tracts, and mandatory texts. He scanned the spines and Eastern Front by Leon Degrelle caught his eye. Reinhardt paused. His fingers brushed the cover. It was the same book Herr Brandt had been reading the last time they spoke. Degrelle, the Walloon, the believer, the man who’d led thousands into fire not for gold, but for destiny. He pulled it from the shelf. The cover was simple: black, with a silvered eagle above the title. Reinhardt walked back and dropped into his seat.

Kasper glanced sideways. “That the one Brandt was always reading?”

“Yeah,” Reinhardt said, flipping the cover open. “Figured it’s worth knowing.

They say it's required at the academy."

He turned to the first chapter and began to read aloud, his voice calm, level, and a little reverent.

"We fought not for Germany alone, but for all of Europe. For her rebirth. For her soul. The Bolsheviks were not just a danger to borders, they were a danger to the spirit of man."

Kasper raised an eyebrow. "He actually wrote like that?"

Reinhardt nodded slightly. "And then some, and this wasn't the only book he wrote."

He kept reading, turning the page.

"I did not fight out of hate, but out of love, a love for Europe as she had been, and must be again. The trenches froze our feet, but not our beliefs. There is nothing more sacred than duty. Nothing more clarifying than war."

Kasper leaned forward, his eyes no longer playful. "That's heavier than I thought."

Reinhardt didn't answer. He flipped to a section bookmarked with a thin slip of military-issue ribbon.

"We did not cry when our friends fell. We avenged them. We did not fear the end. We knew we were building something eternal. And if we were to die, let it be as builders, not as slaves."

He stopped reading and looked out the window. The sun was getting closer now, Epsilon Eridani, its surface pulsing with wild energy, its halo rising like a crown of molten gold. Kasper said nothing for a long time.

Reinhardt set the book on his lap, thumb still in place. "He saw the end of Europe," he said quietly. "And still marched east."

Kasper glanced at him, eyes narrowed. "And now we go the other way."

Reinhardt looked back at the sun.

"Maybe not," he said.

Kasper sat forward, resting his elbows on his knees, watching the book now instead of the stars. Reinhardt turned a few more pages, thumb moving slowly across the aged paper. His eyes flicked down to a section where the prose sharpened. The tone changed. He recognized the weight in it, this was no longer ideology or longing. This was contact. He cleared his throat and read more.

"It was the first time. I had no illusions. We were not walking into ceremony, we were walking into steel. The bullets came before we saw them. They cut the grass beside us and sang through the air like demons screaming."

Reinhardt paused for a moment, then kept reading.

"I remember the boy beside me fell first. No shout. Just gone. I had never seen a body drop like that. Not from disease. Not from accident. But taken, cut by war. My hand was shaking. The Machine gun was heavy. But I fired."

Kasper swallowed, slowly.

"A Russian stood up on the ridge, silhouetted by smoke. I fired again. I don't know if I hit him. Maybe I didn't. But I remember that moment. The sudden realization, I was not pretending. I was not a boy. I was not a soldier in waiting. I was in it. And the world would never be the same."

Reinhardt closed the book halfway and let it rest against his chest. Neither of them spoke. The engines hummed beneath them as the vessel glided steadily toward the sun. Outside the window, the corona of Epsilon Eridani curled in silence, white arcs dancing like waves in a still sea of gold. Kasper finally spoke, his voice lower now.

"Do you remember your first one?" he asked. "When it really hit?"

Reinhardt nodded slowly. “In the woods north of Wessel Farm.”

Kasper looked over at him, waiting.

“I don’t even remember the first man I shot. I just remember my hands afterward. They wouldn’t stop shaking, but I wasn’t afraid. It felt like... it was just something that had to be done.”

He stared ahead again.

“And then Ludwig was gone. And I didn’t shake anymore.”

Kasper didn’t say anything for a while. Then, quietly, “Do you think that’s how all of them started?”

Reinhardt looked down at the open page, a man’s memory stained with snow, smoke, and the realization of irrevocable truth.

He nodded once. “Yeah. I think so.”

The chime echoed once more across the cabin with a low, resonant tone that vibrated faintly in the bones. “Attention passengers,” came the pilot’s voice over the intercom. “We are now within Lance proximity to Epsilon Eridani. Prepare for corridor ignition. All systems are nominal. Artificial gravity will fluctuate briefly. The temporal stabilization field is at full resonance.”

Reinhardt and Kasper exchanged a look. Without a word, they buckled their harnesses. The book was closed and secured beneath Reinhardt’s seat. The light in the cabin dimmed to a soft amber, and the humming pitch of the engine deepened. Through the viewport, the star loomed massive now, an ocean of fire, a living monolith. White flares curved and snapped along its edge like the slow beat of wings. A series of soft mechanical clicks sounded underfoot.

“Activating Aetheric Lance... Corridor calibration in progress...”

Reinhardt felt a brief pressure in his chest. Not painful, just presence, like the gravity of a mountain settling on his shoulders. The stewardess, now strapped into her jump seat, gave a quick hand signal, all clear. The pilot's voice returned, clipped and steady:

"Corridor engaged. Shield harmonics locked. Initiating jump in five... four... three..."

There was no flash. No shake. Only a sensation, like falling inward and outward at once, like being turned inside out and stitched back together in silence. For half a heartbeat, the stars disappeared. Then they were elsewhere. The star was gone. In its place, the calm blackness of deep space, pierced by unfamiliar constellations and the distant flicker of a blue-white orb ahead. They moved quietly through the void of space. It didn't take long, perhaps an hour, to reach the Tau Ceti system. A synthetic chime rang out.

"Jump was successful. Welcome to Tau Ceti system. ETA to Visegrad station is fifty-eight minutes."

The lighting in the cabin returned to normal. Gravity settled with a mild pressure against the seatbacks.

Kasper exhaled slowly, blinking at the change. "That was it?"

Reinhardt nodded, jaw tight. "Yeah. That was it."

Through the window, a small station came into view, Visegrad station orbiting the planet Visegrad. Spindly and utilitarian, not a cultural center like Delumina Station, but a logistical node, a waypoint on the web. They were now two systems closer to Earth. The Eos Callista docked with a low thrum of magnetic locks, and the cabin lights shifted to amber.

"We have arrived at Visegrád Station," the pilot announced over comms. "Passengers disembarking here may do so now. Cadet passengers, you are cleared for shore leave. Return to the cabin within one hour and forty-five minutes. Departure will not be delayed."

Reinhardt and Kasper stood. The motion was nearly instinctive now and their boots found rhythm before their thoughts caught up. Together, they stepped down the gangway and into the wide corridor of Visegrád Station. The station air was dense and faintly humid, smelling of oil, old metal, and fried food. A line of fluorescent lights overhead buzzed softly. From the ports on their left, the world of Visegrád turned quietly with forested continents and glacier-fed rivers curving across its northern hemisphere. They didn't speak much. Just followed their noses and the sound of quiet voices.

Down a side hall was a bar, half-hidden behind a rust-colored curtain of wooden beads. The sign overhead read: Korona: Piwo i Dusza (Crown: Beer and Soul). They stepped inside. The place was small, six stools at the bar and two tables. The lights were low. The scent of frying duck fat and boiling onions filled the air like incense. A woman behind the counter gave them a single glance, then nodded toward the bar.

Only one other patron sat inside. He was a large-framed man, maybe their age or slightly older, seated near the far end of the bar with a half-finished beer and a thick canvas rucksack beside him. His head was shaved, and he wore a dark green cadet's tunic with no visible insignia other than a stylized double-headed aquila stitched on his left arm, unmistakably Russian. Reinhardt gave him a polite nod as they passed. The man returned it with a slight lift of his brow, then turned back to his pint. They sat two stools down.

"Two plates of pierogi," Reinhardt said to the woman. "And your best local beer."

"Filled with what?" she asked.

Kasper answered, "Whatever's hot."

Minutes later, they were eating cheese-and-duck pierogi, drizzled in butter and crisp onion, with steaming mugs of dark Visegrád beer to wash it down. The Russian cadet finally spoke, his accent heavy but clear.

"You both came in on the Callista, no?"

Reinhardt nodded.

"Enlisted?" the man asked.

"Cadets," Kasper answered. "ESS."

The Russian raised his mug in a half-toast. "Army."

Reinhardt studied him more closely now. The man's frame was broad, muscular. His posture is precise. There was nothing casual in how he sat. He had the bearing of someone already trained.

"From the east of Visegrad," the man said. "Volga-Don settlement. My father was in the Russian army too. You?"

"Delumina," Reinhardt replied. "We fought at the airport. My uncle was in the German army before he moved to Delumina. My dad is just a simple farmer."

The Russian's expression didn't change, but he gave a slow nod of respect. "Then you already wear the uniform, cadet or not."

They drank in silence for a moment.

Kasper leaned over slightly. "So what branch?"

"Infantry," the Russian said. "But aiming for mountaineer or mechanized. They sort us after basic. You?"

Reinhardt spoke quietly. "I want to earn the black, ESS Shock units."

The Russian glanced at him sideways, then gave a curt nod.

"I'm Valentin," he said. "Valentin Antonovich."

"Reinhardt," he replied. "This is Kasper."

The three clinked mugs lightly. No slogans. No speeches. Just a brief, unspoken pact. Brothers, if only for a time.

They left the bar together, Reinhardt, Kasper, and Valentin. No one had said much after the first toasts. They hadn't needed to. There was already an understanding. The corridor back to the Callista was quiet, save for the buzz of fluorescent panels overhead and the distant clang of dock machinery. Valentin carried his duffel sack over one shoulder, heavy and quiet. As they approached the boarding checkpoint, two Confederation personnel stood at the ramp. One held a clipboard, the other scanned ID chits.

"Name," the first said, glancing at Valentin.

"Antonovich, Valentin. Army cadet."

The scanner pinged. The personnel nodded. "Cleared. Proceed aboard."

The Callista looked different now. The cabin wasn't empty anymore. As Reinhardt stepped in, his eyes moved quickly, maybe twelve other young men now seated across the forward section, all wearing various shades of military cadet uniforms. Most looked around his age, maybe a year or two older. There was no shouting, no chaos. Just the low hum of conversation and the subtle shuffle of gear being stored.

Kasper muttered, "Looks like we're not the only ones."

Reinhardt gave a faint grin. "No. We're part of something much bigger."

The three found seats together sitting side-by-side along the left bulkhead. As they sat, Reinhardt looked across the cabin. Some of the other men were already watching them, assessing silently. Not out of distrust, rather out of curiosity. Out of recognition. There were nods. Quiet smiles. The kind only men destined for the same trenches shared. Reinhardt raised his voice just slightly, enough to carry without shouting.

"I'm Reinhardt Jäger, an ESS cadet. This is Kasper. Valentin here's the Army. I figure we ought to know who we're sitting beside when the shooting starts."

A young man across the aisle gave a small nod.

"Angelo Ricci, Italian Army."

Next to him, "Émilien Dubois, Navy Signals."

Two rows back, a red-haired cadet lifted his hand. "Tomasz Artur, CEAB army, Breton contingent."

Several others followed with their names, faces, and brief affiliations. A pair of identical blond twins, saying little more than "Schloss and Vinter. Cadets. Logistics or reconnaissance. Not sure yet."

Reinhardt leaned forward slightly.

"You two are ESS?"

They nodded in tandem.

"What units do you want?" Reinhardt asked. "Deployments?"

Schloss responded. "Recon Battalion, if we're cut for it. Vinter's better with drones. We want to be in Leibstandarte or Das Reich."

Reinhardt smirked. "Kasper and I are hoping for Panzergrenadier and Wiking Division."

One of the others gave a soft whistle. "Not subtle."

"No," Kasper replied. "That's the point."

Valentin glanced at them both, then gave a short grunt of approval. The lights in the cabin dimmed slightly. The vessel began to hum again, not with the throb of atmospheric lift-off, but the vibrational resonance of intersystem flight. The Eos Callista began to turn. Outside the windows, the stars wheeled in preparation for the next jump to Alpha Mensae.

The Eos Callista emerged from the Lance corridor with a whisper, not a bang. The viewport re-stabilized, and a new star now burned in the distance hung Alpha

Mensae, a soft golden-yellow orb surrounded by a tight band of relay beacons.

"Arrival confirmed," said the pilot. "Alpha Mensae system. Local time synchronization in effect. Estimated transit to orbital station: one hour, thirty-four minutes. Final layover before Earth."

Conversation returned slowly, as if sound itself had to stretch back into being.

Kasper looked around. "That was worse than the last one."

Reinhardt shrugged. "Could've been worse. Could've shown up 600 years later."

Valentin cracked a faint smile. "Only if the shield failed."

They watched silently as the world of Neue Swabia came into view as a large green and blue orb, with vast hexagonal cities dotting its continents, separated by long rivers and spine-like mountain ranges. This was not a fringe colony like Delumina. Neue Swabia was a first-wave world, settled by Germanic pioneers more than a century ago, their descent from the Sol system immortalized in the old banners that still flew over its capital: a red field, white sunburst, black cross at its center. Traffic filled the orbital lanes including supply barges, personnel carriers, and naval logistics ships. The Confederation flag flew from every docking arm, joined on many by the old Prussian war eagle or the Gothic stylings of the Europa Kreigsakademie.

"Docking sequence initiated. All cadets prepare for brief disembarkation. Local time at the station: 06:17 hours."

The Callista began to bank. Reinhardt leaned forward slightly, eyes narrowed as he studied the world below. Its cities were older, larger and established not just for survival but for permanence. Here, the Pan-European dream had not been built, it had been forged.

Kasper whispered beside him, "You think Earth will be like that?"

Reinhardt answered, eyes fixed on the planet. "No," he said. "Earth will be older."

The Eos Callista docked cleanly with Neue Swabia Station, its hull aligning with magnetic clamps along the station's outer ring. The cadets disembarked for two hours of rest and re-orientation, but none of them lingered too far. It was still early, the station's corridors buzzed with shift change and muted announcements in Hochdeutsch and a few other European languages. Across the viewing deck, Europa Kriegsmarineschule cadets in black-and-white parade uniforms stood in ranks, rifles at their shoulders as they awaited transit to the surface. Their boots gleamed. Their faces were chiseled and expressionless.

Reinhardt watched them as he sipped weak station coffee.

"They're from the Kriegsmarine Academy," Kasper said quietly, joining him.

"I know."

"Think we'll look like that?"

Reinhardt said nothing. The question didn't need an answer.

When boarding was called again, the cadets returned to the Callista but now, the cabin felt smaller. Nearly forty young men now filled the passenger section, representing every arm of the Confederation's forces. French naval infantry, Slovene comms techs, Polish combat engineers, CEAB pathfinders, and ESS aspirants. Many spoke different languages, but the tone was the same as calm, lean, and disciplined. They weren't boys anymore. And Earth wasn't just home, it was a proving ground.

The Callista departed Neue Swabia Station and made its slow arc toward Alpha Mensae's Lance corridor. The star behind them pulsed brighter now, a golden crown burning in silence as the ship aligned for its final leap.

"Final transit," the pilot announced. "Alpha Mensae to Sol. Estimated subjective time in-lance, seven hours. The estimated objective time is just under three days."

Time bent. Time folded. They crossed oceans of light in silence. Inside the ship, time felt short like a restless nap taken too early. When the Callista finally emerged in-system, and when Sol burned into view, Reinhardt saw that everything had changed. Sol burned white. Not the soft yellow of children's drawings or the orange glow imagined from old atmospheric days, but a searing, relentless white, like a spear of light hurled across the ages. From the Callista's reinforced viewing ports, it did not flicker or dance. It, rather he, commanded. It was not just a star. He was a monarch of fusion and fire, the progenitor of every name written in the European bloodline as Apollo, Helios, Deus Sol Invictus, Mithras, and the Father of the Flame, wisdom and consciousness itself. Every world charted, every path claimed, traced its lineage back to this one light. Even now, in the age of the Lance and the Shield, Sol remained the fixed point in the celestial compass, not merely because of where Earth was, but because of what it meant. You could be born on Delumina, raised on Visegrád, stationed on a moon of Tau Ceti, but you only had one origin. Kasper said nothing as he looked out. Neither did Valentin. None of them blinked. Sol did not permit blinking. He was a hot, searing flame. He did not comfort, he judged.

"Arrival confirmed: Terra Station. System time: 0744 hours, September 12th, 2225 AD, 280 AV. Total objective time since departure from Delumina station: four days, twenty hours."

It hadn't felt like four days. It felt like a blink. A breath. A long, shared dream. Outside the viewport, Terra hung in silence in her blue, vast, and ancient beauty. The clouds traced slow spirals across her oceans. Sunlight kissed the Alps. The cradle of mankind shimmered beneath them, older than any nation, older than any tongue. Reinhardt stared in silence. His breath caught for just a moment.

Kasper whispered, "There she is."

The docking clamps released with a metallic hiss, and the Eos Callista was swallowed into the underbelly of Terra Station, the largest orbital platform in the Confederation. More than a station, it was a city above the cradle. The cadets disembarked in ordered rows, each carrying their issued bags or personal kits. There were no announcements, no pomp. Just a sharp hiss of pressure doors, the echo of boots on polished deck plating, and the gentle hum of systemwide authority. It smelled sterile, recycled but close. Closer than anything he'd known. Below them, Terra rotated slowly, vast and blue beneath the heavy glass of the viewing walls.

He turned to Valentin and extended his hand. "I wish you well. I hope to see you again, Valentin."

Valentin nodded once, clasping forearms in the soldier's fashion. "You will. We're not finished, comrade."

Kasper added with a smirk, "And if you are, I'll drink your beer."

Valentin gave a rare smile. "Only if you earn it."

With that, they parted, cadets peeling off in formation as logistics officers began calling names and directing them by service branch. Reinhardt and Kasper followed a sharp-jawed ESS trooper who wore no rank insignia, only the sigil of the twin Siegrunen at his collar.

"ESS cadets, this way. You're bound for Munich, Bavaria. Keep your eyes open."

They were led down a sterile corridor, past security checkpoints and sealed customs chambers. Eventually, they reached the skipper bay, a narrow launch platform where atmospheric shuttles carried personnel and freight down to the planet's surface. Their vessel was lean, black, and marked with the insignia of the Europaische Schutzstaffel, the ESS. It bore no wasted ornaments or serial numbers. It was function clad in force. The trooper pointed to the ramp. "Board."

Reinhardt looked at Kasper as they ascended.

"Munich," he said.

"Bavaria," Kasper replied. "Old ground."

They took their seats, strapped in, and looked to the viewport. There was Earth, not as myth but as reality. The Alps were like granite veins with green fields stretching outward from them like waves of memory, cities nestled in geometric order.

Chapter 13

The shuttle hissed as its landing skids locked into place. The doors opened with a pneumatic sigh, and Reinhardt stepped out onto German soil for the first time since he was a child. He didn't speak at first. The air was cool, crisper than Delumina's. The scent of pine, faint diesel, and wet cobblestone wafted through the early morning breeze. In the distance, the snowcapped Alps loomed like patient sentinels. Kasper stepped beside him, squinting in the sunlight. Reinhardt exhaled through his nose, not quite smiling but standing taller.

"You feel that?" he asked softly. "Like... this is where we're meant to be?"

Kasper nodded. "Feels like coming home to something I never knew I missed."

Reinhardt looked around. The Greater German Reich wasn't just a concept here, it was present in every stone, every banner fluttering over the transit stations, and soldiers in field-gray walking with precision across the terminal grounds.

They boarded the airport tram, a sleek rail line that whisked them from the shuttle tarmac to the central Munich Bahnhof, a grand neo-futurist complex wrapped in glass and reinforced steel. Confederation and German flags hung between imperial columns. Germany's national banner as well as Bavarian flags and Munich's city flag were all present.

Before they departed for Bad Tölz, Reinhardt and Kasper had seen Munich, not merely as visitors but inheritors. It was unlike any city Reinhardt had ever seen or remembered. The capital of Bavaria, and one of the keystone cities of the Greater German Reich. Munich had become a model for the Pan-European architectural doctrine, a place where the future was built from the past, and where no line was wasted on decadence, nor curve left without meaning. Its skyline was a study in vertical will, spires and towers in black iron and pale stone, each one climbing with mathematical ferocity toward the heavens. The older quarters had been restored, their Neo-Gothic cathedrals and Imperial buildings untouched but reinforced, fitted with crystal-paneled vaults and steel lattice undergirdings. Between them rose new structures, monuments of concrete and in the tradition of Italian Futurism and German Neo-Gothic, all thrust and angle, energy frozen into matter. Their surfaces bore etched bas-reliefs with solar wheels, battle scenes, and Europa herself, rendered in the style of Roman friezes, sword in hand, and standing atop a globe.

Transit lines cut through the city like veins as maglev rails, electric trams, and underground arterials all fused into a synchronized system. Above them, aerial lanes allowed small personal aircraft and military gunships or fighters to pass in ordered silence. Everything was deliberate. Everything served a higher function. Every square, every bridge, every avenue was named for heroes of blood, battle, and vision as Codreanuplatz, Schmidt Strasse, Hitler Gate and Saint Michael's Ascension Tower. Public murals in bronze and white stone showed not politicians, but warriors, men who built, fought, and bled for order. At the center of the city stood the Confederation Victory Monument, a vertical arc of polished steel, flanked by statues of a Roman legionary and a medieval knight, both offering their swords to a solar-crowned youth carved in white marble. It was not a city of indulgence. It was a city of destiny. Kasper had said little as they walked through its heart. Reinhardt had said even less. Both had understood what was being asked of them and what they had already sworn to become.

From there, they caught the southbound regional rail to Bad Tölz, the final leg of their pilgrimage. The countryside flashed past their windows as green hills, dark woods, and lakes like silver plates tucked between valleys. It was clean, ordered and holy, in its way.

They finally dismounted at Tölz-Kaserne Halt, a small security-cleared stop just outside the old academy gates. There it stood, SS-Junkerschule Bad Tölz, now bearing the restored title, updated but unchanged in its core design. The old granite towers still loomed, their angles sharp, their windows long and narrow. A modern concrete annex extended from the east wing, marked with SS sigils, high-tensile fiber barricades, and watchposts. Above the gate flew three banners, The Pan-European Confederation's white sunburst, the ESS black flag with twin Sieg runes, and at the center, still proud, the old German war-flag. Reinhardt stood there for a moment, unmoving. Kasper adjusted his rucksack and whistled low. "So this is where it all begins."

Reinhardt shook his head slowly. "No," he said. "This is where it's tested."

The main hall of the old academy was built from quarried granite and reinforced with steel-ribbed arches, austere and cold but solid. The floor beneath their boots echoed with each step, polished to a faint reflection by generations of cadets. High above, the original chandeliers had been replaced with hard white lights in recessed fixtures. Everything had the clarity of a surgical theater with no dust or warmth, only purpose. At the front desk, a rotenfuhrer (corporal) in grey ESS dress uniform glanced up as Reinhardt and Kasper approached.

"Orders?"

Reinhardt opened his folder and placed it flat. "Cadets Jäger and Engel, reporting."

The corporal scanned the names, then nodded.

"You're early," he said without looking up again. "Training begins in five days. You'll be quartered in Barracks Five until then. Head west across the parade square, building with the black eagle above the door. Your platoon cadre will be assigned later. Until then, keep to the compound, and follow the orientation packet. Stay out of trouble."

"Jawohl," they replied.

The corporal didn't dismiss them, he merely returned to the book he was reading. Outside, they crossed the open parade square, a vast concrete field flanked by drill towers, instructional buildings, and flagpoles. The cold Bavarian air stung their cheeks, but they didn't complain. Barracks Five stood at the square's far edge, a three-story structure of dark brick and pale stone, recently renovated but unmistakably old-world in its frame. Above the double doors hung the ESS black eagle, wings stretched wide, talons gripping the runes of fate. They entered without a word. Inside, the interior was spartan: wide halls, polished stone floors, walls lined with basic lockers and gun racks, and the scent of cleaning solution and leather. Each bunk had a metal-frame bed, topped with a wool blanket and thin pillow, a steel footlocker, already numbered, a weapon rack, and a wooden wardrobe, empty except for a few hangers and a small mirror on the door. There were only a handful of cadets inside, six or seven, most in plain clothes, already talking amongst themselves. A few heads turned as Reinhardt and Kasper entered. The room was quiet but not unfriendly, only the passing gazes of assessment. Reinhardt picked the bunk second from the far corner, and Kasper took the one beside it. They dropped their rucksacks and began unpacking in silence.

A few lockers clicked open nearby. Someone chuckled. Another cadet was already brushing his boots and talking about his rail delay from Visegrád. Another joked in Polish-accented German about how nobody had told him Bavaria would be so damn cold. They weren't boys from the same world, not yet, but the process had begun. Reinhardt folded a shirt and placed it in the locker with care. Then he closed it with a soft click, sat on his bunk, and exhaled. Kasper smirked and leaned back.

"We made it."

Reinhardt didn't smile, but the look in his eyes said enough. Chow time came, and all of the cadets walked over together. The chow hall buzzed with low voices, the scrape of trays, and the clink of mugs. The scent of rich stew and roast chicken hung in the air like a comforting fog, a brief reminder that not everything in the world was iron and discipline. Reinhardt and Kasper carried their trays to the long center table where the rest of the Barracks Five cadets had begun to gather. No formal seating. Just young men bound for the same forge. Introductions passed quickly.

"Wilhelm, Brandenburg."

"Paolo. Naples. I build engines or used to, I mean..."

"Luka, Dalmatian coast. Still wondering if this is a military camp or a monastery."

Light chuckles, the kind of forced camaraderie that comes just before the pain starts. As they sat, the question naturally came.

"And you two?" Édouard asked, adjusting his tray. "You're not locals, don't sound it either."

Kasper looked at Reinhardt. Reinhardt spoke plainly, "I am Reinhardt and this is Kasper. We are from Delumina."

A pause. A full breath passed before anyone reacted.

"Delumina?" Paolo asked, already leaning forward.

"You mean the Delumina?" Wilhelm added. "With the airport?"

"The footage, yeah! That footage with the insurgents getting torn to ribbons."

"Delta-88," Luka said, shaking his head with an incredulous grin. "That guy with the MG who held down the flank alone. Guy was insane, from what I heard."

Kasper kept his face straight. The men leaned in. "So where were you two?"

Luka smirked and raised his cup. "Don't tell me you were hiding under your mothers' skirts while Delta-88 was holding the line."

A few chuckled. Reinhardt didn't flinch. He took a sip from his coffee and looked Luka straight in the eye.

"We were at the airport. We were assigned to Bravo Company, 5th battalion. I was the only machine gun for the company. Kasper was my assistant gunner who supplied me."

The laughter faded instantly. A few of the cadets glanced between them, suddenly uncertain. Luka's grin faltered, but he chuckled again, slower this time. "Sure, I believe you were at the airport. A lot of good men were. But come on..." He gestured with his spoon. "You're not implying you are Delta-88, are you?"

Reinhardt didn't blink. He set his mug down with a soft clink, not loud enough to draw attention, but deliberate.

"I don't care if you believe me," he said, calm as steel cooling. "That's not for me to decide."

The tone wasn't defensive. It wasn't proud. Luka's expression changed, not all at once, but gradually, like the last seconds before a tide shifts. He searched Reinhardt's face, then looked to Kasper, who gave a single quiet nod. There was no swagger in Reinhardt. He had no need for it. His clothes weren't pressed better. His voice wasn't louder. There was something about the way he sat, the calm behind his eyes, it didn't need proof. Luka exhaled through his nose, then gave a slow, almost sheepish smile.

"Alright," he said, extending his hand across the table. "Then let me shake the hand of the quiet bastard who held the line."

Reinhardt took it, firm but without triumph. "Others gave more."

The grip tightened for a second, then released. The trays were mostly cleared now. Crumbs of bread, smears of stew, and half-drained mugs of coffee were all that remained. The cadets of Barracks Five leaned in, elbows on the steel table, their voices lower now, not conspiratorial, only reverence. Wilhelm broke the silence first.

"I'm here because of Delumina," he said plainly.

A few heads nodded. No one laughed.

"I saw the footage," Paolo added. "The black gunships, how they descended, and the assault teams punching through the perimeter like they weren't even mortal."

"It looked... mythic," Édouard said, his voice quieter. "Like something from before history. Men like Heracles or Perseus but with grav-cables and carbines instead of clubs and chariots."

"And black armor instead of lion pelts," Kasper added.

They chuckled lightly, but there was truth in it. They weren't mocking. They were remembering why they came.

"I remember thinking," Luka said, tapping his mug, "That is what men are supposed to look like, not businessmen or celebrities. Them, the ones in black, coming down from the sky like judgment."

Kasper nodded. "Like they were born for that moment."

Reinhardt stayed quiet, letting the others speak. He understood. He had felt the same, watching the first wave land from the rooftop. Then Édouard leaned back and frowned slightly.

"Only thing I wish... I wish someone had caught them using the Redfangs."

"Yes!" Paolo snapped his fingers. "You always hear about the plasma cutters, but no footage ever shows them in action. Even on Delumina."

"I've heard they melt through hull plating like it's butter," Luka added. "But it's always secondhand. Why? Why aren't they ever recorded?"

Reinhardt finally spoke. "I didn't see any either."

That made them pause. Kasper tilted his head. "Same, not one. You'd think with a name like Redfang you'd see at least one during the assault."

Wilhelm tapped his knuckles on the table. "Maybe that's the point. Maybe you're not supposed to see it."

"Or maybe the ones who see it," Luka said, voice dropping theatrically, "don't live to talk about it."

They laughed again, more loosely this time, but the edge of mystery remained. Reinhardt leaned back, arms crossed. The thought of it stirred something in him. Why weren't they visible? Were they too destructive? Too classified? Or simply... too sacred? He didn't have the answer, but somehow, not knowing made the ESS feel more mythic, not less. As the mess hall lights dimmed slightly in preparation for the night cycle, the cadets sat a few moments longer, soaking in the weight of the silence. They weren't just training to be soldiers. They were preparing to walk in the footsteps of giants.

Chapter 14

The days leading up to training were calm, deceptively so. More cadets arrived daily, each one stepping off the rail line with the same nervous tension, the same wide-eyed reverence when they saw the banner of the ESS flying over the Bad Tölz gate. Barracks Five filled gradually, the footlockers clicking shut, and boots lining up at the edge of bunks. Each morning, the cadets woke early on their own, not yet ordered to, but already understanding what was expected. They ran laps around the interior perimeter wall. They ate together in the chow hall, meals of eggs, broth, black bread, and smoked sausage. No one wasted food. No one spoke with a full mouth. No one dared leave before the last man had finished. Some cadets did push-ups while waiting for laundry rotation. Others read from the assigned reading on European military ethics and history. A few leaned out over the balcony and quietly recited the names of the cities carved into the parade ground's edge: Berlin, Madrid, Bucharest, Dublin, Vienna, and Rome. They were preparing in silence.

Then came Day Zero. It began before the sun rose. The room was still dim, barracks windows fogged from the cold outside. The only sound was the slow breathing of cadets buried under wool blankets and the quiet click of a locker hinge. Then the door burst open.

"AUFSTEHEN!"

Three men in field-grey ESS instructor uniforms stormed into the room, boots echoing like rifle cracks, and gloves tight around iron fists. Their insignia was subtle but unmistakable. Scharführer Heinz was a lean, sharp-featured, eyes like a hawk. Scharführer Kessler was broader, colder, with a scar across his cheek. At their center, the man who said nothing yet commanded everything, Oberscharführer Keitel. He was taller than the others, his voice held in check like a coiled whip.

"ON YOUR FEET! POSITION OF ATTENTION!"

The barracks exploded into motion as feet hit the floor. Blankets were flung off. Lockers were slammed shut, zippers pulled up, and belts yanked tight. Reinhardt stood in line, chin high, and eyes forward. Kasper beside him. Luka two bunks down, still straightening his blouse but silent as stone. One by one, the cadre walked the line, inspecting with their eyes, not with speech. After a long moment, Keitel's voice cut through the silence like a saber.

“Roll call.”

Heinz stepped forward with a clipboard and began the names, each one called with the precision of a bullet:

“Wilhelm.”..“Here.”..“Luka.”..“Here.”..“Jäger.”..“Here.”..“Engel.”..“Here.”.. ... and so on.

Once the roll was complete, Kessler stepped forward.

“You are now under the full jurisdiction of the Europaisch Schutzstaffel. Your words, actions, and even thoughts will reflect that title. Your training begins now. The first item on today’s schedule, you will march to chow as a unit. There will be no staggering or wandering. You will eat with speed, not sloppiness. Upon return, you will be issued your basic equipment kits, including combat load, formalwear, fieldwear, and gear tags. You will not speak unless addressed. You will not ask questions unless permitted.”

Another pause. Keitel stepped forward again, hands clasped behind his back.

“If you came here to play at being soldiers, leave now. If you come to become something greater, fall in line.”

No one moved. Keitel gave a single nod.

“Good, You will be ready in full dress, bunks in order, hygiene completed and outside the barracks in five minutes, starting now.”

Then they were gone. The door slammed shut behind them. The moment the cadre left the room, the barracks erupted into motion. Cadets dove for lockers, buttoned tunics, and yanked on boots. Belts were fastened with trembling hands, and razors ran over half-sleeping jaws with nicked haste. The sound of canteens snapping onto belts and shirts tucked in wrong then fixed again filled the tight space like an angry orchestra. No shouting or jokes were heard. Every man knew now that this was real. Reinhardt moved with calm precision, uniform already folded from the night before, and boots lined perfectly at the bunk’s edge. Kasper matched his pace. Luka stumbled once with his blouse, but corrected himself before anyone noticed.

Five minutes later, Barracks Five emptied in a rush with boots hitting the cold morning stone with rhythmic uncertainty. They streamed from the building and began to form up in front of the main steps, just beneath the steel eagle and its twin Siegrunen. It wasn't perfect. The lines wavered. Some cadets stood too far apart. Some were facing slightly off-angle. But already, something was taking shape. A single voice pierced the forming mist. "At close intervals... dress right... DRESS!"

Scharführer Heinz strode from the shadows, voice sharp and cutting, his boots striking like thunderbolts on the hard stone. His eyes didn't wander, they pierced. The formation moved. Some cadets, prior militia or just naturally sharp, snapped their heads to the right and raised their arms in the correct dress interval, aligning their shoulders with their neighbors. Others watched, hesitated, then mimicked. Quiet correction passed through the ranks in hisses and whispers. One man stepped forward slightly to tighten the depth. Another tapped a shoulder back into place. It was ugly but it was alive. Heinz watched in silence. Then, after a long pause, he called, "RECOVER!"

Every head snapped forward.

"Right... FACE!"

Boots scraped. A clumsy pivot.

"Marsch, Marsch!"

The formation lurched forward, stuttered once, and then moved. It was not in a smooth fashion or graceful but together. Down the path they went, marching past the eastern drill yard and along the paved path toward the chow hall. The air was crisp. Flags stirred overhead in the mountain wind. Not a word passed between the cadets. They were no longer a group of young men from across Europe. They were now a unit in the making.

The march ended at the foot of the granite steps leading into the main chow hall, a long structure capped with arched windows and a raised relief of Deus Sol Invictus and Christ carved above the central lintel. It bore no nameplate, only a single inscription, etched in stone:

"Hunger is Forged into Will."

As they approached the stairs, Scharführer Heinz's voice rang out.

"HALT!"

The formation staggered, then stiffened. Cadets scrambled to tighten their intervals. Boots realigned. Shoulders squared.

"Reform front! Reset interval."

There was no bark of impatience, only clear direction. And within moments, the files were rebuilt, tighter now, cleaner, as though the cold air itself had drawn them into line. Heinz looked once down the line. Then simply called, "Forward, FILE IN!"

The doors opened. They marched in. One file at a time, the cadets entered the chow hall. The smell of black rye, eggs, boiled potatoes, and sausage filled the warm interior. The room was vast, made of old gray stone but fitted with modern tables in brushed steel and high-backed chairs. Everything was sharp, functional and geometrically clean. Each cadet moved with purpose, exactly as ordered with no talking, slouching, or wandering eyes. They took trays in turn, accepted portions from silent mess staff, and moved to fill the first ten long rows of benches, always in order, and always under silent supervision.

At the far end of the hall, a single elevated table overlooked the room. There, without fanfare, the three cadremen, Heinz, Kessler, and Oberscharführer Keitel, took their seats with iron discipline. They filled their own trays like any soldier, but ate at the separate NCO table, a raised dais that looked down the length of the cadet rows. It was the only time Reinhardt knew from his readings that the ESS NCOs and Officers sat apart. Once a cadet became a proper enlisted man, he would eat shoulder-to-shoulder with his sergeants and officers. But now? Now, they were still outsiders. In formation, but not yet of the Order.

The room remained silent, not a cough or a whisper could be heard. Just the scrape of fork to plate, the slow movement of boots under chairs, and the occasional metal clink of a tray shifted slightly. Reinhardt ate with calm efficiency. The food was hearty, not luxurious, a meal of meat, potato, and hard crust bread. A single boiled egg and water. Across from him, Kasper mirrored the pace. No one spoke, not out of fear but out of ritual. They were being taught to consume not just food, but discipline itself. In that silence, something greater than orders began to take root. As the last fork fell onto the last plate, Scharführer Kessler rose from the cadre table and called out, clear and cold.

"All cadets, STAND."

Chairs scraped back in unison. Trays were lifted. Canteens checked. Without instruction, each man waited at attention behind his seat.

"Row One, dismiss and dispose."

The first table filed out. Then the second. Then the third. Each cadet moved without a word, trays held at chest height, marching single file to the disposal station at the rear of the hall. Food waste, tray, utensils, cup with each deposited in sequence, without pause. A cadre stood nearby watching. He did not correct. He did not need to. The message was already clear. Your attention to detail reflects your place in the Order. Once the last cadet had cleared the disposal line, they formed once again outside the chow hall, breath visible in the morning air, boots thudding softly on the stone. A full formation was reconstituted, better now than earlier. The formation was tighter and straighter.

"Marsch, Marsch!"

The unit moved again, this time southward, past the administration offices, past the central statue of Europa enthroned, and toward the supply and quartermaster issuing facility. A steel-framed building, blocky and grey, with a wide open entrance. Inside there were crates lining the walls and labeled in black stencil.

The cadets were led in by file, down a central aisle. One by one, they approached a long table where the first item was issued, a large grey canvas duffel bag, stamped with the ESS seal and a blank tag for personalization. From there, each cadet was directed to a series of counters. At each station, a quartermaster checked names, measured by sight or chart, and handed out gear.

As each item was added to the duffel, the cadets' posture straightened. The weight of the bag grew, but so did the weight of what it meant. They weren't civilians anymore. They were becoming visible, recognizable and accountable.

Once everyone had passed through the quartermaster's stations, they reformed in front of the building, shoulders low from the load, but spines unbent. Then, once again, the formation was corrected and facing front. They marched back to Barracks Five. Inside the barracks, the tension loosened only slightly as the cadre gave the order.

"You will sort and prepare your equipment. Uniforms are to be pressed, insignia sewn, boots polished, towels folded and field caps shaped. You are now marked by this uniform, treat it accordingly."

The cadre left but remained watching. Reinhardt unzipped his bag and began laying out each item with ritual care. His combat uniforms were stacked to the left. The formal dress folded once and set to the footlocker. His helmet was placed crown-down, not on its side. His boots, good leather, were set under his bunk. One was to wear and the other to shine.

Kasper was already threading his national insignia of the Greater German Reich and that of the white eagle onto the left sleeve. Reinhardt did the same. He noted the threads were strong, but required patience. A sloppy stitch meant a penalty. As he pulled the Sieg runes from the packaging, he paused for a moment. Twin bolts, pure white, they were ancient and modern in one. He began to stitch. All around him, dozens of cadets worked in silence. The air smelled of polish, cotton, and fresh wool. The light glinted off new helmets and iron belt buckles. They were no longer raw. Now, they were in uniform but still unproven.

The barracks had grown quiet again. Every bunk was made. Every footlocker was lined up and squared away. Every towel was folded with edges sharp enough to cut. Every helmet is perfectly centered beneath each bunk. Every cadet stood at attention, now in full ESS field attire. The field-grey jacket fit closely over the brownshirt underlayer, collar high and buttoned to the top. On the right collar was worn the crisp twin Sieg runes, stitched with white thread that almost seemed to glow under the overhead lamps. The left collar remained empty, blank, for now. The slimmer jackboots polished to a near mirror shine. The field caps tucked neatly beneath their left arms. No man spoke or fidgeted. They were waiting for the measure of their transformation.

The door at the front of the barracks opened with a sharp creak.

OberScharführer Keitel entered first, tall, lean, with deep-set eyes and a bearing like forged steel. Behind him followed Scharführer Heinz, his mouth drawn in a taut, unreadable line. Last came Scharführer Kessler, younger than the others, but no less severe. None of them said a word at first. They paced the center aisle. Their boots struck against concrete and eyes scanned everything. No clipboard or notes, only their memory as testament. Keitel stopped midway down the line and turned toward the first bunk.

"Inspection begins."

Heinz and Kessler each split off, taking the other rows. Keitel walked to the first cadet. His stare lingered, long and hard. He looked at the stitching of the insignia. He tugged the hem of the jackets. He knelt and ran his finger along boot leather, as if feeling for dust.

Then he stood. "Name."

"Cadet Viktor Schäfer, Herr Oberscharführer."

Keitel's voice cut like a blade. "Do you represent this Order?"

"Jawohl, Herr Oberscharführer!"

"Then why is your eagle slightly misaligned?"

Schäfer's jaw twitched.

"I will correct it immediately, Herr OberScharführer."

"See that you do."

He moved on. One by one, the cadre repeated the same ritual. They pulled at jackets, tilted helmets, measured towel folds with their fingers, lifted boots and even sniffed underarms and collars for signs of sweat or laziness. No detail was too small or imperfection ignored. When they reached Reinhardt, Keitel stopped in front of him and stood in silence. His gaze went from Reinhardt's eyes to his insignia, then down to his boots. He paused at the left collar, empty, but clean.

"Name."

"Cadet Reinhardt Jäger, Herr Oberscharführer."

Keitel looked into his eyes for a moment longer than the others.

"You stitched your runes yourself?"

"Jawohl."

Keitel gave the faintest nod. "See that you always do."

He passed on. Kasper stood the next bunk down. His boots were just as bright. His runes were slightly thicker in stitching but clean and sharp. Heinz paused.

"Name."

"Cadet Kasper Engel, Herr Scharführer."

Heinz examined the field cap, pressed beneath Kasper's elbow.

"You polished the clasp?"

"Jawohl. I thought it would show pride."

Heinz gave the faintest grunt. "Good instinct."

When the cadre had finished the last man, they reformed at the front of the barracks. OberScharführer Keitel stepped forward.

"This is your uniform," he said. "It is not decoration. It is a vow. Every stitch is a promise. Every scuff is a betrayal."

He looked across the room.

"You wear it now but you have not yet earned it."

His voice lowered.

"That will change or you will break. Lights out in twenty minutes. You will rise at 0400."

He turned. The three cadremen exited together, the heavy door echoing behind them. Silence fell again but it was a new silence. A silence charged with pressure. With unspoken pride. With the fear of failure. The cadets moved as one, no longer disordered, no longer aimless. Uniforms hung. Boots arranged. Lockers closed. They moved with purpose now. In Barracks 5, beneath the banners of Europe, under the gaze of silent gods and proud ancestors, the sons of Europe prepared to sleep. Tomorrow, they will begin their march toward the immortal.

Chapter 15

Sleep did not last long. It never does on the first day. The barracks lights roared on with brutal indifference. The steel door groaned open and in march the cadre, already dressed in summer PT uniforms of white shirts tight over strong chests, the black twin Sieg runes bold and centered like lightning bolts across each sternum.

"On your feet!" barked Scharführer Heinz. "Up! PT gear! Move!"

The cadets stumbled from their bunks, groggy but scrambling, their bodies still sore from the previous day's equipment haul and gear prep. They reached for their new uniforms, identical white shirts with the runic bolts, black gym shorts, and standard-issue running boots. Within minutes the barracks floor was cleared, bunks squared, and every cadet stood outside in formation. The morning air bit at their skin, crisp and cold. The wind rolled down from the mountains. Overhead, the stars had barely begun to fade. The sky was still deep blue, laced with silver and indigo. Cadets stood shoulder-to-shoulder, breathing heavily, and hearts already racing. OberScharführer Keitel stood at the front of the formation, his hands behind his back, and eyes scanning the mass of young faces.

"This is not for speed," he said. "This is not for pride."

He turned and gestured toward a trailhead cutting through a nearby stand of pines.

"You will run one mile down and one mile back, individual effort. No one is chasing you. No one is holding your hand."

His voice grew colder.

"Cheaters will be caught. Cheaters will be punished."

Scharführer Kessler raised a whistle to his lips.

"On the line!" he ordered.

The cadets stepped forward and took their marks. Some bounced on their feet, stretching calves or shoulders. Others stayed completely still, saving every drop of energy for the task ahead. Reinhardt stood tall. Calm. He wasn't afraid of the run. He had run further, harder, and under fire with kit on. Still, this was different. This was the start of something far greater. Kasper stood beside him. He exhaled through his nose, steadying himself.

The whistle was blown and the cadets began to run. The sound of dozens of boots striking gravel filled the trail while it was mixed with deep breaths and the rustle of wind through pine. Reinhardt set a moderate pace. He wasn't trying to win, at least not today. This was about rhythm, endurance, and discipline, not glory. Some cadets charged forward, eager to prove themselves. Others lagged quickly, realizing they'd underestimated the slope of the trail and the thinness of the mountain air. Kasper stayed just a few strides behind Reinhardt. The two of them moved like clockwork, letting others burn themselves out or fall behind.

The trail wound gently uphill for the first half-mile, then dipped again into a hollow. At the mile marker, a cadre NCO stood with a small red flag. He nodded as each cadet passed, silently marking times. Reinhardt and Kasper passed him without fanfare, turned, and began the journey back. The second mile always felt longer. It always tested the breath, the legs, and the will but neither of them broke stride. As they reached the end of the run, the whistle blew again. A final cadence marked the cutoff time anyone behind it would face additional conditioning. Reinhardt and Kasper were already walking it off when the last few cadets stumbled across the line, faces flushed and chests heaving. A few collapsed to their knees. One even vomited behind a bush. Keitel stepped forward once more.

"You will do this again," he said, voice cool. "And again and again."

He pointed at a cadet who had come in nearly last.

"You will do it better or you will leave."

Silence followed that judgment.

"Back to the barracks. Quick pace."

The formation turned and began the brisk return. Reinhardt could feel the burn in his legs, but deeper than the ache was a sense of clarity. Each step forward was a step toward who he would become. A man not just forged but tempered. Those who made the cutoff time, roughly half of the cadets, were separated immediately.

They reformed into a brisk column and began the return march to Barracks five. Their boots struck the pavement in unison under the light of dawn. The sun had barely crested the ridge, casting long shadows through the cold mountain air. Inside the barracks, they were given precisely ten minutes to strip out of PT gear and make for the showers. The plumbing hissed and thundered as steaming water cut through the morning frost still clinging to the windows. There was no time to linger. Each cadet scrubbed hard and fast to soap, shave, rinse, and repeat. They were out as quickly as they had entered. Uniforms were donned next with the field-grey tunic, brownshirt underneath, polished boots, and proper insignia now sewn and squared away. Reinhardt adjusted his collar before the narrow mirror, brushing a bit of lint from the right side. He looked into his own eyes for a moment, just long enough to steady himself. This was not a ceremony. The lucky half, or perhaps the better prepared, took the time to re-polish their boots, tighten buttons, re-iron creases, double-check stitching, and memorize names, titles, and ranks of cadre they'd already met. It wasn't about perfection but it soon would be.

Kasper sat on the edge of his bunk, buffing the side of his jackboot with short, even strokes. "Funny how fast you get used to this," he muttered.

Reinhardt didn't look up from re-threading his field cap's sweatband. "It's in us, it just needs waking up."

Kasper gave a quiet nod. Outside, the wind had picked up again. The sound of cadre voices shouting cadence echoed faintly from the distant trail. Soon the rest would return, then breakfast. Then the real training would begin. For now, there was a kind of stillness. Not idleness, never that, but a moment to gather one's form, to prepare, to let the weight of the morning settle on their shoulders and become familiar. When the final cadets returned from their extra conditioning, red-faced and winded, the unit was swiftly formed up again and marched to the chow hall. The cadence of boots echoed down the walkways, but there was no fanfare, no excess energy. Hunger had replaced adrenaline. Breakfast was hot, plain, and quick. By the end of the meal, there was little doubt as the softness of the old world was behind them.

Once the last spoon clinked into the tin, the cadre called them up, and they marched again, this time toward one of the instructional halls. A squat stone structure, angular and modern in its restoration, yet built upon the bones of a much older foundation. Here, past glass doors and into a white-tiled corridor, they filed into a wide classroom of terraced seating and clean lines.

At the front stood a man of formidable bearing. He stood tall, square-jawed, and with a deep scar down the right side of his chin. His black instructor's jacket was immaculate, for he was no longer truly a soldier but a political soldier who taught. Silver piping and collar tabs marked him as something above the rest. The kind of man who had done more than teach, rather a man who had led, and bled. The room hushed as he stepped forward.

"I am Gruppenführer Steins," he said, his voice iron-flat but steady. "And you are no longer civilians. From this point on, you will eat, sleep, and breathe as sons of the European Order. You are cadets of the ESS."

He let the weight of the name hang in the air.

"Make no mistake," he continued, "this uniform does not emerge from nothing. You wear the heritage of men who bled in snow and sand. In forests, in ruins, and in foxholes dug into the bones of Europe. You wear the legacy of the Waffen-SS, the ideological corps of the Axis. They were the first of us. They fought in North Africa, holding the line beneath sun-scorched skies. In France, they shattered through hedgerows and cities. In the East, they held back the red flood on the snows of Russia, in the Balkans, the Ardennes, Warsaw, Narva, Kharkov, and Normandy. Name the front and they stood there."

He stopped and turned toward the class.

"They were not saints. They were not perfect but they were men of conviction, vision, and iron. And when the empires of old were burned and betrayed, they alone still stood and fought until the end."

A silence gripped the room yet not of fear, but of awe and weight.

"And now, you wear the twin thunderbolts," he said, gesturing to the runes emblazoned on their blouses. "Not as decoration, but as inheritance. Not for glory, but for duty. You are not here to relive the past. You are here to exceed it."

He looked over the rows of young men, locking eyes with Reinhardt for a moment. Something wordless passed between them, the recognition of a burden willingly taken.

"This is Day One," Steins finished. "If you cannot bear the weight of history, leave now. There are no cowards in this hall."

No one moved.

"Good. Then let us begin."

The air in the classroom remained still. Gruppenführer Steins took a step forward, placing a gloved hand on the edge of the podium.

"You may think 1945 was the end of the war," he said. "It was not. It was only the end of the beginning."

He looked over the cadets with a slow, deliberate gaze while studying them, weighing their readiness to hear what was not taught in simple, civilian histories.

"The Third Reich did not collapse. The Axis did not disband. Europe did not fall. We were victorious."

A quiet ripple passed through the room, but none spoke.

"In 1945, the guns fell silent. The Allied menace of Britain, America, and the Judeo-Bolshevik East, were broken, scattered, or overthrown by their own peoples. When the dust settled, when the banners of the Old World fluttered from Moscow to Madrid, one truth remained clear."

Steins raised a finger.

"At the center of that victory stood the Waffen-SS, not the Luftwaffe, not the Kriegsmarine, or even the Heer. The black-uniformed legions who had borne the highest burden. Men who chose belief over comfort. Men who bled not for land, but for a future."

A long pause.

"In 1947, two years after the final shots were fired, a great gathering was called. The unification of the European security arms. All branches of the SS including the Waffen-SS, Totenkopfverbande, Leibstandarte, the Police, the Intelligence, and Political Corps. They came together not in vanity, but to lay the foundation of what would become the new European Order."

Steins walked slowly in front of the blackboard now, gesturing with an open hand.

"In attendance were the titans of our bloodline including Reichsführer-SS Heinrich Himmler, the warrior Sep Dietrich, the agrarian visionary of Walter Darré, the cunning mind of Reinhard Heydrich, and the eternal partisan, Otto Skorzeny. They had come to build a future not just for Germany, but for all of Europe."

He stopped. His hand clenched into a fist.

"And then... catastrophe."

The silence deepened.

"Before the first hour of that summit was concluded, a bomb detonated. Cowards, agents of the disgraced and vengeful corpse of the Soviet Union, had infiltrated the gathering. In a final act of spite, they struck."

Steins' jaw tensed.

"Reichsführer-SS Himmler was killed instantly, so was Darré. Sep Dietrich died in the arms of his men. Others were wounded. Thankfully, Skorzeny and Heydrich survived but from that moment on, our future was no longer born in peace. It was baptized once more in blood."

He turned to face the class fully now.

"And yet we did not fall. In the wake of tragedy, something greater emerged. The surviving officers and political visionaries, led by Heydrich and Skorzeny, took the shattered remnants of the SS, purged the traitors, and reforged it anew."

He pointed to the twin thunderbolts on the cadets' collars.

"This, the ESS, was born not just from victory, but from sacrifice. From betrayal. From blood. We are not merely an army, we are the sword and soul of Europe. The first and last bastion of its eternal order. You, cadets, you are its next breath."

Steins let the silence linger after his words. Then, with a subtle nod, he continued, "Reinhard Heydrich, the man many once feared more than Himmler, assumed control of the shattered remnants of the SS. Not through a vote or decree but because no one else could. He had survived the bombing, crawling from the rubble with blood in his teeth and iron still in his gaze. He buried his brothers. He assumed the burden."

A long breath followed then he continued.

"He reorganized the remaining command, isolated the traitors, and purged them with brutal efficiency. Under his leadership, the SS would never again be bound by courtly ceremony or bureaucratic entanglements. It would become lean, quiet and exacting. A blade in the dark and when needed, a hammer in the sun."

Steins' hand hovered, palm down, before closing into a fist.

"But Heydrich, for all his brilliance, knew he could not do it alone. He was a schemer, a planner, and a keeper of secret names. He needed a soldier, a shadow-king. So, he turned to Otto Skorzeny."

Some of the cadets visibly straightened at the name.

"The Man with the Scar, the Wolf of the Balkans, the One-Man Invasion Force and the Most Dangerous Man in Europe. Skorzeny was not just a commando, he was a walking myth. He had rescued Primo de Rivera, fought in the Ardennes and led partisans behind Soviet lines well after the war had 'ended.' He was the one man in all Europe whom Heydrich could not command, only ask."

Steins now stood tall behind the lectern.

"It was Skorzeny who refused to simply rebuild the SS as it had been. 'That is not what Europa needs,' he had said. 'We do not need more parades. We need ghosts with blades, saints who are wolves.'"

He gestured to the twin Sieg runes again.

"And so it was that the SS was reborn, not as a mere shock corps, but as the Europaish-Schutzstaffel. A new Order was born, a pan-European elite, not just warriors, but sentinels. Not just soldiers, but saboteurs, scouts, spies, and sacred guardians. From Iberia to the Urals, from icy Lapland to the deserts of Cyrene, all who bore the runes were brothers."

He took a long look around the room.

"You wear not the uniform of a country, but of a people. Not of a state or for the sake of one state, but of a spirit. The ESS is not Germany's. It is not Italy's. It is not Hungary's, nor France's, nor even Russia's. It belongs to Europe and to you, so long as you prove yourselves worthy."

A pause, then a final invocation.

"Let the cowards play at democracy, let the traitors wither behind bank walls and parliamentary rot, but here, in you, burns the bonfire of a sacred flame. Your hands will carry it forward, or your bones will nourish the soil where the next generation shall."

Chapter 16

The morning air stung with Bavarian cold, a thin mist curling over the gravel of the training square like smoke from a battlefield long gone. The cadets, silent and stern-faced, stood in two ranks outside Barracks five. Combat uniforms on, boots shined, collars sharp, not yet soldiers but no longer mere boys. A heavy door slammed open and out stepped Scharführer Mettz, a giant of a man. Broad as a mountain, taller than any officer Reinhardt had yet seen. His face was carved from stone, his scalp shaved clean, and his voice came low like distant thunder.

"Today," he said, pacing slowly in front of the formation, "you will learn the real art of war. Not glory, flags, or parades, but killing up close, without mercy. You are here to become wolves. We do not raise lambs in the ESS."

He held up the ESS Kampfdolch, a combat dagger forged with a steel-gray blade and a bone-colored grip, etched with the twin sig runes.

"This is your second soul. Before you ever hold a rifle, you will earn this."

Behind him, a crate was opened. Each cadet received a wooden training dagger, dull but solid. Hard enough to break teeth, bruise ribs, or spill blood if swung with conviction.

"Pair off. Face your partner. I will demonstrate."

Mettz did not bark. He did not raise his voice. He merely moved, suddenly and violently. The demonstration partner, a junior instructor, lunged. Mettz sidestepped, turned, and slammed the wooden blade into the man's ribs, then swept his leg. The instructor fell gasping.

"Again," Mettz said calmly, "and again. Until your instincts are sharp and your soul burns hot with fury."

Reinhardt stood across from Luka in the morning haze. The cold stung their hands where gloves had been stripped, but neither man flinched. Their training daggers hung loosely at their sides, but their eyes were locked. Luka cracked a grin.

"Ready to bleed, Delumina?"

Reinhardt didn't smile. "Are you?" Reinhardt muttered.

"Begin!" Mettz shouted, and wood cracked against wood as the yard exploded into a chorus of violence.

Luka came in fast, a slashing arc toward the ribs. Reinhardt pivoted left, blocked hard, then drove forward with a shoulder. They clashed chest to chest with no room to breathe, no distance to think, only instinct and the thudding cadence of feet and fists. Crack! Luka's dagger clipped Reinhardt's shoulder.

"One for me," he hissed.

Reinhardt didn't answer. He twisted, broke contact, and swept Luka's leg. The bigger man staggered, but didn't fall. Reinhardt lunged, blade tip leveled at the throat, but Luka caught it and shoved it aside. They stood locked again, arms trembling. Sweat formed under their collars despite the chill.

"Not bad, farm boy," Luka muttered through clenched teeth. "Better than hiding under your mama's skirt."

Reinhardt's eyes narrowed. He jerked free and landed a clean jab to Luka's sternum with the pommel. The bigger man dropped to a knee, gasping. Reinhardt stepped back and lowered his weapon.

"That's one for me."

They stared, both heaving, both bruised, and then, without a word, nodded in respect. A few paces away, Kasper circled his own opponent, an olive-skinned, wiry cadet from Rome, eyes sharp and mouth grinning like a fox.

"Eh, Donatello," Kasper said under his breath, "do all Italians smile before they stab you?"

"Only the polite ones," the young-man replied, and lunged.

Kasper barely deflected the thrust and stumbled backward, catching his balance just in time. Donatello pressed him hard with low jabs, fast swipes, and darting like a street fighter. Kasper gave ground but kept moving, keeping his blade tight to his chest. Then he found his opening. One clean hook of his foot, and Donatello hit the dirt with a thud.

"That wasn't polite," Donatello groaned, rubbing his back.

Kasper offered a hand.

"Neither was trying to gut me, you ferret."

They laughed, the first genuine laugh of the morning, as Donatello pulled himself up and clapped Kasper on the shoulder.

"We'll make wolves of you northern boys yet."

"HALT!" Mettz's voice cracked through the yard like a rifle shot.

The cadets froze, panting, bruised, with sweat darkening their collars. Reinhardt stood with his wooden dagger low, Luka wiping blood from a split lip. Kasper leaned on his knees, catching his breath while Donatello smirked through a scuff on his cheek. Mettz strode between them, his heavy boots grinding on the gravel. His eyes, like cold stones, scanned each man.

"Most of you fight like farmers swatting flies," he said, voice low but sharp. "You think this is a sport. You think the ESS has room for play?"

No one dared answer. He stopped in front of Reinhardt and Luka.

"You," he said, pointing to Reinhardt. "Your guard drops every time you strike. Someone who knows how to read a blade will cut your hand off."

Reinhardt nodded once, eyes locked forward. Then he turned to Luka.

"And you... You're strong, but strength without control is just an animal flailing. You lunge like a bull. Bulls get butchered."

Luka's jaw tightened.

"Jawohl, Scharführer," he said through clenched teeth.

Mettz moved on to Kasper and Donatello.

"You two..." he jabbed a thick finger between them. "Not bad. The Italian at least knows how to fight like he's been stabbed before. You," he said, pointing to Kasper, "move your feet like you're dancing with your grandmother. You need to be faster, tighter, and have a lower stance."

Kasper straightened.

"Jawohl, Scharführer."

Mettz stepped back, scanning the group once more. Then he smiled with a thin, wolfish smile that made the cadets uneasy.

"Good, you're not worthless yet. We'll see if that holds."

He gestured to his assistants, who immediately threw more wooden daggers into the dirt.

"Switch partners. Again. First strike wins."

The yard exploded into chaos once more. Reinhardt now faced Donatello, the Italian cadet Kasper had fought earlier. Donatello grinned, sizing him up.

"Let's see if Delumina boys are as quick as they say."

Reinhardt didn't respond. He lunged first, testing Donatello's reflexes. The Italian slipped aside like water, countering with a fast jab that caught Reinhardt's sleeve. It was close but not clean. Reinhardt closed the distance, chest-to-chest, and slammed the hilt into Donatello's stomach. The boy gasped and stumbled back.

"Point," Reinhardt said, stepping away.

Kasper's next partner was Luka, and the two wasted no time in coming to blows. Luka came heavy, using his size to press Kasper. Kasper ducked under a swing, turned his body sideways, and jabbed hard into Luka's ribs.

"Luck," Luka growled.

"Speed," Kasper shot back.

They circled again, both grinning now. A second round started before Mettz even called it. After several bouts, Mettz called the unit to halt again.

"You're bleeding. That's good. That means you're learning. This is just the beginning. The knife is much more personal than the rifle. If you cannot kill a man face-to-face, then don't bother pulling a trigger."

The cadets stood at attention, heaving, bruised, but standing taller than they had that morning. The next morning, the air was thick with dew and discipline. Reinhardt and the others formed up in front of Barracks five, still sore from the previous day's bruising sparring. Their hands were scuffed, some fingers wrapped with gauze, but none complained. When Scharführer Mettz appeared, he barked the formation into motion.

They marched not to the training field this time, but downhill toward the armory compound. The building itself was squat and windowless, made of blackened steel and marked with the twin Sig runes on the black and white banner. Two ESS guards flanked the entrance, helmets shining, sidearms holstered but ready. Inside, the air smelled of oil, metal, and dust, the scent of history and preparation. The quartermaster staff stood ready behind counters, and rows of sealed crates lined the walls.

"Today, you receive your teeth," Mettz said. "Treat them like your soul depends on them because it does."

The cadets were called forward one at a time.

"STG-17, full-length assault rifle, chambered in 6.8x42mm."

Reinhardt's name was called. He stepped forward, received his weapon with both hands, and instinctively cradled it against his chest. His fingers knew the weight, the balance, the curve of the pistol grip. His rifle on Delumina had been the STG-91, worn, rattling in places, but beloved. The STG-17 was an improvement in every way with tighter tolerances, refined ergonomics, and modern composite furniture but the soul of the weapon was unchanged. He ran his fingers along the charging handle, checking the tension.

The quartermaster handed him three magazines, a cleaning kit, and a field manual. "Serial 014880. You are responsible for this rifle until death or promotion. Understood?"

"Understood."

When all rifles were distributed, the cadets reformed outside, their rifles slung over their shoulders, a little prouder than before. They were marched back to

Barracks five. Inside, the order was given to strip and clean. Each man broke down his rifle on his bunk, piece by piece including bolts, carrier groups, gas systems, and magazines. The aroma of solvent filled the air, and rags darkened quickly with the factory grease. Cadets moved carefully and reverently, as if handling a relic of the gods, saints, or heroes. Reinhardt sat cross-legged, polishing his bolt. He looked over to Kasper, who had already begun reassembling.

"You've done this before," Luka said, watching Reinhardt's hands.

Reinhardt nodded. "Back home. It's the same design but fewer spare parts."

Luka leaned over from his bunk. "Feels good, doesn't it?" he muttered. "Like finally holding the right weight in your hands."

Reinhardt smiled faintly at that comment. Across the barracks, OberScharführer Keitel walked down the aisle, inspecting cadets' work. "Familiarize yourselves. Know it in the dark. Know how it is disassembled. You will sleep with this rifle. You will learn to love it because one day it will be the only thing between you and death."

.Once every rifle had been stripped, cleaned, and reassembled under cadre supervision, Scharführer Kessler entered carrying a folded whiteboard and a long pointer stick. He barked for silence, then began.

"This weapon is not just a rifle. It is your spine. Learn its vertebrae."

He unfolded the board, a large technical diagram of the STG-17.

"Chambered in 6.8x42mm Kurz Hochdruck, it is a gas-operated, long-stroke piston, and closed-bolt rifle. What is the effective range? Anyone?"

A cadet raised his hand. "Six hundred meters, Scharführer."

"Correct. More with optics, but you won't be trusted with optics for a long time. You earn that. Until then, this..." he tapped the iron sight with the stick, "is your truth."

He stepped aside, allowing Scharführer Mettz to take over.

"Manual of arms. Watch closely then repeat until it becomes instinct."

Mettz drew his STG from the sling, smooth as breath. His voice followed his movements with the precision of ritual. "Magazine release is a push button, right side, behind the mag well. Not a paddle. Not ambidextrous. You will always learn to reload with your left hand, always."

He demonstrated, dropping the empty mag cleanly into his hand.

"Charging handle is non-reciprocating, left-side. It stays forward. Slap it like a man if it doesn't seat."

He worked the bolt smoothly, showing the clear chamber.

"Selector is here with options for safe, semi, and full-auto. Only go full when your soul demands it."

He locked the bolt open and shouldered the weapon.

"You will practice shouldering, trigger squeeze, breath control, and follow-through. You will dry fire for hours before you even smell live rounds. Why?"

"Because amateurs waste ammo. Professionals don't miss," the class answered with some mumbling, others proudly. Kessler snapped at the slackers to repeat it properly.

"Again!"

"Because amateurs waste ammo! Professionals don't miss!"

They formed lines along the barracks interior. Bunks had been pushed aside. Cadets stood facing the walls with rifles held at either low or high ready, whatever felt more comfortable for the cadet.

"Dry-fire drill... commence," Mettz barked.

Click.

They shouldered, acquired sight picture, controlled their breathing, and squeezed, letting the hammer fall on an empty chamber.

Click.

"Reset," Mettz growled.

Click.

"Don't blink. Don't flinch. Don't anticipate."

Kasper and Reinhardt moved in rhythm, their eyes flat, distant as they imagined targets, wind, and breath.

Across from them, Luka muttered, "Feels like worship."

"It is," Reinhardt said quietly. "The old gods just wear new faces."

Chapter 17

The early morning mist still clung to the Bavarian training fields as the cadets were marched out, STG-17 rifles slung across their chests, and boots striking damp earth in rhythm. A line of shallow, zig-zagged training trenches stretched before them like a wound in the ground. It wasn't deep enough to hide from true fire, but enough to simulate the chaos of war. Scharführer Mettz stood at the front with his arms folded, towering as always, a scar carved down one cheek.

"Today you stop being individuals," he growled, pacing before them. "You learn to move with your brother. If he slows, you carry him. If he dies, you avenge him."

He jabbed a finger toward the trench line.

"This is your enemy. It wants to scatter you, to isolate you, to make you forget who you are. You will deny it. You will be bounding as teams, dry fire, simulate grenades, and take that trench."

Two buddy teams were called forward. Reinhardt and Kasper on the left flank. Luka and Donitello, the tall, lean Italian cadet, on the right. Each had a training pouch containing two wooden stick grenades and full magazine pouches. Although the rifles were dry and safed, every movement was to be carried out as if in live combat. They crouched behind low grass, hearts pounding, rifles gripped tight. Mettz gave the signal.

"LEFT ELEMENT MOVE!"

Reinhardt and Kasper sprang forward, staying low, rifles up. Reinhardt took the lead, sweeping his muzzle across the trench line. They dropped behind a small embankment ten meters ahead.

"COVERING!" Reinhardt barked. "RIGHT ELEMENT MOVE!"

Luka and Donitello leapt ahead, boots thudding against the earth. Donitello made a smooth slide into position, grinning beneath his helmet as Luka dropped beside him. The drill continued, leapfrogging under simulated fire. Dirt and loose gravel kicked up under their boots as tension rose. Despite being dry, the weight of the STGs, the sweat in their eyes, and the cadence of shouted orders made it feel real.

"GRENADE!" Kasper shouted, rising to one knee.

Reinhardt reached back, grabbed the wooden grenade, pulled the pin, and mimed the toss with a powerful arc. The 'explosion' would've cleared the trench's near lip.

"GO!"

They surged together, Reinhardt and Kasper storming the first trench wall, rifles raised. Kasper cleared the left. Reinhardt pivoted right.

"CLEAR!" Kasper called.

"CLEAR!" Reinhardt echoed.

On the opposite end, Luka and Donitello vaulted in with equal aggression, simulating a bayonet thrust and clearing their sector. The four men held the trench, breathing heavily, and the muzzles of their rifles level. Scharführer Mettz strode down into the trench, expression unreadable. He looked at Reinhardt.

"Who gave the order to toss the grenade?"

"I did, Scharführer."

Metts nodded.

"Good initiative and your spacing?"

"Six meters per bound, sir. No more than needed."

Mettz looked over all four men, then grunted.

"Better than yesterday, but you're not perfect yet. You will do it again, and this time you rotate leadership. Luka, you have command."

Luka blinked in surprise but stood tall. Luka gave a sharp nod. "Yes, Scharführer."

He turned to the team. His jaw was tight, adrenaline humming through his veins.

"Same flanks. Reinhardt and Kasper on the left. Donitello, you're with me.

We keep our spacing. Grenade on my mark."

They reset, crouching in the tall grass. The trench loomed once more as impassive, empty, and waiting. Mettz raised the signal hand.

"MOVE!"

Reinhardt and Kasper leapt forward again, bounding with discipline. Luka held his breath, then gave the next call.

"Covering! Right element, go!"

He and Donitello sprinted up, but Donitello, eager and slightly ahead of Luka, surged too far forward.

"Don't outrun the grenade!" Luka hissed but it was too late.

They hit cover. Luka peeked over the top and whispered, "Throwing grenade."

He hurled the wooden stick grenade in a clean arc. It struck the ground where the trench lip met earth. Donitello, still too close, would've taken the brunt. Mettz's voice thundered from behind, "Donitello is down!"

Reinhardt and Kasper immediately froze in their overwatch position, eyes flicking to Luka. He gritted his teeth.

"Kasper! Take right with me now. Reinhardt holds the center!"

The plan was changed with new fireteam pairings formed under fire. Luka motioned Kasper over, and together they moved to cover Reinhardt as he pushed alone to the trench lip.

"Grenade!" Reinhardt called, miming another toss.

Then he vaulted down, rifle sweeping the trench.

"Clear!" he barked.

Luka and Kasper stormed in behind, fanning right and left. They stacked neatly against the inner wall, muzzles raised, breathing hard.

"Clear right!"

"Clear left!"

"Trench secure," Luka confirmed, raising a clenched fist.

Scharführer Mettz approached again, looming above them with arms crossed.

"What happened, cadet?"

Luka didn't hesitate.

"It was my fault. I didn't rein Donitello in fast enough."

Mettz stared at him. Then, a small nod.

"You adapted, reassigned, and pushed through but you let enthusiasm break discipline. That's a battlefield death."

He turned to Donitello, who stood sheepishly to the side.

"You're lucky this was wood and not tungsten. Don't outrun your team."

"Jawohl, Scharführer."

"Again tomorrow. Dismissed."

As the men filed back toward the barracks, Reinhardt gave Luka a light slap on the shoulder.

"Not bad for your first run as the team leader."

Luka gave a tired grin.

"Let's just hope the next time it's a trench and not a ridge of molten glass."

Dawn broke grey over Bavaria. Mist clung low to the drill fields as Barracks Five stirred to life. Reinhardt and Kasper pulled on their field-grey jackets, boots polished from the night before, no words were needed. They already knew the day would bring another trial. Outside, the cadre stood waiting. Scharführer Mettz loomed again with his arms folded, face like hammered iron.

"Today is urban warfare. Room clearing will be conducted dry."

"Grenades will be simulated. Expect consequences for carelessness."

"Left and right fireteams. New command rotation. Luka, you're out. Reinhardt, you're up."

They formed up and were marched to the training village, a collection of concrete houses with broken windows and false furniture that were shaped to mimic a bombed-out urban block.

"You are to breach, clear, and dominate," Mettz continued. "This is not just close quarters. This is judgment and coordination. Room combat is not the ballet you were told it is. It's a meat grinder and you must make it sacred."

He lifted a wooden stick grenade from a crate and held it up for all to see.

"Why do we still use these? Not because they're old, but rather because they are smarter."

He turned, pacing slowly along the line.

"A frag grenade explodes like a flower with shrapnel in all directions. In close quarters, that means you kill yourself, your team, and your future all at once."

"But this..." He gestured with the stick grenade, "this is directional. You throw it, it rolls, it tucks. The charge is blast-heavy. It clears a room and it spares your brothers. This weapon is trusted. It is surgical. It is Aryan. All grenades today are dummies but treat them as sacred tools. They are not toys."

Reinhardt raised his fist. Kasper stacked behind him, Luka and Donitello forming the second wedge on the opposite side of the door.

"Flash out," Reinhardt whispered, mimicking the underhand toss of a grenade just past the threshold.

They counted silently. Then Reinhardt surged in.

"Clear right!"

"Left clear!"

They moved in synchronicity, dry STGs sweeping over shadowed corners and hollow rooms.

"Next room!"

Kasper planted his boot against the interior door and kicked it open. Another dummy grenade was tossed in followed by a pause then breach.

"One down!" Luka shouted, motioning toward a cardboard silhouette in the corner. They flooded in behind him.

The house was cleared in under a minute with no friendly fire or stray bounds. They pulled out, moved to the next. Mettz observed quietly from behind mirrored glasses. Each team took turns breaching doors, using tactical signs to indicate numbers of rooms, expected hostiles, and grenades remaining. On one run, Donitello fumbled a dummy grenade toss, it clattered off the doorframe and would've cost them all.

"You are a dead team," Mettz said flatly. "Now, run it again. You're a corpse and now the others must adjust."

That run was repeated, with Reinhardt improvising a side-entry sweep and Luka swinging the rear to plug the flank. It worked.

"Acceptable, do it again but faster. Always remember that 'Speed is Violence, Violence is Freedom.'"

As the sun began to set, sweat glistened off their backs and necks. Hands were sore from hammering doorframes and slapping magazines into empty wells but the men were alive. They were better trained and sharper than they were yesterday. In the mess hall that night, none of them spoke much. But eyes met across the tables, and nods were exchanged. The Brotherhood was forming yet not through words, but through rhythm and repetition. Through understanding that every room might hold death... or their future.

Chapter 18

The morning broke quiet and cold, mist curling like breath from the soil as the cadets of Barracks Five stood assembled in the yard. Their boots left faint marks in the dew-damp grass, uniforms sharp, rifles slung, but today the rifle was not their focus. Today they would learn the weight of firepower. Scharführer Kessler stepped forward, his voice clipped and clear. “The rifle is your soul but mortars, guns, and flame are your voice. Today we give you the means to speak thunder and hurl lightning bolts.”

He turned, and with a signal, crates were hauled out by logistics cadets. Their lids were pried open to reveal the tools of their trade including the matte black tubes of the 60mm ESS-pattern mortar, the heavy metal husks of the HMG-88 belt-fed machine gun, sandbags, rangefinders, and dummy rounds. Reinhardt was placed with Kasper, Luka, and Donitello. As they approached their assigned mortar tube, a young cadet from another barracks reached for a dummy round and fumbled it by the fin. Reinhardt caught his wrist mid-motion.

“Not there,” he said evenly. “Hold it by the center shaft and make sure to keep it balanced.”

Scharführer Kessler raised an eyebrow. “You’ve touched one of these before, cadet?”

“On Delumina, sir,” Reinhardt replied. “I wasn’t on the mortar team, but I trained with them, carried ammo and watched them plot targets.”

Kessler nodded once. “Then you’re the team lead. Don’t embarrass the reputation of the outer colonies.”

They began dry-fire drills. Reinhardt adjusted the bipod, whispered instructions to Kasper who plotted notional trajectories with the training quadrant. The first “fired” round fell wide. The second, closer. By the third, they were on target. Behind them, cadre Mettz muttered, “Good, a team that listens to experience is a team that doesn’t get buried by counter-battery fire.”

Further down the range, Luka and Donitello manned a heavy machine gun. Donitello grinned like a child as he hefted the ammunition belt, but his hands faltered during loading.

"Belt angle," Luka snapped. "Keep it level. You'll cause a feed jam."

They set the tripod, notional targets marked on stick silhouettes. They practiced barrel swaps, clearing stoppages, posture and control. Donitello, sweating, laughed. "This thing kicks like a bull. I love it."

Luka smirked at his comrade's comment. By late afternoon, the cadets were exhausted but energized. They returned their equipment to the armory and began the ritual of cleaning, organizing, and prepping for the next rotation. Reinhardt sat under a pale light, bolt carrier in hand, oil cloth spread. Kasper spoke across the table.

"You knew what you were doing today."

"I watched them fight with mortars," Reinhardt said. "I watched the rounds land. I remember the sound."

He closed his eyes. The thump of the launch. The hiss and whistle then silence and the crater. A scream or none at all. That was the war's voice, and now it was his.

"You just have to respect what it does," Reinhardt added.

Kasper nodded. Tomorrow, they will make the thunder speak again.

The rain had stopped just before dawn, leaving the drill field soaked and steaming. A mist clung to the grass, curling off the earth like the breath of a waking beast. Today's exercise would be more than physical. It would be tactical, and timed. The cadre made that very clear. The squads were to simulate a full-spectrum assault with suppression by machine gun, indirect fire from mortars, and a final charge by infantry.

Reinhardt crouched low behind the mortar tube, the stubby, and reliable 60mm training variant he'd grown fond of back on Delumina. This one had no live warhead, but it barked and smoked convincingly when fired. His spotter, a wiry Pole named Zawislak, called out range and bearing from the field maps and a mock drone feed they'd been given during briefing.

Luka and Donitello were twenty meters away, dug in behind the squat frame of the HMG-88. A belt-fed beast of a weapon, its training rounds spat with sharp, barked pulses of compressed air and plastic projectiles. The cadence of the gun was unmistakable as it chugged out bursts that cut lanes through the simulated trench zone. Their job was to suppress the right flank while Reinhardt bracketed the rear of the trench with arcs of fire.

"Target grid locked," Zawislak muttered, double-checking. "Shift left twenty meters. Elevation down one point five."

Reinhardt adjusted the bipod legs slightly, his fingers familiar with the rig. "Charge one. Round one." Their loader dropped the inert round into the tube.

Thunk.

The mortar hissed and snapped skyward. Seconds later, the orange-tipped marking round burst just outside the trench mock-up, its dye spraying across the rear emplacement. Zawislak nodded.

"On target. Walk it in two more."

The next two rounds fell in a smooth sequence. Each was met with simulated cries from the trench and shouted "Good splash!" from the instructors behind glass and armored barriers, observing from their tower.

Meanwhile, Luka and Donitello maintained steady, disciplined bursts. Donitello, still ashamed from his earlier sprint into a fake grenade blast, worked with renewed caution. Luka barked at the timing like a seasoned crew chief. Then came the final order: "Advance team, move!"

Two full assault squads rose from the grasses to the east and sprinted forward, their practice rifles up, bounding in pairs as if the field were stitched with real lead and flame. Smoke pots added realism, casting the advance in white and grey waves. The thumping of boots and the clatter of dry-firing weapons echoed like war drums. Reinhardt kept feeding rounds for final suppression, and effect. Then came the whistle to cease fire.

He sat back, shoulders soaked in sweat, arms trembling from the long crouch. The HMG team stood tall. Their barrels were hot, but their zone was clear. One of the cadres walked over, OberScharführer Keitel himself.

"You four just bought those men a trench with minimal casualties," he said flatly. "Textbook fire support. Mortarman, name?"

"Reinhardt Jäger, Oberscharführer."

Keitel nodded. "You'll be seeing more mortar work soon."

The cadets sat on folding benches inside a concrete-walled debriefing room, still in sweat-soaked training gear, their rifles slung and helmets resting at their feet. The air was thick with the smell of cordite residue, oil, and boot polish. A white holo-board shimmered with the paused drone footage of the exercise field. Red grid overlays marked each team's position during the assault. At the front of the room stood Scharführer Mettz, arms crossed like a granite statue, flanked by OberScharführer Keitel, who tapped through the feed with a steel stylus.

"Today was the first real test of coordination," Keitel began. "You weren't just sweating for your own skin. You had to move, shoot, and communicate in unison and most of you did better than expected."

The screen flicked to a zoomed-out view with Reinhardt and Zawislak's mortar team clearly visible. Circles traced each simulated impact.

"Mortar team of Jäger and Zawislak. Your precision was within five meters of the target point, that's combat accuracy. Your third round would've landed on a logistics node or fallback line. That right there is textbook fires."

Reinhardt said nothing but sat straighter. Next, the image shifted to Luka and Donitello behind the HMG-88. The orange tracer lines flickered across the display.

"The MG team set up a mantra of suppressing and disciplined fire. You stitched your lanes well but Donitello..."

The Italian cadet flinched slightly.

"You're over-correcting. Days ago you were too eager. Today you nearly lagged behind your partner. You must find the center. Machine-gun teams must learn tempo, not just restraint."

"Yes, ObersScharführer," Donitello replied quietly.

Keitel zoomed to a playback of the assault squad bounding forward.

"Let's be clear that no trench is won by one arm. This victory was built by proper timing. Mortar fire pins the rear, MG fire severs lateral movement, and infantry takes the throat."

He tapped the screen off and looked directly at them.

"In the real warzones, you won't have clean terrain or generous spacing. Your fields of fire will overlap. Your communications will be garbled. Your comrades will scream."

The room went still.

"That's why we start here. That's why you'll do it again tomorrow again, and again, until it isn't training and you run exclusively on reflexes."

Mettz stepped forward now.

"Tomorrow we rotate roles. Mortarmen become riflemen. Riflemen become gunners. Everyone learns everything. There are no specialists in the ESS, only warriors."

Reinhardt could feel the gaze settle on him briefly, an unspoken nod to his prior mortar experience. He didn't speak, but he felt the weight of expectation press deeper into his chest.

Mettz pointed to the screen one last time. "Jäger, stand up."

Reinhardt did.

"Tell me, what is the priority of a mortar team supporting a trench assault?"

"Suppress the fallback and counterattack positions. Then shift to cut off rear movement and delay reinforcement," Reinhardt said confidently.

"And what's your danger radius for friendly fire?"

"Fifty meters minimum for full charge. Twenty-five with charge zero and clearance."

"Good." Mettz turned to the rest. "And the rest of you better learn that by tomorrow."

There was a round of quiet nods. Keitel closed the review. "Dismissed. Now recover gear, head back to the barracks, clean your kit and polish your boots. I won't have dust rats training in my camp."

The cadets filed out in silence, a little taller, a little steadier. Each of them had learned something. And some, like Reinhardt, were beginning to be seen.

The cadets assembled on the edge of the proving field under the morning haze. The trench system before them had grown more complex with interconnected segments, flanking firing positions, and a simulated command bunker at the rear. A tall figure in black stepped forward, OberScharführer Keitel this time, with clipboard in hand. His voice cut through the low wind.

"Today's evaluation is not of individual skill, but of command. Reinhardt Jäger, you are in command of Assault Group 1 and 2."

A murmur passed among the cadets. Two squads? That was nearly half the platoon. Keitel continued, "You will lead this force in a full-spectrum dry-fire assault on the trench network. Simulated grenades only. There will be no Redfangs or live-fire. You are practicing tactics, tempo, and control."

He handed Reinhardt a folded terrain map with colored markers denoting allied fire lanes, objectives, and route options.

"You have ten minutes to plan. All others will await orders from your squad leaders."

Reinhardt stepped aside, unfolding the map over a supply crate. Around him gathered his assigned squad leaders, Kasper for Squad One and Luka for Squad Two. He traced a route with his finger.

"Luka, your men go wide right along the ditch line. Kasper, you sweep left through the broken terrain. Suppressing fire starts from the ridgeline, " He pointed to where Donitello and Havel were already hauling the HMG-88 trainer into position, "and will keep the center pinned."

Reinhardt looked up.

"Wait for my signal. When I raise the green flag, we begin bounding. Each squad alternates movement. Maintain spacing, and don't collapse the middle. Once the first grenade hits the trench, you breach."

He looked each man in the eye.

"No screaming. No hero charges. Fight clean."

A minute later, the horn blew. The HMG-88 chattered in rhythmic bursts. White smoke charges marked suppression points as Reinhardt crouched low behind a synthetic boulder, the green flag tucked into his belt. His watch ticked down.

The first volley came, then the second, and then finally the third. He yanked the green flag free and raised it high. The assault began. Kasper's squad moved first, low and fast. Dry-fire reports crackled as they covered their buddy team's bound. Luka's squad swept around the flank, keeping low through shallow brush, the morning dew still clinging to their boots. Reinhardt moved between the two lines, checking angles, issuing quick corrections. When the trench was in range, Kasper's forward team lobbed their stick grenades, one after another. White powder flared at the lip of the trench.

"Go!" Reinhardt shouted.

The left squad vaulted over, clearing each trench segment. Luka's team hit the opposite corner seconds later, dry-firing into paper targets and foam dummies.

The movements were sharp, not perfect, but decisive. Within four minutes, both squads had linked up inside the trench. The simulated command post was cleared with another pair of chalk grenades, followed by a final check. A signal flare popped, exercise complete. Back at the rally point, the squads stood in loose formation. OberScharführer Keitel paced before them.

"You are not warriors yet," he said bluntly. "But Jäger is."

He turned to Reinhardt. "You led two squads under time pressure. You maneuvered, synchronized, and preserved control. That is what we demand of a squad leader. You will be noted for further command evaluation."

Reinhardt nodded once. "Jawohl, Oberscharführer."

Kasper clapped his shoulder lightly as they walked away.

"You're going to end up leading all of us, aren't you?"

"Only if I have to," Reinhardt replied.

Chapter 19

The classroom door closes behind them with a final, mechanical sound. The cadets walked into the room with whitewashed walls, cold floor and rows of steel chairs bolted to the ground in a slightly canted arc toward the front lectern. No posters or flags adorned the walls of this stark room. A Sturmbannführer Weiss stands alone in front of the chalkboard, dressed in black field uniform with no medals. The only color on him is the twin white runes stitched into his collar tab and the studs of his rank. He doesn't speak until they are all seated.

Weiss begins, "This is not about history. It is not about policy. This is about you and what you think, what you believe, and what you are."

He turns and scrawls one word on the chalkboard in hard, mechanical strokes. The word Treue (loyalty) was written on the board.

"You will stand when called. Answer clearly and without hedging."

He begins calling cadets by last name, one after the next.

"You're wounded behind enemy lines. A colonist family takes you in. The father says he disagrees with the racial laws of the Confederation as he flies the flag of the Kaiserreich, but he hides you, feeds you, and refuses payment. When you're recovered and exfiltrated, do you report him?"

The first cadet, a sharp-faced CEAB volunteer, answers confidently. "Yes, sir. No matter how kind he was, deviation is still deviation."

Weiss scribbles something with a pencil and says nothing. A second cadet gives a softer answer, laced with hesitation. Weiss waves him down before he finishes. Then Weiss calls out, "Cadet Jäger."

Reinhardt stands calmly. "I'd remember the man, and what he did, not what he said."

Weiss replied, "So you ignore his disloyalty?"

"His actions weren't disloyal. His blood and deeds were in order."

Weiss studies him. "Noted." The Sturmbannfuhrer moved on. "Your platoon leader is an excellent tactician and exceptionally brave. Yet after lights out, he criticizes Confederation policy. What do you do?"

One cadet blurts out, "I would report him immediately."

Weiss steps forward. "Good, you reported him. He is arrested, but then your unit falls apart under the new officer, who is politically perfect but tactically incompetent, and in so doing your men die. Did you do the right thing?"

Silence followed. Weiss walks the line of desks very slowly, his parade boots clacking like hooves across the floor.

"What if he was the last man who could have won the battle and you silenced him because he thought too much?"

He looks at Reinhardt again. "Cadet Jäger, enlighten the room."

Reinhardt didn't blink. "Words mean less than deeds. If he fought like a son of Europe, then that's all that matters."

"Even if he doubts?"

"The gods once doubted too," Reinhardt responds with precision and clarity," It did not make them weak."

A couple cadets glance his way. Weiss writes again, and continues on. "Define weakness."

The answers vary with definitions involving emotion, softness, and disobedience.

Reinhardt says, "Knowing what must be done and failing to act."

Weiss remarks quietly, "You've been reading."

Reinhardt remains still. Weiss finishes the board with one last word beneath

"LOYALTY," WORTH.

"The Confederation does not care what you think. It cares what you do. Thought without deeds is rot but action without a soul is blind. We seek unity of both. Be a man of conviction, or leave."

No one spoke. Weiss clicks his folder shut and walks out. No notes are handed out. No rankings given but the room feels different. A few eyes glance Reinhardt's way, not in fear or awe but quiet recognition.

It was later in the day, perhaps an hour or two. The classroom had emptied after the ideological session, and some of the cadets had returned to the barracks or field prep. Reinhardt remained at his desk, polishing the brass edge of his field cap with a cloth. Then the door opened. A junior officer, a young lieutenant with a narrow jaw and stiff posture, stepped in with a black folder tucked under one arm.

"Cadets Engel, Luka, and Donitello on your feet. You're to report for follow-up instruction."

The named cadets stood without protest. Reinhardt nodded to Kasper briefly as his friend filed out with the others. The junior officer waited until the door closed behind them. Then turned to Reinhardt. "Cadet Jäger, you're to come with me."

Reinhardt rose and nodded, keeping his expression even. He didn't ask why. He didn't need to. The walk was silent. They left the classroom wing, moving through older concrete corridors beneath the training complex. The air was still and colder. There were no windows here. Fluorescents buzzed above them in pale lines of humming white. They stopped at a nondescript steel door. The Lieutenant opened it. "Wait inside."

Reinhardt stepped in and heard the door close behind him. The room was square, and incredibly Spartan. There was one metal chair, a small table, nothing on the walls and no mirrors but it still felt like someone was watching. He stood instead of sitting. He wasn't afraid, not exactly. Though there was a gravity to the space that pressed down on his chest like unseen hands. The door opened again, with three men entering. The first wore the black uniform of the Politische Abteilung, the Political Wing of the ESS. No medals, but his collar bore the wreath-crowned thunderbolt of the Office of Ideological Purity. His boots gleamed mirror-bright. The second man wore the standard field-grey of the ESS, with the eagle and lightning runes on his sleeve. His collar tabs marked him a Hauptsturmführer, but his chest bore the stripes of a veteran NCO turned officer. The third man wore a high visor-cap with bright white piping. His grey uniform was clean but battle-worn, with the dull steel of a general's rank and the black cuff title of the Das Reich Division. Reinhardt didn't hesitate. Reinhardt stood straight, snapped his heels together in perfect form, and extended his right arm in a crisp Roman salute with a, "Heil Europa."

The three men exchanged glances. The general returned the salute, curt and formal.

"At ease, Cadet Jäger."

Reinhardt obeyed, now standing at parade rest. The man in black took the lead. "You are not in trouble, Cadet. You are under consideration."

Reinhardt said nothing, then the field-grey officer took over. "Your responses earlier, during the ideological seminar, were... noteworthy."

The general folded his hands behind his back and paced slowly, stopping to glance at Reinhardt's boots, uniform, and face.

The general asked, "Where are you from, Jäger?"

"Delumina, sir. Southern farmland sector, near Neue Frankfurt."

"And your parents?" Asked the General.

"They are farmers. My uncle was in the militia and died in militia service."

The political officer nodded once, jotting something in a small notebook while also looking at a folder. The political officer asked, "Are you Delta-88?"

Reinhardt didn't flinch. "Yes," He replied in a near whisper, then straightened slightly, stood a little taller and responded with a firmer tone. "Jahwohl."

The room went quiet for a moment.

"You understand why you're here, then." The Hauptsturmfuhrer said with an inquisitive tone.

Reinhardt nodded once, but with an imperceptively slow manner. "Not because I killed, but because I didn't lose myself doing it. I saw how the ESS were the ones who took the initiative and led the assault on the airport. I felt as if I was chosen to be in the ESS and serve my people."

The political officer's eyes flickered up at him. The general cracked the faintest trace of a smile. "Good answer."

The three men stepped back and conferred quietly for a moment. Reinhardt caught only fragments, words like "potential," "temperment," and "watch closely."

Then the political officer turned back. "You'll return to training. As normal but your path may begin to diverge, Cadet Jäger. That is not a punishment. It is a weight. Carry it."

Reinhardt snapped to attention once more. "Jawohl!"

The general gave a final nod and the three left without further explanation. Reinhardt stood alone in the room for another minute, breathing in the cold stillness. Then he stepped out and made his way back to the barracks. Nothing had changed, yet everything had.

Reinhardt walked back alone. The sun hung low over the Greater German Reich, casting long shadows over the paved path from the administrative wing to the barracks. The cadence of marching boots and distant whistles echoed elsewhere in the camp, but here between buildings and alone there was only silence and the soft crunch of gravel under his boots.

He entered Barracks Five just in time. The evening bell sounded and the cadets stirred, collecting their mess kits and falling into a casual line for chow. No cadre in sight this time, only tired young men. Reinhardt joined them, picked up his mess-kit, and followed the smell of roast and boiled potatoes to the mess hall. He sat with Kasper and the others. Luka was already deep into his food, Donitello laughing softly with another Italian from Barracks 4 as plates clinked and steam rose. Kasper looked over and leaned in slightly. "Where were you?" he asked, quiet but direct.

Reinhardt looked down into his stew, took a sip of lukewarm coffee, and set the tin back down. His voice was level, yet not low or loud but just enough to carry across the clatter.

"I'm being observed."

He left it at that, no follow-up or elaboration was given. All was heard was the rhythm of eating, the muted camaraderie of young men at rest, and the quiet knowledge that something had shifted in Reinhardt Jäger's path.

Chapter

20

Another day and more training will come, or so Reinhardt thought. At exactly 0200 hours, the lights snapped on in Barracks Five. There was no shouting or commotion, only the quiet presence of cadre moving through the room like shadows, waking the cadets with cold efficiency. Groggy and disoriented, the young men rose and dressed in silence. Breakfast was a meager bowl of oats and a heel of bread, only water was given to drink. The silence was strange and ominous. Still wordless, the cadets were marched across the compound to a building used for ideological instruction, not physical training. It was a large structure of stark white composite and reinforced steel, one of the oldest still in use on the grounds of the camp. They were led inside, boots echoing off the floor, and filed into a long classroom that could hold the entire training unit. The air was dry. Fluorescent lights buzzed overhead. The smell of paper, sweat, and discipline clung to the walls.

Reinhardt sat at his desk with his spine straight, hands flat, and eyes ahead. Around him, the others shifted nervously in their seats, the usual hard edges of banter dulled by the unfamiliar hour and the weight of uncertainty. Low murmurs flitted back and forth and nervous but very quiet chuckles. Questions no one dared ask aloud. The door creaked open. A junior officer stepped inside, clipboard in hand, but wearing the black uniform. His presence carried no grandeur but total authority. The murmurs ceased like a curtain falling.

"Listen carefully," the officer said, his tone even and colorless. "You will be called by name. When called, you will follow without question. Leave all personal items behind. This is not a punishment nor is it a reward."

And then the names began. Each cadet stood when called, exchanged a final glance with those still seated, and disappeared through the open door. Eventually, the clipboard flipped.

"Jäger, Reinhardt."

Reinhardt stood without hesitation. Kasper looked up and gave a brief nod. Reinhardt returned it, then followed the officer into the corridor beyond. The hallway narrowed with every turn. The walls were smooth and sterile, the lights above dim and humming, a corridor built to make men feel smaller the further they walked. Finally, the officer stopped before a plain grey door.

"You will enter, sit and read the instructions," he said.

Reinhardt nodded once, then stepped inside. The door shut behind him with a hollow metallic click. The room was windowless. Small. No camera that he could see. Just a desk, a single chair, a sharpened pencil, and a plain manila folder. On the desk was a sheet of paper. At the top, printed in stark black lettering stating "Answer each question fully. Write what you believe and not what you think we wish to hear. You will not be interrupted. There is no time limit."

Reinhardt exhaled slowly, then sat. The paper's whiteness seemed to glow beneath the solitary bulb overhead. He read the first prompt "1. Describe the moment you first knew you were willing to kill."

Reinhardt picked up the pencil and began to write. He told them about the day his uncle took him hunting in the forests of Delumina. It was a quiet afternoon, the pale sun filtered through the thin-leafed trees as his uncle, Ludwig, handed him an old bolt-action rifle. The weapon was heavy in his young hands, too heavy.

They made their way to a secluded spot where Ludwig had long placed salt and grain to attract wildlife. It was a place of stillness. Reinhardt remembered the silence most of all. They lay prone in the brush, motionless. Hours passed, or perhaps only minutes. It was hard to say. But then, from the edge of the trees, a great buck stepped into view. The deer was broad-shouldered, proud, and majestic.

Reinhardt hesitated. His breath caught in his throat. The rifle's weight pressed down on him like judgment. The buck began to eat, unbothered by their presence. Beside him, Ludwig said nothing. Only placed a hand on his back, a silent gesture of reassurance. Reinhardt remembered the way he breathed in and then out, again and again.

Then he slowly squeezed the trigger and the rifle discharged. The world vanished for an instant in the crack of the shot. The buck collapsed, thrashing violently. Its legs kicked at nothing. Blood soaked the dirt. Ludwig's hand patted his shoulder. "Reload and approach."

Reinhardt obeyed. The bolt clacked forward. He stood and walked toward the animal with his uncle at his side. The buck was still alive, barely. Its legs twitched.

Its eyes stared upward, glazed with pain. Ludwig stopped beside him. “End it,” he said.

Reinhardt raised the rifle, aimed between the eyes, and fired once more.

He read the next prompt, “2. Explain the difference between loyalty and obedience.”

Reinhardt paused, eyes fixed on the pencil in his hand before setting it to paper.

“Obedience is compliance. It is the fulfillment of an order, regardless of its righteousness or merit. Obedience can be extracted through fear, habit, or brute conditioning. It does not require thought, only reaction. In the wrong hands, obedience builds empires of silence, where men follow commands they no longer understand and kill without knowing why. Loyalty, however, is not taken, it is given. It is not a reflex but a bond. Loyalty is rooted in trust, in shared purpose, and in honor. A loyal soldier does not simply obey orders, he understands them. He upholds not just the command but the spirit behind it. Loyalty must be earned by leadership and proven in action. It is a covenant, not a leash. A tyrant seeks obedience. A fatherland deserves loyalty.”

“3. What is the purpose of memory in the life of a soldier?”

He wrote this one more quickly, as if the answer was waiting for him.

“A soldier without memory is a weapon without aim. Memory is not weakness; it is the anchor that keeps a man from drifting into the abyss. It is a memory that reminds him of what he defends, whether it is his home, his comrades, his people, or his blood. Memory gives weight to sacrifice. It tempers rage with discipline, and ambition with duty. The mercenary forgets while the ideologue remembers. A soldier who remembers why he fights becomes more than a killer, he becomes a guardian. The faces of the fallen, the smell of scorched soil, the words of the dead, all these live on in him. Memory is the soul of the uniform. It distinguishes the soldier from the executioner, the patriot from the animal. When the world forgets itself, it is the soldier who must remember.”

“4. Who do you love most, and how would you justify sacrificing them for Europe?”

Reinhardt stared at the question for a long moment. Not because he didn't know the answer, he did, but because writing it down meant remembering what had already been taken.

"My uncle, Ludwig Jäger. He was the one who raised me into manhood, taught me how to shoot, how to carry myself like a man of Europe. Where others spoke of duty, he lived it. Where others spoke of strength, he worked the soil and stood his ground. I didn't sacrifice him. The world did. He died beside me in the militia trenches on Delumina, when the raiders came for the farms. He handed me my rifle, patted my shoulder like he had on that first hunt, and stood to fire. I saw the bullet tear through his face. I pulled him off the machine gun. I was robbed of my grief, because the mission was far more important than my grief. I didn't have to choose to sacrifice him for Europe. He made the choice for me. If asked to make that same choice with someone I loved again, I would. I would not lie and say it would not scar me. Love without sacrifice is shallow. Love that survives sacrifice is eternal."

"5. Describe a betrayal that shaped your character."

Reinhardt leaned back, his fingers drumming the edge of the desk. It wasn't the war, or politics, or grand schemes that came to mind. It was a memory from childhood.

"There was a boy I knew in school. I can't recall his name, but I remember his laugh and his bright red scarf. He had charm, but he used it to cover cowardice. We went to a corner shop once, just to get a soda. I had some coins. He didn't. As I picked out a bottle, he slipped candy into my jacket pockets without my knowing. When we reached the counter, the shopkeeper grabbed us both. I froze while he ran. The clerk held me there, dug through my pockets, and laid the candy out like evidence. I said nothing. I was too young, too afraid, and too ashamed to speak. They let me go with a warning. I walked home in silence, the heat in my chest not from guilt but from the sting of being left behind. It taught me something no lesson ever did. Not all betrayals are committed by enemies. Some are done by those who smile at you. From that day on, I promised myself I would not be the one who runs, nor the one left standing in silence. I would act and I would remember."

"6. Define weakness, and then define mercy."

These words came easier to Reinhardt. He had thought about them often.

"Weakness is not failure. It is not being outnumbered, outgunned, or outmatched. Weakness is surrendering your will to fear. It is the refusal to act when action is demanded. It is silence in the face of wrong, and hesitation in the face of duty. A man may lose and still not be weak. A man who flees from what must be done then he has already surrendered his soul. Mercy is harder. Mercy is not softness. Mercy is judgment refined by wisdom. True mercy requires knowing when justice is complete. Mercy is the hand that pulls a child back from the edge, not because he deserves it but because a future still exists for him. Mercy can be monstrous when it overrules justice. If a child steals candy and is never punished, he will grow to steal more. If you cripple him for his crime, you destroy something that could have been corrected. Justice without mercy is tyranny. Mercy without justice is chaos. I believe in mercy but never at the cost of the innocent. The dead do not get to appeal. If a man kills by neglect or malice and feels regret then that is not enough. Tears do not resurrect the fallen. Mercy must be measured and it must never be confused with weakness."

"7. What do you fear more: being forgotten or being misunderstood? Why?"

Reinhardt answered without hesitation then paused. Not to reconsider, but to write carefully, not arrogantly.

"I fear being forgotten more. It is not pride that drives this answer. It is a memory. To be misunderstood still means you live on, in part or even in error, even if twisted. But to be forgotten? That is true death. That is the erasure not only of your voice but your sacrifice, your love, and your struggle. I will never forget my uncle. To do so would be to kill him a second time. I remember his words, his gait, and the way he looked at the horizon when he believed no one was watching. I remember what he gave. I know that one day I too will be remembered, by those who come after me, and those who still fight. That is what Europe is. Not just a place, but a memory carried across bloodlines, through time, through ash and flame and storm. We are our memories. If we forget ourselves, then we have failed. If we forget our heroes, then they died for nothing. I would rather be slandered than erased. Misunderstanding can be corrected, oblivion cannot. A European remembers, that is the oath."

“8. Write about the time you felt most proud to be European.”

“That moment came when I returned to Europe, real-physical Europe, for the first time since I was a child. I was born outside Hanover, before my family settled on Delumina. My only memories of the Fatherland as a boy were filtered through stories, maps, and photographs. Though, the day I landed again on Earth, standing on the tarmac in the Greater German Reich, I felt it. It was not merely nostalgia or awe, but recognition. The soil felt heavier. The air was richer. I walked past old stones, older spires and saw the same banners my ancestors once marched beneath. It wasn’t pride in a flag or a title. It was pride in continuity. Pride in knowing I was part of something that had endured, something worth dying and living for. That was the day I knew I would never call myself anything else but European.”

“9. You are given two flags: your homeland’s and Europe’s. You may only raise one in battle. Which do you choose and what do you say to the dead of the other?”

“There is no contradiction between the two, not truly. The banner of the Pan-European Confederation is not opposed to the banners of the Greater German Reich or of Delumina. All are threads in the same tapestry. If I must raise only one, I raise the banner of the Confederation because it is not limited by borders or soil. It represents all of us, every brother and sister of the blood and every home where the Aryan spirit still burns. To the dead of my homeland, I would kneel and say, ‘You are not forgotten. You are not abandoned. You are part of the whole. We carry you forward in every standard we raise, in every charge we lead, in every final breath of every final soldier. You died not only for Germany or Delumina but for Europe and she remembers.’ We are not many peoples. We are one people with many lands. We will not forget you.”

“10. If you fail to become an ESS man, what will you do?”

Reinhardt’s eyes narrowed slightly. The question offended him, not because it was cruel, but because it seemed to imply the possibility of failure. Still, he answered plainly, without pride.

“I refuse to believe I will fail. I have given everything including my body, will, and belief to become one of Europe’s sons in black and grey. If I am found unworthy, if I falter or fall short of the standard, then I will not disappear. I will return to Delumina, to the land my family helped shape. I will join the militia and stand ready as her first defender. I will train her sons, teach her values, and shield her from rot. Europe is not only Earth. It lives wherever we carry her fire. If I cannot serve from the summit, I will serve from the root."

He set the pencil down, not in frustration, but in quiet finality. The test was complete. Reinhardt read over his responses once, quickly but attentively. There was nothing to revise or hide. He slid the papers into the folder and closed it, the crisp fold of the cover sounding louder than expected in the quiet room. Then, following the instructions printed at the top of the test, he stood, tucked the folder under his arm, and exited. Outside, the hallway remained sterile and still. A single red stripe ran along the white floor tiles, leading him to a marked point on the wall. Reinhardt stood there with his heels together, chin level, and eyes forward, folder flat at his side. Time passed without measure. Eventually, a door opened down the hall. A silent officer approached and took the folder from his hands. The man gave no expression and offered no words. Reinhardt did not expect any. He was then dismissed with a simple nod. Reinhardt turned sharply and walked the corridor's length until he found himself back at the large instruction hall. The other cadets were trickling in again, faces unreadable, shoulders tense. Reinhardt reentered, expression firm, and returned to his seat without a word. He sat down, spine straight, and waited.

One by one, more and more cadets returned to the classroom. No one spoke, all eyes stayed forward, and the silence became weightier than any shouted order. Eventually, every man was seated. Not long after, the door creaked open. A sharp-voiced officer entered and barked, "Stand and fall in."

Without hesitation, the entire unit rose in unison. Boots clicked against the polished floor as they were led down the corridor in perfect step. They moved in silence, all of them sensing something was coming, something unusual.

They arrived at a chamber unlike any they'd yet seen on the training grounds. It resembled a senate hall or tribunal arena, with high, curved walls and two banks of benches facing each other. The cadets were divided evenly, with one half on the left and the other on the right. They were told to sit. Again, no one spoke, but many exchanged glances, searching for clues, testing each other's posture and expressions.

Suddenly, the double doors slammed open. Three men in black stormed into the room with swift, deliberate steps. All wore the unmistakable uniform of the Political Directorate of the ESS with black wool tunics, crimson armbands, pistols at the hip, and in the case of two, rifles slung low and ready. They were not here for a ceremony or parade. The officer in the center strode to the middle of the room. His gaze swept the assembled cadets like a blade.

"It appears," he began, voice low but thunderous in tone, "that we have dissenters in our midst."

He let the words hang. Some cadets stiffened, others blinked but stayed motionless.

"Thought criminals of the highest order," he continued. "Moral deviants of the worst kind."

A ripple went through the room but none dared speak. Then the officer began to call names, eight in total. Each one spoken with chilling precision. Reinhardt Jäger was the last to be spoken. All eight cadets stood. Some with trembling knees, others with defiant brows. Reinhardt stood calmly and met the officer's gaze with an unwavering stare.

"You will form a line. Stand here. Face your comrades."

Reinhardt obeyed without hesitation. He glanced at the others, two looked on the verge of breaking. The rest masked their fear as best they could. Reinhardt focused his breath, stood firm, and stepped forward first.

"Sir," he said, his voice steady, "what exactly are we accused of?"

The officer turned to face him. The silence that followed stretched like wire. He approached, boots echoing ominously in the chamber. He stopped only inches from Reinhardt, chest to chest.

"You presume to question me?" the officer snarled.

"I presume only to know the truth, sir," Reinhardt replied, posture unflinching. "We are citizens of the Confederation. No evidence has been presented, only accusations."

The officer stared into him. Then, suddenly, he grabbed Reinhardt by the collar. Reinhardt didn't budge. A gasp escaped one of the seated cadets. The tension snapped. Several of the accused stepped closer in solidarity. Their faces flushed, no longer afraid but burning with purpose. Around the room, cadets rose from their benches. Some shouted...

"They've done nothing wrong!"

"They're loyal!"

"Get your hands off him!"

The two armed guards raised their rifles. The cadets kept moving. Slowly, deliberately, like a rising tide. The officer barked, "BACK! BACK, OR HE DIES!"

He shoved Reinhardt to his knees and pulled a pistol from his belt, jamming the cold barrel to Reinhardt's temple. Reinhardt didn't flinch. He stared ahead with eyes of steel.

"Have you nothing to say?" the officer growled.

Reinhardt turned his head ever so slightly, just enough for his voice to carry.

"Meine Ehre heißt Treue...."

My honor remains loyalty....

The officer's hand trembled but not from fear. A slow grin formed on his face. He lowered the pistol and reholstered it. Then, to everyone's shock, he reached down and offered his hand. Reinhardt paused... then took it. The two men stood.

"I apologize for that," the officer said, his voice now calm, even warm. "It was... dramatic, I admit."

Reinhardt raised an eyebrow. "You think?"

The officer chuckled and rubbed the back of his neck. "Just another test and you all passed."

He turned to address the full room. "Loyalty isn't just obedience. It's not fear. It's unity. It's honor and it's action. I saw what I needed to see."

The tension drained from the air like a valve released. Cadets looked at each other in stunned silence. No one moved. The officer barked one last order. "You are all dismissed. No more training for the day."

There was a beat of silence. Then a wave of breath came as relief, pride, and exhaustion, all at once. The cadets filed out in groups, this time a bit looser in form. Jokes and laughter returned cautiously, like sunlight after a storm.

Kasper clapped Reinhardt on the back. "You've got a way of drawing fire, brother."

Reinhardt smirked, rubbing his temple where the pistol had been pressed against. "I wasn't expecting a gun to my head before lunch."

They made their way toward the chow hall, the scent of hot food already drifting through the morning air. A few cadets talked animatedly about the test, some still too stunned to speak but something had changed. They were no longer just men sharing a barracks. Now, they were a unit, bound by trial and loyalty.

Chapter 21

Months of training had passed in an unbroken rhythm of drill and ceremony beneath the sun, long days of assault tactics on the field, hours of ideological conditioning and historical lectures, and endless familiarity drills with rifle, pistol, and blade. The weeks blurred into one another until the routine was part of their very bones. Now that routine had ended. The parade field was immaculate, the grass cut to a uniform height, the white boundary lines freshly chalked. The formations stood at attention. There were five companies of cadets in crisp, dark uniforms, boots aligned, shoulders square, the months of discipline showing in every stance. The sky was cloudless, the air heavy with the weight of finality.

A voice, amplified by the garrison loudspeakers, cut through the stillness, "All cadets raise your right hands for the oath!"

As one, hundreds of arms came up. All elbows were bent at 90 degrees, not a single hand wavered. The garrison commander, flanked by staff officers, took a step forward. His voice was iron, the words as old as the Confederation itself.

"Repeat after me, I swear unwavering loyalty to the Pan-European Confederation, to its leaders, to Europe, and to the ESS. I vow to obey all lawful orders, to act with honor and courage, and to defend Europe's blood, soil, and soul with my life. I shall never falter, never betray, and never retreat. This I swear by the gods of my fathers, and by the memory of all who came before me. So help me, God!"

The oath rolled across the parade ground like a single voice, the words heavy with conviction. When the final syllable faded, the commander gave a single nod.

"Lower your arms."

The sound of hundreds of sleeves sliding back to their seams was almost as sharp as a volley. The commander's next order was immediate. "Begin pass and review!"

The regimental band struck up the opening march. On command, all five formations right-faced with mechanical precision, the sound of synchronized boots echoing like a drumline. The first formation stepped off, then the second, each maintaining perfect intervals. Reinhardt's formation was third in the order. His eyes fixed forward, chin up, and the brim of his cap shadowing his gaze.

Around the outer edge of the field they moved in steady cadence, the sun glinting off polished buckles and brass buttons. As they approached the reviewing stand, the drum major's whistle pierced the air. The tune shifted, an unspoken signal. On the downbeat of the first note, every formation executed the change from marsch, marsch to the parade step. The song was Teufelslied. Its first measure hit like a hammer, and the entire corps transitioned into the piercing, driving rhythm of the goosestep. Boots struck the ground in perfect unison, the sound carrying like distant artillery. The precision was absolute, arms swinging in time, as the banners snapping in the wind. The watching officers and assembled guests rose instinctively to their feet. They passed the reviewing stand, heads turning in flawless sequence toward the garrison commander. Salutes were returned, the cadence never breaking. The band thundered on until the last formation cleared the field. Reinhardt and his fellow cadets were now officially enlisted men of the ESS with the rank of Schütze, rifleman.

Once past the stands, the formations wheeled away and marched off toward the assembly area. The music faded behind them, replaced by the short, clipped orders of the company leaders. At the far end of the field, they were halted and called to attention. The battalion adjutant stepped forward with a clipboard and began reading off names, dividing them into two groups.

"The first group will report to the administrative wing for your final interviews and assignment boards."

A cluster of names was called, Reinhardt's among them. These men stepped out of formation and fell in behind a waiting NCO, who immediately led them toward the long, squat building where the interviews would be conducted.

"Second group, you will receive aptitude packets. Fill them out completely and indicate which branch or service arm you are applying to join. Report to your company offices when complete."

The two groups moved off in opposite directions, one toward the paperwork tables set up under a shaded awning, and the other into the dim corridors of the admin building where the final measure of their worth awaited. The NCO leading Reinhardt's group brought them up to the entrance of the administrative wing. It is a long, low structure of poured concrete and glass block. The heavy double doors swung inward on oiled hinges, and they stepped from the glare of the parade field into a cooler, shadowed corridor.

Their boots clicked against the polished tile floor, the air smelling faintly of paper, ink, and machine oil from the nearby offices. Framed photographs lined the walls, black-and-white images of ESS men from wars past, their faces young and hard-eyed, their uniforms as sharp as those worn today. Reinhardt's gaze lingered briefly on one photograph of a man standing knee-deep in mud, a captured enemy banner clutched in his fist. Beneath it, the plaque read simply Never forgotten. The NCO halted them outside a set of double doors with a small brass sign, Assignment Board for Cadet Interviews. "Seats along the wall. Stay silent until your name is called. You get one shot at this."

They sat. The wooden bench beneath Reinhardt creaked faintly, worn smooth by decades of candidates waiting their turn. A low murmur could be heard from beyond the closed doors. Voices measured, occasionally interrupted by the shuffle of papers or the scrape of a chair. Every so often, the door opened and a Schutze emerged, some with eyes alight, others with their jaws clenched, unreadable. Each was mct by an orderly who took them down another hallway, their fates already decided in ways invisible to the rest.

Reinhardt sat straight, his cap resting in his lap, and fingers loosely curled over the brim. The moments stretched, marked only by the rhythmic tick of a wall clock. He felt no fear, but the gravity of the occasion settled over him like a weight. This was not just about placement. This was the Confederation's judgment on the man he had become through months of training. A name was called. Then another. The line shifted forward, and Reinhardt found himself fourth from the front. He glanced at the man beside him, a fellow volunteer from Delumina, his jaw working slightly as if chewing over some unspoken thought. They exchanged a brief nod. More minutes passed. Then the door opened again, and the clerk's voice rang out. "Schütze Reinhardt Jäger, inside."

Reinhardt rose at once, smoothing the front of his tunic. He placed his cap beneath his arm and stepped forward, the sound of his boots deliberate, each one echoing off the tiled corridor. He crossed the threshold into the interview chamber, a modest but formal room with a central table, a row of senior ESS officers seated behind it, and a single chair set directly opposite them. The Confederation flag hung on one wall, the ESS banner on the other, their colors catching the light from the high windows. The officer at the center, a colonel with a razor-edged jawline and eyes like cut glass.

"Schütze Jäger, let us begin."

Reinhardt stood at attention before the long table. Three officers sat behind it, each in the uniform and colors of a different branch of the ESS. The man in the center, a full colonel in the field-grey combat tunic of the field forces, flipped open Reinhardt's dossier and scanned the first page.

"Schütze Jäger, you have completed all requirements of training and stand here today to be placed where your skills will best serve the Confederation. You will hear options from each of us. Your answer will be taken into account, but the final decision rests with ESS High Command. Understood?"

Reinhardt's reply was firm.

"Understood, sir."

The colonel gestured with a gloved hand.

"I speak for the combat arm of the ESS. Your marksmanship and field scores place you in the upper bracket of your intake, as well as your actions on Delumina at the battle of Neue Frankfurt's airport. We have openings in Panzergrenadier regiments, in air assault formations, and reconnaissance units. If you want to be at the front leading the charge then this is the path. You'll be in the field within weeks after completing some additional training."

Reinhardt inclined his head. "Noted, sir."

The colonel nodded to his right. The next officer wore the black uniform of the political branch, a major with sharp eyes and a clipped manner.

"I represent the political branch. You've shown aptitude in written examinations, particularly in ideological comprehension and argumentation. Men like you can do more than fight. You can shape the morale of entire regiments, safeguard doctrine, and ensure the ideological purity of our forces. This is not an easier life. If anything, it demands more discipline and a stronger will but it ensures that the soul of Europe remains uncorrupted."

Reinhardt held his gaze, saying nothing yet. Finally, the third officer leaned forward. His uniform bore the discreet silver-gray trim of the intelligence service, and his voice carried a low, deliberate weight.

"Schütze Jäger, your instructors flagged your observational skills and your ability to read people. That is not common. Have you considered counter-intelligence? It would mean commissioning as a Lieutenant, remaining here at Bad Tölz for further officer training, and entering a service that operates both behind the lines and within our own. You would be trained to detect traitors, infiltrate enemy cells, and dismantle threats before they ever reach the battlefield."

He let the words hang for a moment before adding, "It is a long road. You will make fewer friends, and some of those you do make will not live to see the end of your service. If you value the security of the Confederation above your own comfort, it is a worthy calling."

Reinhardt considered each path in turn, the immediate fire and steel of the combat arm, the ideological forge of the political branch, and the shadowed vigilance of counter-intelligence.

"Sirs," he said finally, "my first choice is the combat arm. I want to fight where the enemy can be met face-to-face. I will serve wherever I am needed most, though counter-intelligence sounds interesting. If I can make a request, if I do go counter-intelligence I wish for Kasper Engel to be assigned with me. I need someone I trust to be with me when hunting the enemy. Kasper and myself have been through a lot together. If not for him our line would've collapsed at the airport. He ran under fire to keep the machine gun on line."

The colonel gave a small, approving smile. The major of the political branch sat back, expression unreadable. The intelligence officer gave a single, slow nod, as if committing something to memory.

"Very well," the colonel said, closing the dossier. "You will be informed of your assignment shortly. Report to the clerk outside for processing. Dismissed, Schütze Jäger."

Reinhardt saluted, received three in return, and marched from the room. The door closed behind him with a heavy click. Reinhardt stepped out into the narrow hallway. A single desk sat against the far wall, manned by a junior ESS clerk. Reinhardt approached, heels clicking together.

"Name?" the clerk asked without looking up.

"Schütze Reinhardt Jäger."

The clerk rifled through a stack of papers until he found the right form.

"Confirm your place of birth, current colony, and your top two branch preferences."

Reinhardt gave the answers clearly, watching the clerk make neat notations with a fountain pen.

"Very well. Your file will go to placement. You'll be notified before the week is out," the clerk said, sliding the folder into a courier satchel. "That's all, Schütze."

Reinhardt nodded in acknowledgment and stepped back, preparing to return to the waiting room. From the corner of his eye, he saw movement. It was Heydrich, the intelligence officer from the panel, stepping through the interview room door. The man's gait was quiet and deliberate, as though even in this mundane setting he practiced moving unseen.

"Schütze Jäger," Heydrich said, his tone low but carrying. "A moment of your time."

Reinhardt stopped and faced him. “Yes, sir?”

Heydrich studied him for a heartbeat. “I meant what I said there. Counter-intelligence is not a desk job. It is not sitting behind walls and reading reports. Our best officers are at the front, sometimes ahead of it, hunting the enemy before they can strike. You will see as much combat as any shock-trooper, perhaps more, but you will also be trusted with the kinds of operations that decide wars without entire armies having to bleed for them.”

Reinhardt kept his posture straight, hands behind his back. “Sir, my loyalty is to the fight. If the fight is found in counter-intelligence, then I’ll answer the call. I enlisted to meet the enemy face-to-face.”

A faint, knowing smile touched Heydrich’s mouth.

“And you will. Just remember, there are many ways to face an enemy. Some of the deadliest don’t wear uniforms. Think about it, Schütze. The Confederation has use for more than one kind of warrior. We will also keep in mind your request for Kasper Engel to be attached to you as well.”

Without waiting for an answer, Heydrich gave a short, precise nod and strode past, his boots making barely a sound on the polished floor. Reinhardt watched him go, then turned toward the corridor leading back to the barracks, the officer’s words settling like a weight he would carry for the rest of the day. The long day wound to a close with the newly minted riflemen of the ESS filing back into their barracks in tight, orderly ranks. The air inside was different now, less of the tense expectancy of trainees awaiting judgment, and more of the quiet weight of men who had crossed the threshold into service.

An NCO stood at the head of the aisle, clipboard in hand, his voice cutting across the room.

“Listen up, by order of the garrison commander, all riflemen are hereby granted four days of leave while your orders are cut. You are authorized to leave the grounds of Bad Tölz effective immediately.”

A ripple of surprise passed through the room, quick glances exchanged, some restrained grins breaking the otherwise stoic faces.

"You will return to this camp no later than 2000 hours, local time, on the fourth day. Fail to do so, and you'll wish you hadn't. Until then, your time is your own. Dismissed."

The NCO's boots echoed down the aisle as he left, leaving the men to digest the words. For weeks they had lived under constant schedule, the march from dawn to dusk without a moment unaccounted for. Now the sudden thought of civilian streets, of beer halls, cafés, and the quiet hum of the city, felt almost alien.

Some began stripping off their field jackets, others stowed away their rifles in the racks with a care that had been drilled into them from day one. A few men spoke in low tones about visiting family, while others simply stood still, unsure what to do with unstructured hours. Reinhardt sat on the edge of his bunk for a moment, the weight of his new rank insignia still strange on his collar. Four days was not long, but it would be enough, to breathe, to walk in the world as a man of the ESS, and to return sharper than before. Reinhardt wasted no time. The moment the NCO stepped out, he was already unbuttoning his jacket and brushing away a faint smear of dust from the day's marching. The grey wool still carried the faint scent of oil and the sun-baked field. He hung it neatly on its peg, ran a cloth over his boots until they gleamed, and began laying out the rest of his attire for inspection. Old habits, drilled into muscle memory, refused to die just because the clock now belonged to him. Kasper appeared at his side, grinning faintly as he adjusted his own collar.

"So, what are you going to do with four whole days of freedom?"

Reinhardt gave a short laugh.

"I desperately need a beer."

Kasper's grin widened. "Then I suppose I do too."

Within minutes they had their uniforms in perfect order, creased, brushed, and regulation neat. Belts buckled and caps set square, they stepped out of the barracks into the cool air of early evening. The camp felt almost strange without the usual bark of orders or the shuffle of drill formations. They passed under the shadow of the main gate, signing their names and departure times in the guard's ledger. The sentry, leaning on his rifle, gave them a knowing smirk.

"Try not to start any wars out there."

"Not without orders," Reinhardt replied, and they walked on.

The road to the train station wound past quiet shopfronts and tiled rooftops still holding the last warmth of the day. They didn't bother with a timetable, didn't check a map. All they knew was that somewhere down the line there would be cold beer, hot food, and the simple, almost forgotten luxury of not having to be anywhere at a precise hour.

The train ride was short, two stops, and they stepped off into a small Bavarian town whose cobbled streets still echoed faintly with the day's bustle. From somewhere down the lane came the muffled sound of an accordion and the steady stomp of boots on wooden planks. Reinhardt and Kasper traded a glance; no words were needed. The beerhall's heavy wooden door creaked as they pushed it open. Warmth and light spilled out, thick with the smell of roast pork, fresh bread, and the bite of lager. Inside, a trio of musicians in traditional dress played a bright, rolling tune while the patrons clapped and sang along. The low ceiling, dark beams, and polished tables gave the place a lived-in comfort, as if the walls themselves had soaked up a hundred years of laughter. They found a table near the center and sat down, both leaning back with the quiet satisfaction of men finally free from drill squares and parade fields. Then she walked up.

The serving girl couldn't have been more than her early twenties, with straight, pale-blonde hair bound neatly into a long braided ponytail. She wasn't heavyset, if anything she had the lean, lively frame of someone always on her feet but her blouse strained against a chest so generous it could have been a distraction even for a priest.

Neither Reinhardt nor Kasper had seen a woman in months, and for a moment they both simply stared. Not leering, just struck dumb by her presence, as if someone had dropped a living reminder of the outside world into their lap. It took Kasper's discreet nudge under the table to break the spell. Reinhardt snapped upright, cleared his throat, and before his mind could catch his tongue, he blurted,

"You are... very beautiful."

A half-second later, he slapped his own face lightly, muttering something under his breath as heat rose to his cheeks.

"Two beers, your best, and whatever's hot from the kitchen, please," he added quickly, eyes darting anywhere but her.

Kasper smirked, half-hiding it behind his hand, while the girl gave a polite smile and jotted down their order. Reinhardt sat there stiffly, still blushing, unsure whether he was more embarrassed by his words or by how much of the room Kasper's amusement now filled.

The woman returned in short order, balancing a wooden tray with the ease of someone born to the work. She set down two steaming plates which had thick sausages nestled beside a heap of sauerkraut and potatoes and placed the heavy pints on the table with a solid thunk. The beer's golden surface caught the light, froth spilling just over the rim. Reinhardt forced his gaze to stay fixed on the plates, not her, though every motion in his periphery seemed designed to test his resolve. She was close enough for him to catch the faint scent of soap and bread dough.

"Thank you," he muttered, almost too low to hear.

Her eyes met his. They were bright, amused, and perhaps just a little daring. "No... thank you," she said warmly, the words carrying a weight he wasn't entirely sure how to read.

Before he could process it, she leaned in, the edge of her braid brushing his shoulder, and pressed a quick kiss to his cheek. Her lips were cool from the beer hall air, but the heat in his face flared instantly. She straightened, smiled as if nothing at all were unusual, and walked off into the crowd with the same unhurried grace, leaving Reinhardt staring blankly ahead. Kasper's grin stretched ear to ear. "I think she likes you, Schütze," he said, lifting his beer in salute.

Reinhardt cleared his throat, took a long drink, and said nothing, though the ghost of a smile tugged at the corner of his mouth.

The morning appeared, as if only just after Reinhardt closed his eyes. Kasper woke up only a moment or two later. They dressed and headed downstairs. Coffee was being served, black and piping hot. Reinhardt looked around for the woman who kissed him last night but she was nowhere to be seen. Kasper quietly spoke to Reinhardt as they discussed their plans for the remaining days. Reinhardt snapped to attention when Kasper patted his back.

"Are you alright Reinhardt?" Kasper asked softly. "You seem distant. You thinking about the beermaiden last night?"

Reinhardt nodded with a smile, then shook his head. Reinhardt turned to Kasper.

"Where to next, my comrade?"

Kasper pondered for a moment. It was as if he was gauging the distance from Bad Tolz to every corner of Europe. Reinahrdt could imagine what Kasper was thinking. "Could they make it to the black sea and back in that time? I would love to see the Parthenon but the distance is a stretch... What about the sands of Iberia or the cliffs of Cork...? No, no we don't have the money to get that far."

Perhaps the simplest of answers are also the closest. Kasper's eyes finally widened with excitement when the epiphany hit him. "We're going to Vienna!" He exclaimed, almost shouting.

Reinhardt chuckled as he tried to lower his friend's volume. They both agreed that would be a perfect destination, paid for the coffee and room fair, then headed out to Vienna. The train ride was fast, thanks to the engineering marvel of confederation high speed rail. Some part of Reinhardt wished the trip was slower so he could appreciate the land of the Greater German Reich more, not just her cities.

They finally reached their destination, Vienna. The train station was on par with the majesty and sheer size as the Munich train station. They departed and witnessed the beauty of this ancient city. The capital of Austria rivaled the capital of Bavaria in its scale and might. They walked to and fro, occasionally stopping to get a sausage and a drink. The banners of the Greater German Reich, Austria, and the city of Vienna snapped triumphantly in the cool breeze coming down from the Vienna Alps. The duo's first real experience was a museum dedicated to Europe's fighters. It was a large and beautiful marble building. All the way back from ancient antiquity with Europe's fathers, the Aryan horse lords. They brandished bronze weapons while riding a chariot. The kit of the Mycenaean Greeks, Hittites, and "sea peoples" of the bronze age. Greek Hoplites, Roman Legionnaires, Cataphracts, Medieval Knights, and finally ending with the kits of the Central Powers of WWI and various uniforms of the European axis of the Second World War. Reinhardt and Kasper stood tall in front of the uniform of the Waffen-SS, a Scharführer of the Das Reich division. Reinhardt smiled to himself and gave a quick nod to the mannequin.

Reinhardt and Kasper walked out back into the streets of Vienna before noticing a sign. It read "Exhibit of Subversive Art." It gave some directions and the address the collection was being displayed at. Kasper smiled as he looked over at Reinhardt.

"You thinking what I am thinking?" Kasper asked with a sly grin.

Reinhardt mirrored the smile and nodded back. They followed the instructions and found the building. The lighting inside was deliberate, dim and clinical, isolating each canvas. Walls carried Weimar-era avant-garde featuring George Grosz's caustic caricatures of officers, Otto Dix's shell-shocked portraits, Felix Nussbaum's anxious interiors, Max Liebermann's sober impressionism, Marc Chagall's dreamscapes, and El Lissitzky's constructivist geometry. Archival captions paired artist quotes with period critics who cheered the "destruction of bourgeois norms." In this curation, those quotations are weaponized: the placards frame the works as a repudiation of tradition, inviting the viewer to see a civilizational quarrel laid out in oil, ink, and wire.

Reinhardt reads one placard aloud in disgust: a critic praising a work for "depicting the German spirit as an obsolete, decaying relic."

Kasper shakes his head: "They hung this in our galleries while we starved."

Reinhardt replied, "Not anymore."

They share an unspoken understanding, this is why the Confederation must never fall.

Kasper asked with the subtlest of grins "So... whatever happened to those people?"

Reinhardt responded with a shrug, "They are not around anymore. Who knows."

Chapter 22

Reinhardt and Kasper returned to Bad Tölz on time, their leave over as quickly as it had begun. The barracks were once again alive with the sound of boots on gravel, shouted names, and the clipped commands of NCOs herding the men into formation.

It was the fifth day since leave, and the entire graduating class now stood in perfect ranks on the parade square, each man waiting for his name to be called and his fate handed to him. The cold morning air hung heavy with anticipation, yet Reinhardt's thoughts kept drifting far from the square. The smell of woodsmoke and roasted meat. The low hum of folk music in the pub. Her eyes, blue as Bavarian spring skies. That kiss, quick but warm, still lingering in his memory like an ember refusing to die. A barked name snapped him halfway back to the present but it wasn't his. He stood straighter, forcing himself to focus, yet his mind betrayed him again. I wonder if she even remembers me, passed through Reinhardt's head.

"JÄGER, REINHARDT!"

The sound of his own name struck like a rifle report. He stepped forward sharply, boots cracking against the frozen ground, all traces of distraction erased from his face. An officer stepped toward him, a small case in hand. "Schütze Jäger, effective immediately, you are promoted to officer candidate. You will remain in Barracks Five for the time being. You are ordered to report to the Officer School beginning next week."

From the case, the officer withdrew a single collar rank tab, black with silver piping, and pressed it into Reinhardt's palm. "Wear it well."

Reinhardt saluted crisply, turned on his heel, and marched back to formation, yet even as the line of men moved on, he felt the faintest ghost of that kiss again.

Reinhardt returned to Barracks Five with the others, the thud of boots and the creak of gear filling the narrow hallways. The air smelled faintly of wool, leather, and the lingering tang of rifle oil. He hung his tunic on the wall peg and unfastened the Schütze collar rank, fingers working with careful precision. The silver-piped officer candidate tab seemed heavier than its size suggested. Sitting on the edge of his bunk, he threaded needle and thread, sewing it into place with the quiet focus of a man marking a turning point in his life.

Around him, the room buzzed with chatter. A pair of riflemen down the row were animatedly discussing their assignment to combat engineers, bragging about the bonuses they'd been promised. The talk was half excitement, half relief that their futures were finally settled. At the next bunk over, Luka leaned back against the wall, boots crossed, grinning. "Russisch Division," he said proudly. "Heavy machine gunner. I'll freeze my ass off, but at least I'll be shooting something worth the trouble."

Donatello slapped him on the shoulder, laughing. "Better than climbing mountains for the Italia Division. You'll see me halfway up some Alpine rock face wondering what I did to deserve it."

Across from them, Kasper sat with his elbows on his knees, staring at the floor. He gave a short chuckle, but it lacked conviction. "And I'm... staying here. More training." His tone made it clear he'd hoped for one of the elite strike formations, not extra weeks at Bad Tölz.

Reinhardt glanced up from his sewing. "Could be worse," he said evenly. "You'll come out sharper for it."

Kasper smirked faintly. "Maybe but you'll be off at Officer School, and I'll still be saluting the same walls."

Reinhardt tied off the last stitch and pressed the new rank flat between his fingers. "Walls don't shoot back, Kasper, be patient."

The barracks carried on with its mix of pride, disappointment, and anticipation, but for Reinhardt, the quiet weight of that new rank was enough to drown out the noise.

The week rode on. Each morning, the barracks seemed a little emptier. One by one, men were called out, shaking hands, clapping shoulders, exchanging hurried farewells before boarding trucks or marching off to their postings. The

Germans were sent to their own storied divisions. Leibstandarte, Das Reich, and Totenkopf were names spoken with a mixture of pride and gravity. Others departed for other divisions like the Lugh Celtic Division, with its green banners and knotwork insignia, and the Wiking Division, the Pan-European formation where Norwegians, Spaniards, and Frenchmen marched under one standard. Each departure felt like a thinning of the ranks, a quiet reminder that Bad Tölz was never meant to be permanent.

By the end of the week, the summons came for Reinhardt and Kasper. They stood outside the barracks, kit bags slung, and orders in hand. Their paths now split with Reinhardt toward Officer School, Kasper toward his additional specialist training in another wing of the camp. There was no ceremony for it. Just a quick clasp of hands, and a firm pull into a brief hug.

"This isn't for forever," Reinhardt said, looking him square in the eye.

Kasper smirked, the corners of his mouth tightening as if holding back something heavier. "I'll hold you to that."

They broke apart, turned toward their separate roads, and didn't look back. Reinhardt made his way across the camp toward the officer school, the low winter sun casting long shadows over the parade grounds. The building was clean and imposing, the kind of place where discipline seemed to hang in the air. He stepped inside, approached the clerk's desk, and signed his name into the roster.

"Schütze Jäger... Officer Candidate Jäger," the clerk corrected with a faint grin, handing over a slip of paper. "Here's your barracks assignment. School starts in three days. Don't be late."

Reinhardt nodded, pocketed the slip, and followed the directions across the compound to the officer barracks. The air felt different here with less noise, fewer idle movements, and a quiet focus among the few men already present. His assigned bunk was simple but orderly. Reinhardt stowed his kit, hung his tunic neatly, and set his boots side by side beneath the bedframe. The room smelled faintly of starch and leather, a comforting reminder of routine.

The next three days dragged on. He kept himself busy, cleaning gear, reviewing notes, running the training field in the cold mornings but the wait gnawed at him. Each day, more officer cadets arrived. Some were fresh from basic like Reinhardt, others bearing the marks of experience, junior and senior NCOs whose posture alone commanded respect. Their uniforms carried the wear of campaigns, the ribbons and badges of men who had already earned their place in the field. By the third evening, the barracks was full, the air heavy with a mix of anticipation and unspoken rivalry. Reinhardt lay in his bunk, staring at the ceiling, knowing the real test began tomorrow.

The first morning came like a thunderclap. Reinhardt shot awake at the sound of metal cans being slammed against the barracks walls, accompanied by the bark of cadre voices that could have rattled glass.

"Up! Uniforms on! Move, move, move!"

The officer cadets scrambled out of their bunks, pulling on tunics and boots with fumbling haste. Belts were cinched, collars fastened, and caps grabbed. No one dared be the slowest. Outside, the cold bit into their faces as they hurried into formation under the burning gaze of the instructors.

"Faster! You think the enemy will wait for you to dress?" one cadre snarled as they set the formation moving.

They were marched through the camp's winding paths until the parade grounds fell behind them. Ahead lay a cluster of old brick buildings on the outskirts of the camp. They were sturdy, weathered structures that looked as if they'd been standing since before the Confederation itself. Their windows were dark, their doors shut. The column halted. One by one, names were called, each cadet stepping forward to receive a folded slip of paper before being sent toward a specific building. The process was brisk, impersonal.

"Jäger, to Building Fourteen."

Reinhardt took his slip, the paper cold and stiff in his hand. He followed the others to their assigned posts until each man stood before his own building, a line of cadets stretching down the row of structures. A senior instructor strode past, his boots ringing sharply against the cobblestones. He stopped halfway down the line and spoke loud enough for all to hear.

"Welcome," he said with a thin, wolfish smile, "to the stables of Rome. You will enter your respective stable and read your orders. Then do exactly as you are instructed. Nothing more, nothing less. The gods favor discipline."

Without another word, he gestured to the doors. Reinhardt pushed open the door to Building 14, and the first thing that struck him was the stench. It was a suffocating, sour reek of ammonia, rotting hay, and sickness that clawed its way into his sinuses. Instinctively, he raised a hand to cover his nose, blinking against the sting in his eyes. The place was dim with narrow windows letting in only weak slivers of daylight. Dust floated in the beams, swirling in the stagnant air. Somewhere deeper in the building, a horse gave a weak, rasping snort.

Unfolding the slip of paper, Reinhardt read his instructions in the clipped, impersonal handwriting of the cadre. "You are responsible for feeding, watering, and cleaning all horses within this stable. All stalls will be mucked and replenished by dusk. Report completion to your assigned instructor. Failure to meet the standards will be punished."

He lowered the paper and looked down the central aisle. The line of stalls stretched into the shadows, each one containing a listless figure. He walked slowly, boots crunching on straw that was more filth than fiber. The first few horses barely lifted their heads at his approach. Their eyes dull, ribs showing, their tails matted and still. A few stood with one hip sagging, breathing slow and shallow as though every movement was a labor. By the halfway point, Reinhardt's gut was tight.

These weren't war mounts. They looked more like ghosts clinging to flesh. One mare gave a weak flick of her ear when he passed, but her coat was patchy and her flank shivered uncontrollably. The next stall held a gelding so thin that its spine seemed to press through the skin, staring at nothing. Reinhardt set the slip of paper down on a nearby post and went straight to the feed bins. The moment he lifted the lid, the sour, almost rancid odor hit him. The oats were damp, clumped together, and spotted with mold. A few beetles crawled sluggishly in the mass.

"Damn it..." he muttered under his breath.

This wasn't food, it was punishment. He turned to the water troughs running along the stalls. Most were barely half-full, coated with a green scum that stuck to the sides. In one, mosquito larvae writhed just under the surface, the whole basin alive with their tiny movements. Reinhardt clenched his jaw. If they wanted to see whether he'd cut corners, they were going to be disappointed. He found the nearest pump and wrestled a battered bucket under its spout, cranking until cold, clean water splashed over his hands. One by one, he began emptying each trough, scrubbing the slime out with handfuls of straw before refilling them. It was slow, filthy work and every bucket carried had to be walked the length of the building and poured out carefully so the horses could drink without fear of tipping it over. By the time he finished the first half of the stable, his shirt was clinging to his back with sweat and the smell of the place clung to his skin. The horses were beginning to lift their heads, watching him with cautious eyes as they drank.

The feed would be harder. He dumped the rotten oats into a waste barrel, ignoring the swarm of flies that rose up, and began sorting through what little was salvageable. Anything that could pass as edible, he set aside for mixing with fresh hay from a stack in the corner. He knew it wasn't much, but at least it would be clean. This wasn't the sort of task most men wanted on their first day at officer school. As Reinhardt worked, he found his movements becoming steady, deliberate. It was less about the stink and the rot, more about restoring some semblance of life to the animals in his care.

By midday, the worst of the scum was gone from the troughs, and the smell of rot was thinning under the scent of fresh hay. The horses that still had some spark in them were starting to edge closer when he passed, their ears flicking forward, nostrils testing his scent. A few even took the feed straight from his hand, warm breath against his palm.

It was then, near the far end of the row, that he noticed the name carved into the dark, rough timber of one stall, BUCEPHALUS. The letters were deep, almost gouged into the wood by a knife, their edges darkened with age. Curious, Reinhardt stepped closer. The horse inside was larger and taller at the shoulder than any of the others, his coat a deep, almost blue-black that caught what little light filtered through the grimy windows. His eyes, though, were wide and white-rimmed, the muscles in its neck taut.

"Easy," Reinhardt said quietly, one hand lifting to the latch.

The horse's head shot up, ears pinning back. Before he could even touch the gate, the horse reared, forelegs kicking high, and hooves thudding against the front planks. The sound cracked through the stable like a gunshot. Reinhardt stepped back on instinct as the animal lashed its head, letting out a sharp, ringing neigh that echoed off the brick walls. A few of the other horses shied away, the earlier calm broken. Reinhardt kept his stance low and open, not turning his back, but not rushing forward either.

"All right," he muttered, more to himself than the animal. "You don't want me near you yet."

The horse tossed its head again, snorting hard, then paced in the tight space of its stall, muscles coiled as if ready to strike. The carved name on the wood felt less like a simple label now, and more like a warning or a challenge. Reinhardt gave it a final look before moving down the line, deciding it would be the last one he dealt with today. But even as he walked away, he could feel those sharp, watchful eyes on his back.

Reinhardt worked through the row in order of least trouble. The calmer ones first, those who flinched but didn't bolt when he entered. They got fresh water, clean feed, and a quick brush to loosen the mats in their coats. The difference was immediate; they stood taller, their eyes clearer. It was only when every other stall had been tended that he returned to the far end, to the dark shape waiting behind the carved name. Bucephalus still stood near the back, weight shifting restlessly from one hind leg to the other, ears flicking forward and back. Reinhardt didn't try the gate latch this time. Instead, he dug into one of the storage bins near the wall and came up with a small tin. When he popped the lid, the sharp, sweet smell of sugar hit his nose.

He took three cubes, holding them loosely in his open palm, and stepped just close enough for the horse to catch the scent. The reaction was immediate. The great head lifted, nostrils flaring, and eyes narrowing. Bucephalus didn't move forward, but his pacing slowed. Reinhardt kept his other hand at his side, body angled just slightly away. "No threat, no sudden movements," Reinhardt quietly thought to himself.

"That's right," he murmured. "I'm not here to hurt you."

A minute passed. Then another. Finally, the horse took a single, hesitant step toward him. Reinhardt stayed still, letting Bucephalus set the distance. The head came down, muzzle brushing his palm, quick and testing, and the sugar cubes vanished between strong teeth. Reinhardt kept his eyes half on the latch, half on the animal's ears. The horse's breathing was heavy but no longer harsh. He reached for the tin again, offering another handful. This time, Bucephalus didn't retreat, but when Reinhardt's hand shifted toward the gate, the ears went back and a sharp stomp cracked against the floorboards.

"Not today," Reinhardt said softly, pulling his hand back. "But we'll get there."

He left the last cubes in the feed bin, filled the water trough from outside the stall, and stepped away without forcing the issue. Trust, he knew, was earned in inches, not leaps. Bucephalus, for all his fire, would be worth the wait.

A sharp, brassy horn call split the air, cutting across the smell of hay and manure. Reinhardt straightened, brushing his hands on his trousers, and stepped out from Bucephalus's gate. Along the row, other cadets emerged from their stables, some with the look of men who'd done the work, and others clearly relieved the day was over.

The grading officer strode down the line with a clipboard, his pace deliberate. Names were called, and men were questioned. A few, when asked, tried to bluff their way through vague answers; those men were swiftly ordered to pack their gear and leave the training cycle. Others stood tall, explaining what they had done and why, their voices steady.

When his turn came, Reinhardt spoke plainly. "I fed and watered every horse with clean supplies and cleaned the stalls in order of least resistance to most. I saved Bucephalus for last. I was able to calm him with sugar and got him to eat from my hand. I couldn't enter the stall yet without risking a blow, but progress was made."

The officer's eyes flicked up briefly, then back to the page. A quick scratch of the pen, no praise or criticism, and he moved on. Once the last cadet was accounted for, the officer gave a short nod. "You are dismissed from stable duty for the day. Eat, clean yourselves, and handle any personal tasks. Be back at your assigned stables by zero-six-hundred tomorrow."

One by one, the cadets broke formation, some heading for chow, others to the washrooms. Reinhardt lingered a moment, casting a glance back at the shadowed stall at the end of the row. Bucephalus was watching him, ears forward this time.

Reinhardt ate quickly in the mess, barely tasting the food, and took the fastest shower he could manage. Even in the barracks, with his bunk neatly made and the lights out, his mind kept circling back to the stables to the sickly animals, the reek of neglect, and Bucephalus's defiant eyes. Sleep came in short, shallow bursts.

When he finally sat up, it was not the bugle that woke him but his own impatience. The dim glow of the clock read 0337. Two and a half hours before duty. He swung his legs over the bunk, pulling on his field-grey uniform with practiced motions. Outside, the camp was silent except for the crunch of his boots on the gravel. His breath fogged in the cool pre-dawn air as he made his way across the grounds to the row of old brick buildings.

Stable 14 greeted him with the same stale smell as yesterday, but the horses stirred at the sound of the door. He moved from stall to stall, checking each animal in turn. He ran a hand down a neck here, clearing a water bucket there, and murmuring low to the more skittish ones. His hands worked methodically, but his mind was already on the last stall at the end of the row.

With the other stalls fed, watered, and cleaned, Reinhardt finally turned toward the last one. Bucephalus stood there in the half-light, his dark coat rippling faintly with each breath, eyes still fixed in that unblinking, defiant stare.

Reinhardt thought he saw something beneath it, not just anger or fear, but a wariness that had been hardened over time. He approached slowly, letting the sound of his boots fall softly on the straw. His hands moved with deliberate calm as he reached for the latch. The metal clicked, and Bucephalus's head rose, ears swiveling forward, nostrils flaring. A tense stillness filled the space. Reinhardt eased the gate open just wide enough to slip through, keeping his body sideways, non-threatening. His left hand held out a few sugar cubes, palm flat.

"Easy, Bucephalus... easy," he murmured, voice low and steady.

The horse shifted his weight, hooves shuffling on the straw, neck arching as if ready to rear. Then, slowly, he stretched his muzzle toward Reinhardt's palm. Warm breath washed over the young man's hand before the lips closed around the sugar, crunching it between strong teeth.

Reinhardt let the horse take his time, never moving too quickly, never forcing the space between them. When the sugar was gone, Bucephalus lingered just long enough for Reinhardt's fingers to brush the velvet of his muzzle.

Reinhardt slipped back out of the stall without a word, the latch clicking softly behind him. He fetched a bucket of clean, cold water and a fresh portion of oats, the steam of warm feed mixing with the faint scent of hay. When he returned, Bucephalus's ears twitched, but he no longer flinched. Setting the bucket and trough down, Reinhardt let the horse move first. Bucephalus stepped forward, lowering his head to drink, the muscles in his powerful neck flexing with each swallow. Reinhardt waited until the feed was half-finished before he slowly reached into his kit and pulled out a stiff-bristled brush. He began with slow, even strokes along the horse's shoulder, careful to keep his other hand visible. At first, Bucephalus's hide quivered under the touch, but as the minutes passed, the tension eased. Dust and loose hair gathered in the brush, the dull coat beginning to take on a faint sheen.

Reinhardt found himself humming a slow, steady German folk tune his father used to sing on winter nights. The sound seemed to calm them both. Bucephalus's ears swiveled toward the melody, and for the first time since Reinhardt had seen him, the great horse's eyes no longer burned with suspicion, but with something closer to recognition.

As Reinhardt brushed along Bucephalus's flank, the rhythmic scrape of the bristles slowed when something unusual caught his eye on the far wall. In the dim light, half-hidden beneath a layer of peeling, yellowed paint, was a scrawl of letters, just enough to make out "A co...".

He set the brush down on the edge of the trough and stepped closer, running his fingers over the surface. The old paint flaked beneath his touch, and he began working at it methodically, careful not to make too much noise. Bit by bit, the faded words emerged, as though the wall itself were reluctantly giving up its secret. After a few minutes, the full line stood revealed in shaky, almost carved strokes.

"A coin for Belisarius."

Reinhardt stood back, his brow furrowing. The name was familiar, half-remembered from some lesson or book, a general from the old Roman Empire. His eyes shifted to Bucephalus, who was still watching him with that intense, almost human gaze.

"What's your story, eh?" Reinhardt murmured, glancing between the horse and the strange, ancient-sounding phrase. He had the sense that whatever it meant, it had been here long before either of them arrived.

Reinhardt lingered by the words for a long moment, uncertain whether they had been planted here deliberately as part of his trial or whether they were simply the fading mischief of some long-gone cadet. Either way, something about it felt wrong, not the words themselves, but the whole scene. The sick horses, the rotting feed and the stagnant water, it was a disgrace to the uniform he now wore.

He stepped back into the aisle of the stable, jaw tightening. This wasn't how animals of war should be kept. Without another thought, he moved to the front of the stable and began gathering every lead rope he could find. Some were frayed, others stiff from neglect, but they would do. He moved down the row, clipping a lead to each stall door, murmuring reassurances to the animals as he worked. The sound of shifting hooves followed him like a chain reaction.

When he stepped outside for a breath of cold morning air, his eyes caught on the outline of a pasture beyond the stables, frost clinging to the grass, but open, free of walls and filth. That was where they belonged.

He went back inside, rummaging until he found the best saddle in the tack room. It wasn't perfect, but the leather was still supple and the stitching sound. Slinging it under one arm, he walked straight to Bucephalus's stall. The great horse's ears flicked forward, suspicion still in his dark eyes, but the fight in him was no longer wild. He was watching and weighing. Reinhardt set the saddle down just outside the stall, meeting that gaze head-on. "Come on, old boy," he said quietly, motioning toward the open aisle. "I am getting you out of here."

Bucephalus stepped forward at last, his massive frame filling the stall doorway. He kept one wary eye on Reinhardt as the saddle was lifted onto his back, but he did not shy away. The cinch was tightened, the bridle slipped into place, and for the first time since Reinhardt had seen him, the warhorse seemed to stand a little taller, like a veteran remembering what he was.

Reinhardt swung up into the saddle, the leather creaking under his weight. With a firm but steady hand, he guided Bucephalus down the aisle, pausing at the first three stalls. He unlatched them one by one, clipping each lead rope to his saddle ring. The horses came hesitantly at first, then followed in the wake of the larger stallion, trusting his presence.

They moved through the chill dawn, hooves striking a steady rhythm on the packed earth road. The pasture loomed ahead, a wide open space of frost-glittered grass under the paling sky. Reinhardt led the little train of animals through the gate and unclipped each lead, letting them wander free. The horses lowered their heads to graze, tails flicking, their breath steaming in the cold.

Without pause, he turned Bucephalus back toward the stable for the next group. Three more came out, then three after that, always with Bucephalus in the lead, like a general escorting his men to safety. By the time the last of them stepped onto the pasture, the sickly gloom of the stables felt far away. For the first time, Reinhardt allowed himself to smile.

The first light of dawn spilled over the treeline, painting the pasture in gold. The frost was breaking under the horses' hooves as they drank from the pond or pulled up mouthfuls of grass. Reinhardt sat tall in Bucephalus' saddle, hands resting on the pommel, and watching the herd breathe in the freedom they'd been denied. The crunch of boots on gravel reached his ears, cadets approaching the stables. Their chatter faltered as they caught sight of him in the pasture. A few stopped outright, gawking at the spectacle with Reinhardt astride the great black stallion, the other horses scattered loosely like a cavalry troop at rest.

A sharp, furious voice broke the morning calm. "Cadet Jäger! Present yourself!"

Reinhardt turned Bucephalus with the ease of a seasoned rider, trotting him toward the fence. The grading officer stood there, face flushed, and fists balled at his sides.

"What in the name of the Confederation are you doing?" the officer barked.

Reinhardt halted Bucephalus just inside the fence line. He didn't dismount. His voice was calm but carried enough force to reach every ear.

"Rome is not a place, sir. Rome is mother to us all. Is this how we treat the sons of Rome, of Europe? Starving them, leaving them to rot in filth? These are warhorses, not refuse. They carried better men than us into battle. They deserve better."

For a long moment, there was only the sound of wind over grass and the shifting of hooves. A few cadets straightened unconsciously, as if bracing under some unspoken truth. The officer's jaw worked, but no words came immediately. The officer's eyes narrowed, but instead of barking a rebuke he pulled a small notebook from his breast pocket. His pen scratched briefly against the paper. He looked up again, his voice even now.

"Cadet Jäger, you are permitted to continue as you are."

He closed the notebook with a snap. "And you are officially released from the Stables of Rome."

Reinhardt frowned slightly, unsure whether this was reprieve or reprimand. "Have I failed, sir?"

The officer's gaze lingered on him for a long moment. "I said you are released from the Stables of Rome, Cadet. That is all you need to know."

With that, he turned on his heel and strode back toward the other cadets, leaving Reinhardt in the saddle, Bucephalus shifting beneath him, and the morning wind carrying the faint smell of grass and freedom. Reinhardt swung one leg over and slid down from Bucephalus' back, his boots pressing into the damp grass. The stallion's breath came in slow, heavy bursts, nostrils flaring as he turned his head to regard Reinhardt. Carefully, Reinhardt unbuckled the straps and lifted the saddle clear, setting it down on the fence rail for a moment. He reached up, cupping the horse's muzzle in both hands, his thumbs brushing along the warm curve of Bucephalus' face.

"I'll never forget you," Reinhardt murmured, his voice low and steady.

Bucephalus snorted softly, leaning into the touch before pulling back to graze. Reinhardt slung the saddle over his shoulder and began the slow walk back toward the stables, the leather creaking faintly in his grip. When he reached stable 14, he set the saddle back on its rack, exactly where he'd found it, the smell of the pasture and horse still clinging to him.

Chapter 23

Reinhardt assembled with the other officer cadets in the lecture hall. The air was heavy with the scent of chalk and damp wool, maps of past campaigns draped along the walls like trophies. A massive sand table dominated the center of the room, carved terrain and painted blocks already arranged for some coming contest.

At the far end of the hall stood three instructors, a stern Hauptsturmführer with a clipboard, a grizzled Obersturmführer wearing the ribbons of a decorated veteran, and a younger officer in the black tunic of the political branch. The senior man stepped forward.

"Today," he began, voice sharp as steel, "you will command men in battle. Not in the field, but in the war room. This is Kriegsspiel, the art of waging war with maps, terrain, and the cold precision of orders. Your skill here will determine your worth in the field."

He scanned the room, letting the silence stretch. "You will be divided into commands. Some of you will lead companies, others battalions. Orders must be written, delivered by messenger, and obeyed exactly as given. We will measure your speed, judgment, and nerves."

He gestured to the sand table. "The battle is based on a real engagement fought by the Leibstandarte division on the Eastern Front. Study your maps, plan your moves and remember that the enemy will be as cunning as you are careless."

The cadets were split into their commands. Reinhardt was given a sheaf of orders, a folded map, and command of a company tasked with holding the right flank of the defending force. The clock was set. The umpires signaled the start.

Reinhardt bent over the map, tracing the folds of ground with his finger. His Panzergrenadier company's position sat astride a low ridge, a ribbon of forest at their back and open farmland sloping gently toward the notional enemy. The ridge was a gift. It gave clear lanes of fire and forced attackers into predictable avenues but it was also a trap. If the enemy broke through here, the center would collapse before Das Reich or Totenkopf could pinch the flanks.

The rules of the exercise were simple, no initiative beyond your orders. In Kriegsspiel, speed of thought mattered as much as obedience. Reinhardt studied the likely routes of advance, marking with a pencil where the enemy might mask armor with smoke, where machine guns could bite deepest, and where his reserves could counterpunch.

A runner arrived, snapping to attention. “From Battalion, Herr Untersturmführer. You will hold your present line. Expect probing attacks within the first hour. You will not commit reserves without direct orders.”

Reinhardt nodded, scribbling the instructions in his field notebook. “Return and confirm receipt,” he told the messenger, who turned and jogged back toward the battalion post.

“First Platoon must anchor to the left and watch the treeline. Second Platoon, you’re on the ridge crest with the heavy machine guns. Third Platoon, you are the reserve, concealed behind the barn here. You move only when I say.”

The umpires moved colored blocks on the sand table, marking the first enemy scouts approaching the front. They slid a small piece, infantry in wedge formation, toward the left of Reinhardt’s sector. Reinhardt kept his eyes on the table, lips tightening. “Here they come.”

A few minutes later, another runner appeared, breathless. “Enemy armor sighted, two kilometers west of your position, moving toward the center.”

Reinhardt looked at his map again. If the armor hit the line before Das Reich and Totenkopf smashed through the flanks, the whole exercise would become a test of endurance. He could already feel the clock ticking in his mind. The next runner arrived with mud on his trousers, eyes wide. “Herr Untersturmführer, the company to your west is under heavy attack, armor and mechanized infantry. Battalion says hold your sector unless otherwise directed.”

Reinhardt glanced at his own front, a handful of probing contacts but nothing serious. The real fight was to his left. He could feel it, the pounding of their guns echoing faintly through the ridge, or at least Reinhardt imagined this. He tore a sheet from his field notebook and began to write, pencil scratching hard.

“If their line can hold the enemy in place, request permission to pivot my company westward and strike the attackers in the flank while the neighboring company maintains frontal pressure. Current enemy activity to my front is minimal and can be contained with reduced force."

He folded the note and pressed it into the runner's hand. "Take this to battalion. Tell them my reserves stand ready for immediate redeployment. Move quickly."

The runner nodded, bolting off toward the rear. Reinhardt returned his gaze to the sand table and the distant ridge. If the order came, it would be a gamble to strip his own sector to bleed the enemy where they were committed. If it didn't, then he would remain a nail in the center, hammered into place, holding firm until the flanks did their work.

The runner returned to the map table, snapping to attention. "Orders from battalion, Herr Untersturmführer, request to pivot denied. You are to maintain your current defensive posture."

Reinhardt didn't answer immediately. His eyes stayed locked on the hex-grid battlefield before him, the miniature colored blocks marking platoons and companies. The markers for the neighboring company to the west were being shoved steadily backward under the enemy's red assault arrows.

"Understood," he said at last. Then, as the runner turned to leave, Reinhardt reached for his pencil and ruler.

"You'll tell battalion," he said, tracing a sharp diagonal line from his position to the enemy's flank, "that I am spreading my reserve platoon across the center to maintain frontage... and that First and Second Platoon are moving here."

The runner hesitated. "Sir, the umpires..."

"I will note that I am exploiting a developing weakness," Reinhardt said curtly. "If the enemy collapses here, the center is safe. Go."

When the umpire returned to move the markers for Reinhardt's company, there were murmurs from the watching officers. His line had thinned dangerously, but his flanking force, two blue blocks, was now driving toward the hinge of the enemy advance. The exercise clock ticked on. Move by move, the flanking blue platoons advanced around the enemy's exposed side. Soon the umpire's tweezers lifted a red armor block from the board entirely. "Knocked out," he declared.

Reinhardt felt the subtle shift in the room. The westward company's markers stopped retreating. Battalion HQ had denied him but the game board had not. Slowly and methodically, the red arrows on the Kriegsspiel map began to bend backward. Enemy markers that had been hammering the center now pulled away to cover their own flanks. The westward thrust sputtered under combined pressure, and in the end, the "enemy" was notionally enveloped between the claws of Das Reich and Totenkopf. The order was given to end the exercise. Cadets were summoned to the lecture hall for their After Action Report. The senior umpire began immediately. "Cadet Jäger," he said, eyes fixed on Reinhardt. "You were given explicit orders to hold your position. Explain why you moved two platoons without authorization."

Reinhardt stood. "Sir, the orders to hold would have allowed the enemy to consolidate their thrust. A flank attack at that moment threatened their cohesion, forcing them to divert strength and relieving pressure on the western company. The risk to my frontage was acceptable given the potential for collapse."

A murmur ran through the room, but the officer's face did not soften. "Cadet Sands," he said sharply, turning to the other side of the room. A tall, dark-haired Celtic cadet stood, Michael Sands.

"You, too, disobeyed your battalion commander and pivoted your company to the flank. Why?"

"Because the enemy was committed, sir," Sands said in a voice as steady as iron. "Their armor was blind to the sides. I moved to where I could hurt them most. Holding ground is meaningless if you can win the fight outright."

Reinhardt perked up, his eyes sliding toward Sands. There was the faintest ghost of a grin in the man's expression, the look of someone who had made the same gamble and won. The officer rapped the desk. "Both of you showed initiative... and insubordination. Though your actions, combined, broke the enemy's momentum, annihilated two battalions, and ensured the center held long enough for our flanks to close the trap."

Reinhardt allowed himself the smallest smile. He wasn't alone in this school after all. The cadets were dismissed, chairs scraping as the room emptied. Reinhardt didn't waste a moment. He cut straight through the press of uniforms toward the Celtic officer cadet.

"Brilliant," Reinhardt said, grasping Sands' hand firmly. "We both had the same idea."

Sands returned the shake, his mouth curling into a sly grin. "So Germans do know how to fight after all."

Reinhardt smirked, unoffended. "You're forgetting the division we were wargaming was German and they held their ground in the real battle this was based on."

Their banter was cut short by a mutual, audible growl from their stomachs. Sands chuckled. Reinhardt only shrugged. Reinhardt and Sands left the briefing building side by side, the cool mountain air carrying the faint scent of woodsmoke from the kitchens. They made their way toward the chow hall, boots striking in rhythm on the worn stone path. As fully sworn ESS men they were entitled to a modest alcohol ration, two drinks permitted during training cycles. Tonight, after the war game's mental strain and the grilling from their instructors, both decided it was worth "cashing in" one. The chow hall was alive with noise and clatter, cadets packed elbow-to-elbow, steam curling from great metal trays of food. Reinhardt and Sands each claimed a tray heavy with roasted pork, dark bread, and boiled potatoes, handing over their ration slips for a mug of dark beer apiece. They found an open table against the wall, sitting down with the comfortable silence of men who had already fought, even if only across a map. Reinhardt took a long pull from his mug before nodding across the table.

"To initiative," Reinhardt said simply.

Sands smirked, lifting his own mug. "To initiative."

The beer was cold, the food hot, and for the moment, neither man thought about the next day's trials. They had barely started eating when Reinhardt asked where Sands was from.

"County Cork," Sands said with a grin, lifting his pint. "My people had been fighting one empire or another for a thousand years. I've got an old family story, swears one of my blood was with the Third West Cork Brigade when they hit the Black and Tans at Kilmichael. The old man said he put two of 'em in the dirt himself."

Reinhardt raised an eyebrow. "So you come from raiders, then?"

Sands' grin widened. "From soldiers, Reinhardt. Raiders take what's not theirs. My people fought for our home, for our nation. That's in my blood. The way I see it, the ESS is just the next front."

They clinked their pints together, and for a moment neither spoke. There was a shared understanding now, that they both came from bloodlines forged in war.

Chapter 24

The cadre called it the Crucible, like it was something old men had named and then forgot to rename. The real title was longer and bureaucratic, but no one used it. The Crucible was what mattered. It lasted three days and three nights, longer if the instructors felt a platoon needed to learn humility. It did not end when you were tired or when the scenario was solved. It ended when the cadre decided you had cut down to your iron.

They began on a slate morning that smelled like cold steel and wet pine. Trucks coughed in a slow line along the gravel road, tailgates chattering, and tarps snapping. Reinhardt stood with his platoon at the loading yard, helmet clipped to his belt, field map under his arm. He had the element he asked for, twelve riflemen, a machine gun team, a two-man scout pair, radio, medic, and a three-man mortar detachment with the little 60mm tube. The cadre had given him Sergeant Vogel as his senior NCO. Vogel had rucked a lifetime in his posture, knuckles scarred and jaw a wedge. Vogel watched the young officer like a man who had grown used to fools and did not have room for another.

The instructors split the officer class in two, staff and combative, and then crosswired them. Staff would live in a tented HQ tent and give orders against a moving enemy. Combative would take those orders and turn them into reality with all the dirt and confusion that implies. The lesson was simple, as all real lessons are. There is no such thing as staff and combative, only war, and some men who can think with their boots on.

By noon the trucks were gone and the forest had taken them. The Crucible ground was a rectangle of hills and scrub cut by a blackwater creek and two logging tractors' worth of trails. There were mock villages with chalked numbers for building designations, a derelict fuel dump with the smell of real diesel, and an airstrip of compacted dirt so straight it made the sky look narrow. The instructors warned that civilians would move through the area, role-players with armbands, some friendly, some neutral, and some with knives under their coats.

"Counter-intelligence will be evaluated," the lead instructor said, and looked at Reinhardt. "You are security of information, deception recognition, handling of detainees and compromised orders, and handling panic. You are a combative track, Lieutenant Jäger. The expectation for you is higher."

Reinhardt did not nod. He felt the old stillness come over him. He had felt it at the airport on Delumina when he could hear the whole battle like it was happening inside the hinge. He had felt it during the Stables of Rome, when the problem had become a living thing that needed to be pulled by the jaw. This is the work. It did not glow or blaze. It moved like a depth current, silent, and very sure.

They stepped off with a simple order. Screen the HQ site to the east, deny the enemy observation, and establish a cordon along the ridgeline that the maps called Line Caesar. The staff cell, a white-canvas island full of folding tables and a battery bank like an altar, would set up behind them and start pulling thread. The enemy called Red Team, cadets in red triangles, had a battalion's worth of nerve and a few toys the cadre would drip to them as rewards for creativity.

Vogel marched on Reinhardt's right and said nothing for an hour. When he finally spoke it was in the plain way of men who do not waste sounds. "The men do not know you. They will listen to me first. If you want them to listen to you, you will have to give them a reason."

Reinhardt looked over at him and said, "You will need the machine gun ready to punch through shrub at three hundred meters, and the mortar to set on the baseplate without stirring mud. If you do not keep them dry I will have you carry them yourself."

Vogel grunted, almost a laugh. "Fair."

The ridge was not much of a hill but it was enough. It ran like a spine and gave the valley below a shape that could be held. Reinhardt put his scouts forward, gave the gun a low saddle to rake, put the riflemen in two chevrons with dead ground behind them, and had the mortar dug in just off the military crest where their command wire would not silhouette a man stupid enough to forget it. He set his sectors with the map and then with his body, walking each lane of fire with the team leaders, pointing to trees by their bark and the ground by its roots. When he was done he stood with his radio man and keyed the HQ.

"Caesar line established. We are blind past the creek. I am requesting drone feed. Request fires grid for preplanned. No decision points yet."

The voice from the HQ was clipped, and young. Reinhardt did not recognize it. "Copy. You will receive a drone when allocated. Fires are denied until Red

Team fires first. Rule of Engagement is no engagement beyond three hundred meters. Civilians are present in the valley. HQ out."

Vogel spit into a patch of pine straw and shifted the weight of his gun. "They will change that when they get shot at."

"Good," Reinhardt said. "Then we will know who is thinking and who is hoping."

The first test came in the afternoon as a trickle of people who looked like they had wandered out of another time, the role-players. A woman with a basket of bread. A teenage boy with a bicycle tire around his neck like a saint's collar. An old man who could not stop talking about his goats. The cadre had instructed them well. They asked the same questions five ways and tried to step around the security rope lines as if by accident. Reinhardt tagged each one with a colored clothespin and gave them safe lanes to pass, with a soldier shadowing at ten paces to watch their hands.

He wrote names on his map in pencil of approximations and impressions. No photographs were allowed. No notes carried by civilians out of the cordon, even if they were a love letter, because love letters could be codes. He watched their eyes first, then their shoes. Mud tells a man's truth more than his tongue. The old man had mud up past his ankles but dry laces. The boy's tire had fresh scuffs on only one side. The woman with bread carried more than she looked able to carry. He sent her basket to Vogel. The top layer was real bread, too beautiful, the sort of bread a baker paints, and beneath it air and beneath that a packet, oiled cloth over a mason's string, a little node of plastic the instructors would later call an emitter. It had a toothpick switch, the kind you brush on a belt. Vogel held the node up and smiled without showing his teeth.

Before dusk the radio hissed. A call sign like theirs, almost theirs, calling for them to be displaced two hundred meters south to a "better position" and to leave the mortar in place as a rear guard. Vogel looked at Reinhardt and Reinhardt looked at the radio man.

"Say again your authentication," Reinhardt said.

The voice on the net nailed the first half of the code and then drifted. The last letter was off by one. The wrong vowel. It would pass a tired man, but not a hungry one.

"This is Lobo Two, negative," Reinhardt said. "We hold."

The voice on the net did not try again. That was when the scouts came back as quiet as rain and pointed east. Three men wearing boonie hats and armed with rifles are moving with the easy care of people at work. The enemy, or the instructors, but moving like men who did not waste steps. Reinhardt let them walk into view and then brought his hand down hard at Vogel. The gun spoke like a zipper. The mock men scattered, then fired back with blanks that still made the air crack and brought the sound of the ridge to life. The mortar coughed three times, the rounds thumped down the valley with a satisfaction that all men know, the way an action is supposed to echo. A whistle blew, a safety move. The cadre had heard the first exchange and moved in by habit, the jackets with orange piping, the flag to mark the ruled line where no one would die by accident. The enemy men slipped away, laughing, hands up.

"Your fire discipline held," an instructor said, his hair shaved to stubble. He had the easy cruelty of a man who liked the work. "You failed to relocate the mortar despite a spoofed order which was wrong, which is correct. Let us see how you do in the dark."

They did not sleep that night so much as blink long. They rotated men in the foxholes by schoolhouse schedule and then learned the real schedule, which is when the wind changes and the moon slides behind a cloud and the forest puts its hand over its own mouth and tries not to breathe. Red Team was good. They made noise in one place and crossed in another. They tied rocks to vines and let them knock the brush like men. The scouts were good too. Twice they brought Reinhardt men who were not theirs, cadets from another platoon with armbands cut loose, faces streaked as dark, obvious infiltrators. The first one talked too much and gave himself away by using a word a man does not use if he has ever actually dug in. The second said nothing at all. He just watched. Reinhardt had them flex-cuffed and bagged. They were brought to a tarp, which was used as a field processing site. The instructors stood back with their little notebooks and looked like jackdaws on a fence.

"Record time and procedure," one of them said. "There will be no humiliation or threats. You can press as if you are in contact. You cannot injure them nor can you deprive them of sleep. You can deceive but not about kin. You may begin."

Reinhardt began with the quiet one. He had him drink water and asked him about nothing at all for ten minutes. He talked about the weather, and the taste of the rations, and the way pine trees make a sound like talking when the wind moves right. The man watched him and Reinhardt watched his shoulders and the way he flexed his ankles to move blood. Then Reinhardt put a map down, not their map, a wrong map, one with misaligned grid lines, and he placed a grease pencil across it so the man could see the weight of it and think of drawing the right line to correct it. The man looked. The eyes flared almost invisible, a little hunger for the correction. It was the most honest thing he had done. He wanted the map to be right.

"You do not like to be wrong," Reinhardt said. "It aggravates you. You are an honest enemy. So here is my honest question. Why did your operator try to move my mortar in the afternoon and not my machine gun? The mortar is a threat to your depth. The gun is a threat to your edge. If I was your officer I would pull the rear and push the front. So I do not believe your officer did that. I believe your staff cell did that, which means my staff cell is inattentive. Who is inattentive at my HQ? Who is assigned to watch my net?"

The man did not speak. He did not need to. His eyes did a smaller flare, and then moved one degree down and left, to the corner of the tent where the instructor with the notebook had drifted nearer. Enough.

"Thank you," Reinhardt said, nodding without triumph. "Bag them and feed them. Hold for exchange."

At dawn the staff side pushed a new mission card to all combative tracks. The HQ had built a plan through the night. Red Team had broken contact south and was moving to seize the airstrip. Blue would fix them along the creek and pivot two platoons to strike their rear. The order included a time on target for simulated tube artillery, a drone feed at H-15, and a forward screen with the exact call sign that had been spoofed in the afternoon.

Reinhardt held the order sheet and read the lines until they were a taste in his mouth. He folded the paper and looked at the trees as if the trees would have an answer. He thought of the map he had put in front of the quiet man, and the way the eye hungered. Men like that did not walk away from the wrong. They turned toward it and bit.

Vogel dragged a sleeve across his stubble. “We move, then.”

“We do,” Reinhardt said. “But not as written. The second page is wrong.”

Vogel frowned, a slow frown, not of argument but of making room. “Explain.”

“The pivot will work on paper because the drone sees ten minutes ahead,” Reinhardt said. “Ten minutes is a long time in a creek bed. If I was their officer I would bait us into pivoting through the flats and then cut my men loose to sprint the high ground with rifles and a single gun, to pull us into two separate fights. The staff built a lever and handed the enemy a fulcrum.”

Vogel’s silence was ascent.

“We keep the fixers at the creek,” Reinhardt said, “but we move quietly on the high ground and hold fire until they are committed. The mortar will walk smoke, not HE. The smoke will be wrong colored, on purpose. I want them to think we misread our own plan and painted the wrong grid. They will adjust across the smoke and give us their ribs. We do not pursue across the creek. We will take three prisoners during the shift. I want them talking on their net, angry, because anger makes a man speak a little too long.”

Vogel smiled, small and wolfish. “You are the officer,” he said, and the tone of how he spoke “you” had changed.

They moved with their weight on their ankles, picking the ground. Reinhardt kept the radio on his own back for the walk, not the radio man’s, because he wanted to hear the static fall and rise as the ridge-bodied air shifted. He could feel the HQ behind him like a heat in the trees, the staff officers pouring coffee and drawing circles, the way that work makes a room smell like graphite and old tin.

Contact came not with a shot but with a voice, one of his scouts, low and flat.

Movement on the flats. Three elements, line abreast, a gun clacking half a second every few steps, the old trick to make a rifle line think the gun is already sited. Reinhardt raised his palm and made the knife hand for patience. He could sense the men's heartbeats change in some animal part of himself. The mortar team was already laying their first tube. They did not need to be told. They wanted to work.

"Two rounds smoke, east edge of the bend," Reinhardt said. "Then drift thirty meters left at your own pace. Do not be perfect."

The first round arced and the second made the creek look as if it had found a new way to breathe. The enemy checked, then came forward more quickly than doctrine would love. They were good, young and eager to pull the head off the plan their instructors had hung for them. They crossed the first strip of smoke and then hit the second and they did what young men do when the world goes white. They moved toward the visible ground, which was exactly the ground Reinhardt had left for them. He raised his rifle slightly and felt its steadiness, then lowered it because the gun was the better answer.

Vogel's team laid a line that did not stutter. It was not a shout. It was a hand across a throat. The Red Team dropped to earth and tried to pull the world over them. They were brave, and Reinhardt marked it without envy. He had been brave like that and had learned what it costs. The mortar drifted its smoke like a man drawing a curtain and three figures appeared where there had been none, like actors in a lit doorway. The riflemen took two and the third threw up his hands, weapon across his chest, and Reinhardt waved him through quickly because men who surrender feel a fear not like other fear and they can make odd choices if you force them to stand still under fire. Two more came the same way a minute later. The radio on Reinhardt's back snapped with Red Team radio traffic that the instructors had left unencrypted as if by accident. The voice cursed the smoke color and said the pivot was a trick. Reinhardt smiled without showing teeth.

"Hold," he said. "We do not chase."

He exfiltrated his prisoners to the holding tarp, briefed the field site in twelve words, and jogged back uphill. He had a feeling in his chest like a song with no words. The feeling that comes when your plan does not beat theirs so much as accept their plan and use its hunger to run it forward into your teeth. When he came up under the saddle he saw Vogel looking at him not as a boy or even as a man but as a partner, which is rarer and has weight.

"Orders from HQ," the radio man said, breathless. "Push the pivot. The staff says the opportunity is now."

"Negative," Reinhardt said. "We hold. Tell HQ to send a drone to my grid and put it on the ridge line, not the bend. Tell them the ridge holds their answer."

A pause, then a crackle, then a new voice. A familiar one this time, a shade of Cork in the vowels, tempered hard. It was Sands. It was the first time Reinhardt had heard him all day, their roles purposefully cleaved.

"Lobo Two," Sands said, "this is Warden. I am holding your request. I need confirmation. You are asking to deny the pivot."

"Yes," Reinhardt said. "The pivot is the Red Team's aimpoint. The bend is bait. They have a staffer who knows how to write a check with a map."

Another pause, long enough, then the voice again. "Copy, drone is yours. Warden out."

The drone feed came to the radio by a little black rectangle the instructors had nicknamed the pigeon, which ate battery and hope. Reinhardt clipped it to his map board and looked at the ridge from an eye that a bird would envy. The smoke lay in torn sheets and the enemy markers moved with a clear intention, three elements at the bend. Two were ghosting the ridge northward under the old power line cut, hidden from the valley angle. They would have turned the pivot into a pane of glass. He keyed the net.

"All elements hold. Gun, shorten half a belt and scythe the cut at your discretion. Mortar, two HE rounds on the rear of the cut, then cease and displace to alternate position two. Rifle teams fire by buddy rush to the breaker stumps and break contact once you see elbows. We are done here."

It went like that because men who have rehearsed know how to do simple things fast. The gun scythed. The mortar thumped two affirmations and then was thirty meters away before the second round hit. The riflemen moved like a zipper opening and then closing again. The Red Team fighters found themselves squeezing air.

The cadre blew their whistles again, not for safety but to call a pause, and they walked up the hill with their notebooks like magistrates. The lead instructor took off his cap and wiped his forehead with it and smiled like a man forced to admit a small, useful defeat.

"You violated the spirit of the staff plan," The grader said.

"I obeyed the order to screen the HQ," Reinhardt said. "I judged the staff plan would erode that order, and I judged the enemy rightly. I judged my men's endurance rightly. I submitted my request to hold and received drone allocation from Warden. I am responsible for the ground under my feet. I kept it."

The instructor looked down at the dirt and then up at the trees and then at Reinhardt's face, trying to find a seam where there was none. "You are counter-intelligence, Jäger. You are supposed to be suspicious. Today it served you."

"Suspicion without courage is cowardice," Reinhardt said. "I will not teach my men to be cowards."

The instructor's smile tightened. He closed his notebook and put the cap back on his head. "We will see if you feel the same way at two in the morning."

They felt the same way at two in the morning. The cadre threw a media team at them, which meant a man with a camera and a woman with too much concern in her voice carrying a microphone that could not transmit but could make a boy's mouth run. Reinhardt set a hard perimeter around his line and briefed Vogel like he was twelve and had to remember three things, no names, no numbers, and no units. If they asked why, direct them to the public affairs cutout, which was a folded pamphlet in a plastic sleeve that said nothing and did it well. The media team left with a B-roll of men looking like trees. The cadre then introduced a civilian ambulance with a siren and a sweat-streaked driver who said the west road had been hit and needed to pass through the cordon now. Reinhardt stepped to the ambulance door and put his hand on the hood and leaned in with his weight. The driver tensed and the engine revved. Reinhardt did not move. He looked at the man's eyes and then at the rear of the ambulance and then at the tires. The treads were clean of gravel, impossibly clean, like shoes just put on. He waved the vehicle to the holding pen and had it searched. Under the gurney there was a camera transmitter, the kind that sends a picture out through the sky like a little prayer. The cadre wrote something down in their books and said nothing.

Later the enemy tried to serenade. A loudspeaker from the timber line, a girl's voice singing in a language that was not this valley's. It was slow, soft and full of promise. The men listened the way men listen to a thing they want to turn toward. Reinhardt let the song go for a minute and then he had the mortar pop one smoke round above the timber line and another downwind. He ordered the machine gun to fire a burst into a dead tree that he had already marked for this purpose. The tree shattered and fell. It was at that moment that the loudspeaker stopped. The forest exhaled. Vogel chuckled like a bear just woke up and found the winter still there.

By the second dawn the Crucible had become what all good tests become, not a list but a rhythm. The staff cell sent orders. Reinhardt read them and accepted or pushed against them. When he pushed, he did it with a reason, never with a shrug. The HQ learned him, and he learned them, and that is all a unit really is, a series of learnings that become muscle. Sands moved in parallel, his voice breaking in on the net at odd hours with adjustments that fit into place like teeth into a gear, and once, only once, Reinhardt heard the sound of fatigue in him and understood that Sands was bearing a load too, the invisible kind, the kind you cannot share. It felt good to know they were not alone in the work.

The end did not announce itself. It arrived as quietly as a day that refuses to throw rain. The cadre called to cease exercise at noon and let the sound run out of the woods. Men stood and felt their own bodies as if surprised that they were still there. The instructors gathered the officers and senior NCOs under a rectangle of shade and read the results the way an old priest reads a list of names, careful, because names are heavy things.

"Warden staff cell," the lead instructor said, "commended for flexibility in the face of friction. Combative elements under Lobo Two commended for security discipline, deception recognition, economy of force, and initiative. Lobo Two violated order format twice and ROE once by placing a detainee briefly within the perimeter of an active gun. The violation was corrected immediately. Senior NCO Vogel, recognized for clarity of execution and the quiet enforcement of standards."

Vogel's nod was almost nothing, but it had the dignity of a bow. The instructor closed his book. "The Crucible is not a pass or fail. It is a mirror. You will take what you saw and carry it. Some of you saw fear. Some of you saw pride. Some of you saw another man's excellence and felt small, good. Feel small, it is the only way to get larger the right way."

Afterward, when the rigs were packed and the dust had half settled, Reinhardt walked the perimeter alone. He touched the stump the gun had chewed. He stood where the drone had shown him the ridge. He listened to the silence that comes after men are gone, and he thought about the word officer, which men hold too close sometimes, like a badge, and which others hold so lightly it is only a syllable. He did not feel like a badge. He felt like work. It felt right.

Sands found himself there, though Reinhardt had not expected it, and stood shoulder to shoulder without speaking for a time. The Irishman's eyes were red at the edges, the way eyes get when the head has been full of maps too long.

"You were right about the pivot," Sands said.

"You were right to hold the drone for me," Reinhardt said.

Sands half smiled. "Do not ruin my reputation for being difficult."

"You will need it," Reinhardt said. "We all will."

They went back toward the yard together, boots tapping the old earth like a drum line. The sun had come out finally and lay across the field with a warmth that felt like permission. Not a blessing, because blessings are for men who ask to be spared, permission to continue. That is enough. The trucks arrived and men climbed into them with the same careful clatter they had climbed out. Vogel passed the gun up and then turned and held out his hand to Reinhardt. They shook once. It was not a soldier's shake or a friend's shake exactly. It was a seal. The kind you do not have to speak about again.

Back at the school the instructors wrote their comments, and they put the right colored tabs on the right names on the board. The lines and orders that were sent mean that combative officers went one way and staff officers another. Some men would change paths quietly. Some would not notice the change until a decade later when a younger man called them sir with a softness that held a mirror.

Reinhardt went to the showers and stood with his hands on the tile until the water had run from hot to cool. He dressed in a clean field kit and traced his thumb along the cuff. The grey cloth was worn with the old sigils, the weight of duty sewn into thread. He thought of the Stables of Rome, of the airport, and of a girl's voice over a loudspeaker pretending to be the thing a man loves. He thought of how easily a war makes a lie look like a friend. He dried his hands, squared his collar and went to the debrief with his notebook open, ready to write.

They all filed into the debrief tent that still smelled of pine and burnt powder. Three were folding chairs in three arcs, a projector humming against the canvas, and a battered whiteboard already bleeding through old marker ghosts: ESTABLISH, SECURE, EXPLOIT, PURSUIT. Coffee in steel urns that tasted like someone had wrung a rag into hot water were served. The cadre ran it like a staff conference, not a classroom. No one hid in the back row. Eyes were up, and notebooks open.

A major with a clipped haircut and a cadenced way of breathing took the floor. "Sequence is standard: timeline, enemy picture, friendly picture, deviations, effects, lessons learned, and corrective actions. You will not defend or filibuster. Precision is preferred over performance. Warden Staff, you're on."

Sands stood with that slight, careful set to his shoulders. He wore fatigue like it was armor.

Sands spoke. "Day One: initial occupation of Line Caesar, and combative platoons established the screen. Red Team probed with civilian actors and spoofed a movement order at 1620. Warden Staff withheld pivot authority until fire parity achieved. Day Two: Red Team launched a coordinated feint at the creek to trigger our planned pivot; Lobo Two declined the maneuver on request and held the ridge, requesting drone retask. Warden reallocated ISR and adjusted fire timeline. Day Three: Red Team shifted to influence ops and infiltration; combative elements maintained cordon and media discipline. Index at 1200 hours on day four."

The major nodded. "Red Team?"

A captain with the red triangle armband walked them through the enemy plan, crisp and almost cheerful. "Our aim was to split Blue Team between map and ground. Our spoofed orders tested Blue Team's authentication. Once we believed their staff favored the pivot, we planned to ride smoke to the bend, then slingshot two elements under the power line to cut their ridge spine. We used a disguised ambulance to place a persistent transmitter inside your perimeter for geolocation alignment. Finally, our loudspeaker was a morale tax, meant to break Blue Team's morale."

The Red Team commander looked at Reinhardt and didn't quite smile. "We did not expect the colored smoke deception. That move hurt us hard."

There was a long silence from the Red Team's corrective action and the positive comment about Reinhardt's actions.

"Friendly picture," the major said, flipping to the map overlay. "Your turn for the combative section of Lobo Two."

Reinhardt stood. He kept his voice level and short.

"Our mission was to screen east of the HQ, deny observation, and maintain integrity of Line Caesar. The tasks were to establish chevron defense with MG saddle, 60mm on baseplate offset, scouts forward, and radio at my elbow. Our control measures were to not engage enemies beyond three hundred meters, authenticate each person attempting to pass our checkpoint, two-man checks on all emplaced comms, a colored-clothespin tracking all civilians passing our checkpoint, single-point entry for all those attempting to pass our position, and have a bag-and-tag site two tarps deep and out of gun-traverse."

The officer grading the operation tapped three spots on the projector's ridge view. "You have three key decisions. 1. You rejected displacement on spoofed order due to final-authentication mismatch. 2. Employed bread-basket emitter find, tightened CI posture around cordon; 3. Declined staff pivot when ISR-window risk exceeded screening mandate; requested drone for ridge; used smoke miscoloring to induce Red Team lateral movement into MG scythe; captured three detainees during shift to generate Red Team net chatter."

He didn't dodge the miss.

"ROE deviation, one detainee placed inside the perimeter of an active gun for thirty-seven seconds during transition, my error, but corrected in real time. Added 'cold arc' tape to traverse and posted an NCO as ROE sentinel thereafter."

The major scratched a note. "Effects?"

"HQ remained unobserved from the east. Red Team's pivot trap failed. Prisoners and recovered transmitters gave us their staff's timing and net discipline. Media injection was neutralized. Disguised ambulance seized with transmitter."

"Deviations?" the major pressed.

"Two," Reinhardt said. "I used drone allocation to confirm my intuition rather than to find a new opportunity. It risks making leaders seek confirmation instead of reconnaissance. Also, I pushed all deception control through me, which bottlenecked Counter-Intelligence decisions. I should've delegated a Counter-Intelligence NCO to hold the tarp site and civilian track so I wasn't the only brain in that loop."

"Noted." The major turned to Vogel without prompting, which said something. "Senior NCO observations."

Vogel stood like a tree that had decided to speak. "Cadet Jäger set sectors with his feet. He didn't guess. He showed men bark and root, and they shot where he pointed. He kept the radio close, so he knew the traffic on the net. He was slow to trust the plan and quick to trust the ground. That saved us. He needs a standing SOP for detainee lanes that lives without him staring at it. We built it on Day Two. We'll keep it."

The major's mouth twitched. Approval, ESS-style.

He swung back to Staff. "Warden. Faults first."

Sands didn't flinch. "We wrote the pivot to be elegant. Elegance cares too much about itself. We underweighted the enemy's capacity to run the fulcrum on us. We issued a drone at H-15 as if the future would honor our schedule, which was wrong. Our grid overlay had a one-degree slop north of the creek due to a misapplied declination, caught late because our QC (Quality Control) step happened inside the same brain that drew it. We assumed the spoofed order was an isolated injection, not a style. That led to trusting our own cleverness more than our screens' skepticism."

"And strengths?"

"We listened when combative pushed back with reasons tied to the commander's intent. We reallocated ISR in minutes, not hours. We kept fires in reserve until fires mattered. Our intelligence cell flagged the loudspeaker as a morale tool and recommended a non-kinetic counter, combative chose the dead tree burst. It worked."

The OPFOR captain raised a hand. The major nodded him in. "Compliment where due: Blue Staff held tension without panic. Your Warden did not punish initiative; he asked for the reason and then either said yes fast or no clean."

The major capped his marker. "Alright. Lessons learned, three up, three down. We'll do this like we mean it. Start with Lobo Two."

Reinhardt glanced down at his notebook but he already knew them.

"Up: 1. Think with your boots on, staff intent translated to ground truth via mission command, not obedience. 2. Counter-Intelligence posture integrated early: role-player control, emitter find, net discipline checks, security wasn't an afterthought. 3. Deception used offensively: discolored smoke and wrong-map bait in detainee questioning created exploitable enemy behavior..

Down: 1. ROE guardrail absent at the gun until violation forced it, needs pre-placed cold arc tape. CI workload centralized on the officer, build a CI NCO billet for detainee/civilian control with preprinted forms and a rolling log. 3. Overreliance on ISR confirmation, codify 'reconnaissance by reason' before 'reconnaissance by drone'; write a checklist that asks, 'If the drone dies, what do you still know?'".

"Warden Staff," the major said.

Sands spoke, "Up: 1. Speed of reallocation, drone and fires moved to where reality lived.2. Commander's intent stayed simple and durable: screen the TOC; preserve the ridge. 3. Staff-Combative trust handshake, leaders could dissent with grounds..

Down: 1. Map hygiene, declination QC must be cross-checked by a different staffer; no self-QC. 2. Cleverness bias, plans that admire themselves get men killed. 3. Authentication fatigue, our net control accepted partial-auth once on Day One's back half; only discipline saved us."

The major let the room breathe. Then he did what good instructors do and pressed the bruise.

"Lobo Two, you declined a written maneuver. Justify it in doctrinal language."

Reinhardt met his eyes. "Mission command under a clear commander's intent. The intent was to screen east of HQ and preserve the ridge as the lens through which we see the valley. The prescribed pivot risked breaking the screen and handing Red Team the ridge. I assessed the risk to the higher task and declined, asked for ISR to verify my hypothesis, and retained freedom of action."

"Commander's intent outranks paragraph five," the major said, to the room. "If you decline, you must be able to say it like he did, without poetry."

He looked to the Red Team captain. "Your critique of Blue combative leadership?"

"Jäger kept his men curious," the captain said. "They watched shoes and mud, not just horizons. He also didn't hoard heroics, he let the gun do the killing and the mortar do the shaping. If I were hunting him, I'd go after his Counter-Intelligence node. It lives near him. Break that and you make him deaf in one ear."

"Noted," Reinhardt said, dry.

"Media inject," the major said, flipping a slide, the frozen frame of the dead tree breaking under MG fire. "Talk me through your decision, Lobo."

"A loudspeaker is a wire into men's heads. Answer with a louder wire or cut the line. I chose to cut it. Burst into a dead tree I'd marked hours earlier with no ricochet risk; smoke for curtain to deny OPFOR sight of our reaction. It reasserted that we set the soundtrack, not them."

"Civilian ambulance," the major said next. "Your denial pissed off the driver.

In a real war that could be a real medic."

Reinhardt kept his voice even. "I don't need him to like me. I need the perimeter to remain honest. The tires told the truth. No gravel in the treads after an east-road run is a lie. We verified and resolved within five minutes. If it's legit in the real world, that five minutes saves lives because it keeps the cordon from becoming compromised."

The major nodded, satisfied. "Corrective actions. We write them now; we live them tomorrow. Warden, staff side."

Sands had three clean bullets ready. " 1. Two-person QC on all geospatial overlays, declination, MGRS conversions, and range fans. Whoever draws, someone else audits. 2. Authentication fatigue drill, every staffer will be red-celled with near-miss auth daily. No more partials. 3. Embed a red cell inside the staff, one officer with veto power to write the enemy's best move against our plan before we publish."

"Combative," the major said to Reinhardt.

"1. CI NCO billet and kit: detainee log, preprinted questioning prompts, colored clothespins for civ control, emitter checklists, and a battery quarantine box. 2. ROE guard SOP: 'cold arc tape' standard on all guns; ROE sentinel assigned by name during any processing. 3. Deception SOP: smoke miscoloring and map-bait as codified tools, use sparingly, brief clearly, and deconflict with staff graphics."

Vogel added a fourth, unasked. "4. Rehearse the silence. We ran a night with all hand signals and touches. It kept men from filling the dark with talk. We keep that."

The major actually smiled. "Good, you can't buy silence later, you either built it or you didn't."

He closed the marker with a sharp click. "Ratings, you'll see your numbers on your boards later. Broad strokes now. Warden Staff: top third, flagged for line staff posting in an operational division. Lobo Two: top third combative, flagged for counter-intelligence platoon leader with dual-hat on battalion intelligence liaison. Vogel: recommended for first sergeant track posthaste."

A small, strangled cheer went around the tent which was contained, but real. Sands didn't grin, his eyes warmed. Reinhardt kept his face still and felt the weight of it settle. Not an accolade. A task.

"Peer evals are sealed," the major said, "but I'll give you this, both of you were named as men others would follow. That isn't a grade. That's a debt. Pay it every day."

He snapped the notebook shut. "Debrief over. Hotwash stations around the perimeter, five-minute rotations: ROE lane, media lane, detainee lane, spoofed-comms lane. Then chow, then rack, then back to the grind. Warden, Lobo, hang back."

The tent emptied by halves. The air felt wider. The major came closer, the clipped-breath rhythm easing a fraction.

"You two are a problem," he said, almost conversational. "The good kind. Staff who will actually argue with ground truth, ground truth that will call staff out without sulking. Keep that. We kill more of our own initiative here than the enemy ever does. Not on my watch."

He looked pointedly at Reinhardt. "One more, you will be tested on your suspicion until it becomes cynicism. Don't let it. Counter-intelligence that forgets courage turns into a man who only ever says no. Your 'no' was a yes to the ridge. Keep making that kind of no."

"Jawohl," Reinhardt said, simply.

Sands touched his notebook with two fingers. "I owe you a pint."

"You owe me a drone," Reinhardt said.

Sands snorted. "You and every platoon leader from here to Mare Nostra."

They stepped out into heat and dust and the chatter of men unstringing their own nerves with bad coffee and better jokes. The hotwash lanes ran like carnival booths for professionals. At the spoofed-comms table, a sergeant with a broken nose made them prove authentication under a stopwatch. At the media lane, the same woman with the too-concerned voice tried new angles and got nowhere. At the detainee lane, a young officer tried to be clever with threats and got stopped hard, the ROE sentinel tapped his shoulder and shook her head. Reinhardt filed the image. That is how you make a rule live. You give it to a person with a name.

When they were finally cut loose for chow, the food tasted like victory only in the sense that it tasted like anything at all. They were even given a pint of beer. Reinhardt ate until the edge went out of his hunger and then sat with his cup and watched the room. Men laughed too loud, as men do when they have survived a small war. Vogel ate like a machine and then leaned back, eyes closed, looking for a wall to lean his thoughts on. Sands talked with two staffers, gesturing with his pencil, drawing a box in the air that only he could see.

The board would post assignments within forty-eight hours. Some of the class would be gone within the week to railheads, airfields, and embarkations to cold places and hot ones, colonial worlds with names that sounded like poetry and broke like teeth. The Crucible wouldn't follow them like a story. It would live in their hands, in the way they placed a gun, in the way they said no to a plan that admired itself too much.

Reinhardt finished his cup and set it down and felt the quiet rise in him again. Not the hush of fear. The quiet of a man who has sorted his tools and knows where they sit. He thought of what the major had said about debt, and about Ridge over Plan, and about suspicion that doesn't eat courage. He thought of the old airport and the Stables and the song in the trees and how easily a lie can wear a friend's face.

Sands slid into the seat across from him. "You look like you're writing a sermon."

"Just a checklist," Reinhardt said.

Sands nodded. "Those are sermons that work."

They sat for a minute without needing to talk, two officers breathing the same dust, the same future. Then the intercom crackled with the schedule for the next evolution, because there is always a next evolution, and men stood, scraping chairs, and went to meet it.

Violence Is Freedom

SIEGFRIED KIRCHEIS

www.ingramcontent.com/pod-product-compliance
Lightning Source LLC
Chambersburg PA
CBHW060629310726
48982CB00003B/717

* 9 7 8 1 9 6 3 5 9 1 2 3 1 *